The Rose
in the Wheel

Books by S.K. Rizzolo

The Regency Mysteries
The Rose in the Wheel
Blood for Blood
Die I Will Not

The Rose in the Wheel

A Regency Mystery

S.K. Rizzolo

Poisoned Pen Press

Poisoned Pen Press
6962 E. First Ave. Ste. 103
Scottsdale, AZ 85251
www.poisonedpenpress.com
info@poisonedpenpress.com

Printed in the United States of America

For my father, Charles Farmer Pitts (1916-1995).

And for my daughter Miranda, the inspiration for Penelope Wolfe's little girl Sarah.

Acknowledgments

Thanks are due to many people who helped this book reach publication. I owe my gratitude to Susan Chen and Laura Wallace of the Regency Library and to Bob Whitworth for answering research questions; to my colleague Julia Lawrence for assistance with Thorogood's Latin; to John and Roxane Quinn for practical assistance and moral support; and to my friends Kathy and Cy Caruso for their willingness to come along on the journey.

Thank you also to Daphne Wright and Kathryn Skoyles for taking the time to read the manuscript and offer feedback; to Pat Wynn, a fine writer, who offered advice and encouragement when they were most needed; to Jane Dystel, Miriam Goderich, and Stacey Glick at JDLM who were all unfailingly supportive. And especially to Barbara Peters and Rob Rosenwald for their expert guidance.

Finally, I must thank my co-author and husband Michael J. Rizzolo, who made rich contributions to the story, spent countless hours in the library poring over old books, and tramped all over London with me in retracing the footsteps of our nineteenth-century characters.

—

"Oh hope and glory of virgins, Jesus, good King,
I beg of you that anyone who honors the memory of my passion,
or who invokes me at the moment of death or in any need,
may receive the benefit of your kindness."

St. Catherine's prayer
from *The Golden Legend* by Jacobus de Voragine

Chapter One

London, November 1811

The clatter of wheels broke the stillness. Two horses strained in harness, nostrils flaring, breath steaming in the night air. Wrapped in a greatcoat and low-crowned hat, the driver rode hunched over, face hidden by his scarf. A gloved hand cracked the whip. Faster.

The woman lying in the road seemed unaware of her peril. She kept her eyes fixed on the church rising against the night sky. As the mists parted, the rose window emerged, a circle of textured shadow patiently awaiting the sun's fire.

The horses reared, and the woman's body tumbled beneath hoof and carriage, arms and legs a-tangle. Whipping around the wheel, her cloak yanked her back and up so that for one instant she was held suspended. Down she tumbled to land in a heap. The coach tilted wildly, regained control, and sped on. Hoof beats echoed away. The silence closed in with the fog.

❧ ❦

Penelope tumbled out of sleep, stifling a scream. Someone was in the room. A step shuffled; a drawer edged open with the scratch of old wood. Her arm reached instinctively for the child at her side, but Sarah still slept, warm and sweet, breathing softly.

A form detached from the shadows by the bureau and moved toward her. She heard a thud followed by a muffled curse.

"Jeremy?"

"Who left that blasted thing in the middle of the room?"

As he bent to right the rocking horse, Penelope slipped out of bed, groping for the tinderbox on the nightstand. Fingers trembling, she struck metal against flint until a spark caught. She lit her candle and turned to face him.

Jeremy stepped into the flicker-glow, slivers of light illuminating eyes, nose, or mouth, each in turn then thrust back into darkness. He was smiling.

"What do you want?" she said.

"You're not curious about how I breached your defenses? Quite simple actually. You should remember to lock your windows."

"However you entered, you can exit by the same route."

He looked hurt. "Now is that any kind of greeting after so long an absence? That trellis is deuced rickety. I could have been dashed to my death."

"You'd have landed in the rosebushes. And perhaps a bed of thorns is in order here." She loosened her grip on the candlestick. "Keep your voice down or you'll wake Sarah."

Jeremy bent closer to the bed and grazed the child's cheek with his fingertips. "She'd sleep through the storming of the Bastille. All's well with her?"

"What do you want?" she said again.

"I am short of funds at present. I hoped you might spare a few pounds out of the household money."

Anger quickly flamed in her: a familiar anger, a warm and secure anger that set her jaw. "Scorched again? Well, I won't have it, Jeremy. Besides, we've little to spare as you should know." But she knew she had no choice, for he might take everything if he so desired and she could not stop him. A few pounds would satisfy him for now.

Penelope took his arm and pulled him into her tiny sitting room. Turning up the lamp, she perched on the settee, indicating he should take the chair opposite. Instead, Jeremy removed his cloak and squeezed next to her.

He leaned closer so that she could smell the brandy on his breath. "Listen to me, love," he said. "I've had a run of ill luck.

I need a trifle to tide me over until I finish my commission. Just to pay my shot with a few of the more pressing duns and get my shirts out of hock from the laundress."

"What commission?"

"Constance Tyrone. The daughter of a baronet. Possessed of a face like the Virgin's, but there's fire beneath. Sixty-five guineas for a full-length, no less." His voice was reflective.

"You should see my sketches of her," he went on. "Best work I've ever done. And there's more, Penelope. She's got influential friends. If I play my hand right, I'll be awash in solicitations for portraits."

"Why should she do that for you?"

Jeremy looked mischievous. "A favor for a favor. I know some and suspect more."

"What can her private affairs mean to you?"

"Why nothing, of course. Except that handled delicately, she may not be averse to lending aid to one who understands her so well." He chuckled, leaning back against the cushion. His eyes fluttered shut.

For the first time she looked at him in the light. He wore dark breeches and a white waistcoat traced with silver thread under an evening coat that fit perfectly across the shoulders. She had not seen this particular ensemble before and eyed him with some disgust, calculating how much it might have cost.

"Understanding women is rather a specialty of yours. Don't you dare fall asleep. Mrs. Fitzhugh stirs early, and I won't be put in the position of explaining your presence here."

His eyes flew open. "I need your help. Would you have me beg for it, Penelope?"

As his long artist's fingers closed about her hand, his gaze met hers. She could see the faint lines forming at the sides of his mouth and along his cheeks, looking strangely out of place on his youthful features. Not marks of character or of wisdom, but of dissipation. Countless nights spent drinking and wenching were beginning to take their toll even on Jeremy's beauty.

"How much do you need?" She pulled away, rising.

"A trifle, just to see me along."

Penelope walked across the room to her desk and removed a small enameled casket. For a moment she stared at the lid, which depicted a scene from Shakespeare's *The Tempest*: Miranda and Ferdinand embracing in their brave new world. True lovers. She flipped it open to expose a small roll of bank notes and some coins. Handing him about half the roll, she said, "Here. Take it."

He took the money, but kept hold of her hand. "You shall have it back, my sweet, and perhaps tenfold should Fortune smile." He gave her a searching look. "Any word from your father by the by, or is the Great Man yet to forgive his erring daughter? Not that I should be concerned so long as he does not neglect your allowance."

She snatched her hand away. "I imagine he's busy if the talk we hear of unrest in Palermo is true. Father will be in his glory if the republicans can wring some concessions from King Ferdinand."

"No doubt," said Jeremy, losing interest. "I suppose you keep up your scribbling? Any luck on the literary front?"

"Just my work for Father's printer friend. Several little poems and a piece about Sicilian cookery. None of which qualifies as literature."

"Ah well. The lot of the artist is rarely without its perils, and frittering away one's talent on Philistines is the worst of them." He shot a sidelong glance at her. "Still using your *nom de plume*, I trust?"

She knew why he asked. He was perfectly willing to grant a woman her right of self-expression. Write by all means, make money if possible, but do so anonymously, savoring any triumphs in secret. Whatever you do, do not attract the world's vulgar notice. She felt again the old disappointment.

"Not to worry, Jeremy. Mrs. Fitzhugh insists upon maintaining the respectability of her lodgings. A woman alone with a child is bad enough. If she were to discover she harbors a lady writer as well, we'd be in the street by first light."

She became aware that Jeremy's gaze had drifted down from her eyes. And suddenly she realized she stood clad only in her shift, the lamplight revealing her body through the sheer material. Disconcertingly, she felt her nipples harden.

"Don't look at me like that." She crossed her arms over her chest, backing away.

"I didn't come for that, love. Though I can't say the notion doesn't have appeal."

"You know me better than that. Not with liquor on your breath and likely another woman's scent elsewhere."

"That's just it; I do know you." He slid his fingers across her throat, gripped her shoulders, and bent to kiss her cheek gently. "Not to worry. I've an engagement." He put on his cloak and walked to the window.

"In the middle of the night?"

Laughing, he waved his hand and was gone.

Ten minutes later Penelope was back in bed listening to Sarah's quiet breathing. Remembering that instant of yearning, she felt ashamed, then angry again.

"Damn you, Jeremy," was her last thought before she fell into a dreamless sleep.

❦

"Who found her, Constable?" John Chase let his gaze sweep down the line of terrace houses and back to St. Catherine's church, imposing in the early light. There was something about the colorless dawn that made the day start bleak. It was not a cleansing light. Dirt from the day before looked that much dirtier, ugliness that much uglier, and human frailty that much more frail.

He looked down at the woman at his feet. They would have to move her soon. Already a line of drays and carriages had formed and tempers grew short, drivers shouting curses at the street-keeper who waved them toward a detour.

A small crowd had begun to gather on the pavement, the curious eager to sniff out any lurid details. And soon the Grub Street hacks themselves would arrive. Someone was bound to have informed them since the journalists paid a shilling for any tidbits.

"Who found her?" Chase repeated.

Constable Samuel Button pulled his eyes from the body. "Sorry, sir. The curate Mr. Thaddeus Wood discovered her before daybreak. Unlocking the church gates he was, sir, when he shines his lantern into the street and sees her lying there."

The constable's broad, bovine countenance wore a troubled expression. Lord knows, most men avoided the year-long stint as an unpaid official more studiously than the plague itself, especially given the possibility of facing something like this. Most, in fact, employed a substitute to execute this duty.

Unlike many of his colleagues, Chase always tried to turn the parish authorities up sweet since a little honey produced better results than the usual bitter rivalry. "I'll warrant you wish you'd nabbed a Tyburn Ticket when this business ousted you from your fireside." A Tyburn Ticket, purchased at an enormous price, exempted one from parish duties.

Button gave a rather strained smile. "Indeed, sir." He cleared his throat, produced his occurrence book from somewhere, and began to flip through the pages. Then, like a child about to recite a lesson, he darted a nervous glance at Chase. "Upon finding said deceased, Mr. Wood calls the Watch who summons me. A matter for the Runners, I say to myself, knowing Bow Street won't say no to a murder inquiry, fees arranged or not. It's a queer situation, I don't mind telling you."

"Is it now?" Chase smiled at him. He groped in his pocket for his spectacles and put them on, squinting irritably at the smudges on the glass. It was not yet half past seven, and already his forty-one years weighed heavily. In addition to the frustration of the spectacles, only of marginal help to his failing vision, Chase was enduring the usual pain in his bad knee.

Suddenly impatient, he lifted the book from Button's hand and scanned the rest of the report. Not much there thus far, merely a few remarks recorded in the man's rather laborious hand and the name and direction of the curate who had found the victim.

The constable said slowly, "You see, sir, I thought at first she was killed accidental while crossing in the dark, but directly I spied her neck 'twas plain we had ourselves a nasty one."

He paused for confirmation, but Chase just nodded at him to continue.

"Though I reckon she was struck after the fact. We get a number of complaints about night coaches rattling through the streets keeping honest folk from their rest. And drivers so intoxicated as to be a menace to any poor soul what crosses their path." He lapsed into silence.

Chase circled the body. The woman's thin muslin gown, torn and filthy, had bunched at the waist, exposing her shift and a hint of white flesh where this garment too had ridden up. Cloak in a similar tangle about the shoulders and upper torso. Neck at an odd angle, obviously broken. Thick dark hair matted with mud had tumbled from its pins although smooth curls still clustered around her face. She looked like a child's outgrown rag doll tossed in a pile of refuse.

Bending down to examine her more closely, he saw at once what Button meant. Blood had trickled from her nose, and her neck was bruised with livid finger marks. Death by strangulation. Yet she was not as disfigured as such victims customarily were. Very often the tongue protruded through swollen lips; the cheeks displayed a garish blush. This woman was pale, her features unmarked.

"Anyone touch her?"

"Only to examine her pockets."

"Have you identified her, Constable?"

"Certainly, sir." He puffed out his chest. "The curate knew her, you see. She's one Constance Tyrone of the St. Catherine Society. The curate says as how she and her women let the old rectory on the church grounds. One of them charitable societies what's been springing up all over."

"Not a prostitute then."

"Indeed not, sir."

Chase fingered the folds of the woman's cloak, a thick, soft merino, obviously of the highest quality. Peering more closely, he plucked a few strands of a lighter coarse thread that were stuck to the fabric and slid them into his waistcoat pocket. Later he would have a look around and try to match the threads with something in the vicinity.

"What on earth was she doing roaming the streets?" he wondered aloud. "She must have been on her way to or from the Society, but why would a lady be out on her own in such weather? Now were she a barrow woman or a serving lass, I could fathom it."

"Odd, wouldn't you say, sir?" said Button. "Mr. Wood says as Miss Tyrone's coachman always collected her at dusk. Seems last night she wasn't here, so the coachman drove home, thinking perhaps she'd gone early. Then she turns up this morning."

"She been robbed?"

"I'd say so, sir. No wipe in her pocket, no gloves nor reticule neither. And the curate says as she were wont to wear a fine gold cross round her neck, and, as you see, it's not there now. Of course, she may have had other valuables on her as well."

Chase stood up. "I'll speak to Wood once I've finished here. Have your man keep this area clear for a few moments more."

Scanning the spectators automatically, Chase noted that the journalist Fred Gander was present. A small, sharp ferret man, Gander stood next to an enormous woman with two children clinging to her skirts. Elbowing the woman out of the way, he minced toward the curb where he waved his ink-stained fingers at Chase and held his notebook poised.

"Seems rather unorthodox to deposit one's victim in the center of the road," Chase said, louder than before.

"It is at that," replied Button.

"Witnesses?"

"One woman has come forward to say as she spied a hackney coach strike the victim, but she wasn't close enough to see much."

"And I'll wager she describes everyone from the devil to the Prince Regent himself driving the thing!"

There was scattered laughter from the crowd while Gander scribbled furiously.

Chase turned back to the constable and pointed to the marks visible on the paving stones. "See here, Button. Observe these horse and carriage tracks. It looks as if she were dragged along here after being struck by the horses and caught by the wheels. The impact probably snapped her neck."

"But was she quite dead before it struck, sir? I'd hate to think of her lying in the cold suffering all to herself." Button lifted somber eyes from the ground.

Meeting his gaze, Chase lowered his voice. "'Tis hard to say. It depends on whether or not the throttling killed her first." He paused. "I'll see the Watch now."

"He's here, sir." Button indicated a frail, stooped old man sitting on a low wall nearby, a stave and grease-encrusted lantern at his feet.

The old man approached, his rheumy eyes glaring at Chase. "Get on with it. I need my sleep and can't afford to waste time standing here freezing my arse."

Button was embarrassed. "Show some respect, Old Tom. This gent's from Bow Street."

Tom merely snorted, but Chase addressed the old man politely: "Were your rounds regular last night, Tom? Any business delay you?" He purposely gave the old man an out in case he had been sleeping in his box, tippling, or talking to the dollymops, all activities popularly attributed to the Watch.

"Like clockwork! Every half hour in the rain and all."

"Did you notice anything out of the common? Any strangers? Any disturbances?"

"No more 'n usual." He started to shuffle away, but Chase waved him back.

"You see, Tom, the attack must have occurred after the rain stopped as the loose dirt on the front of the victim's cloak has not been washed away. Nor is her clothing as damp as one might expect. When did the rain end, do you recall?"

"After three, I reckon."

"Might you have overlooked her on your circuits? Oh, not through lack of diligence," he put in hastily as Old Tom's hackles rose. "In the dark."

"Couldn't say." He folded his lips together as if determined to add nothing more.

Button broke in. "Verifying the gates are fast is part of Tom's duty, sir. He'd have seen her, that's certain." He pointed to a narrow iron gate set in the churchyard wall.

"What's on the other side of that wall?" asked Chase.

"Just the garden, sir, and the Society's buildings beyond. The women use this gate, I believe, as it's most convenient."

"What about the other gates? Are they kept locked as well?"

"Yes, sir. I did ask the curate, and he unfastened them as usual this morning."

After regarding him frowningly a moment, Chase looked back at the Watch. "One more question before you seek your bed, Tom. What time did Mr. Wood summon you?"

"He called to me as I was making my six o'clock rounds. So I springs my rattle and folk come running. Logical, ain't it?" He brandished the rattle in Chase's face.

Moving aside, Chase nodded in dismissal. "That's all for now." The old man snorted again and hobbled away through the muck, his tracks joining the welter of smudged markings in the street.

"The horse and wheel traces are still plain," Chase remarked, "but as for footprints, I'd swear a herd of bullocks plowed through here. We won't distinguish hers in all this."

"Perhaps we rubbed 'em out, not looking where we were stepping." The color came up under Button's round cheeks.

Chase moved toward the curb with his head down. "Clear these people away, Constable."

"You heard him, Pinch," Button called to a man at the front. "And you too, Meg." He and the other parish officer moved through the throng, addressing people by name, urging them to disperse. The fat lady made a face at Button and turned to go, a child draped over each massive arm. Gander retreated to the doorway of the bakery across the way.

Returning to the dead woman, Chase studied her once more. This time he felt a heavy regret he knew would linger rather like the perpetual ache in his knee.

Constance Tyrone had rich, yet delicate lips, a high forehead, and gray eyes, death clouded. The curve of her profile was lovely. He stooped to pick up one white hand stiff with rigor. Chase replaced it gently, his gaze traveling lower.

On her right foot she wore a pale blue slipper tied at the ankle. A white satin rosette adorned the toe. Strange footwear for walking on a wet night, no hat in evidence either. And where was the other slipper? Her left foot was covered in just a ripped stocking. He motioned to Button.

"She's missing a shoe. Have a look around and see if you can spot it."

"Must have flown off when she was struck."

"Flown where? Surely no farther than we can see."

The constable looked helpless.

Chase fingered the slipper. "And I've a mystery for you, Button. Do you suppose she was a witch?" He smiled at the constable's blank amazement. "No muck on the sole, man. See for yourself. Unless she was in the habit of flying through the streets of London, I cannot think how she got here. She assuredly did not walk."

Chapter Two

When the Coroner and jury filed in, Penelope straightened on the bench and closed the journal in her lap. Recording the particulars of the scene had beguiled the waiting. Though she had not wanted to come today, she had promised. And now that she was actually here, her curiosity had quickened in spite of herself. Suddenly aware of the scratching of pencils, she glanced at a cluster of men seated nearby. Journalists, no doubt, easily identified by their notebooks and their narrow-eyed scrutiny of the room.

The large front parlor of the Crown public house was packed almost to bursting with spectators all determined to plumb Constance Tyrone's life. Why had she ventured out alone in the bitter November night? No gently bred woman ever did, even one who so resolutely pursued her own ends. But perhaps that was it: she had not been like others of her class.

All this Penelope had gathered by listening to snippets of the conversations swirling around her. Mostly, those in attendance were tradesmen of the parish, but a few heavily veiled ladies sat in the private booths. A fire blazed in the hearth, adding the smell of wood smoke to the sweat and perfumes of close bodies.

She was relieved when the proceedings began. After the Coroner offered his initial remarks, an officer escorted the jury into an adjoining room to view the body. Upon the panel's return, the Coroner called the first witness, Sir Giles Tyrone's coachman, who reported his failed attempt to collect his mistress on that final afternoon.

Then a spindly young man stepped up to the table in the center of the room. Voice quavering, he gave his name as Thaddeus Wood, curate for the parish of St. Catherine. Upon the Coroner admonishing him to speak up, he sat in the chair provided and steeled himself for what was patently an unpleasant duty. But his ordeal was brief, for he had little more to relate than his discovery of the body early the prior morning.

"Have you any notion why Miss Tyrone might have been abroad?" asked the Coroner before dismissing him.

"No," replied Wood, barely audible. "An errand in the parish perhaps."

Next the Coroner called a woman who appeared to be about six- or seven-and-thirty. Wearing a frayed gown and a dusty, flamboyant hat, she scowled at the jury as she sat down. Her face was pale under hectic spots of rouge, her hair scraped back into a knot. Penelope felt a stirring of pity as the hum of disapproval rose.

The Coroner glanced up from his papers. "Name?"

"Joan Snowden of Milk Alley near Dean Street." She smoothed her skirts and folded her hands in her lap.

On her way home from an engagement with "friends" at just after one o'clock on Tuesday morning, Joan had seen a hackney coach driving north at a spanking pace.

"I'd have thought nothing of it, sir, but for seeing as how it near toppled when it hit something in the road by the church."

"Did you observe the hackney's number plate?"

"No, sir."

Irritation darkened the Coroner's expression. "Did you go closer to ascertain what—or who—it was the carriage had struck?" he inquired, sarcastically polite.

"No, sir, I didn't. It wasn't my lookout. Anyway, someone else got there first. He could've been aiming to lend a hand or up to no good. How was I to know?"

A murmuring broke out, and the Coroner said sharply, "You saw someone in the street? Can you describe him?"

Joan looked scared. "No, sir, except to say as he looked uncommon big. Leastwise from where I was standing."

When she stepped down, a Mr. Reginald Strap, surgeon on staff at St. Thomas's Hospital, gave his testimony.

"I understand you are intimately acquainted with the Tyrone family, sir?" began the Coroner.

"Indeed. Mr. Bertram Tyrone and I are friends from our school days. We renewed the acquaintance in town some years ago when the family consulted me about fainting spells Miss Tyrone had been having. Nothing serious, exhaustion merely, but I referred her to a physician." He spoke with authority, his purposeful eyes fixed on the audience.

"I am afraid my friend Mr. Tyrone is in some distress as he and his sister were devoted. I've had to administer laudanum drops to give him ease. You see, he feels to blame for failing to protect her, particularly as he and I spent a rather convivial evening together the night before she was found." Strap looked up, adding bleakly, "We didn't realize."

"You weren't to know. Would you tell the jury, sir, what is your connection to the St. Catherine Society?"

"As an old friend, I offer my medical services *gratis* to Miss Tyrone's *protégées*."

"And I make no doubt she was grateful, Mr. Strap. It seems this noble endeavor had become her life's work?"

"Indeed, the family would likely say the work consumed too much of her time, for her health was uncertain and the demands of this self-imposed duty burdensome." Strap's voice dropped. "I wonder if she was attacked while performing some charitable errand in the parish that night. Although it can only be considered…unwise for a young gentlewoman to be abroad alone, Miss Tyrone was not always amenable to the advice of well-wishers."

Shaking his head, the Coroner glanced at the jury to see if they got the point. They did. Penelope looked away.

Her gaze fell on a man who sat taking notes in his pocketbook. She somehow knew he wasn't a journalist. Too large, she thought illogically, and too relaxed, half lounging in his chair. There was humor, solitary and acrid, in his face, and a fierce intelligence in the eyes glinting behind spectacles. He wore creased, nondescript clothing and highly burnished boots. His gray-streaked hair was tied in an old-fashioned queue. Before she could be caught staring, Penelope's attention was pulled back to Mr. Strap, who was reporting his examination of the body.

"Actually, it was rather difficult to determine the exact cause of death. She suffered two grievous injuries, either of which could have been mortal.

"There are severe contusions indicative, of course, of an attacker's hands pressing upon the throat, yet the victim also sustained fractures of the cervical vertebrae." He surveyed the room. "In layman's terms, her neck was broken."

"Was her neck broken in the attack, or is it more likely the carriage accident was the cause of this injury?" asked the Coroner.

"A particularly violent throttling could indeed have snapped her neck. However, the lack of significant swelling in the face would seem to support that a severed spine rather than asphyxiation by choking is the likely cause of death."

Strap added that when he had examined the victim at eight o'clock in the morning she had been dead for at least six hours, and rigor mortis had set in. At length, when the Coroner dismissed him, he made his way to one of the booths near the rear of the room.

The Coroner called Elizabeth Minton, Constance Tyrone's assistant, who described the work of the St. Catherine Society.

"We are engaged in helping women of humble station, especially unmarried females who are thrown upon the world. The Society offers practical assistance and also some rudimentary education enabling a young woman to find respectable employment."

Miss Minton's testimony was delivered in a prim, colorless tone as if she had memorized it. In her early thirties, she was a slight woman with large, waiflike blue eyes. Her cumbersome mourning dress seeming to swallow her up, she looked like a child playing dress-up in her mother's clothing. Her back was stiff, however, her gaze alert and oddly guarded.

Responding to her apparent fragility, the Coroner seemed at first inclined to lavish his rather ponderous gallantry upon her. After assuring himself she was comfortable, he said, "You must be especially qualified to shed some light on Miss Tyrone's final hours, madam. Though to speak of her must bring you great sorrow, I can only hope that sacrificing your own feelings in the service of truth will be of comfort to you in your affliction."

Contempt in her eyes, she retorted, "Fear not, sir. I am more than ready to answer any question you may put to me; still, I very much doubt that anything like truth is obtainable here."

"Why what do you mean, Miss Minton?"

"Only that my friend is dead, and nothing you can do will alter that fact. We do not know what was in her mind that day, nor what brought her out in the night to be attacked so cruelly." Her tone implied that the Coroner at any rate was likely to remain in ignorance.

"She did not in general confide in you?" he asked after a short silence.

"No, Miss Tyrone was one to keep herself to herself."

Without any further prompting Miss Minton went on to summarize what she knew of the victim's final day: a morning spent in the usual activities, luncheon with members of the Society, and an errand in the afternoon.

"She didn't tell me what her errand was, but it may have been connected to a letter delivered at luncheon."

"Did this letter appear to alarm her?"

"I couldn't say. She merely pressed a coin into the hand of the urchin who brought it and slid the letter under her plate for later perusal. When I saw her a short time later, she mentioned she would be going out about two o'clock."

Miss Minton had not seen Constance again and returned to her own lodgings about four.

The last witness turned out to be the man whom Penelope had noticed earlier: John Chase, a Bow Street officer. Casually removing his spectacles, he sauntered forward to take his place. And as soon as he opened his mouth, there wasn't a person who could look away.

"Upon examining the body and speaking with the Watch, I found that some curious facts had emerged." Chase went on to explain that since the victim's clothing had not been saturated, he could presume she had been accosted sometime after the rain stopped.

"The watchman Old Tom reported that the sky cleared about three o'clock, but it seems he mistook the time. If you recall Joan Snowden's testimony, she observed the hackney coach striking something in the road rather earlier: a few minutes after one, in fact.

"In subsequent inquiries, I ascertained that the rain actually ceased about half past twelve, which added further credence to Miss Snowden's report. But if she did indeed witness the trampling, it seems odd that during Tom's regular circuits he should not have discovered a body in the middle of the road. Of course, with the weather so inclement perhaps Tom felt himself called upon to repair to the watchhouse. I believe there is one placed hard by the church grounds in order to discourage grave robbers and other villains." His tone was dry, and Penelope could envisage the parish authorities seething.

"What are we to make of this, sir?" put in the Coroner.

Chase turned to him politely. "Initially I assumed that sometime between half past twelve and one o'clock Miss Tyrone was the victim of violent thievery only then to be struck by a passing carriage. But I must tell you, gentlemen, certain circumstances seem passing strange in my view."

The Coroner frowned. The journalists, however, looked pleased.

"Her footwear was entirely unsuitable for walking abroad," Chase continued. "Indeed, one of her slippers was missing, and the sole of the one remaining was free of filth in spite of the muddy street.

"And why would Miss Tyrone be on her way to the Society? The curate has told us he did not unlock the gate until just after six o'clock in the morning. She had no key in her possession, either to the gate or to her office. I thought perhaps her keys had been stolen, but later discovered one in her desk and the other hanging in its place on the wall."

He looked around the room rather triumphantly, Penelope thought, and for good reason. No one had the faintest idea how to answer the questions he posed. The Coroner merely shrugged, gesturing at the officer to continue. The journalists, gorging on every word, knew good theatre when they heard it.

"There remains another matter which it is my duty to bring to your attention." He paused again. Truly, thought Penelope in amusement, this man should have been on the stage.

"You see, gentlemen, I think I know what Miss Tyrone's errand was the afternoon of Monday, 11 November. Searching her study, I found a portfolio of sketches drawn by the artist whom Sir Giles had engaged to complete her portrait." He picked up some sheets from the table and held them up.

Addressing the jury directly this time, he added, "As you will see in a moment, these drawings portray Miss Tyrone in the guise of St. Catherine—she who was put to the wheel to be tortured."

They nodded. Chase added, "I am afraid the drawings are of an indecent nature."

"Indecent?" said the Coroner.

"Yes, there is something in the subject's expression and posture. I leave it to you to see what I mean."

As a loud buzzing broke out, the Coroner called for order, and the Runner sat, unselfconsciously enjoying the effect of his words. But Penelope's smile had shriveled to ashes.

Chase rose, handing the sketches to the Coroner, who picked up the first one and stared at it, entranced. Tearing his eyes away, he dropped it on the table with an exclamation of disgust.

Penelope ducked her head for a moment as if somehow the people around her would be able to read her thoughts. But no one was paying her the least attention. The avid whispering intensified, the journalists craning their necks and edging forward to get a glimpse of those sketches. One even planted himself directly behind the Coroner's bewigged head and thrust his skinny neck into viewing position. From behind, his cronies hissed, begging for details.

It might have been comical if one did not recall exactly what it was they were falling all over themselves to look at. A woman had died, and there was something obscene in her exposure to public censure and titillation. Damn Jeremy. Nonetheless, her anger at his folly warred with anxiety that this time his charm would pay no toll; he was in deep trouble indeed. How could he do this to her and to Sarah? The room seemed to press in.

"…with the sketches was a letter which I believe was the very one Miss Tyrone received at luncheon Monday last. It is from the artist, one Mr. Jeremy Wolfe, soliciting a private interview with the victim on unspecified but 'urgent' business. I submit to you that for the next step in this investigation we must apply to this Mr. Wolfe."

Penelope had heard enough. She slipped her notebook into her bag and gathered her gloves and hat. Pushing her way out of the room, she took a deep breath upon gaining the corridor. At least the walk to Jeremy's lodgings would allow her time to regain her composure. She would need her wits about her.

It wasn't every day, after all, that one's husband was likely to be taken up for murder.

Chapter Three

Edward Buckler leaned back, his feet occupying the one uncluttered spot on the desk. For several hours, he had sat immobile in his chair, reading the past few editions of the *Times*. The report of a deadly fire in Crown Court had made him shiver with horror. On a lighter note, he'd learned that Mr. A.S. Thelwall had delivered an address on the progress of the Great Comet, which had been visible now for months. Moreover, a series of lectures by the noted poet Mr. Coleridge was to commence soon at the Philosophical Society. Two guineas for the course, or three "with the privilege of introducing a lady."

He stretched, yawning, and the newspaper slid from his lap to join the pile on the rug. "Damn," he croaked. He pushed back his chair and stood, frowning down at the desk crammed with papers, open books, and dried-up ink pots. Beside the desk a small table held the remains of more than one meal, including a half-empty teacup, which Buckler retrieved on the way to the window.

Throwing back the curtain on another hazy day, he slumped against a pedestal supporting a battered bust purported to be Dante. Someone had scratched an inscription on its base: LASCIATE OGNI SPERANZA VOI CH'ENTRATE!

"Abandon all hope, indeed, Dante old boy," he murmured, patting it affectionately, "for all who enter here will find the tea has gone cold. Not only that, but this room is a bloody jumble."

Even in the dim light the furniture looked faded and lumpy, dust coating every available surface. Stacks of books and periodicals dotted the carpet, and the coat rack had tipped over to spill its garments on the floor. In the far corner stood a long case clock that lost precisely one minute and fifteen seconds every twelve hours, something Buckler had discovered in a week-long experiment.

Turning his back, he leaned his elbows on the sill and gazed at the mist that had rolled up from the Thames to smother his view of the garden. Somehow the gospel of getting ahead had been less insistent of late. Those maneuverings designed to browbeat a witness or mislead a credulous jury—too often in defense of a cause one knew to be unjust—now seemed as unreal as half-remembered dreams. All in the great tradition of the English Bar, he thought wryly.

But here the Temple had stood for over six hundred years, originally as the seat of the Knights Templar, that abolished order of warrior monks, and later as a preserve for lawyers. In the Elizabethan period it had offered a fraternal, collegiate lifestyle and sound legal training to young men of good family. The barristers remained, but the days of revels were ended: no gentlemen dancing in the Hall for the Benchers, no feasts lasting for days, and no more moots or mock trials testing the mettle of all participants. Today, life at the Temple was eminently less colorful and more practical, as suited the modern era. Business, the all-absorbing, vital business of law. One defendant's misfortune could be the making of a barrister's career.

At that moment he realized that he himself, still in his red brocade dressing gown in the middle of the afternoon, was in no better condition than his chambers. Surely at thirty he was too young to retire from the world, even if he had nothing better to do than to idle at the court with all the other briefless barristers. Perhaps he merely needed some companionship, preferably female, an excellent bottle of claret among friends, or a ticket to Mr. Coleridge's lectures.

"I shall make a new start of it," he said aloud with a mock salute in Dante's direction.

With that he moved toward his desk, determined to do battle with the mound of papers. Bending down, he yanked at the drawer where he kept his pins, expecting it to stick as usual. Instead it flew open and expelled its entire contents.

"Damn, damn, damn," he muttered, crawling about on hands and knees like some pacing beast with red fur.

He was in this position when he heard the stairs creak. The door banged open.

"Come in, Bob. Don't stand on ceremony. Have some cold tea," he called, still focused on the pins, pens, wafers, and blotting paper all over the floor.

Someone cleared his throat with a blusterous "Ahem," and Buckler groaned in recognition. When he looked up, instead of his clerk's bony frame he beheld the rounded, imposing figure of Ezekiel Thorogood, attorney, reformer, and general pain in the…. But Thorogood was not alone.

In the doorway stood a small woman, made that much smaller next to Thorogood's bulk. Wearing a serviceable gray cloak, she had warm skin and wide eyes of a rich brown. Her dark hair was dressed simply. The style gave her an air of vulnerability until one noticed the strong bones of nose, cheek, and jaw. She was young, five-and-twenty perhaps, and held a child, a girl of about three years who resembled her. The woman waited, not diffidently, but with an air of sizing up her surroundings.

Peeking like a tiny, eager bird, the child giggled to see him on his hands and knees. "Horsey, Mama!" she chortled as she squirmed in her mother's arms. And Buckler bounded to his feet, grabbing ineffectually at the belt which trailed on the floor.

Advancing into the room, Thorogood lifted the coat stand and draped his fur-lined cloak and white hat over it. "I trust we haven't come at an inconvenient moment."

"Do make yourself comfortable," said Buckler.

The woman set her child on the threadbare carpet. Her gaze swept the room.

"Edward Buckler, ma'am," he announced with the slightest of bows. "I fear you have the advantage of me."

She had stooped to loosen the child's wrap. Now she rose, incredulity writ clear in her face. "I do apologize, sir. I am Penelope Wolfe. This is my daughter, Sarah." Again her stare lingered on the dirty breakfast dishes and the clothing strewn on floor and furniture. "Perhaps we are intruding?" The child tugged at her cloak so hard that the woman staggered. She bent again to issue a low-voiced reprimand.

"No, no, my dear," said Thorogood. "Buckler, we've need of your help. This young woman's husband is under a cloud."

Buckler emitted another groan, which he turned into an unconvincing cough. He had known Thorogood for a mere two years, but somehow it seemed longer. Long enough at any rate to have embroiled him in a number of tangles, for the old lawyer had a genius for wreaking havoc in any well-ordered existence. More than once Buckler's "payment" lay in a few bolts of cloth or, on one memorable day, in a brood of chickens that had taken to his chambers like ducks to water.

In a country where in theory one could be hanged for stealing merchandise valued at a few shillings, Thorogood stood for a new ideal. He actually believed there was something more important than the preservation of rich men's property. Some of his colleagues gave him the disparaging title of "thieves' attorney," claiming he worked hand in glove with the criminal element. Thorogood saw it differently. His career had been long and successful, and now, approaching retirement, he offered his services only to those who were poor or in desperate need. The original impulse for Thorogood's altruism had sprung from his second wife, a Quakeress, who had left the faith of her upbringing to marry for love. But he had become so wholly keen on his own account that even she had trouble restraining him.

Buckler slanted a scowl at his friend, then with a flourish swept debris from one armchair to the floor. "Won't you sit down, madam?" He essayed a smile at the little girl, who ignored him. The woman removed her cloak and sat, her unflinching gaze fixed on Buckler as he took the chair opposite.

Thorogood perched somewhat precariously on a stool. Retrieving a silver timepiece from his pocket, he intoned, "*Tempus fugit.* Though apparently not so swiftly around here. Buckler, your clock is off by ten minutes." He clicked his watch shut. "Well then, here it is. Yesterday this lady attended the Coroner's inquest looking into the death of Miss Constance Tyrone." Pausing, he beamed. Mrs. Wolfe, taken aback, opened her mouth to clarify.

Buckler picked up the newspaper he had been reading and pointed to an article. HORRID MURDER, said the headline. "Baronet's daughter found dead outside the church?"

The lawyer nodded as if commending a favorite pupil. "You've heard the verdict? Murder against person or persons unknown. Only it seems some are inclined to name that unknown person, and rather prematurely I might add. A not unusual state of affairs for our esteemed authorities."

Sighing, Buckler turned to Penelope Wolfe. He had a feeling he knew what was coming. "Are you connected with the family, ma'am?"

"No. It is my husband Jeremy who knew the victim. He is an artist, you see, commissioned to paint Miss Tyrone's portrait. Now, through an unlucky chain of circumstance, he has come under suspicion."

Buckler had little desire to get involved in this matter, whatever the "chain of circumstance" that had brought Jeremy Wolfe to the notice of the authorities. "Ah, tea?" he said awkwardly. Then he noted her all too obvious appraisal of the pile of used crockery.

"We won't put you to any trouble," said Thorogood. "We'll be on our way once we've made the arrangements."

"Arrangements?" he echoed with foreboding. He tried to catch Thorogood's eye, but in vain, for the lawyer was muttering over a gravy stain on his waistcoat.

The woman spoke again. "Jeremy has been remanded to Newgate, awaiting evidence. We had hopes you might visit him."

Barristers did not visit persons held under suspicion of murder in filthy prisons. That lot fell to solicitors and attorneys. Barristers stayed comfortably holed up in their own comfortable if insular milieu with nothing to say to the scaff and raff. If this was Thorogood's way of pushing him back into the world, he could think again.

But if Buckler didn't interview Jeremy Wolfe, there was no doubt that Thorogood would. And for all his vim, the man was getting on in years. Allowing him to enter a damp den like Newgate would hardly endear Buckler to Mrs. Thorogood. Although she knew her husband to be perfectly capable of driving himself and anyone fool enough to accompany him into an early grave, lately she had looked to Buckler to moderate his sudden enthusiasms. Or, persuasion failing, to serve as Thorogood's proxy. Persuasion always failed.

Buckler looked down to see the child Sarah reaching her hand toward the table where lay a tiny quartz figurine that he had absently set in his saucer.

"No, love, you mustn't touch," said Penelope Wolfe.

But when the child's eyes shot to his face, he smiled. "That is Philomela, the nightingale, lover of song. You may hold it."

The little girl nodded wisely and repeated to herself, *night-in-gale*. After exploring the bird with her chubby fingers, she set it in the middle of the saucer.

Curiously, this brief byplay seemed to unnerve the mother, for she looked away for the first time, her fingers pulling at her skirt. Then she said, "You were about to wish me at Jericho, were you not? Oh, politely, I have no doubt." Her expression reflected a mixture of doubt and hauteur.

Buckler sighed. "Have you no one else to act in your interests?"

"You mean, why isn't some gentleman here in my stead? I assure you I shall do better without. Besides there's no one."

She looked around the room again as if seeking visible evidence of his credentials. He felt a prick of annoyance.

"Youngest son of a country gentleman of good repute and middling estate. Harrow. Then Cambridge. Called to the Bar of the Inner Temple some three years past. Won a few cases, lost a few more. That's all I can tell you, I'm afraid."

She laughed, and her face thawed into sudden, surprising beauty. Hearing her mother, Sarah laughed too. Thorogood grinned at all and sundry, clearly delighted his little gathering was proving a success.

Buckler gave in. "What would you have me do, ma'am?"

"Since my husband has refused to give good account of his whereabouts on the night in question, suspicion has attached to him all the more strongly. I'd like you to question him, impress upon him the seriousness of his position. And I'd like you to defend him should it prove necessary."

"I will have little choice but to do so if the brief is properly tendered."

She raised her brows. "If you are asked to argue a cause you yourself do not wholeheartedly endorse? What then, sir? Would you work to free a man you thought guilty?"

"It is quite simple, madam. The integrity of our system, indeed the very liberties of England, depend on doing just that." Ignoring Thorogood's bark of laughter, he continued. "You see, as Lord Erskine said in defending the radical Tom Paine, the minute counsel prejudges the guilt or innocence of his client, justice can never be done. That judgment belongs only to the court."

"You've learned your lessons well, boy." Thorogood left his stool to retrieve a pipe from his coat. "My one remaining vice," he said as Mrs. Wolfe nodded her permission.

Lighting it, he stood in front of the fire and declaimed, "*Non potest gratis constare libertas. Hanc si in magno aestimas omnia parvo aestimanda sunt.* Freedom cannot be bought for nothing. If you hold her precious, you must hold all else of little value."

"That's well enough, sir," said Mrs. Wolfe. "But Seneca aside, sacrificing one's integrity is too high a price to pay, even for freedom. I have heard that honest diligence can be a rare commodity among those engaged in criminal work."

She knows the classics? Buckler was surprised and not entirely certain whether he liked it. On the whole he approved of education for women, yet there was something rather disconcerting in the sharpness of this rejoinder.

But what she said was true enough. Barristers taking criminal cases were often not highly regarded in the profession, and many used this work merely as a stepping stone to more eligible pursuits in civil suits.

"Not this man, missy," said Thorogood. "He's quite the most honorable and...er...diligent man I've ever met, though perhaps one wouldn't think it on first acquaintance. You should see him in his barrister's robe and wig. A different animal entirely."

He waved his pipe and sent a plume of smoke to curl around Buckler's head, adding, "But you really ought to engage a maidservant, my dear fellow."

Penelope stepped out of Buckler's chambers into Crown Office Row, glad to escape the narrow stairwell. But it seemed she had only entered a more stifling corridor as she pressed through a thick, yellowish fog that made it impossible to see beyond a few yards ahead. It was beginning to rain again, a dreary drizzle that soaked through the brim of her bonnet and trickled down her face. She wondered if she had been wise to take leave of Mr. Thorogood and the hackney so graciously offered, yet she'd no wish to impose upon the old gentleman any longer or to reveal the need to preserve her own slender resources.

She walked up to Fleet Street. Though it was only four o'clock, the lamps were lit, and the occasional flicker of a linkboy's torch added its bit to dispel the gloom. Caught in the flow of their own business, people drifted in and out of view, moving in currents up and down the street, some resting briefly in a doorway only to be swept once more into the course. It was nearly a mile to her lodgings in St. Martin's Lane, and Penelope couldn't use the umbrella under her arm since she needed both hands to carry the child. So she quickened her pace, trying to avoid the puddles washing over her ankles, her skirts quickly saturated with filth.

By the time she paused at the crossing, trying to catch her breath and fruitlessly shifting a Sarah grown heavy with sleep, she began to think that perhaps she ought to give in and take a hackney after all. But how this sensible resolve was to be enacted with no coach stand in sight, she could not at that moment apprehend. The carriages flying past were so full of purpose and importance while she, standing there, felt so unequivocally and irredeemably alone...

"Come away from the window," Jeremy said. "You'll catch a chill." She moved closer to him on the seat and braced herself as the coach lurched. Shutting her eyes, she wished she could drown out the incessant clopping as each blow of the horses' hooves pounded between her eyes.

In contrast, Jeremy was in high spirits, the habitual discontent for the moment eased. On the way home from an evening at the theatre, he was full of restless energy, crossing and uncrossing his legs, squirming in his seat, and flexing his fingers as he talked.

"Aphrodite rising from the sea foam? Not that mushroom's over-ripe daughter! I had to remind them of their place, of course. Never mind it cost me the commission."

"Cost what?" She had been so intent on his face that his words did not immediately sink in. It was often like that with Jeremy.

Suddenly irritated, he said, "Dash it, you've been like this all evening. Are you sickening for something?"

"Just a headache. I heard what you said, however. I take it we shall be practicing economies for a time?"

His hands stilled. Then he sighed audibly and pressed his head back against the squabs, his face finding the only slash of lamplight in the coach. "I didn't mean anything," she began, "but if—"

"You do not have to say it. I could tell precisely what you were thinking."

It was true enough that her expression often betrayed her.

"Jeremy, I would not have you immortalize merchants' daughters unless you wish to. At least not on my account."

After a quick sidelong glance, he stretched his legs and returned to the contemplation of his gleaming boots, a perfect picture of artistic isolation.

Penelope watched him. Sometimes she got so tired of the constant playacting—the endless reassurances, the blithe schemes, the unspoken agreement that Jeremy had with everyone in his sphere that no sordid realities need intrude.

Before she'd remembered to guard her tongue, the words were out: "But why not a merchant's fat daughter, Jeremy, if she also has a fat purse?"

Splash. A passing barouche had driven a sheet of water into her face. She transferred the child to her hip, angrily brushed at the water, and trudged on, thinking with longing of sun-warmed Palermo and of her father.

It had been too long since she'd seen him, and indeed, Sarah had never met her grandfather, whose standing as erudite radical made him celebrated in his adopted country. Penelope remembered him as always the dynamic figure at the center of some gathering, she the observer. After her mother's death she had become his hostess, learning to smooth rifts in conversation with a prompting question or provocative remark. And there were the slow, happy days when it seemed she had nothing to do but read and study and take long walks.

Here in London it was hard to imagine the isle of Sicily with its orange and lemon groves and glorious mountains. No, more real in the growing darkness was the fear Constance Tyrone must have felt in the last moments of her life. Though the larger streets were kept fairly clean and well lit these days, the city still harbored myriad foul, hidden places where wealth and family would be no protection and brutality lashed out all too often.

Yet Penelope believed that Jeremy, for all his faults, was not capable of such viciousness. He was vain, self-serving, shallow, but no murderer. She had not been able to turn him away when he returned the day after his midnight visit. Pale, almost sick, with no trace of his usual jauntiness, he had begged her to attend the Coroner's inquest. And she had gone. Now, arms tightening around Sarah, she saw with relief that a coach stand was just ahead.

A quarter-hour later she entered her lodgings to find Mrs. Fitzhugh hovering in the entry. A woman in her middle fifties with a lined, sour face, the landlady grumbled, "Rather late, Mrs. Wolfe. I'm afraid your dinner will be spoiled. Moreover, a gentleman"—she hesitated over the word—"awaits you in the parlor."

"Hungry, Mama," whined Sarah, awakening fully.

"Soon, darling." No doubt the caller was merely the printer Mr. Cotton, there to offer her a bit of work destined to swell the pages of his newest periodical. Though Mrs. Fitzhugh thought him some sort of cousin to her lodger, she never scrupled to show her disapproval of his occasional visits despite the fact that his was a gray, inoffensive presence. As for Penelope, she appreciated the printer's uncommon willingness to oblige by coming to her, understanding full well that he acted at her father's behest.

But when Penelope thanked the landlady and walked into the parlor, it was to find a stranger standing near the window. A small man with slicked-back, oily hair and glistening eyes, he reached into his waistcoat pocket and presented her with a card: Mr. Jedidiah Merkle, Solicitor.

"An honor, ma'am. Most…grateful for an…opportunity to broach a certain…matter with you." He spoke at a curiously measured pace with frequent pauses as if he found it necessary to feel his way through each sentence.

Mystified, Penelope said, "Pray be seated, sir. If you will give me a moment." She gestured to a nearby chair.

"Thank you…good lady, but this one…will suit me… better." He pointed to the window seat.

She put Sarah down, but the child immediately clung to her leg. After struggling out of her own damp cloak and bonnet, she removed Sarah's wet garments.

When at last Penelope took a seat, the man leaned forward, coming uncomfortably close. Mr. Merkle wore a loud, flowered waistcoat and puce colored breeches. She could smell his pomade.

"Your unfortunate…husband…is not without…friends."

"Really, Mr. Merkle." She looked again at his card.

"Oh yes. And these…friends have…entreated me to set your mind at…ease as to the…ah…affair of your husband's… Let me assure you that he will soon be…restored to the… bosom of his family." He put his hand into another waistcoat pocket and removed his snuff box. Lifting the lid, he took a pinch of snuff and inhaled with great enjoyment.

"My own mixture." Merkle waited for her response.

"Oh indeed." She wondered if he expected a compliment.

"Of course, dear…lady I came at…once to allay your very natural…concern. But no…need, ma'am, no not in the…least."

Sarah tugged at Penelope's sleeve. She reached down to pull the child into her lap, but Sarah continued to wiggle and whine. At this time of day, she wanted nothing more than her dinner, a story, and bed. Penelope didn't blame her. Merkle, quite at his ease, sat patiently.

"Are you acquainted with my husband, sir?" she said at last.

"I have not…the pleasure."

Penelope's eyes met his. "I'm afraid I don't understand you, Mr. Merkle. Be so good as to speak plainly."

His fingers slid into yet a third pocket. This time he held a bank note. "I have been…instructed to bestow…this upon you and to…assure you that Mr. Jeremy Wolfe stands in no…danger from this…misunderstanding." Smiling, he picked up her hand, stuffed the bill into it, and patted her arm. He seemed to think the matter settled, for he rose to his feet.

Penelope stood also. "I cannot accept this. Who are these friends of my husband's?"

"Now think…nothing of it." He walked across the room to retrieve his coat and hat. "The twenty pounds is not a…loan, but monies…owed to your husband for…services already… rendered."

"For what sir?"

"Do not...trouble yourself about the...details, ma'am. Everything has been...taken care of. Good evening to you... and the child."

She marched forward to intercept him. "Sir, will you not tell me who sent you here?"

"Why, no...ma'am. Would you have me...betray my client's...confidence?"

With that he bowed and left. Penelope stared after him, holding up the bank note. "Well, what do you make of that?"

"Hungry, Mama," said Sarah.

Chapter Four

ONE HUNDRED GUINEAS REWARD
(To be Paid on Conviction)
BRUTAL MURDER!!
WHEREAS,

in the early morning hours Tuesday last, Miss CON-STANCE TYRONE was most foully Murdered by some person unknown. Barbarously Strangled and Trampled in the street, she was discovered outside the East Gate of St. Catherine's Church. A Hackney Coach which it is supposed may bear some connection to this Crime was seen in the vicinity.

Missing is One Slipper, pale blue satin with white satin Rosette and Grecian Tie. Also missing, believed stolen, is a Crucifix in Gold Filigree bearing the victim's initials and set on a fine gold chain. Any Person having knowledge of such articles, or who witnessed any Suspicious Activities on the night aforementioned, is earnestly requested to give immediate Information.

By order of the Churchwardens, Overseers, and Trustees
Joshua Border, vestry clerk, Wednesday, 13 November 1811

Edward Buckler read this handbill, one of many thrust his way as he walked along Fleet Street, the others extolling the wonders of cure-all medicines, waterproof boots, or beauty enhancers. The eastward route he took today between the two churches of St. Dunstan's and St. Bride's once served as a path of atonement for the faithful when so many medieval prelates inhabited the area. Now, a chaos of vehicles vied for room to maneuver, inching toward Ludgate Hill and St. Paul's or pressing west with equal futility to the crush around Temple Bar.

Buckler had risen early, determined to turn the morning to good account. Accordingly, he had spent several hours perusing the press accounts of the Constance Tyrone inquiry. The authorities had moved quickly for once, arresting Jeremy Wolfe two days after the body had been found. Not surprising, Buckler reflected. Street scum may murder one another with impunity, but as soon as violence touches one of Society's own, the voices cry out.

The papers had all struck the same note of outraged virtue tinged with panic. Moreover, the debate about London's lack of a centralized police force had been revived with the usual arguments both for and against reform. Supporters insisted the time had come. The lawlessness of London's streets demanded it. Opponents waxed poetic about the need to safeguard English liberties—just think of the abuses of the powerful, secretive French police. Both sides, however, agreed upon the need to resolve the matter quickly. The pressure to find, convict, and execute Constance Tyrone's murderer would be intense, a fact which boded ill for Buckler's potential client.

As for Jeremy Wolfe, twenty-four hours could seem an eternity to one unaccustomed to Hell: Newgate with its well-earned reputation for filth, debauchery, and inhumanity. Felons, whether tried or untried, small thief or brutal killer, all herded together, though debtors were separately confined, and women had their own cramped area of the prison. It was said that first time offenders thrown in with hardened criminals were so thoroughly corrupted in this school of vice that a life filled with depredations inevitably followed.

Passing St. Bride's, Buckler continued to the Old Bailey and turned north to approach the prison's grim façade. The stark, soot-stained walls rose unrelieved to the heavy cornice, the only ease for the eye offered by a series of empty niches originally designed to hold figures. With almost no windows to the exterior, Newgate presented a blank face to the world.

Ringing the bell, he waited for the turnkey to descend from the lodge. The turnkey, clad in a shabby tailcoat and carrying a lantern, merely grunted in response to Buckler's request and led him through a heavy, nail-studded door and down a stone passage toward the Felon's Side.

It was hard to tell which direction they headed as they followed the damp, gloomy corridor through a series of gates and gratings, each one unlocked and locked in turn by Buckler's companion. The passageway was crowded with streams of visitors shuffling with heads down: women with hungry children at their skirts; men with furtive faces probably come to plan new robberies with the prisoners; journalists visiting one of their number imprisoned for seditious libel; pie men hawking their wares.

"How much farther along, my man?" Buckler murmured.

"The name's Gus." The turnkey stopped in front of a gate with bars through which Buckler could see a narrow courtyard. Gus took him through the yard and up some stairs into one of the wards.

It was not the worst Newgate had to offer, at least not compared to the common felons' wards where a prisoner who lacked the desire or the funds to indulge in the general licentiousness might be stripped of his clothes and tried by mock tribunal. Jeremy Wolfe must have paid the entrance fee to the master side as well as the required "garnish" money to his fellow inmates.

This room was large with benches, a deal table, and wooden barrack beds where the prisoners slept, eighteen inches allotted to each. About two dozen men loitered as close to the sea coal fire as possible, wrapped in rugs against the chill. No one was shackled; all apparently had the funds to pay for "easement," as they called it here. A handful of prisoners played cards, several others looking on listlessly. Some men perambulated about the ward; a few lay with eyes closed on pallets. Most looked drunk.

Wolfe was easy to pick out. He sat on a low stool with drawing pad in hand at work on the profile of a fellow prisoner. A candle flickered beside him, casting uneasy shadows on the wall.

The turnkey blustered over and placed a heavy paw on the artist's shoulder. "Painter man," he growled, "your lawyer's here."

Jeremy Wolfe stood and laid his work on the table. Straightening his coat, he stepped away from the turnkey to take Buckler's measure. "Indeed. You're not what I expected."

Gus said, "You ain't his lawyer?"

Buckler addressed himself to the artist. "Mrs. Wolfe asked me to pay you a visit."

"My wife sent you? I thought…well, I am glad to see you, sir. Won't you sit?" Wolfe indicated a corner of the room where they perched on a bench. The turnkey remained, but at a respectful distance.

The artist wore buff pantaloons and a well cut coat, but his linen was soiled, his cravat untied. The stubble on his chin and unkempt hair betrayed that he had endured an uncomfortable night.

Buckler said, "I need to ask you a few questions. I don't yet know if I can assist you, but anything you divulge will remain confidential."

"I have not been formally charged. They can't keep me here forever."

"No. Unless the magistrates decide to commit you for trial."

"On what grounds? A trumped-up charge? A few drawings and a letter that says precisely nothing? And all this due to nothing more than a bunch of doddering fools in a panic lest the public see them for what they are."

"You did write to Miss Tyrone?"

"Yes, I was dissatisfied with our progress. She had missed several sittings, and it had begun to seem unlikely I would complete the project by year's end. You knew I had been commissioned to paint her?"

"So your wife has told me." Buckler took out his notebook and pencil. "Who proffered the commission?"

"Her father, Sir Giles Tyrone." He chuckled. "You see it's not enough to have wealth if one wants to cut a dash in polite society. One must also possess the finer accouterments."

"A portrait."

"A professional portrait," corrected Wolfe. "After all, 'twould be a comfortable possession, hanging quietly on the wall for all the world to admire. More restful than its model certainly."

"You mean, I take it, that all was not well with Sir Giles and his daughter?"

"Who's to say? I did wonder why she had consented to the sittings. Not at all the sort of thing to interest her. One can but conclude it was at the behest of her father."

"What makes you think she didn't enjoy it?"

"Champing at the bit from beginning to end. Quite a challenge, I must say. The problem was she had no vanity. Usually I can count on that to keep the ladies in place."

Wolfe himself was hardly a restful person. He had the trick of listening to his interlocutor's words with another part of his mind someplace else. In some men this might be a sign of greatness. In Jeremy Wolfe it seemed to indicate both a high-strung temperament and an intellect busily seeking its own advantage. Fingers drumming, one booted toe tapping, he appeared to find sitting still a torture. God knew how he would manage should his incarceration prove lengthy.

"Where did you hold your sessions with Miss Tyrone?" asked Buckler.

"One day when I've secured a proper patron I shall have rooms for painting and a gallery to display my work. And assistants with books of engravings scurrying to do my bidding." He smiled. "In the interim, I am forced to content myself with visits to my clients, in this instance the family home in Great Queen Street."

"Did she talk to you much?"

"No. That was part of her fascination. I had the feeling she didn't have much to say to anyone, about personal affairs at any rate. Though she'd blow the gaff about her work readily enough."

"Fascination?" Buckler wondered what the artist had felt for his client. Though his tone was flippant, he seemed to have observed Constance Tyrone keenly. Part of his stock in trade or something more?

"Yes, she was intriguing. Fearfully independent, didn't give a tinker's curse what anyone thought, yet she could charm when she chose. I know only one other woman who can hold her own quite that well." He looked up, his expression regretful, and Buckler felt the pull of liking for the first time.

Wolfe continued, "But if you're wondering whether I was in love with Miss Tyrone, the truth is she scared me out of my wits. Too intense by half for a frippery fellow like me. God knows I've gone that road before."

Their eyes met in sudden understanding.

"What did Miss Tyrone tell you of her work?"

"You heard she founded the St. Catherine Society? I suppose it was a respectable endeavor for a gentlewoman initially. It's one thing to help serving maids and paupers learn their Bible. It keeps them humble, in their place so to speak. If they hope for something better, they don't expect to get it in this life.

"But she talked a lot of nonsense about everyone having the right to a thinking life. Even the Irish, mind you, and the lightskirts off the street. She raised a breeze or two with that." He laughed again, maliciously.

"You find that ridiculous apparently," commented Buckler. "And I suppose it was an attitude that would win her enemies, yet she must have had courage."

"She did," replied Wolfe, serious now. "When you listened to her speak, the least likely things sounded not only obtainable, but utterly desirable." His mouth twisted mockingly. "A pity, isn't it, sir, that such delightful fancies trouble so few of us?"

"How did you obtain knowledge so intimate?"

"By any means possible. I make it my business to know my subjects. It's the only way I can create, the only way to stimulate the imagination." He paused, pointing to the man he had been sketching who sat nearby staring into the fire.

"That man in the shabby cap was once an able seaman in His Majesty's navy, that is before he killed someone in a drunken brawl. I could have guessed something of the sort brought him to this pass without his telling me. It's there to read in the face."

"And what was there to read in Miss Tyrone's face?"

Wolfe squirmed a little. He seemed to be weighing the odds, playing out his hand. Buckler's sympathy evaporated as the silence lengthened.

"Sir, your wife has told me of your visit to her lodgings on the night of the murder. You implied you had discovered some potentially 'useful' intelligence which concerned Miss Tyrone?"

Silence.

"If you choose not to be frank with me, there's really nothing more to say." Buckler stood. He had the feeling Jeremy Wolfe had been leading him a dance during this conversation. He didn't like it.

"No need to take one up so quickly," the artist said, motioning Buckler to resume his seat. "But isn't that just like a woman? Discretion seems to be a virtue which escapes the best of wives."

"What of the sketches the authorities found? They were hardly discreet."

"Part of my artistic process, sir. I envisaged Miss Tyrone as the beautiful Saint Catherine of Alexandria. You know the tale?"

"Did she not convert the fifty philosophers the pagan emperor brought to debate her? And then was bound on spiked wheels because she still would not renounce her Christian faith and marry the emperor."

"Exactly. But God smote the machine with fire, slaying her executioners, so the emperor ordered her head chopped off. It's said that milk flowed from her body, not blood, and that the angels bore away the corpse to be buried at Mount Sinai. Catherine went up to heaven to be espoused to Jesus himself. Anyway, I was trying to capture Miss Tyrone's powerful will as well as the fires she kept well banked."

"From what I've heard, your impression is not exactly in keeping with her reputation."

Jeremy fingered his creased neckcloth. "I still say I pegged her nature right."

Buckler said flatly, "Mr. Wolfe, you must see that your refusal to cooperate in the magistrate's inquiry has added in no small measure to your difficulties. If you will tell me of your whereabouts throughout Monday evening and early Tuesday last, I may be able to help you."

Before Wolfe could respond, the door was flung open. A second turnkey entered with someone else in tow. When Gus pointed out Wolfe and Buckler, the turnkey's companion advanced into the ward, gesturing at both prison officials to stay back. He was a small man wearing a dark coat over a waistcoat embroidered in large daisies. In one gloved hand he held a packet of herbs, which he wafted continually under his nose. The other hand clutched his overcoat and cane as if he feared someone might wrest them from him.

"Jedidiah Merkle, solicitor," he said as they stood to face him. "I find you in good…health and…spirits I trust, Mr. Wolfe, in spite of this lamentable…error."

He bowed to Buckler. "It is my charge this day to…report that Mr. Wolfe will not be in…need of your…services, after all…though it's indeed a…pleasure to meet you, sir. I've heard of you, for you have earned quite a…name in some…circles." He placed a card in Buckler's palm and bowed a second time.

There was something terribly irritating about Merkle's measured speech, particularly in contrast to the hand fluttering about his face. "I regret I cannot return the compliment, sir," Buckler replied, glancing at the card.

The solicitor took Jeremy Wolfe's arm. "You will be eager to depart this foul…den, so ruinous to the…health. Let us not waste an instant, sir."

Gus made a motion toward Jeremy, but the other turnkey intervened. "Leave be, Gus. This one's bought and paid for. He's off with this carrion bird to Bow Street."

"What?" said Buckler.

"Quite simple, sir. A witness has come forth with… testimony completely clearing my…client. The… gentleman with whom Mr. Wolfe was playing cards on the evening of Monday last has been…located. He was at first a trifle… reluctant to come… forward, but was induced to see reason once he apprehended that the life of an innocent…man was at…stake."

"One moment." Shrugging off Merkle's arm, Wolfe picked up his sketchpad and approached Buckler.

"I am grateful, sir, for your kindness and hope to offer you better hospitality should we meet again." Relief and triumph mingled in his voice. He shook hands, adding, "I cannot but think that the authorities will find another pigeon to pluck, but apparently I'm to keep my feathers for the present."

With that they were gone.

"You'd best be off too, sir," said Gus, "'less you want to stay and feed on any of these carrion."

❦ ❦

"Been expecting me, I see," said Noah Packet as he slid into a chair. From under Noah's broad-brimmed beaver, his muddy eyes flicked from table to table, to the doorway, and back again.

Chase pushed a full glass of gin across to him. The smoke hung like fog about the room, each breath bringing the varied and pungent odors of humanity mingled with the sweetness of tobacco. The din of voices swelled.

This was the Russian Coffee House, vulgarly known as the Brown Bear, a most disreputable flash house where the underworld plotted iniquitous acts only a few yards from Bow Street public office opposite. Here John Chase would come for good drink, mostly unadulterated, and for the occasional arrest. Today he sought information. Someone had gone bail for Jeremy Wolfe. He wanted to know why.

"Buck up, Friday-face." Packet threw back the gin in one swallow. "Though it queers me how it all come about."

Chase looked at his companion. Noah Packet was most certainly a thief, though in a small way only. Because he was one to keep his ear close to the ground, he often came by useful tidbits of news. Of indeterminate age, he was slight with bowed shoulders, neatly dressed in a black suit. His complexion bore the pasty, haggard finish common to night creatures.

Packet always had money, but never much, so he was glad to get a dram or two of liquor in exchange for his assistance. It was well known at flash houses that certain of the Runners would nurse a culprit along until he "weighed forty," or was indictable on a capital offense, his ultimate conviction garnering the officer a portion of the forty-pound reward. But Chase knew Packet trusted him as far as that went. In a strange way they had become friends.

"Wolfe knows something, Noah. Curse him."

"You'd best let it lie. You got plenty else on your plate, I warrant. If you want to find the one as nobbled the gentry mort, I'd smoke out that necklace what's missing. That's my advice. And have another." He saluted Chase with his empty glass and grinned, showing a mouthful of rotting teeth.

When Chase ignored him, he continued, "Besides, I hear the Tyrones are sure it was some lackwit as put her away. It may be so. I ain't heard no whispers."

"Better a random attack by a lunatic than scandal visited on the family. Sir Giles has made it quite clear my inquiries are unwelcome."

"There you are then. Forget the artist. Go for fences, pawnshops, and such. Why flog a dead horse, especially when those most concerned ain't prepared to pay for your trouble?"

"Too many unanswered questions." Leaning forward, Chase captured his companion's gaze and forced Noah's flitting eyes to halt. "I want to know, Packet."

"If that ain't the main thing I can't abide in you, Chase. You always got to know. Like some kind of plague from God, you is. You don't quit." Gesturing to the serving maid to refill his glass, Packet sat back, trying to look innocent.

"Have you learned anything about the fellow who laid Wolfe's alibi at Bow Street? Arthur Bennington claims the two of them spent the entire evening of the murder together enjoying an intimate supper and a few hands of piquet."

The thief smiled.

"You know something, Noah. Out with it, or you'll be clapped in irons before morning."

Packet gave the hoarse rattle that served as his laugh and coughed, gaze on the door again. He never looked Chase directly in the face when about to spill information.

"Word is tradesmen are starting to dun 'im."

"Bennington? Deep play?"

"Dunno." He shrugged. "He lives high, but it's a hollow purse if you take my meaning."

"Anything more?"

"Well, it's a curious thing: Bennington's servants can't precisely call your man's face to mind. And it seems Bennington himself were home on the night in question nursing a cold in the head. Ain't likely he felt up to entertaining."

"Perhaps I ought to pay Mr. Bennington a visit tomorrow just to determine if he's recovered from his indisposition. What do you think?" He dropped a few coins on the table, gulped his drink, and picked up his coat and hat.

"I think you'd do well to leave be before someone decides to shut your bonebox for you," said Packet mournfully.

Chase pushed back his chair. "If Bennington's fortunes are at low tide, perhaps he was bribed to provide an alibi. But where would Jeremy Wolfe have found the money? See what else you can discover, Noah."

He left Packet sitting over his gin.

❧ ❧

After dinner Chase bid his landlady Mrs. Beeks good night and went upstairs. Closing the door behind him, he removed his boots and waistcoat and trod to the bureau to find a clean nightshirt. As he was rummaging in the drawer, his fingers touched a small packet wrapped in cotton wool.

He removed the wrappings to examine the miniature by lamplight. Framed in silver, it showed a young woman with blue eyes, wide and intense, looking levelly at him. Straight nose, a smiling mouth. Full lower lip, the upper thin but with an attractive lift. Her rounded chin had the tiniest pocket of excess skin. She was wearing a pale muslin gown trimmed in ribbons that just matched her eyes. Chase cataloged each feature, thinking, as he always did, that the artist had done fine work; he had not made Abigail too pretty.

The child held standing on her lap was much like any other infant, for an artist's skill can do little with features as yet unformed. Clutching his rattle, he looked like any other fat, happy baby captured for posterity. Yet perhaps the artist had caught something in the set and shape of the eyes, or perhaps Chase merely imagined the likeness. Carefully, he wrapped the miniature and replaced it in the drawer.

He poured himself a brandy and wandered into his sitting room to stoke the small fire and recline in the armchair drawn near. Strange how the memory of Constance Tyrone's empty eyes had troubled him for a moment during dinner when Mrs. Beeks had inquired about the business. He had thought almost simultaneously of Abigail's eyes, brimming with life, but most of all asserting the proud independence that was peculiarly her own.

It was her independence and his stubbornness that had separated them, he realized. For Chase had not wanted to return with Abigail and her father to her home in Boston, and she refused to accompany him to England. Her father was aging, she said, and needed help in his business. And never mind that she was pregnant with Chase's child. She could manage.

Abigail was good at managing. She had saved his leg, after all, when he was invalided out of the navy with an injured knee after Aboukir. Nelson's victorious but wounded fleet had anchored in Naples, and while the hero was off being coddled by his mistress, Lady Hamilton, Chase had found his own haven.

An American woman a few years his senior, Abigail nursed him back to health, and they fell in love. For both, it was the first time. Chase's father, a poor country parson with five children to establish, had secured him a place as a cabin boy at the age of thirteen, and Chase had spent his youth in the West Indies and the Mediterranean, protecting the British merchant fleet and fighting a war. He had eventually advanced to first lieutenant. Abigail, a thirty-three-year-old spinster, had traveled widely with her father, somehow never finding an opportunity to settle.

They parted amicably enough, he supposed, in spite of Abigail's rejection of his marriage proposal; it hadn't proved so difficult for him to give up a child he had never seen. He made his way back to England, tried rusticating for a few years, and ended up in London working for Bow Street. One of the magistrates, whose only son was a naval officer, had offered him the post over eight years ago.

And Chase's son had just reached his twelfth birthday.

Chapter Five

A massive dark wall guarded the London docks from the infectious touch of thieves and scavengers. Since its construction, the district had grown ever more dangerous, for those who once preyed upon the vessels now resorted to assault or begging. These were hard times. Napoleon's Continental Blockade had crippled the country's European commerce, war with America appeared likely, and the harvest had been poor. Many would go hungry this winter.

It was here on the Ratcliffe Highway in Wapping that the hackney deposited Chase. Intent upon his own business, he wended his way purposefully through a crowd of stevedores, watermen, coopers, and rat catchers. Sailors, pockets to let after a few weeks ashore, swaggered: bored, drunk, and quarrelsome. The smell of fish mingled with the waft of the Thames. East and West Indiamen and a plethora of other craft creaked at anchor.

Just outside the great barrier in an alleyway off Old Gravel Lane, Chase paid his gate fee and entered a warehouse. Dust hung thick in the morning sun streaming from a window overhead. He could feel this was a cavernous place, empty of goods, though the upper floors and the far walls were lost in shadow. He looked about, experience having taught him that caution was in order at gatherings like these, for the quick flash of a blade might be the only warning of trouble. English and foreign seamen skirmished often; just last month a Portuguese had been fatally knifed.

Even so, mingling with the pickpockets, dock workers, and sailors were a few of the Quality: wild, young blades and sporting types, willing to brave the stink in order to gorge on a different sort of energy. Chase, too, felt it, but also sensed a new edge. Over the last few months he'd noticed a subtle shift in the working men he encountered. Hard to pinpoint but definitely there, a certain wariness toward anyone in authority, a surly cast to the countenance.

At one end of the warehouse, men clustered about an excavated area where someone had contrived a round, sunken stage about ten feet in diameter, ringed with a low bulwark to prevent the combatants from fleeing. As Chase approached, voices crested in excited shouts, and he caught the stench of fowl. Arthur Bennington stood a little apart, scuffing his Hessians in the dust.

Bennington wore a long driving coat and a belcher handkerchief. His artfully arranged hair surrounded a well worn, cynical face. Chase knew his like. Aging London exquisite, a favorite for rounding out the numbers at dinner parties, someone a hostess could count on to be suitably amusing. And Bennington was said to be a devotee of all blood sports. Probably added a little spice to a life immersed in nothing more important than the cut of his coat. He didn't look up until Chase was upon him.

"A word with you, Bennington."

The dandy eyed him up and down.

"John Chase, Bow Street. I should like to ask you a few questions, sir."

"If you are here to inquire further about Wolfe, I thought we'd dealt sufficiently with the matter."

A few of the men nearby turned their heads.

Chase moved closer. "I'd speak softer if I were you. I'm not for trouble today. Unless you are?"

Bennington, perhaps two or three inches the taller, looked down his long nose as if Chase were an insect buzzing for notice. "What can I do for you?" he said after a moment. "Ah, another battle. You'll have to talk whilst I observe." He stepped closer to the bulwark.

Two men, the "setters-to," entered the makeshift cockpit, each holding a fighting bantam. Chase caught the glint of steel gaffles, cruel spurs attached to each cock's legs. As the birds, one black and one red, were brought into the ring, guttural sounds issued from both and echoed from the crowd.

"Black," Bennington murmured. "Observe that one," he said to Chase. "Excellent bottom. Not too large, nor indeed too small. See how he holds his head upright and crows vigorously."

The two cocks were brought beak to beak. Making eye contact, they struggled in the grip of their handlers who drew back to either end of the ring. Men called out bets. Upon the birds' release battle was joined as they struck at each other, turning and twisting for dominant position.

"Nothing to choose between 'em so far," said Bennington, satisfied.

Chase tried to curb his impatience. "Wolfe played piquet at your house into the morning hours of Tuesday last?"

Bennington didn't bother to look at him. "So I have informed your superiors."

"An intimate of yours?"

"No, acquaintance merely. Town is thin of diversions at this season, and a snug game of cards passes the time. Who wants to be abroad in such weather we've had of late?"

"I take it you and Wolfe passed a tolerable evening in spite of no servants to wait at table?"

Bennington swung toward him. "What the devil is that supposed to mean?" Then, as more betting erupted, he concentrated again on the cocks. A thin trail of crimson oozed from the black's left eye.

"Damn! First blood; it'll come about, however." Out of the side of his mouth, he added, "I only told the truth, man. Can't allow an innocent man to stand wrongly accused."

"Yet you waited until a full day after he was arrested to speak."

"Lord, how the bird struts. The black is just sparring, biding his time; you'll see."

Chase leaned in again, his voice rougher this time. "How is it that no one in your household recalls seeing Jeremy Wolfe?"

Bennington arched his brows. "Servant's prattle? I've a bachelor's establishment, nothing elaborate. Friends often come and go with none the wiser."

The black suddenly stumbled, and the other bird struck a sharp blow at its neck. The black reeled back.

"Relish games of chance, do you?" said Chase. "I heard you lost a tidy sum to Wolfe. Strange, he doesn't strike me as being up to your weight. Not long in the purse either."

Bennington stared at him coldly. "You gamble?"

"Not for money." Chase returned the look.

The black bird had retreated and was now pinned against the wall below them. The other cock dived at it viciously, tearing feathers and drawing blood. A sudden spurt sent red droplets across the arm of Bennington's coat.

"Blast." Taking out a handkerchief, he dabbed delicately. "Quite spoiled, damn it."

Chase said, "Blood stains the hands worse," and waited with interest to see the effect.

Bennington's eyes glittered with humor. "So I am to be cast the villain of this piece? How entertaining. Yet providing an alibi for Wolfe would hardly be astute of me."

"Unless you act to protect someone else."

The match reached a crescendo. The black bird, in serious trouble now, attempted a final rally, launching itself at the red in desperation. Bennington, however, showed no concern. Still frowning at the marks on his coat, he waved a dismissive hand.

"You begin to fatigue me, sir. It's a pretty thing when a Bow Street officer persists in annoying his betters."

"I am engaged in a murder inquiry," Chase reminded him, "and persistence must serve a man well in such case."

"I had no part in any villainy and neither did Wolfe. I suggest you seek other game; there's no profit for you here."

"Nor for you. Your bird is finished."

Just that fast the black bird lay dead amid the dirt and blood.

The crowd reacted with cheers and muted growls. Bennington cursed and extracted his purse from his pocket. His debt satisfied, he drew his coat around him, obviously ready to depart, but gave a loud sigh when Chase barred his path.

"Look," said Bennington. "Upon occasion one has an opportunity to do a friend a small favor, and one must take it, the opportunity, I mean. But nothing wrong."

"You're telling me you did Wolfe a favor?"

"No, not him. He didn't kill the girl, any more than I did. However, the fool was treading on some prominent toes, someone who can't afford the glare of public view just now."

"Who?"

"I cannot tell you that. I will say that this person had nothing whatever to do with Miss Tyrone's death. Of that I assure you." Nodding curtly, Bennington stepped around Chase and ambled toward the door.

Hard by Westminster Abbey, St. Margaret's church attracted the wealthy and fashionable as well as members of Parliament. This November day Constance Tyrone's funeral had drawn genuine mourners, many from the lower orders, as well as the merely curious. Indeed, the throng spilled onto the pavement where observers strained necks and ears to follow the proceedings inside.

Penelope had grown thoroughly chilled lingering on the outskirts of the crowd. When, at length, the service ended, she pushed her way inside, no longer surprised to note the marks of grief on the faces of many she passed. Hoping to observe something of the Tyrone family, she strolled up the nave and paused in front of the church's east window.

A crucifixion scene, the window was divided into five compartments, three of which depicted Christ and the two thieves. A hovering angel bore off the soul of the penitent to heaven. A little demon had the unrepentant thief on its back. At opposite ends were the warrior St. George, a red dragon at his feet, overlooking a youthful Henry VIII at his prayers, and St. Catherine, flanked by her wheel and bedecked in a crown of glory, guarding a similarly kneeling Catherine of Aragon.

By turning her head slightly, Penelope could observe the family standing a few feet away with the pastor. About sixty years old, Constance Tyrone's father had deep-set, faded eyes under thick brows, patrician features, and white hair falling back from a knobby forehead. He responded politely to remarks addressed to him, yet seemed remote.

Next to him stood two young men, so different it seemed impossible they could be related, though Penelope nonetheless took them to be Miss Tyrone's brothers. The younger boy, with his poor posture and unhealthy, bloodless complexion, looked more sulky than grief-stricken. The elder, perhaps seven-and-twenty, was tall like his father with features cut in the same cast. As Penelope watched, the boy laid a hand on his brother's arm and spoke a few words. She was leaning forward to catch the reply when a voice at her elbow made her jump.

"Why does the devil need yet another bad seed when Hell is already full to the brink?"

The Bow Street officer John Chase stared contemplatively up at the window. Penelope didn't know if his remark had been meant for her ears, or if the Runner merely thought aloud. But she felt compelled to answer.

"The demon is covetous of the poor fellow's soul, of course." She couldn't resist quoting softly, "And mine eternal jewel given to the common enemy of man."

Chase laughed, causing several people clustered around the Tyrones to look up in disapproval. "Having carted off more than a few villains myself, I have never found their souls to be of great value, if, indeed, they may lay claim to such a boon at all."

"Everyone is possessed of an immortal soul, sir," she said stiffly, "even a contemptible being like that thief."

"Many thanks for the reminder. Though I have yet to discover evidence of anything so hallowed in many, if not most, human creatures." He bowed. "John Chase, Bow Street, ma'am. May I have the pleasure of knowing your name?"

Chase had been watching her for several minutes, tantalized by the conviction that her face looked familiar. Then he'd placed her; she had attended the inquest. He remembered finding it odd to see a young, well-dressed woman sitting unaccompanied among the journalists and assorted riffraff. Seeing her again today, he was intrigued. And when she'd tarried in the church, clearly with the intent of observing the Tyrones, he had decided to approach her.

Defiantly, she told him her name.

"Penelope Wolfe," he murmured. "Wife of Jeremy Wolfe, the artist detained in Newgate, then providentially released. I wonder what brings you here. Inspecting a rival, albeit a dead one?"

"My husband is still imprisoned, sir."

There was no mistaking the astonishment on her face, and he could tell his insinuation about Wolfe and Constance Tyrone had failed to penetrate. But quick to recover, she added, "As you are no doubt well aware."

He bowed again. "Your husband was brought up at Bow Street yesterday afternoon and discharged. I've been round to his lodgings several times, but his landlady hasn't seen him. You reside elsewhere apparently?"

"We live apart." She clamped her lips shut.

"A gentleman named Arthur Bennington has come forward to claim he played cards with your husband at his house in Jermyn Street on the night of the murder. They were playing deep from about nine o'clock till dawn and never stirred from the table. The two of them even breakfasted together. Bennington claims he didn't know Mr. Wolfe had been taken up."

Observing the thoughts chasing across her face, Chase knew immediately she didn't believe the alibi either. Certainly it didn't seem Jeremy Wolfe was plump enough in the pocket to play for the usual high stakes.

"A true disciple of Lady Luck, is he?" he asked as an angry red tide suffused her cheeks. "But perhaps your husband prefers not to confide his peccadilloes to you?"

"On the contrary, sir. I am well informed of his pursuits. You may, however, ask him yourself." She walked away.

He caught up with her as she stepped outside. "You see, ma'am, there's something very wrong here, and I mean to know what it is. A young woman found dead in the street. A family who won't talk. Someone making sure your husband isn't around to answer any questions." He laid a restraining hand on her arm. "I mean to know," he repeated.

She opened her mouth, no doubt to offer a blistering reproof, but instead looked at him in sudden speculation. What now, he thought?

"Mr. Chase, I confess I am anxious to learn the truth also, and not just for my husband's sake. These past few days I have found myself wanting to know more of Constance Tyrone." Ignoring the jostle of pedestrians, she moved aside and signaled for him to join her in the shadow of the Abbey.

"I believe Jeremy must be in some kind of trouble," she continued. "He may be somewhat…impulsive, but he is incapable of harming anyone. And he certainly had no liaison of the nature you imply with Miss Tyrone."

So she had understood his earlier remark; not such an innocent, this one, and no fool. Chase smiled. "Many women have been surprised on both counts, I am sure."

She was struck to silence, looking miserably uncomfortable. "She was not the sort of woman to appeal to him," she said at last. "But why would anyone want to harm Miss Tyrone, who from all accounts has done so much good?"

"I cannot say. Mrs. Wolfe, allow me to escort you to your husband's lodgings. Let us hope he has returned and can answer some questions."

"Now why should that be necessary, sir, if, as you say, Jeremy is in the clear? Still, perhaps together we may unravel this tangle a bit."

He gave a wry smile. "I suppose any ministering angel may, upon occasion, elect to throw in her lot with the demon, ma'am. Still, should you not be in fear of a soul snatcher like me?"

Chapter Six

The rooms of the St. Catherine Society lay in a corner of the churchyard, a high hedge supplying privacy so that one almost forgot the bustle of the parish church next door. Following the curate's instructions, Penelope made her way down a path, her steps unnaturally loud, for here the city's noise was dampened by foliage and the calling of birds. Another late autumn day threw a gloomy canopy overhead. She was quite alone.

As she emerged into the open, two whitewashed, creeper-covered structures, one little more than a cottage, the other somewhat larger, confronted her. Mr. Wood, the curate, had told her that these close-set buildings once served as the old rectory, but today's incumbent lived elsewhere. Penelope wondered why this property was not given over to Mr. Wood, who looked impecunious enough, but perhaps the rector garnered a greater profit letting it.

Choosing the larger dwelling, she lifted the door knocker, muffled with a black swatch, and plied it vigorously. No response. Finally, she put her hand on the latch and pushed.

When the door opened with a decided creak, Penelope stepped into a small receiving area. Chill and rather dismal, it was furnished with a couple of scratched chairs and a faded needlework settee. Next to the settee a small coal fire smoldered in the hearth. A workbox sat on the floor near a stack of brown paper bundles. There was no one about, which seemed odd for the middle of the day. However, another door beckoned to Penelope's right, and, after a cursory rap, she entered.

Sunlight leaked through a gap in heavy damask curtains over a French window, probably a recent addition to this old dwelling. She went across the room and looked out on a terrace and tiny back garden encircled by a path disappearing into the shrubbery. In contrast to the rundown churchyard, the flower beds of pansies and marigolds had been carefully tended.

Turning back, Penelope considered the chamber. In the middle of the carpet was a mahogany writing table untidily strewn with papers. Behind the desk, a silk firescreen painted with a Grecian motif flanked a simple chimney-piece. Running along the far wall were enormous bookshelves decorated with several urns and a world globe. She was drawn across the room.

The selection ranged from the classics and books on horticulture to volumes of chapbooks and bundles of penny magazines such as the common folk read. Taking one down, she smiled. A ghost story: *The Tale of the Cock Lane Ghost.*

Sliding the chapbook back into place, she thought that she really ought to leave before someone discovered her where she had no business to be. But Jeremy was gone, no one knew where, and many would place a sinister construction upon his flight, make a presumption of guilt, in fact. Penelope preferred not to consider what role guilt might play in her own presence here—disobedient daughter, errant wife…

She paused, her eye caught by an open cabinet on the lower shelf where a stack of pamphlets and books seemed about to topple. Instinctively, she put out a hand to straighten it.

A cursory examination told her that the books comprised works by Bentham and Godwin and pamphlets by Cobbett, Paine, Wilberforce, and Cartwright, all reformists or radicals to whose ideas Penelope had been introduced by her father, a man unconventional enough to believe in providing his daughter with something beyond the usual lessons in music and drawing.

Thoughtful now, she lifted up one of the books and began to page through it. Why would Constance Tyrone possess these writings? In Penelope's experience most philanthropists would rather preachify on the virtues of Christian humility than contemplate real social change. She set down the volume and took up another: Godwin's *Political Justice*. But as she opened it, a slim bundle tied up in blue ribbon slipped out and landed at her feet.

Yet another sampling of political tracts, she saw when she picked up the bundle, these composed by one Daniel Partridge, current firebrand of the House of Commons. Penelope remembered her father mentioning this man as the hope of the new generation of reformers; the remark had struck her because her father so rarely spoke in praise of others.

On an impulse, Penelope slid out a pamphlet, setting the rest atop the desk, then went to the window to peruse her find in the light. But when she unfolded the tract, she saw immediately that it held numerous handwritten notations. Afraid the writing might be private in nature, she folded it up again, and suddenly stiffened.

Creak.

In the next room the outside door had opened. She heard garbled mutterings and the chink of coals. Footsteps crossed the floor. Someone fumbled at the door of Constance Tyrone's office.

With no time for anything more, Penelope slid through the curtains and let herself out the French window into the garden, turning to shut the window behind her. Strange it wasn't kept locked, but she could only be grateful for the escape route.

Safe in the garden, she released the breath she'd been holding and put Partridge's tract into her reticule. I'm for it now, she thought. John Chase will be knocking at my door to whisk me off to the hell of the unrepentant thief. She would have to find a way to replace the pamphlet before it was missed.

After smoothing her gloves and straightening her hat, she followed along the path and so was able to approach the frontage again. This time when she knocked an old woman opened the door.

"You the lady Mr. Wood sent along? I looked for you, but you wasn't on the path."

"I rather lost my way," faltered Penelope.

The old woman didn't seem interested. "I'll take you to Miss Minton. This way." She stepped over the threshold to indicate the smaller building. Proceeding to a door off the tiny entry, she called to her mistress and gestured for Penelope to walk in.

The women were gathered around a large deal table, tall tapers at intervals providing light as they stitched at some sort of plainwork. Elizabeth Minton rose from her place and came forward, her surprise evident. Penelope's heart was pounding as she introduced herself.

"Wolfe?" Miss Minton echoed warily. She wore a severe dress that did not become her. Her cheeks were pale, her expression unyielding.

"Yes, I am Mrs. Jeremy Wolfe. May I have a word with you?"

Miss Minton glanced back at the circle of faces and frowned. The women did not appear to mind the interruption; they had set down their sewing and were observing avidly.

"As you can see, I am occupied at present."

"A moment only." Penelope bowed toward the open door.

She nodded. "Keep at your tasks, if you please," she said over her shoulder as they passed out of the room.

The women bent back to their work, but Penelope could feel eyes boring into her back. Facing Miss Minton, she tried a friendly smile. "Thank you for agreeing to speak with me."

"I must be candid, Mrs. Wolfe. I do not much care for your husband, nor can I imagine what we have to discuss."

"I must be equally candid, Miss Minton. I cannot blame you in the slightest, but you see, ma'am, I must be acknowledged something of an expert on his character. Feckless he may be, but he did not harm your friend."

"Oh, but he did. He did great harm to her reputation. And once lost, a lady's good name may be mourned in vain."

"In common fairness, you must see that my husband did not intend for his sketches to be exposed to public view. However, I am not here to make his defense, ma'am. I came to beg your pardon and to offer my help."

"Help? You are very good, but I cannot conceive of your meaning. You should return home to your husband and discover what the example of a loving and virtuous wife may do to reform his character."

Wrestling with her temper, Penelope had to draw a deep breath before she could continue. "Your counsel perhaps does not come amiss, madam, but I have yet to explain my purpose in coming here. In the last few days, I have read the newspaper reports about Miss Tyrone and also heard the evidence at the Coroner's inquest. And I have felt that the authorities are merely groping in the dark. Somehow they cannot see her."

Damn, she thought as her throat tightened, but she had Elizabeth Minton's attention now. "You must have loved and admired her greatly," Penelope said, pressing her advantage. "May I offer you my sincere condolences?"

"Thank you, Mrs. Wolfe." Miss Minton looked down on tightly clasped hands.

"I thought I could sit sometimes with your women. I do not know how you are fixed at present, but perhaps other duties impose upon your time and resources?"

Her gaze lifted. "As it happens, one of our most devoted and competent young women recently left us due to illness. Perhaps…"

At that moment the aged doorkeeper reappeared from next door. Several gray locks had escaped from her sparse bun to straggle about her face. Her eyes gleamed.

"What is it, Winnie?" asked Miss Minton.

"Here's a queer start, mum," the old woman said hoarsely. "Someone has been prowling in Miss Constance's office. We got housebreakers!"

Penelope clutched at her reticule.

❦

"I knew something wasn't right soon as I saw her desk and the vase what's smashed on the floor!" said Winnie.

Abandoning their sewing, the women had surged outside to investigate the commotion. Now with the old doorkeeper in the vanguard, they swept forward, Elizabeth Minton's repeated pleas for calm falling on unreceptive ears. Penelope was borne along with them.

In the waiting area, the women clustered around Winnie to pepper her with a shrill volley of questions, but Miss Minton dispersed them firmly and sent a young, red-haired woman called Maggie off to fetch the curate. Then she drew Winnie into the office with Penelope trailing behind.

Winnie said, "Look how the window be open, Miss 'Lizabeth, and I always lock up tight night and morning."

Penelope stared at the open French window. She was certain she had closed it as she fled. Perhaps the latch had not caught? No, she could distinctly recall hearing the click. And she assuredly had not broken the lovely Meissen vase that lay in shards on Constance Tyrone's carpet.

"Calm yourself, Winnie," said Miss Minton. "Sit down while I determine what has been taken." She walked to a heavy armoire in the corner. Pulling the doors wide, she lifted out a silver candle snuffer and a carved wooden box, turning them over thoughtfully in her hands. Next she crossed to the mantel to finger the clock.

Winnie sat, fanning herself with a clutch of paper. "Why just look at that desk, mum, and Miss Constance always neat as ninepence, poor soul."

The directress approached the desk, her expression grim as she checked each drawer in turn. "I straightened it myself this morning. I cannot understand this. Do you suppose one of the children crept in here to play?"

Winnie's face crinkled. "Ain't likely, mum."

Miss Minton looked at Penelope. "I apologize for troubling you with our affairs, Mrs. Wolfe. Please do not feel you need remain."

It was a dismissal. Penelope said quickly, "I hope you will consider my offer of assistance, ma'am? It was heartfelt, I assure you."

Miss Minton nodded. "I will consider the matter. Perhaps you could sit with the women of an occasional afternoon." Her smile was a little stiff, as if she found it difficult to unbend. She was not a woman easy to know, Penelope felt, though her friendship once won would be rewarding.

Remembering that damned tract in her reticule, Penelope felt her guilt grow, but if she admitted her transgression now she would lose all the ground she had gained. Inadvertently, she glanced over at the desk and had to swallow back her shock.

The bundle of pamphlets was gone. That could only mean that someone, perhaps Winnie, had moved it unless... Good Lord, she thought, what if there was a thief, and I interrupted him at his work? That would explain why Winnie found the window ajar and the vase broken. He would have had to hide somewhere.

Shivering, she glanced around. The shadows round the enormous armoire were deep. Could someone have crouched in that corner watching her then removed the political tracts upon her departure? And had he seen her take one of the pamphlets? This thought was particularly unnerving.

"What's amiss?" Winnie had hauled herself out of the armchair and hobbled over.

Before Penelope could respond, the red-haired woman burst into the room followed by the curate. They were accompanied by a footman dressed in resplendent livery.

The woman's words spilled out. "I went to fetch Curate, mum, but he was already halfway here."

"I was bringing along Sir Giles' footman, Miss Minton," said Mr. Wood, "when Maggie told me of your trouble."

"We got housebreakers!" said Winnie.

The curate's shy countenance grew pink with amazement. "Indeed? How distressing for you. Have valuables gone missing?" He held out one hand to the directress as if to offer reassurance, but immediately withdrew it, blushing the more. "Shall I send to the authorities for you?"

"Nothing seems to be gone, sir, but perhaps we had best report the incident in any case." She stooped to pick up the pieces of broken vase, then, rising, turned to the footman. "Oh,

I beg your pardon. Has Sir Giles sent his carriage? As you can see, we're at sixes and sevens here. Will you wait please?"

Obediently, the footman moved to stand near the door. After sending Winnie back to her post, Miss Minton drew Penelope aside.

"Mrs. Wolfe, if you truly wish to help, you may do me a kindness. I was to call upon the Tyrones this afternoon to return some of Constance's personal belongings. Would you be so kind as to go in my stead? I would not entrust so delicate an errand to one of the women." She hesitated. "To be truthful, you should be doing me a service, for I was dreading the prospect of an interview with Miss Tyrone's family just now, and in any event I'm needed here if the authorities are to be summoned."

"Yes, of course, Miss Minton," Penelope agreed warmly. "I do think, however, that I should use my maiden name. I doubt the Tyrones would welcome a call from Jeremy Wolfe's wife."

She looked uncomfortable. "That is true, of course, yet it cannot be right to deceive them."

"As it hardly seems likely I shall encounter the Tyrones again, I see no need to distress them to no purpose."

"Then you must do as you think best," she said. "The items are ready bundled in the outer room, and Maggie will go along to assist you."

Anxious to get a closer look at the paper in her reticule, Penelope would rather have gone alone. The tract looked to be valuable if it could provide a clue as to who had broken in and why. It seemed, however, that she would have to wait. And if she did discover something, she would have to confess her own involvement in the incident, if not to Elizabeth Minton then to the officer from Bow Street. Penelope did not at all relish the prospect.

Chapter Seven

As the carriage threaded its way through traffic, Maggie was quiet, seeming content to examine the interior with its highly varnished panels, brass mountings, and mahogany shutters.

After a minute or two, Penelope extended her hand. "We were not properly introduced, I believe. Penelope Sandford Wolfe."

Her open, freckled face broadening in a grin, Maggie shot forth her own hand. "Mrs. Margaret Foss. You can call me Maggie, as that's all I ever answer to anyway."

"How long have you been at the Society, Maggie?"

"Nigh on a year now. I started just after Jamie was born. He's never known nothing else. I left him napping today, but he'll be shouting for his supper if you know what I mean." She grinned again, surveying her expanse of bosom complacently.

"Ah well," she continued, "perhaps we'll be back before matters get to that pass. Specially because Miss Elizabeth won't understand, being without chick and all. You married, mum?"

Penelope looked away. "Yes, I am. But my husband is away at present."

"That so? My Danny is wont to take himself off too, but he usually turns up, looking to line his pockets. I don't mind except that I find myself with another babe to feed nine months later. No matter, mum. Men is all the same."

She gave an emphatic nod, which sent her rather flyaway red hair into further disarray and lowered her gaze in a parody of servitude. "Beg pardon, mum. I got no call to be speaking thus to a lady. It's just that I get to talking, you know."

Even when her tone was serious, Maggie had irrepressibly laughing eyes. Yet there was also a quick compassion underneath the laughter, for she had observed Penelope's embarrassment and was ready to conduct the conversation single-handedly if necessary.

At the risk of opening the floodgates further, Penelope remarked, "You must have had many opportunities to converse with Miss Tyrone, Maggie. What was she like?"

She cocked her head, considering the question. "I'd say she had some strange notions, though I don't mean to speak ill of the dead. She was smart, but not up to snuff in some ways. Too innocent like, expecting folks to share her manner of seeing. Miss Elizabeth was always trying to tell her."

"What sort of notions?"

"Well, mum, she used to talk of her flowers as if they were living and breathing. It fussed her just as much to see something green dying for lack of care as to come across a child with naught in its belly. She used to say the world could be one big garden with plenty for all, but Miss Elizabeth is right. We is poor and will stay so." She hugged her arms to her body.

"Surely…surely well-intentioned people can effect a change."

Maggie gave her a pitying glance. "Yes, mum. You know, I'm sorry for Miss Elizabeth. She must feel right terrible 'bout that brangle she had with Miss Constance on the day she died."

"They argued?"

"Lord yes. We all of us heard. Miss Elizabeth wanting to know where Miss Constance was going and Miss Constance a-telling her to mind her own affairs."

"When exactly was this, Maggie?"

"After luncheon. Then Miss Constance took herself off, and we never saw her again. Maybe Miss Elizabeth had a notion what would happen."

Thinking of Elizabeth Minton's careworn face, Penelope nodded. "How awful for her. Did they often have differences?"

"Oh, they were both godly women, and they loved each other, no mistaking that. Most wise they agreed just fine, particularly when it come to not needing no man. You know, Miss Constance used to tell me I could manage on my own, and maybe she was right. Still, if nothing else a man keeps your feet warm of a cold night."

Penelope smiled, repressing a qualm that this conversation smacked of impropriety. "From what I have heard, Maggie, Miss Tyrone was a woman of great presence. Did she have no suitors?"

"'Tweren't for lack of trying on their part. I heard they buzzed round when she was younger, and even now she could cast her spell. Not knowing, you understand." Stretching her legs, Maggie leaned back and affected a pensive air. "She was well blunted too. What man ever resisted the lure of gold?"

"Only a few perhaps," said Penelope soberly. "You are most observant, Maggie."

"Ah well. A woman can learn a good deal if she keeps her eyes open. You have to look at things square on, I always say. And help yourself to a little luck when you find it."

They had pulled up in Great Queen Street, Westminster. The brick buildings on either side had a pleasing uniformity, an understated, graceful refinement that spoke of real wealth. Like some of the other dwellings, Sir Giles' town house featured a lovely carved wooden canopy over the door.

When the coachman let down the steps, Penelope descended, followed by the footman and Maggie, who carried Constance Tyrone's belongings. As befitted a house in mourning, the front curtains were closed, the door adorned with a black mourning wreath. In the marble-floored vestibule the butler took their cloaks while another servant appeared to assist the footman with bearing the bundles away. After she saw Maggie comfortably bestowed in a chair to await her, Penelope was conducted after Constance Tyrone's possessions and so into the withdrawing room. It was appointed in the French style with white brocade and gilt furniture and an ornate looking glass over the mantel.

The ambience was far too formal for Penelope's taste, but elegant nevertheless.

The footman had apparently hastened to report the burglary of Constance's office, for when Penelope was announced, Sir Giles and his elder son were both on their feet, their stance adversarial.

When she stated her errand, they greeted her politely enough and introduced themselves. Sir Giles asked her to be seated, sat down himself in one of the chairs, and instructed the footman to bring refreshments. After the briefest of niceties, Mr. Bertram Tyrone knelt down and began sifting through the stacked bundles on the floor.

"I am told these things were not in the office at the time of the disturbance."

"Yes, sir, so I understand."

"Thank God for that." He held up a handsome volume bound in morocco leather. "Livy, you know. Quite valuable. But worth the more to me as once belonging to my sister."

Sir Giles broke in. "Kind of you to have brought it, Miss Sandford. In our extremity, it is the smaller gestures which bring the most comfort."

"I was happy to be of help, Sir Giles. Miss Minton would have come herself, but she was constrained to wait for the arrival of Bow Street."

"Ha, Bow Street." Bertram flashed a contemptuous glance at his father and jumped up. Crossing the room, he laid the book on an occasional table and paused for a moment as if to collect himself.

Penelope searched for words to break the taut silence. "I had not the honor of an acquaintance with Miss Tyrone, yet everything I have been told of her has evoked my profound admiration." She found herself addressing Bertram's back.

He swung around. "Oh, she was universally admired, but not always understood." His father, sitting like a statue, did not look at him.

Penelope said, "Perhaps it is difficult for ordinary mortals to fathom those who are quite out of the common way."

Sir Giles cleared his throat noisily, staring down at his gleaming shoes.

Bertram laughed, a bitter sound. "You're right in that, ma'am. No one ever accused Constance of being a mere mortal." He quickly added, "I do apologize, Miss Sandford. Family troubles are no excuse for ill manners. But, you see, as the days pass we are losing hope that the animal responsible for my sister's death will ever be apprehended." As if he couldn't bear to be still, he strode back across the carpet and bent again to inspect Constance's possessions. He pulled out a few more books, a clock, and several pairs of stylish, immaculate gloves, laying each item aside carefully.

"Surely the authorities will turn up something, sir. Has there been no progress?"

"Not to speak of, ma'am," said Sir Giles. "And since they seek a desperate thief who would commit murder that he may leave no witness to his villainy, I do not believe the authorities will get on. 'Tis likely he has taken himself off by this time."

"You presume the motive to be robbery?"

Sir Giles raised his brows. "Of course. Why else should the culprit have stolen her cross?"

The footman entered, carrying a large silver tray with tea service. Sir Giles nodded curtly. "Pour out, if you please. May I offer you some refreshment, Miss Sandford?" He frowned at his son. "Sit down and have some tea, Bertram."

Their gazes locked. Bertram opened his mouth to speak, then changed his mind. Turning away, he sat on the sofa.

Sir Giles ignored him, saying to Penelope, "Let us speak of something more pleasant, ma'am. Are you connected to the Sandfords of Wiltshire, ma'am? A fine old family."

"Only remotely, Sir Giles."

They were her cousins, but she wasn't about to tell him that. The family had disowned her father years ago after his marriage to Penelope's mother, the Catholic daughter of a Sicilian

bourgeois. And later when Eustace Sandford had become noto-
rious for his political views, the Wiltshire branch had sent him
several vituperative letters.

The silence grew again as the footman passed around tea
and a plate of cakes. Accepting a cup, Penelope said, "Your
daughter's work was most worthwhile, Sir Giles, for the plight
of her *protégées* must touch the hardest heart. They so desire to
better their lot."

His lips tightened. "I am not convinced that the lot of the
poor can be materially improved. They will only breed all the
more and again outstrip their means of sustenance. Then too
you will encourage them to fancy themselves misused when,
as naturally and inevitably occurs in our system of free trade,
conditions alter with the times. You have heard, ma'am, of the
recent outrages in Nottingham, the riotous spirit, the smashing
of valuable stocking frames? You see what can come of wrong-
headed 'philanthropy'."

Bertram flushed a little. "Constance would applaud your
sentiments, Miss Sandford. We are not unfeeling people, but
her determination to right the wrongs of the world caused her at
times to neglect nearer ties. I've often thought that my mother's
death when she was twelve played no small part in the formation
of her character."

Resolutely lowering her gaze lest she lose all sense of discretion, Penelope replied, "A tragedy of such magnitude overwhelms
anyone. I myself lost my mother quite young."

"Yes, it's true. My sister may not have been so...consumed
with her work had her early experience been otherwise. Constance never enjoyed the normal life for a woman of her station."

"Normal life?"

Sir Giles spoke. "Pretty dresses, balls, routs, suitors, that sort
of thing. All that a father could desire for his daughter."

"Did she not have a Season, sir?"

He smiled without mirth. "Only because I insisted, ma'am,
and she despised every instant. As far as Constance was concerned, it was all a colossal waste of time."

"Certainly, Sir Giles, your daughter received great satisfaction from helping others. She accomplished—"

"Charity may be suitable in its place, but it seems lately there is always some canting methodist preaching at one. It wasn't so in my day. And nothing is more fatal to the charms of an attractive young woman than to betray a priggish earnestness." His eyes meeting hers significantly, Sir Giles smiled. "More tea, Miss Sandford?"

"May I have a word, Miss Sandford?"

Following in the butler's wake, Penelope halted in surprise as a pale, somewhat disheveled young man stepped into her path.

"I'll show her out, Jewkesbury," he told the butler. "You go about your business."

Giving an elfin smile, the young man introduced himself as Ambrose Tyrone, brother to Constance, though she had at once recognized him from the funeral at St. Margaret's church. It didn't suit the proprieties for her to be drawn into a *tête-à-tête* with a strange young man, but this was a boy really. A boy moreover who studied her, eyes startlingly bright in the dimness, as if she were a rather intriguing but unlikely species.

"Will I do?" she asked, diverted.

"Hard to say. I think perhaps you will one day. You remind me of my sister."

Penelope bowed. "A compliment, Mr. Tyrone, I thank you. In what way?"

He pondered for a long moment before answering. "The same intensity, I think. Also the same fear."

She stared at him. "Fear of what, pray?"

"Of life…and death. What else is anyone afraid of? But some people let it keep them from what they most desire. Constance wasn't one of those." He pushed aside his hair impatiently. "That wasn't what I wanted to speak to you about, Miss Sandford. You're from the Society, are you not?"

"Yes, I've come on an errand and been most hospitably entertained by your father and brother, and now you."

"I rather think you were not received with much warmth by my father," he said dryly. "A woman with her own will and a voice to speak it sets his back up. Which is why Constance was something of an embarrassment to him and even to Bertram actually."

"But not to you?"

"No, not to me." He moved closer. "That wasn't what I wanted to say to you either. I've a message to charge you with for Miss Elizabeth Minton. Will you deliver it?"

Surprised, she nodded her agreement.

"Tell her that Sir Giles does not intend to contest the terms of Constance's will. For once, the lawyers have been forthright enough to admit the futility of such an attempt."

"Why should he wish to dispute your sister's wishes?"

Ambrose's eyes glowed. "You knew she was an heiress? Oh yes, my aunt left Constance some four or five thousand pounds per annum. Aunt Emily had no liking for Bertram or me for that matter." His face wrinkled in mock dismay. "Now Constance has left one-third of her fortune to be held in trust for her charitable society with Bertram as executor. The rest to my brother and me in equal shares, nothing to my father."

"He disapproves?"

"You've met him. I am sure you can imagine his sentiments. And now that Bertram has means of his own, even my father won't be able to keep him on such a tight rein." He darted a quick look at her face as if to see if he had disconcerted her. "Not that my brother is not a dutiful son. You know he's soon to be wed? A most respectable match, Sir Giles says." A chuckle escaped him.

"Your father must be pleased to have one of his children suitably settled. Sir Giles mentioned that your late sister had little interest in such matters?"

"Oh, Constance was far too clever to be caught thus. Told my father she wouldn't marry until a truly worthy suitor presented himself. But somehow none of 'em ever came close to deserving her."

"No, they wouldn't, would they?" She felt a sudden sharp sadness. "Your sister's bequest will be welcome news to Miss Minton. Sir Giles does not intend to relay this intelligence?"

"He chooses to leave her in uncertainty for a time." It was as if he spoke of strangers.

"Would Mr. Bertram Tyrone choose likewise?"

"Part of him desires to respect Constance's wishes. The other part thinks the money would line his own pockets a good deal more comfortably."

"And yet he seems so grief-stricken. It must have been quite dreadful for you all when she did not return."

"No one was worried at first. I had told the servants she had an errand. I almost believed it myself."

"But why?"

"Because it might have been true. If she had forgot to send a note, I didn't want to give Father any more fuel for his ranting."

His gaze shifted, going out of focus, and he seemed to be in rapt contemplation of the wall in front of him. Penelope looked into the raw, glowing embers that were his eyes and wondered how this fey boy managed living with a man like Sir Giles, who had probably never had an original thought in his life. There was something so alone about Ambrose.

"I must go now," she said softly.

He nodded and as though issuing a royal command said, "You will carry my message to Miss Minton."

Chapter Eight

Ignoring the discomfort in his leg, Chase knelt by the French window outside Constance Tyrone's office. The daylight was beginning to fail; he would have to hurry his observations. The lock had been damaged, not in itself surprising under the circumstances. But it looked as though someone had merely made a few jabs with a sharp object, scratching the metal on either side of the keyhole—hardly an efficacious method of gaining entry. A rank amateur might have smashed in the door. A cracksman would have picked the lock delicately, with precision.

He sat back on his haunches. Elizabeth Minton had assured him she could find nothing missing. Many of the valuables had been in the receiving room, packed up to be returned to the family. But there were still items worth the taking in Constance Tyrone's office. Why run such a risk and steal nothing? And how could a thief be certain no one would be around to nab him? Surely it would have been more prudent to wait until the women went home.

Chase walked through the office and entered the anteroom where the doorkeeper Winnie Skirl stood by the fire, trying to ward off the chill of the coming darkness. She had packed up her mending basket and shut the curtains. Her shawl lay ready on the table.

"Hell itself wouldn't warm these old bones," she muttered. "Eh, Mr. Chase, you gave me old heart a turn. You finished in there? I can't be staying longer. Not easy in my mind after sundown."

He watched her closely. She had not been present on his prior visit, and he had questioned her only briefly today. "Have you far to go, Mrs. Skirl?"

"Not far. I'll just tell Miss 'Lizabeth and take my leave." She made as if to shuffle toward the door.

"I've a few more questions, but I shall only keep you a minute. That is, if you answer me true." Chase used his most officious voice, but softened it as he took in her huddled form. "You've been ill?"

"Wait till you've my years," she said sourly. "My joints ache awful bad with the rheumatism, my teeth is loose, and nothing settles on my stomach proper no more. Ain't fun, not that I expect life to be."

"I see they treat you well here. Miss Minton seems a kind mistress."

Perching on the edge of a chair, she sniffed contemptuously as if his spurious pity had somehow reassured her.

"What was you wishful to ask me? Sure isn't the state of my health you'd be after."

"Did you observe Miss Tyrone's departure on that last afternoon, Winnie?"

"No, sir. I went home early that day, feeling poorly. I don't reckon as anyone saw her go. Miss 'Lizabeth was busy with the women."

"Aren't the children cared for upstairs in this building?"

"They are and a rare rumpus they makes."

"Little devils, eh? Do you suppose one of them may have scratched the window?"

"But...but that was the thieves, of course. You're not accusing one of the children?" She grabbed at her fingers as if trying to loosen the gnarled knuckles.

"I've known mere babes to turn criminal, not that I mean to imply such a thing of this lot. But you see, Winnie, it's an odd kind of thief who takes his knife and slashes the outside of a lock. More like child's play, wouldn't you say? Especially since the vase was shattered, and nothing seems to have been stolen."

A strange expression flickered across her face. It didn't look like relief although his suggestion ought to have reassured her. A bit of mischief from a high-spirited child would have caused no real harm.

"I suppose as that may be," she allowed. "You'll have to ask Bet, the nursemaid."

"You've said the French window in Miss Tyrone's office was fastened this morning. But what about in here?" He pointed at the door leading to the churchyard. "That door remains unlocked during the day, does it not, so that the business of the Society may be conducted? Were you away from your post at all?"

"No sir, I told you. I sat right here all morning, and when I heard a noise I went to look, but he was already gone." She stared stolidly ahead, her heavy jowl quivering.

Chase sensed she was not telling him something. But why would Winnie lie? If she knew she had been careless about securing the office and didn't wish to own up, perhaps. And with the rest of the women at work next door for much of the day, she was alone here.

"You're a brave woman, Winnie. Do you realize you must have frightened away the thief before he could take anything? It was a close run thing."

Instead of preening at his compliment, she went still, watching him, eyes drawn to his.

"I wouldn't be surprised had you forgot to check that window what with all the flurry around here lately. Could it be it was getting late last night, and you were thinking of getting home?"

"I…I been in a fidget, there's no doubting. Perhaps I did forget." As if on cue, tears began to well up in her already red-rimmed eyes.

Chase was about to press further when Penelope Wolfe entered, accompanied by a young woman dressed in the Society's sober garb. What the devil is happening here, he thought in astonishment.

Mrs. Wolfe regarded him with the look of consummate disapproval he had come to expect in their short acquaintance. She looked every inch the lady, down to the polished half boots on her feet and the beaded reticule in one gloved hand. The sight of her filled him with intense annoyance.

As if a spell were broken, Winnie stood and moved toward her with an awkward step, a few tears trickling down her flabby cheeks. Taking the old woman's shawl from the table, Penelope draped it gently around her.

"Good afternoon, ma'am," Chase said. He nodded to the red-haired woman who waited beside her.

Penelope spoke. "Maggie, why don't you take Winnie to Miss Minton? That is, if Mr. Chase is quite finished."

"I rather think I am. For now."

Her eyes gleamed. "I do beg your pardon for the interruption."

"You're sure, mum?" asked Maggie, studying Chase with some doubt.

"Just go, if you please." Penelope smiled in reassurance. "I hope to see you again, Maggie, and I thank you for your company."

"Do you have some stake in this affair which is yet to be revealed, Mrs. Wolfe?" he said when the door had closed behind the two women. "Or is it idle curiosity that draws you?"

"Is it idle curiosity to desire the truth? I do, after all, have reason, as I told you when you attended me to Jeremy's lodgings. My husband has vanished."

He saw that underneath her bravado she was worried, yet saw also that she wanted to know merely for the sake of knowing. If anyone could recognize the signs of that particular trait, John Chase could. He walked around Winnie's worktable to stand in front of her. "You might find that 'truth' is rather less palatable than you had imagined."

She grinned at him. "You are no doubt correct, sir. I might."

Disconcerted, he added in a brisk tone, "Why are you here, ma'am?"

"Oh, I called this afternoon just prior to the housebreaking's being discovered. I wanted to make Miss Minton's acquaintance and see if I could offer any assistance. I also came to apologize on my husband's behalf for those sketches."

"She knows your identity yet has made you welcome?" He didn't trouble to hide his disbelief.

"She is willing to give me a chance, I believe."

"A chance to do what precisely?" he said impatiently. "Deceive these women into thinking the impulse of charity has brought you here? I see you are not above a little manipulation of circumstance."

"I see you are not above browbeating old women," she retorted, adopting the lecturing tone he remembered from their last encounter. "When I came in, your face wore the precise look of that merciless devil on the window at St. Margaret's. You looked as though you intended to cart off poor Winnie."

"That may just be more appropriate than you realize. If you hadn't interfered, I might have obtained a better notion of this so-called robbery. I am convinced she lies about something."

As they talked, the darkness had grown subtly so that the rich color of Mrs. Wolfe's gown had begun to blend with the shadows. Strangely, the gloom only seemed to accentuate the expressions playing across her face. He watched her irritation fade to be replaced by eager interest.

"You mean, sir, that you suspect her of connivance with the housebreakers? That would explain—" A telltale blush mounted in her cheeks like a beacon.

"Explain what?"

"Why, your distrust of that pitiful, old creature!"

That wasn't what she had been about to say. The second woman to lie to him in less than half an hour…

He eyed her speculatively. "If you seek a clue to your husband's disappearance, I take leave to doubt that you'll find it here. Have you considered where he might have gone?"

"No. Are you planning to interrogate me, Mr. Chase?" She drew herself up.

"Not a bad notion. Why don't we step into Miss Tyrone's office for a few minutes?" Before she could object, he opened the door and bowed politely; perforce, she preceded him into the chamber. He left the door ajar as a sop to the proprieties.

Walking to the desk, Chase turned up the lamp and perched on the chair to begin poking around in the drawers. When he glanced up, he surprised an incredulous expression on her face and realized it was because he had dared to sit while she remained standing. Not the act of a gentleman, but then he had long ago renounced whatever claim to that honor he once possessed.

He waved a hand at the wing chair across from him, and she took a seat, trying to appear unconscious of his lapse in manners. So Penelope Wolfe, who seemed to enjoy flouting convention, was not entirely free of that ingrained upper class code. Her circumstances were not affluent, he believed, yet he sensed an arrogance in this woman that spoke of breeding.

"Where did you and Maggie go this afternoon?" he asked.

"Miss Minton asked me to supervise the return of Miss Tyrone's belongings to her family."

"You saw Sir Giles? What do you make of him? He'd rather give Beau Brummell the cut direct than cooperate with the likes of Bow Street."

"He was most gracious," she said with faint sarcasm.

Chase smiled. "Miss Tyrone was heiress to a tidy sum held in a trust to be administered by Sir Giles until her thirtieth birthday, which would have been in the new year. Poor girl. She could have tweaked her nose at them all."

"Perhaps she did anyway. Ambrose says the Society is to gain one third of the estate with the two brothers sharing the remainder. And Constance named Mr. Bertram Tyrone as trustee."

He gave a low whistle. "So not a farthing to compensate Sir Giles for the loss of a thoroughly unsatisfactory daughter? A pity for him and for me since I had supposed he had a pecuniary interest in her death. What of Bertram Tyrone?"

"While he disapproved of his sister's activities, he seems genuinely grieved at her death."

"Still, one wonders whether Bertram knew of the arrangements. Maybe he thought to inherit all."

"Sir Giles recently arranged an advantageous match for him; the girl is well dowered, I believe, though I am not certain whether Mr. Tyrone himself favors the marriage. He and his father are at outs." Penelope went on to describe her impressions of Ambrose. "An odd boy, secretive and self-contained, yet he admired his sister. Certainly greed would never govern him."

Chase remarked, "A boy of his age and class ought to be away at school. There are whispers about him—he's a bit 'touched,' according to one servant I questioned. Apparently, his father deems it better to keep him under the family's eye."

Penelope sat up straighter. "What persuades you that the attack wasn't random robbery as Sir Giles claims? Surely Ambrose, at any rate, was tucked up at home on the night of the murder? Where were the others?"

"The boy remained in his bedchamber, according to his valet and several other servants. As for Sir Giles, he spent the evening at his club, but it was a quiet night, and he spent some time alone in the library. The porter is unable to vouch for his uninterrupted presence."

"And Mr. Bertram Tyrone?" she inquired.

"He was with that surgeon fellow, Strap. Witnesses place them in various low taverns."

Chase perceived that she didn't like to think of villainy so cold-hearted as to disregard close ties of blood. He could have told her that much garden variety viciousness was perpetrated by husbands, fathers, wives, sisters, brothers.

Elizabeth Minton appeared at the door. "Mr. Chase, you wished to speak with the curate? He awaits you in the sewing room."

"Thank you, Miss Minton." He stood and turned to Penelope. "Wait here, ma'am. I shall see you safely to your lodgings."

"That won't be necessary."

He bowed. "I insist. It's the least Bow Street can do."

When he walked out, Miss Minton hesitated. She looked frail and exhausted, but when she spoke again, her lips twisted in scorn. "Many of the ladies we usually call upon for assistance find themselves otherwise engaged at present. Should your offer hold, Mrs. Wolfe, I shall be obliged if you would return tomorrow afternoon. I have some business to attend to in the parish, and I prefer not to leave the women on their own."

"Of course, Miss Minton." She went on to relay Ambrose Tyrone's message. The directress listened, her shoulders easing a fraction.

"I shall sleep the better tonight," she said when Penelope finished. "Good evening then, Mrs. Wolfe."

"May my little girl accompany me tomorrow? I am afraid I have no one to mind her."

Miss Minton's lips curved up in the barest of smiles. "She will be most welcome." Dropping a brief curtsy, she withdrew.

Penelope relaxed gratefully. At last she was alone. Making her way to the desk, she saw that the packet with the blue ribbon was definitely gone while the other papers seemed undisturbed.

Well, she thought, it must be now or never. She had had to will herself to stop thinking of that pamphlet while talking to John Chase, else have her guilt writ large across her face. Loosening her reticule with fingers a trifle clumsy in her excitement, she at last brought out the tract into the open. Quickly she unfolded it, reading the title in bold print: *An Examination of the Present Day Condition of the Working Poor* by Daniel Partridge, M.P. Underneath a subtitle read, "A Treatise on the Appalling State of Health and Well-being among the Most Vulnerable Inhabitants of the Metropolis." The pamphlet itself consisted of several pages of densely printed text.

Penelope skimmed through it, noting that the rhetoric was impassioned and eloquent in the manner of the reformers of the time. There was also much marginalia, some written in a decisive scrawl, the rest in a fine copperplate. She thought the latter must be Miss Tyrone's hand; points of exclamation and references to "my friend" punctuated the glossing. She was about to put the pamphlet away when her fingers came across a slip of paper folded at the back. It was penned in the first distinctive, bold hand:

> *To Constance: I doubt there has ever been a woman named so aptly as you, my Dear. May you always be Constant to the ideals we share and to our Friendship which, I must confess, gives me the greatest Pleasure I have ever known. I shall strive to remain Worthy of it—and to temper my regard with all due Honour.*
>
> *Yours, Daniel*

If this were any indication of the rest of the stolen papers, no wonder Mr. Daniel Partridge had found it expedient to retrieve them, if indeed Penelope's suspicions were correct. She read his note to Constance again, struck by the power of the emotion expressed in so few lines. One could not doubt the sincerity or the magnitude of the writer's feelings, yet the language was moderated, crafted, each word carefully chosen. Restrained. Did Mr. Partridge have himself as firmly in check?

He wouldn't risk coming to repossess the papers himself, but a man in his position could easily employ someone to do a dirty task. One conclusion was certain. Should his involvement with Constance Tyrone become known, Mr. Partridge would have much to explain to the public, to his fellow reformers, and to his wife, if he had one. No lady would think to question a husband's dealings with his *chères amies;* a gentleman, after all, was expected to indulge in such affairs. But Constance Tyrone was a young woman of good family, a conspicuously virtuous woman, moreover. Knowledge of her relationship with Partridge would provide an unscrupulous individual with the perfect weapon…

"Jeremy?" she whispered, suddenly horrified. But then an even more frightening thought occurred to her. Daniel Partridge had a strong motivation for wishing Constance dead. What if their friendship had soured, and he had feared betrayal? No, Penelope could not imagine Constance turning on a friend. But what if Jeremy's meddling had precipitated some sort of crisis? Dread made her feel almost ill for a moment.

Penelope was roused from contemplation by Mr. Chase's return. He walked straight to the French window and opened it. A blast of cold air hit her face.

"What are you doing?" Unobtrusively, she slid the pamphlet and note back into her reticule.

"We'll be off in a minute. I wanted another look at this lock first." He glanced up. "Mr. Wood was no help whatever. It seems people may come and go around here more or less unnoticed."

"Is there something amiss? With the lock, I mean. I thought the window had been left open, fortuitously for the culprit."

"It looks as if somebody attempted to force the lock, but if that is the case, we've got a sadly inept cracksman."

Kneeling on the flagstones, he motioned for her to come and see. Penelope bent down and peered. The scratch marks on the metal had not been there when she fled this way earlier, and the window had been unlocked in any case. It didn't make sense, though at least she now knew what the thief had been after.

She came to a decision. "Mr. Chase, will you please step back into the office? I have important intelligence for you." He looked surprised, but obeyed.

When they faced each other once more, she said, "I must tell you that my husband visited me near midnight on the night of the murder. He was in high alt about good fortune he imagined might come his way." With the officer's sharp eyes never leaving her face, she had to force herself to continue.

"He...he mentioned Miss Tyrone by name, in fact, and said he thought she might be useful in furthering his career. He seemed to know something to her discredit. Moreover, he had an engagement later that evening, but did not tell me with whom."

"Your husband pays you visits in the middle of the night, Mrs. Wolfe?"

"We live apart, as I told you," she replied through stiff lips. "But he does on occasion turn up." Like the proverbial bad penny, she thought.

"Then he couldn't have been with Bennington all night," said Chase with satisfaction. "I knew that knave was protecting someone. He admitted as much."

"You knew Jeremy's alibi was fabricated? But you must believe me, sir. He couldn't have murdered Constance Tyrone. He hasn't the stomach for such horror."

"Perhaps so, though you'll forgive me for reserving judgment. But I do think there's someone in the shadows behind your husband and Bennington. I'll wager this person wants desperately to keep his entanglement quiet."

She met his gaze squarely. "You'd win that wager, sir." She told him of Merkle's visit to her lodgings after she returned from consulting the barrister Edward Buckler. Next, she pulled Partridge's pamphlet from her reticule and handed it to him wordlessly. Donning his spectacles, Mr. Chase glanced through the pamphlet, found the note, and read it.

"Where did you get this, Mrs. Wolfe?"

There was nothing for it; she would have to confess. Relating the events of the afternoon, she felt the heat in her face again and wanted to swear with vexation. She wished she could read his thoughts, but he remained impassive.

Finally, with a glint in his eyes, he said, "It seems my warning about the dangers of curiosity hit the mark. Have you stopped to think that the thief must have been in the room with you?"

"I thought it a possibility," she admitted. "But perhaps he came after I departed?"

"No. You said the desk was already in disarray. Elizabeth Minton was quite clear that she had tidied it this morning. No, you must have interrupted him, and you inadvertently led him to what he sought."

"Perhaps so. Yet if I had not found this pamphlet we should not know of Daniel Partridge."

The officer moved to the door. "We must see if Miss Minton can shed some light on this new development. Wait here."

He was back a few minutes later with Elizabeth Minton.

"I've told Miss Minton of your 'discovery'," said Mr. Chase. He handed Partridge's pamphlet to the Society's directress and waited while she read the note it contained.

A frown settled on the woman's brow. "I am afraid I don't know what to make of this."

"Are you acquainted with Mr. Daniel Partridge, ma'am?" asked Chase.

"Yes, he visited here February last with a parliamentary inquiry committee. I have not set eyes on him since."

"Apparently your friend Miss Tyrone has."

Miss Minton turned on him fiercely. "What do you mean to imply, sir?"

Penelope put in, "It's just that Mr. Chase needs to know more of this man, Miss Minton, especially if he is behind today's break-in."

The directress hesitated, then said, low voiced, "I knew Miss Tyrone well, or thought I did, and she would never be involved in anything dishonorable. Yet it's true she had been absent a great deal of late—and preoccupied. On the day she died, in fact, I taxed her with it."

"What did she say?" asked Chase.

Her fingers curled around the edge of the desk. "Oh, she smiled in that way she had. Never cruel, but determined on her own path regardless of other people's opinions. Then she suggested I attend to my own affairs." She laughed shortly.

"Perhaps she merely sought to enlist Mr. Partridge's support for the Society," said Penelope. "Except the note he's written makes it seem much more..."

Miss Minton walked to the door and paused, turning. "It appears he was a trusted friend, and it may be he abused that trust; I would not know. I do know that Miss Tyrone believed she could see inside people, finding always the good at bottom. But only a fool refuses to acknowledge the darkness that is also there."

Without another word, she stepped into the hallway and closed the door behind her.

Chase took Penelope's arm. "I think we should be going too. That is, unless you have any further disclosures?"

She had thought he would be angry with her, but if anything he seemed pleased. Certainly he now had a vital trail to follow, one that might lead him to Constance Tyrone's murderer.

Could it be Daniel Partridge? Though she had never met him, she admired his devotion to the downtrodden. So few people ever saw beyond their own narrow complacency. Yet she realized that just because a man professed noble aims did not mean he could elude the same human frailty that besets others. Like everyone else, he might experience ungovernable passion. Or hatred.

After Mr. Chase secured the window, they proceeded down the path and entered the churchyard. Without sunlight, the yew trees had turned black, pressing closer. These grounds were terribly neglected, as if the rector didn't care to spend the funds on upkeep. Chase kicked a fallen branch out of Penelope's path and took firmer hold of her arm.

Shivering a little, she asked, "Will you seek out Mr. Partridge?"

"Yes, but cautiously. The papers were full of his doings during the last session of Parliament. He is quite the hero of the moment, for the common folk at any rate. He's made enemies among his own kind with him and Burdett playing the House gadflies. Though God knows those asses could do with a few stings, especially after that turn-up last year with Burdett being clapped up in the Tower. Let us hope Partridge does not inconveniently recall to his memory the fact that Bow Street assisted in his friend's arrest."

"My…my father always spoke highly of Mr. Partridge."

"Your father?"

"Yes, you see, he is Eustace Sandford. I don't know if you will have heard of him?"

"Who has not?" He gave her a considering look. "Rather full of surprises, aren't you?"

"I suppose so," she said, smiling. "But you needn't worry that I have any notion of interfering. I shall be occupied enough here."

"Be careful. Danger may hide behind a seemingly innocent face."

Penelope halted, her eye caught by a single rose blossoming on a bush at the side of the path. Its color was washed out by the lengthening shadows.

"Bit late in the year for a bloom, don't you think?" Idly, she cupped the flower.

"The autumn has been warmer than usual. Careful of the thorns."

The church bells began to ring out the hour, the clamor drowning the bird song and the rattle of carriages passing in the nearby street. The din was echoed throughout the city as a hundred other churches took up the call.

"Quite a peal," said Chase. "Five o'clock."

"The darkness comes early at this season."

"Soon time for the curate to lock the gate."

"'Twould be about this time that the coachman came for Miss Tyrone," Penelope said.

She could imagine the man stepping cautiously in the gloom. He would be tired, thinking of his dinner and a warm fire; probably he would keep his eyes fixed on the path. But, of course, Constance had not been there, and the coachman had gone home alone.

Their eyes met, but neither spoke until the bells faded.

Chapter Nine

The next day the fog was back, and Penelope and Sarah got a late start. After a breakfast of toast and tea, they settled to their various pursuits, Sarah playing happily in her nightgear, and Penelope braving the latest assignment from Mr. Cotton: the first installment in the tale of a singularly foolish heroine and her efforts to choose between two suitors, one a steadfast if rather dull country gentleman, the other a dissolute London spark. Penelope had merely to fill in the plot already outlined for her, but it was tedious, trying work.

The heroine had just received a letter from her childhood friend, offering sage advice on the topic of the worthy gentleman's foul breath which had heretofore proved an effective deterrent to romance. Frowning, Penelope picked up her pen and wrote: *A discreet and gentle prompting may serve to make a loved one aware of a shortcoming, which once remedied, is soon forgot. Should the problem prove intractable, however, it is well to remember that a physical imperfection pales to nothing beside the more solid virtues, and that which appeals to the senses may provide ill nourishment for the spirit…*

A sudden image of Jeremy, handsome in his new coat, popped into her mind. Smiling ruefully, she banished him and glanced over to check on Sarah. This morning her daughter had found an absorbing task: lining up Penelope's hair pins and perfume flasks across the floor and interspersing them with buttons which she continually shifted from one pile to another. Then she had taken all the pillows from the beds, chairs, and sofa and crafted a burrow.

"Oh, Sarey. Must you wreak such havoc, my darling?"

Sarah was indignant. "The dollies are sick, Mama. They have to go to hospital!" She picked up a red button. "See, here's the medicine." Bending down, she ground the button against her doll's painted mouth. She looked up hopefully. "You sick too, Mama?"

"I've a terrible pain right here." Clutching her stomach, Penelope got up from the writing table and draped herself across the pillows. She gave a theatrical moan.

Small face intent, Sarah ran to the bureau, grabbed a handkerchief, and bestowed it across her mother's nose. "A cloth for your forehead. That helps you, doesn't it?"

"Much better," came Penelope's muffled voice.

"And here's your medicine." One of the buttons was pressed against the cloth.

"Just pretend, sweet," she protested. "Mama can't breathe." She pulled off the handkerchief and swept up the little girl for a kiss. "Do you realize what time it is, miss, and you still in your nightgown? Come now. We have an appointment this afternoon."

But it took a full hour to get them both properly washed and dressed. Penelope had never known anyone who could dillydally like this child, and telling her to hurry only made her worse. Sarah wanted to do everything for herself, so something as simple as putting on a shoe took on monumental proportions. Then, of course, she announced she was hungry just as they were finally ready to go.

Thus it was later than planned that they caught a hackney to the St. Catherine Society. Street noises filtered through only faintly to where they sat in the smelly, drafty coach, marooned cocoon-like in the mist. Penelope kept her arms around the child, who simply couldn't understand why the sun disappeared, and everything familiar was blanketed with this wet, unpleasant stuff.

When they arrived, Penelope introduced Sarah, who promptly lowered her head. She had always spent her days with her mother and didn't take to strangers well. Having seen little of her own parents as a young child, Penelope had been determined to do things differently. She was finding out, though, that there was a price to pay for this kind of closeness: black terror at the thought of something happening to her daughter and the worry that she was smothering her, making it difficult for the little girl to grow strong and fearless.

Miss Minton looked as if she wanted to be friendly. "You'll enjoy meeting the others, Sarah," she said heartily. She held out her hand, but the child backed up into her mother's skirt. Taking Sarah into her arms, Penelope followed the other woman up the tiny staircase to a low-ceilinged room under the eaves.

The furnishings consisted of an ill-assorted collection of chairs, a scratched dining table, and a few cradles and straw pallets. A group of about ten children stood regarding Sarah. In her simple calico dress and thick stockings she must have appeared strange indeed to these little ones, clad as they were in a mixture of rags and adult clothing cut to fit. Looking closely, Penelope could see that an effort had been made to turn them out well: hands looked clean, hair combed. Her heart ached to see it.

"We intend to have new garments made up for them as soon as the funds are available," said the directress, watching Penelope's face.

"That will be lovely." She smiled all around. Still, she felt uneasy about leaving Sarah here. The nursemaid, who had approached bobbing a curtsy, seemed respectable enough, and the children were just that…children. It was an instinctive reaction, this urge to protect her child from the taint of poverty, yet it sickened her to feel it.

She nudged her daughter forward, saying, "This is Sarah who's come to play with you today."

The child gripped her mother's knees, refusing to look at anybody, and Penelope felt embarrassed. She was sure Miss Minton would find Sarah abominably spoiled. But then Maggie came in, set her baby in a cradle, and led over a little boy who was about the same age.

"Good morning, Miss Sarah," she said cheerfully, bending down to address her eye to eye. "This here's my son Frank. He is a special sort of person, and if you're lucky he'll show you what he's got in his pockets."

The little boy regarded Sarah gravely. He had his mother's red hair coupled with lucent green eyes. As his sensitive mouth parted in a smile, Penelope felt herself relaxing. If Sarah took one of her sudden likings to him, all would be well.

A few minutes later Sarah and Frank were sitting on two chairs examining the contents of his pockets—bits of yarn, rocks, and marbles. When Penelope stooped to kiss her goodbye, Sarah's lips came up willingly, her arms encircling her mother in a brief hug.

"I'll see you established before I depart," said Miss Minton as she and Penelope walked to the sewing room. "Your duties are simple really. Sit with the women and keep them to their work. You may choose to read aloud from the Bible or converse on improving topics. Later in the day, they will have a reading lesson, but I shall be back for that. Satisfactory, Mrs. Wolfe?"

"Yes, indeed, ma'am."

The women were seated at the round deal table. As Miss Minton introduced them, each in turn stood and curtsied. They all wore the same demure, dark gown with an apron. White caps covered their hair. Slipping into her place, Maggie lightened the rather somber mood with a broad wink at her companions which the directress, fortunately, did not see.

"It might be helpful for you to know something of their histories." Miss Minton indicated a woman to her right who was small and thin with a wrinkled face and sharp, birdlike features.

"Dorrie here was once employed in a cotton mill until the joints in her fingers swelled, and she could no longer work expeditiously enough. They turned her off, and she made her way to London where for a time she became a beggar and a hawker of old clothes."

Next, Miss Minton held out her hand to a young girl called Fiona who rose and listened quietly. Tall with delicately rounded arms and fine-boned wrists, she had a lovely, artless face.

In a hard, colorless voice, the directress said, "Fiona came from the workhouse originally. At the age of eleven, she was apprenticed to a mantua maker who abused her without ceasing for some years. She complained to the parish overseers and was discharged with no means of subsistence. In desperation she turned to petty thievery until she found her way to us.

"And here is Nora. For many years she kept a green stall selling turnips and radishes in the Fleet Market. Unable to earn enough to keep her family, she was compelled to resort to unclean acts and was frequently sent to the Bridewell..."

After Miss Minton departed, Penelope and the women sat down to their work. Though it was early afternoon, they needed working candles since shadows played across the circle of faces. Penelope took up one of the pocket handkerchiefs to hem, and for a time the room was quiet, the women obviously feeling awkward with a stranger in their midst. Penelope too felt shy. She wanted to talk to them, yet didn't want to seem intrusive. But they had listened to Miss Minton's introductions with no trace of resentment in their expressions, had seemed, in fact, to approve.

A woman called Lil broke the silence. "Miss Elizabeth brought my old mistress to mind. Ah, but she was a downy 'un." Lil's former mistress had been a fruit-seller until sent to debtor's prison, Penelope recalled.

A few of the others gave Lil a quelling look, but she just grinned, showing blackened teeth. "She had a proper good lay going with oranges, particularly. You boil 'em, and they plump up beautiful. Makes them look fit for a lord, it does, and they sell right brisk. But when the flat gets 'em home, they turn black as coal in a couple of days." A general laugh went up.

"For shame, Lil," hissed Dorrie.

Lil ignored her. "My poor mistress. She was doing just fine till she took that rakeshame to her bed. He feathered his nest nicely with her money."

Thinking that this hardly qualified for "improving" conversation, Penelope found it expedient to intervene. "Shall we have a story?"

"From the Good Book?" asked Lil, her face falling.

Penelope smiled. "Well, something else perhaps."

The faces swiveled toward her. "Oh, yes, miss," breathed Fiona. "Miss Constance used to tell us a tale for working hard. Days like this specially when the sun is never coming out."

"We had a bang-up one last time," said Maggie. "I didn't sleep for a week I was that scared. Do you know any ghost stories, mum?"

An idea came to Penelope: an old folk tale she hadn't thought of in years which seemed somehow appropriate for this gloomy day. It had certainly given her a few nightmares when she had first heard it as a child. Still, it did have a moral, one she would want Sarah to understand when she was older.

The current attitude toward fairy stories puzzled Penelope. So many condemned them as irrational, superstitious nonsense that only encouraged profitless fantasy. But she knew the imagination craved stimulus; indeed, she suspected that without healthy nourishment, it could turn dark and perverted. Perhaps that had happened to the villain in this tale.

So she told of the young woman and her sister, both courted by the charming, powerful lord with the long blue beard. Though he was extravagantly rich, the world whispered about Bluebeard, for he'd already married several wives and nobody knew what had become of them.

"Ultimately, it was the youngest and most naive of the sisters who succumbed to Bluebeard's lure, wed him, and went to live in his castle. And she was content there until her husband, embarking on a journey, left her with a ring of keys to the castle's numerous doors. She might open all the doors except one, he said. But then, of course, her curiosity allowed her no rest…"

Outside, the wind lashed against the trees, making them creak and groan. Penelope saw that sinuous fog snakes curled about the windows. She went on, not stopping to chastise the women for having abandoned their work.

"At the end of a long corridor, the young wife came upon the forbidden chamber and opened it with her key. It was too dark to see, so she lit a candle—and screamed. She had discovered the corpses of Bluebeard's former wives: rows of skulls and piles of bones."

Penelope's audience sat up straighter, eyes unblinking, then gasped with relief as she described how the woman fled the evil chamber.

"She was safe, it seemed. The young wife removed the key, intending to restore it to her pocket. Yet when she looked down, it was oozing blood in fat, round drops that were no sooner wiped away than they welled up again. No matter how hard she scrubbed, the bleeding continued. In due course Bluebeard returned and asked for the key."

"Gawd," said Dorrie, "she better watch herself."

"Shhh," said the others, and Fiona looked as if she expected Bluebeard to jump out at her.

Maggie spoke up. "You know, this fellow ain't so very different from the general sort of man. They all have their secrets, though I don't expect they murder their wives usually. And they're cross as bears if you ask too many questions."

"That's so." Nora nodded. "Why, my Gordie used to keep back a few shillings from his pay. It got to where I'd be turning out his pockets every night."

A spirited discussion about the perfidy of husbands ensued until Fiona said plaintively, "I want to know what happened to the lady in the story."

"Oh, the bride's brothers rescued her in the nick of time, and they ran Bluebeard through with their swords." Penelope glanced around the table. "Please continue your work now. Miss Minton will observe, in justice, that I have encouraged you to waste your time with frivolity."

"No, indeed, mum." Fiona obediently took up her needle. "I learned something important. I'd not be disobeying my man. He told her not to look in that room."

"Heaven's above!" cried Dorrie. "How's she supposed to know she wed a monster?"

Upon these words, the door banged open, and Winnie lurched in, weaving on her feet, her face covered with the sheen of perspiration.

"You been tippling?" demanded Nora. All the women gathered around, talking at once.

"Quiet now." Penelope took Winnie's arm. "Are you sick?"

The old woman's eyes bore into hers. "I couldn't help myself, miss. Is you aiming to tell Miss 'Lizabeth?" She slumped forward.

Together Penelope and Dorrie lowered Winnie into a chair, and Penelope laid a hand on her forehead. "She's burning up. We shall have to fetch some assistance."

"It's the Comet Fever," said Dorrie.

"Nonsense. Is there an apothecary nearby?"

Nora shook her head. "Mostly Miss Constance and Miss 'Lizabeth dose us, ma'am. Though when Ursula were so desperate sick, we sent for the surgeon."

As Winnie moaned and thrashed, Maggie said, "I reckon you ought to go look in Miss Constance's cupboard. There's raspberry vinegar and some fever powder in there for emergencies."

The door opened, and the nursemaid entered, carrying Sarah.

"Mama, I want you." Though clearly ready for a sleep, Sarah would not settle in a new place without her mother. But Penelope had Winnie to cope with, and she didn't want Sarah anywhere near the sick woman. Heart pounding with fear, she started forward, but Maggie got there first.

"No closer, Bet. Not to worry, mum. I'll look after the child while you tend to Winnie." She shepherded the nursemaid and Sarah out of the room.

"Go fetch the medicine, mum," urged Dorrie.

"Yes, directly. We shall need something to keep her warm as well."

Penelope sped to Constance's office, approached the armoire, and threw the doors wide. Rummaging through several drawers, she located a canister labeled "Dr. James' Fever Powder," a bottle with cherry colored liquid, and a flask of brandy. Now if she could only find a blanket and a pillow, they might make

Winnie more comfortable. Her gaze swept down to the bottom of the armoire and lighted on a woolen blanket. Reaching down to snatch it up, she knocked something over.

It was a woman's boot: a sturdy walking shoe of nankeen. She set it upright next to its mate and was stepping back to close the armoire door when a thought suddenly struck her. If these boots had belonged to Constance Tyrone, why were they still here? Deciding they must have been forgotten when Miss Minton returned the dead woman's belongings, she shrugged and shut the armoire.

The women looked up in relief when Penelope re-entered the sewing room, carrying the blanket and medicines. Winnie was still slumped over mumbling to herself and shivering, but she had a little more color.

"I been sponging her with cool water," said Fiona.

Somehow this little mouse had established herself at Winnie's side, and observing her gentleness, Penelope was glad of it. Dorrie and Lil, who argued in loud whispers and chafed the victim's hands unmercifully, were another matter.

She glanced around the group. "You've all been of enormous help, but she will need some quiet. And if her complaint is infectious, we should remove her to another room as soon as possible. Is there someplace she might rest?"

Two of the strongest women supported Winnie down the hall to Elizabeth Minton's shabby sitting room, small enough to warm quickly, Penelope saw with relief. As Lil built up the fire in the tiny grate, Fiona helped Winnie to the divan and wrapped her in the blanket. The old lady shook her head at the fever powder and the raspberry concoction, reaching instead for the brandy.

"Let her have a nip, miss," urged Dorrie. "It'll warm her much better than that rot." She looked with loathing at the medicines.

After a few generous swigs, Winnie lapsed into sleep, snoring loudly. Reassured, the women trooped out.

Left alone with Fiona and the sick woman, Penelope said, "You seem to know just what to do."

"Yes, miss. You see, I was used to looking after my grandma before she passed on. Of course, that was when I was quite little, but she used to say I had the healing touch." Fiona spread her fingers on her lap, palms up. Her hands were gracefully shaped, but toil-reddened and marred by prickly-looking blotches.

As Winnie whimpered in her sleep, Fiona moved to her side to touch her cheek. "She don't seem so hot now, miss. I'll keep wiping her down." She bent to her basin of water and dipped the cloth.

Winnie opened her eyes. "I ain't been right since that doctor dosed me. The Lord never intended such mucking about with a body's innards." She stirred restlessly. "I needed the money for food, or medicine maybe. All's I did was leave the window open…"

Fiona said, too fast, "Oh, she's talking about the vaccination for the smallpox what Mr. Strap give us. Hush, you silly old thing."

Penelope said, "Do not worry, Fiona. Winnie will come to no harm from me. She is too ill to realize what she says." All the same, she thought, if Winnie had accepted a bribe from Daniel Partridge's minions in exchange for leaving the window ajar, John Chase would have to know.

Fiona looked down at the old woman's feet. "You think she'd be easier with her shoes off? It's warm enough."

Agreeing, Penelope was reminded of the boots she'd seen in Constance's office. "Fiona, when I was fetching the medicine, I noticed some walking boots in the armoire. Do you happen to know to whom they belong?"

"Why, to Miss Constance." She bent to pull off Winnie's cracked, old boots. "I put 'em there myself. But I'd have thought Miss Elizabeth would've sent them back to the family." Reaching into the pocket of her apron, she took out a knife and began scraping at the dirt on the soles.

"Well, they were partially hidden under the blanket, so perhaps she didn't see them."

Fiona nodded and went to the door. "I need a bit o' rag to do them proper." A moment later she was back, kneeling at the fireplace and rubbing away at the other boot. Penelope watched her, troubled by some half-formed thought that tickled the edge of her consciousness.

"She wasn't wearing them then?" she said slowly.

Fiona stared in wonderment. Then she looked from the shoe in her hand to Winnie.

"No, no. I meant Miss Tyrone. Why wasn't she wearing her boots the day she died? The weather was wretched, remember? And when she was found the next morning, she had on only one thin slipper."

Fiona dropped the boot and covered her face. She began to cry silently, her shoulders shaking.

"What is it?" Penelope went to her. "Don't cry, Fiona. Tell me what I've said to upset you. Is it hearing me speak of Miss Tyrone?"

"I'm that sorry, miss. The others are always saying I'm a wet goose. But she was kind to me, you see." She pushed Winnie's boot away and took several deep breaths, her eyes far away. Then she resumed her task.

"Why did you put the boots in the armoire?"

Fiona looked at her as if she were ripe for a lunatic asylum. "To keep them safe, of course. They were covered in muck, miss, and I was afraid they'd be spoiled. So I cleaned 'em pretty before putting them away." She added anxiously, "I didn't know Miss Elizabeth would miss them when she went to pack up. I done right, haven't I?"

"Yes, of course."

"I found them underneath her desk when I was closing up for the night. And the next day when I come in, Miss Elizabeth told me…" She faltered a bit, but sniffed bravely and wiped her eyes.

It was Penelope's turn to look blank. "Fiona, what are you saying? Precisely when was it you found those boots?"

"'Bout half past five on Monday last, mum. I remember distinctly. Winnie had gone home, and I was to set all to rights."

She sounded thoroughly frightened now, and Penelope forced herself to soften her tone. "Fiona, listen. This is important.

Would anyone have seen Miss Constance leave for her errand that afternoon? Anyone at all? Please think."

"Not likely. We were all in the sewing room, you see. Not unless someone had to go to the necessary."

"I imagine Mr. Chase has already inquired about that," said Penelope with regret.

"Why don't you ask, mum, just to be sure?"

They had both forgotten Winnie. With a guilty start, Penelope heard her stir. Fiona got there first, cloth in hand, and resumed her sponging.

"Better now," she said.

The door opened, and Maggie came in. "I came to tell you young Sarah's gone down for a sleep," she announced.

Penelope thanked her.

"How's Win? She looks like she's resting fine."

Penelope said, "She seems to be. Maggie, do you know if anyone at all would have seen Miss Constance leave on that last afternoon?"

"I saw her." Maggie strolled to the fire and sat down near the warmth.

Penelope restrained her excitement. "Have you told anyone?"

"No one asked. I was on my way back from the privy, and I saw her walking toward the gate. I didn't call out because I knew she'd send me about my business. Truth to tell I was taking a wee rest on the bench."

"I told you, mum," cried Fiona. "Didn't I say it might've been someone as had to go to the privy?"

"Maggie," said Penelope urgently, "did you happen to notice what Miss Tyrone had on her feet?"

She looked surprised. "Why her nankeen boots, mum. Them what she always wore."

Struck silent with amazement, Penelope looked from one to the other. If the victim had been wearing those boots when she left at two o'clock that afternoon and Fiona had cleaned them at half past five, there was only one conclusion. Constance Tyrone had returned after all.

Chapter Ten

Having received yet another summons from the St. Catherine Society, Chase duly presented himself in the morning. As he walked through the churchyard, he pondered the information about Daniel Partridge, M.P., provided by Noah Packet the prior evening.

Chase was lucky Partridge was even in town, for many of the upper classes had retired to their country estates until the next Parliamentary session began in the new year. But, as Packet had said, Partridge rarely slowed down, his charities and speaking engagements keeping him and his family in the metropolis. Not that the M.P. didn't enjoy the usual pleasures of a gentleman. He dined often at Brooks's club and attended the Whig elite's soirees at Holland House. His wife was also an asset, Chase gathered, for she was of good family and an accomplished political hostess.

In fact, what made Partridge different was not his ardent devotion to reform which others shared, but his magnetic personality. Even Packet seemed to respect the man. It was the M.P.'s reputed charm that intrigued Chase because he sensed that such a man could command admiration even from a single-minded spinster like Constance Tyrone.

A gathering later this afternoon would afford an ideal opportunity to seek out Partridge as he addressed a select group about his most recent project to assist the poor. And for reasons Chase did not care to examine too closely, he had decided to ask Penelope Wolfe to accompany him. He told himself that if for some reason access to the M.P. proved difficult, he could always convince Mrs. Wolfe to identify herself as her father's daughter. No doubt that would open doors.

He spotted her now, picking her way through the high grass, stepping around the piles of muddy leaves which someone had gathered but not yet swept up. Idly, he wondered why she hadn't stayed on the path, but supposed she had been reading some of the epitaphs on the rows of headstones.

"This is become something of a habit," he called.

"Good day, Mr. Chase," she said blithely as she approached. "Good of you to obey my summons."

The day was bright, the sun illuminating every corner of the yard. The newer headstones glowed, standing tall and clean. But far more numerous were the older, moss-covered memorials whose legends had been obliterated by the omnipresent London smoke, stones falling askew or toppling altogether. No one was near, though Chase could hear the murmur of a service being conducted in the church.

He drew her down on a bench. "What is it, Mrs. Wolfe?" he asked, watching her face. Her message had said only that she had important intelligence to impart and would be glad of his presence. But suddenly he felt he knew this woman. For all her prickly decorum, she found the challenge of a murder inquiry exhilarating. It was an intellectual puzzle that elevated her above the mundane, the dull. Though his own curiosity was aroused, Chase sat calmly with arms folded.

She smiled at him and stretched out one leg to regard a neatly booted foot. "'Tis a fine day, but the ground is yet muddy after yesterday's damp. A good thing I am possessed of the appropriate footwear."

Chase waited. When he didn't say anything, she went on, "Particularly if one has errands to perform abroad at this season, one cannot rely upon accommodation from the weather. And what a pity to risk the ruination of a pair of slippers, for instance."

"You've found her boots. I suppose I should have thought of that. Where were they, and why the deuce wasn't she wearing them?"

Penelope looked annoyed; then her face brightened. "Oh but she was when she left at two o'clock that last day. Maggie saw her. And Fiona found the boots much later, cleaned them, and placed them in the armoire."

"Where you just happened to stumble upon them."

"Yes. Winnie was ill, and I was looking for some medicine to ease her." She waved an impatient hand. "Don't you see what this means, Mr. Chase? Constance must have come back at some point that afternoon."

"Another conundrum," he murmured. "Why should she change a pair of sturdy boots for those slippers if her design was to depart soon after?"

"Perhaps she was called away suddenly and didn't have time to replace her outdoor garb. But I have some further intelligence for you, sir. I believe you were right about Winnie's involvement in the housebreaking." She described the old woman's unguarded comments during her delirium.

"Ah, your helpless old woman has helped herself to an opportunity. I cannot say I'm surprised."

Her expression was troubled. "It may be so, but she is dreadfully poor, Mr. Chase. I do not think we can truly imagine…"

Out of the corner of his eye, he saw that the church doors had been thrown back. Two men bearing a wool-wrapped bundle stepped into the yard, followed by the curate. With the curate were another man and a veiled woman who moved with a faltering step, as if she had just disembarked from a ship. Her companion held her up grimly. Chase looked again at the shroud, noticing for the first time how small it was, and knew that it held a child.

The sight took him back to the many times he had seen his father perform this sacrament. Death had come frequently to the bleak village where the family lived. Indeed, death had been a regular visitor in their own house, taking seven of

Chase's twelve brothers and sisters before their fifth birthdays. Whenever he thought of these children, it was to imagine an inexorable shadow advancing over their tiny forms, at length to darken hearts and eyes. It was no wonder his mother had lost her faith. But it was the horror of her struggle to live in peace with herself and her churchman husband that had marked the boy Chase had been.

Now, the group had reached the graveside marked by a small mound of fresh dirt. As the curate began reciting the traditional words, the woman raised her veil, and Chase heard Mrs. Wolfe's gasp. Dead eyes, utterly blank. It wasn't right to look at them.

Turning away, he took Penelope's arm and led her down the path skirting the churchyard. Her arm felt stiff beneath his fingers, and he saw that her happiness was gone. But by unspoken consent, neither said a word about the tableau upon which they had unwittingly intruded.

She said, "Perhaps if you were to inquire again, you would find someone who saw Constance later that day. It seems odd no one has spoken up so far."

"It is odd. Perhaps Miss Tyrone returned, changed her footwear, and departed. In a carriage probably—which would explain why her remaining slipper was not soiled when we found her. Then, returning late that night, she was attacked before she could reach safety."

"But at the inquest you said she had left her keys in the office. She would not have been able to enter."

"That is so. Then maybe the man in the carriage was the murderer. They argued; he killed her and decided to discard her body in front of the church. That would account for any number of puzzling facts; a dead woman needs no key, for instance."

"It's possible." She thought a moment. "Do you suppose Joan Snowden erred in her statement? She might have mistaken a private equipage for a hack. We shall need to find out if Daniel Partridge, or indeed anyone else, was in the habit of taking Constance up in his carriage."

"I see someone who might know," said Chase, coming to a sudden halt. "Isn't that Winnie Skirl? What do you suppose she does here?"

He pointed to a figure half hidden in the shadow of a yew tree. Leaning heavily on a headstone for support, Winnie seemed intent on the final words of the service. Enveloped in a dirty green shawl, she clutched a wilted posy in one hand and a battered prayer book in the other.

As they approached, Penelope spoke first. "Winnie, you should not be out of doors. This warmth won't last, and if the weather alters suddenly, you'll catch your death."

"Death is all around me." Winnie nodded at the grave markers. "It comes to us all, but when it visits the little ones, I got to pay my respects. That's Peggy Anson, burying her youngest."

She gestured at the black-clad woman who stood with a handful of dirt trickling through her fingers, dull horror fixed on her features. Her husband, who had already tossed his offering into the hole, waited at her side. Curate Wood reached down, gently took the woman's rigid hand, and helped her sprinkle the last of the soil. Then he guided her back toward the church.

Winnie watched the little cavalcade go. "I been acquainted with the family for years. Lost three of my own, you know. George, Clementina, and my youngest, Thomas. He'd be nigh on thirty years old now, which is a thing not possible to conceive. They's all laid here, and I know where each one is, though there's nothing left to mark 'em. But I always come to see the children get settled proper." She smiled.

"You must go inside now," said Penelope.

"Curate is a good man, mum," said Winnie as if she hadn't heard. "He do his best by us. The whole service; don't scrimp none. Flowers too and a bereavement call upon the family."

"Most commendable. I am certain that such consideration affords enormous solace."

Penelope didn't look very certain, thought Chase, and truly he doubted whether a clergyman, no matter how well meaning, could do anything to assuage such grief. Were it his child...

Cutting off that thought, he said, "How much were you paid to leave the French window unlocked, Winnie?"

Her jaw dropped. "How'd you?…it were a guinea," she muttered. She looked as if she wanted to cry. "I meant no harm. I wouldn't do nothing against people what has been good to me. Are you aiming to tell Miss 'Lizabeth?" She gripped Penelope's hand.

"Mr. Chase? Surely it isn't necessary to mention it."

"Should it become necessary to the success of this inquiry, I'd not hesitate for an instant." But he knew that a guinea was a fortune to someone like this old woman. The temptation had been severe.

"Tell me something," he said. "The thief must have bid you keep out of the way. Was it he who put the scratches on the window lock?"

"No, I done that myself. I was afraid, you see, after I seen the scramble he'd made. I wanted it to look like someone had bust in."

"Who gave you the money, Winnie?"

Hanging her head, she stared down at her straggling bunch of flowers and whispered, "I didn't ask his name."

✽ ✿

Daniel Partridge paused to wipe his brow. The pause was calculated, occurring as it did at the height of his speech, and it produced the desired effect on the spectators, who launched into tearful, enthusiastic applause. He finished his speech and waited on the platform, taking a moment to catch his breath and survey the room before jumping into the fray.

Bedecked in the finest muslins and silks, the ladies had relished his histrionics—entertaining enough to these jaded appetites. But they enjoyed their own virtue even more, for in giving nodding homage to a worthy cause, they proved the tenderness of their hearts and the liberality of their opinions. He knew it made them feel good to cry about the cruelties visited upon the poor. At the same time, he knew that the money any one of these women spent on a seasonal wardrobe or carriage trimmings would feed a family of Spitalfields or Seven Dials for years.

Yes, Daniel Partridge, one time fiery radical, had become a cool statesman, a practiced player. As a young man back in the nineties, his overriding concern had been the great issue of the day: the much needed reform of Parliament. While he and his friends had shared an interest in the sufferings of the destitute, they believed that only by modifying the existing political structure could this problem be alleviated. Ultimately in their quest to uphold the individual's natural and inalienable rights, they had gone so far as to promote universal male suffrage.

It had seemed then that anything was possible and that a more enlightened age had been ushered in. But in the wake of unremitting government persecution, the movement had dwindled, and though it had revived in the last few years, today's reformers were a different breed: less quixotic, more practical in their aims, less certain of their eventual success. At least Partridge was.

Yet sometimes the charade of it all sickened him, as now when faced by an assembly of ladies given over for the moment to charity. And looking out unseeingly on the rows of faces, he thought of Constance, a woman who embodied truth. Her sincerity and friendship had given him brief hope. But truth, after all, is a risk few men are willing to take...

The sea of eyes shifted slightly, and he sensed a new presence, a penetrating gaze trained upon his face. He peered in that direction, but the afternoon sun pouring through the windows was making it difficult to see. After a moment, he could just make out a rather ordinary looking young woman standing a few yards away. Partridge was used to being stared at, but there was something oddly focused in this woman's expression. He inclined his head politely, raising his brows in inquiry, but her companion touched her arm, and she pulled her eyes away. Partridge should have been glad, but he wasn't. Perversely, he wished she would look at him again.

The crowd was beginning to disperse, so he stepped off the platform and approached a bevy of ladies who were waiting to speak to him. As he gave himself over to their exclamations, he caught one last glimpse of the woman as her friend led her off.

"What did you make of it, ma'am?" asked Chase, escorting Penelope to some chairs against the wall.

"A brilliant address, Mr. Chase, but most disturbing. Who can bear to think of eight-year-old children whipped to make them work harder in the mills? Parish apprentices starved and neglected. Chimney sweep boys dying of terrible lung complaints. Truly only a nation of barbarians would allow it."

He saw with amazement that she had tears in her eyes. Brushing them away, she fumbled in her reticule for a handkerchief.

"I meant what did you make of the man?" he said hastily.

"Do you want to know what logic tells me, or would you rather hear my intuitive response?"

Chase grinned. "Favor me with both, I suppose."

"Well, 'tis obvious he is most charming and persuasive. I can see Miss Tyrone may well have been captivated enough to endanger her reputation. That, of course, gives him a possible motive for wanting her dead had she threatened a scandal."

"Just what I thought," said Chase, pleased.

"But that doesn't seem right somehow. I cannot believe she would have relations of that nature with a married man, nor, I'm persuaded, would she seek to hold hostage his good name."

Chase's lip curled. "You have remarkable faith in human goodness, else you've yet to experience certain aspects of life. Have you forgot the sketches your husband drew? He apparently glimpsed something quite other in Constance Tyrone."

Penelope gripped her hands in her lap as if to restrain herself, but replied composedly enough, "I do not deny she may have felt a powerful attraction for Mr. Partridge."

"I could tell you were rapt in his speech like every other woman here. But I wouldn't trust the man if the angels themselves were to vouch for him." He got to his feet. "Come now. We shall attempt to waylay him."

Daniel Partridge had disengaged himself from the crowd and was making his way toward the exit, a small entourage in his wake. His progress was slow, for he had to stop every few feet to bow to acquaintances. Chase and Penelope attached themselves to the train and pushed forward until they were right behind the M.P.

"Mr. Partridge. John Chase, Bow Street. I need to speak to you about Constance Tyrone."

Partridge swung round. For an instant his smile wavered, but his self-command was paramount. He schooled his features into civil inquiry, ignoring the speculative glances and whispers that erupted from those around him.

"Of course. How may I help you, sir? Shall we speak privately?" Without waiting for an answer, Partridge made his way into a small office, Chase and Penelope following.

Light from the window illuminated his face as he turned to confront them. Partridge had clear olive skin, even features, and vivid, dark eyes. One felt immediately his enormous energy and strength of purpose.

Leaning against a desk, he said in a carefully nonchalant tone, "This has to do with that unfortunate woman's death, of course. I read of it in the papers."

"I understand you were acquainted with Miss Tyrone," said Chase, giving Penelope a quelling glance as she opened her mouth to speak. For the first time, Partridge looked at her also, eyes widening, but didn't comment upon her presence.

"Yes. She was an exceptional person, and if there's something I can do to help you catch the villain who took her life, you need only tell me. I presume that's why you're here, sir?"

"When was the last time you saw her?"

"Sometime toward the end of October, when we toured a local almshouse. Much of what you heard me speak of today we observed on that expedition. She was anxious to advance her proposals for the education of the destitute."

Penelope appeared to absorb his every gesture and intonation as if she analyzed some foreign object, yet at the same time she also radiated a warm empathy that Partridge must sense. Chase wondered what her "intuition" was telling her. To him, Partridge seemed a smooth customer who wouldn't hesitate to lie outright to gain an advantage.

"So Miss Tyrone was your…colleague in the quest for social betterment?"

Surprised, Partridge replied with dignity, "Indeed, she was. The very best sort: intelligent, dedicated, and immensely talented. I shall miss her."

"I believe your relationship was closer than you let on. Would you care to describe it?"

"No. I would not."

Icy hauteur had replaced Partridge's former cordiality, and Chase recalled suddenly that this was not a man to antagonize with impunity, but he never considered backing down.

"A pity that. Your reluctance to be candid may perhaps be misconstrued."

"Not by anyone who knows me." The M.P. had lost his too-casual stance. The bridge of his nose looked pinched; the worry lines about his mouth had deepened. And he was looking again at Penelope Wolfe.

"Ah, but who truly knows anyone?" Chase inquired softly. "Even the most public of men has his secrets to be kept hidden at any cost."

At that Partridge blanched, and Penelope broke in. "Mr. Partridge, you say you had great esteem for Constance Tyrone. Will you not help us find her killer?"

"That's presuming you are not speaking to him right now, ma'am," Chase bit out. "In which case, I take leave to doubt he would make a push to help you."

The astonishment on Partridge's face should have been comical. "You cannot think I killed her?" He began to laugh, an acid sound that grated on the ear. He said to Penelope on a rising note of desperation, "You don't think that of me?"

"How can I know, sir? But you must tell the truth."

Damned interfering woman. What did she mean by gazing fondly upon the man like she was the bloody Virgin Mary and he a sinner seeking absolution? Chase pulled the pamphlet from his pocket and tossed it at Partridge. "Have a look at that. Perhaps you'll see why we have paid you a visit."

With shaking hands, Partridge pulled out the note at the back. There was a long silence as he read it, his face inscrutable.

Chase plucked both pamphlet and note from his fingers and returned them to his pocket. "Evidence, I'm afraid. You may perceive, Mr. Partridge, why one might misconstrue your motives." Then as the M.P. still didn't move, he said, "Look, perhaps this can remain a private matter between us. That is, if you'll make a clean breast of it."

Partridge ducked his head, staring at the carpeting at his feet. "I see I have no alternative, but I want to know something first." He addressed Penelope. "Who are you, ma'am? I should appreciate an introduction."

"She's Mrs. Jeremy Wolfe. I am persuaded you remember him. He's the man you had released from Newgate."

In other circumstances, he might almost have felt sorry for Partridge, who was being dealt one blow after another. First, his indiscreet letter had surfaced, and now he was confronted by the wife of the man who had made him the mark of an extortion scheme. Or so Chase believed. To test his theory, he said, "Arthur Bennington told me he recently did a favor for a friend, someone in a bit of a scrape who could not afford the glare of unpleasant publicity."

Partridge met Chase's eyes frankly. "Anyone might have need of such a friend." He pointed at a grouping of chairs in front of the desk. "Why don't we sit, since it seems this is to be a lengthy conversation? Though I must warn you, I have an appointment in an hour's time." After they each took a chair, Partridge leaned forward. "I did ask Bennington to provide the alibi for Mr. Wolfe, but only because I knew Wolfe to be innocent and didn't wish to expose my own interest in the affair. We have an important measure pending at our next session. I would not risk the outcome."

Penelope nodded. "I am grateful to you for helping Jeremy. I suppose it was you who sent Mr. Merkle with the money?"

"Yes. I thought you might be in difficulties."

"Kind of you," said Chase flatly. "But the truth is, you asked—or bribed—Bennington to perjure himself. How do you know Wolfe is innocent?"

"I was with him that evening. We shared a supper at a local chophouse; then I left him for a few minutes at a lodging house in St. Martin's Lane while he fetched something from Mrs. Wolfe. We went on to another establishment to have a few drinks and didn't part until well after four in the morning. I understand from the testimony at the inquest that Miss Tyrone died sometime after midnight?" When Partridge mentioned the dead woman's name, a horror came over him, but he stifled it quickly.

Penelope turned to Chase in triumph. "My husband did say he had an engagement." Her face glowed with relief. As much as she had denied Jeremy Wolfe's guilt, clearly some shadow had lurked in her mind.

"You can prove this, I take it?" said Chase.

"I've no doubt any number of people would have noticed us. I am rather well known." This was said without conceit. He swept an unruly piece of hair away from his brow and sat back in his chair.

"Are you telling us you and Wolfe were friends?"

"Well, acquaintances perhaps."

He appeared uncomfortable, as if trying to convey some warning. It took Chase a moment to realize what it was, and when he did he almost laughed aloud. Like a true gentleman, Partridge wished to spare Penelope Wolfe any embarrassment.

"Shall I make this easier?" said Chase. "The fact is Wolfe thought to feather his nest in exchange for keeping quiet about your relationship with Constance Tyrone, and you met with him to placate him, or maybe to stand the nonsense. Is that it, Mr. Partridge?"

The M.P. glared with real dislike, but Penelope said, "He's right, you know sir. You must tell us."

Partridge sighed. "Wolfe sent Miss Tyrone those sketches as well as a letter requesting a private interview. When she confided in me, I told her I'd attend to the matter.

"I saw him the next day. He talked of how a man in my position could be of enormous assistance to a young artist and said he would value our friendship, always striving to be of service to me in a discreet fashion."

"Hush-hire."

Penelope looked wretched. "He wouldn't call it that himself, Mr. Chase. He'd see it as a mutually satisfying arrangement."

Partridge began to launch into elaborate apologies which Chase thought would only increase her distress. He headed him off with another question. "Have you any idea where Jeremy Wolfe is now?"

"None." Partridge smiled regretfully at Penelope. "I imagine he is quite safe, ma'am, and will return when the furor dies down."

"You'd better tell us the rest," she said. "Exactly what was your relationship to Constance Tyrone?"

"I met Miss Tyrone some months ago when I toured the St. Catherine Society…"

As the words came faster, Partridge seemed to find a release in speaking. Clearly, he hadn't been able to share his grief with anyone. Listening to him, Chase had to admit he appeared sincere, but he knew that many murderers were able to force their guilt into a little compartment of the mind, fooling themselves and the rest of the world in the process.

"I wish you might have known her," Partridge was saying. "Any words I use to describe her seem so ineffectual, so paltry. She had a miserable childhood. Lost her mother young and was left to the tender ministrations of a series of prudish governesses and a father with ice in his blood. For all that she emerged with a spirit so strong it made one weep.

"I am not a sentimental man. I have learned that practicality and decisive action are the qualities most needed in a world so filthily unjust. That's the mistake many reformers make, I think. Who can afford sentiment? It only gives the enemy ammunition. I'm married, you know, and married well to a woman who furthers my career and manages our home with diplomacy and grace. God knows, I never asked to have my life turned topsy-turvy by a contrary spinster who didn't have a circumspect bone in her body."

Chase nodded, feeling a grin tug at his lips. "Fate has a way of playing inconvenient tricks. But you've told us very little, sir. Where did you meet? Did you see her often?"

The M.P. shook his head as if trying to slough off an unpleasant dream. "We used to meet for tea in the private parlor of a pub. Sometimes we went out together to investigate conditions in the poorer parishes. Or we just talked, made plans."

"Plans?"

He gave a bleak smile. "She wanted to open a school for poor women and children, Mr. Chase. She believed they ought to receive more learning than just their letters and the Bible— Milton or Shakespeare, for instance. A 'march of intellect,' she called it, to add meaning to lives of unceasing drudgery." His smile widened at their evident amazement. "Not very pragmatic, I grant you, for where would the poor find the means? Their coin comes too dear to spend on books instead of bread even if an hour of leisure can be found. And such learning would only breed discontent. Miss Tyrone's notions were hardly calculated to win her many friends."

"I confess I find it hard to imagine the lower orders developing a taste for the Bard," Chase said.

"It's a marvelous idea," said Penelope. "So she awaited her inheritance to put her design into practice?"

He nodded. "The allowance her father made her out of the trust wasn't nearly sufficient, a fact of which he was well aware. Even her brother, whom she had always thought an ally, was not above undermining her behind her back."

"What precisely did Mr. Bertram Tyrone do?" Penelope asked.

Partridge frowned. "She didn't tell me all, but she mentioned he had consulted her physician without her knowledge, then discussed the matter with Sir Giles. I imagine they sought ammunition to convince her to abandon her work."

"Perhaps they were merely concerned," said Chase. "I heard that Miss Tyrone had been courting fatigue. Possibly she needed some inducement to curtail her exertions."

Partridge merely looked at him. "She would never have allowed frail health to stop her, sir. Anyone who truly loved and understood her could not expect it."

"Anyone—meaning you?"

"Yes, though our relationship remained that of friend and colleague. I cannot tell you, Mr. Chase, what I would have done had she been willing for more, though I like to think I should have resisted temptation."

"Did she return your regard?"

"Yes. There was one time, only once, she told me so." His expression softened at the memory.

So Chase was supposed to accept that Partridge had carried on some sort of high-minded friendship with a beautiful young woman in the private parlor of a public house? Nonsense.

"If this relationship was so innocent, why did you find it necessary to send someone to steal back the letters and papers you had given to Miss Tyrone? Or perhaps you performed that little task yourself?"

Consternation distorted Partridge's handsome features. "Well...well, I thought it best to have them retrieved."

"And had your man bribe the doorkeeper."

"There's no end to your perspicacity, sir," he said, stretching out his arms in a gesture of defeat. "You must also know then that I did not murder anyone."

"Well, I ask you once again, sir. When was the last time you saw Constance Tyrone?"

Face guileless, Partridge replied, "About a fortnight before she died. The last part of October. We met at the Bull's Head in Gerrard Street."

Chapter Eleven

"Eh, your ladyship," called a jeering voice. "Your carriage is waiting." A raucous burst of cheers and laughter went up around the street outside Bow Street office.

"Careful, me lovely," screeched a woman standing near the back. "You don't want to ruin them fine togs."

Observing from the edge of the crowd, John Chase watched as the young girl shielded her eyes with one hand. The light was perhaps too bright after the dim interior from which she and the others had emerged, or the crowd had frightened her. Dressed better than most, she stepped over the pavement, delicately avoiding the muck. By the time she reached the shelter of the prison van, the tears ran down her cheeks.

Probably a maid fresh from the country, thought Chase, yet another come to London to seek her fortune. She would have done better to spit insults right back, for that they could understand. It was an everyday affair: a motley group of the usual thieves and whores on their way to gaol. And the street rubbish watching the show were themselves likely to make one of the prisoners' number before long.

Chase had stopped by after the meeting with Partridge to see if any more arrests had been made in the Tyrone matter. Already four or five people had been rounded up for questioning with no results. But they were brought up before the magistrates if only to show due diligence in the public interest.

He pushed his way through the herd and entered the building, ignoring the grumbling that erupted behind him. Inside, with court in session, another crowd had gathered to watch the proceedings in the begrimed, stuffy chamber. Well screened from the populace, the magistrate and his clerk sat behind the bar. Guarded by two officers, prisoners languished in the dock. The rancid odor of unwashed bodies filled the air.

"Chase." A man suddenly faced him.

"Good day to you, Farley."

"Glad you're here," said Dugger Farley. "Step outside." He drew Chase into the corridor. "New development in the Tyrone matter. The Old Man is sending us to make an arrest. Wants it done quick and quiet like."

Farley leaned against the wall, his florid face lit with excitement. He clutched a blunderbuss in one hand and his hat and coat in the other.

Chase said, "That is progress indeed. Who is it?"

"I know precious little myself, and what I do know says we may be heading for trouble." He met Chase's eyes. "It's Strickland's game."

Chase scowled. "Strickland, eh?" He doubted whether the arrest would be either quick or quiet.

"A pawnbroker in the Dials laid information this morning. Seems he was approached by a bloke wanting to peddle the little rose from the Tyrone woman's slipper. And stroke of luck, the dealer had the handbill what described it."

Not luck. It was supposed to work that way.

"Pawnbroker knew the chap too," Farley added. "He's a dangerous 'un: Irish and a Papist to boot. Strickland's taking in some special constables."

As if conjured by name, the Runner appeared. In his thick hand was the Bow Street ensign of office: a tipstaff, hollowed to provide storage for the warrant and topped with a removable brass crown. "So, Chase, you're joining us common folk for once," he said, grinning.

Barrel-chested with rounded shoulders and an overlarge head, Strickland was born ready to charge. Though he possessed the rudiments of a cunning intelligence, he was often defeated by his own belligerent impulses. Behind him stood a half-dozen men, armed with pikes and cudgels.

"I see you favor the discreet approach," said Chase. "You'd best hope they don't take you for a press gang. Just where is your man hiding?"

Strickland stepped closer, expelling the reek of onions. "We're going into Bethnal Green. I need a proper force at my back." He started to walk away, then turned back. "I know you've an interest in this. You'll get a piece of the blood money."

"We need a conviction first," Chase said skeptically. "But I'll see you through anyway."

Outside, the crowd had thinned. The prison van had rattled off to deliver its charges, and there were only a few stragglers left to see the second wagon roll up. The wind brought a sharp chill to Chase's bones which he attempted to ignore. God, he was tired. In younger days he could have had a jolly round in a pub, stayed up late, and been about his work the next morning without so much as a yawn. No more. And with Strickland in charge, it was bound to be a long day. He felt for the brace of pistols, one in each of his greatcoat pockets, and climbed up after Farley into the wagon.

The driver immediately whipped up the horses. They swung up Long Acre to Drury Lane and continued to High Holborn, proceeding east over increasingly shabby streets to come eventually to Bethnal Green. The parish, once rural, had been overrun with the spillover population of weavers from Spitalfields. Augmented by unskilled poor seeking employment in the silk trade, the area now consisted largely of choked alleys populated by inhabitants who could only escape their misery through drunkenness and riotous amusements.

Strickland addressed the men. "The man we're after is called Kevin Donovan. Wife's a weaver, and he works her trade too when times is good. When times is bad, he takes up another line or turns to thievery. We know where he lives, but I warn you, he's not likely to come like a lamb."

The men listened attentively, holding their weapons at the ready. Farley looked over at Chase and rolled his eyes.

"The way I reckon," Strickland continued, "Donovan was out to line his pockets that night, and maybe he decides to kill her so no questions asked. Then the hackney come along as he was stripping her. He run off with almost no gain."

His logic failed to impress. For one thing, it didn't explain what Constance Tyrone had been doing in the street. Also, the livid finger bruises on her neck suggested passion, a loss of control. Wouldn't a petty thief like Donovan be more likely to sneak up on her from behind, bludgeon her, snatch the goods, and run?

"You'll need to get Joan Snowden in to see if she can identify him," Chase said. "She saw an uncommonly big man bending over the victim. That fit Donovan?"

Strickland gave him a dismissive glance. "Ah, she's a whore and a sot. Who cares what she's got to say? Like as not she couldn't set one foot before t'other."

The sky had darkened in a low cloud cover. As the party pushed on, Chase grimaced at his surroundings. Dark buildings in filth-strewn lanes, the odor of stagnant sewage overwhelming. People milled about, men and women lurching drunk, children dejected and undernourished.

The wagon halted, able to progress no farther as their way lay though a passage into a warren of narrow courts beyond. As the men climbed down to form a ragged band, Strickland designated the driver and one other to stay with the vehicle while the rest moved ahead on foot. Chase could feel furtive eyes upon them, peering from windows and doorways and around corners.

"Spread them out, Strickland," he said as he joined them. "This ain't a parade. Why cause more of a stir than you need?"

Strickland smiled unpleasantly. "These people like a good show. I don't aim to disappoint."

The men gave nervous laughs and followed with Chase and Farley in the rear trying to look at least somewhat disinterested, Farley keeping his blunderbuss hidden beneath his greatcoat. Slowly they penetrated deeper into Bethnal Green. It began to rain, a thick drizzle that quickly turned the ground to a quagmire.

Here was a labyrinth of obscure streets and alleys terminating in tenebrous courts. Every five buildings or so housed either gin house or pawnbroker. Less frequently they passed butcher shop, chandler, or grocer, some with whey-faced proprietors standing guard in front of decaying façades. Chase yanked Farley away from a particularly unappealing puddle in the road and walked on, stepping gingerly. Ahead Strickland had finally sighted his goal: a dilapidated building, which probably housed three or four families and which was indistinguishable from a hundred others they had passed.

Now the rain pelted down. Strickland elbowed toward the doorway, shoving aside a costermonger and his wheelbarrow packed with tiny metal odds and ends. Cursing, the coster shook one fist and bent to fumble with his wares. By the time Chase and Farley caught up, a circle of onlookers had materialized.

Strickland's voice seemed to rise unnaturally loud. "Open up." He pushed against the door until it gave, then marched in, his men remaining outside to face the crowd. Chase entered behind him.

Climbing the stairs, the stench of excrement hit them like a blow. At the top they found a cramped room. The only furnishings in evidence were a plank table, one ancient bedstead, and a loom. No fire for warmth. Paper had been painstakingly pasted over cracks in the oversized window to protect the silk and provide some semblance of comfort, Chase assumed.

Strickland had cornered Donovan, a short, prematurely bent man, eyes blazing in a thin face. Gaze locked on Strickland's, he took one step backward. Huddled against the wall were his wife and a child, so small they could have been dwarfs cowering in some cave. The woman's tiny hands clutched at her child.

"You come along quiet," bellowed Strickland.

"Not till I know what I done," came the answer. Donovan glanced wildly at the door, back at his wife. She wept silently, and the child burrowed its face in her apron.

"You'd best come with us, lad," said Chase quietly. "We mean no harm to your family."

"Who are you?"

"Bow Street," said Strickland, a joyful demon light in his eyes. He picked up Donovan by his hair and pushed him against the wall. Against the officer's beefy arm, Donovan was a pitiful bag of bones. As the Runner slung him higher, Chase said, "Strickland."

"I'll handle this," Strickland said over his shoulder. "These people need to respect the law."

Letting Donovan slump at his feet, he slapped cuffs on him and dragged him across the floor to the stairs, the family in the corner watching in dull silence.

But the gathering outside showed no more respect to Strickland than the weather did. In spite of the driving rain, the circle had tightened.

"Turning ugly," said Farley, meeting them at the door.

Chase felt a current flow through the spectators. He heard someone shout, "They come for Donovan today, they be coming for you tomorrow." Voices roared in agreement.

"You Irish back off now," Strickland shouted.

Holding their pikes lengthwise, the constables pushed against the bodies, trying futilely to create a pathway. When the people saw Donovan clamped under Strickland's arm, they pressed even closer.

"Take him that way," called Chase urgently. He pointed at an opening between the buildings, presumably leading to an alley. Nodding, Farley began to edge forward. Strickland, swearing now, tapped one of his men on the shoulder, jerked his head toward the gap, and began to struggle toward it.

In the scuffle the costermonger's barrow tipped and came crashing down, scattering metal bits to be ground under foot and buried by mud. The vendor let out a howl, dropping to his knees. The water poured down his bent head. Almost falling over him, Strickland recovered and stumbled on. He kicked aside the coster's goods as he went.

Chase had just reached the mouth of the alley when suddenly a great bullock charged out of the street opposite, a shouting, laughing mob in its wake. By chance, the throng had picked this narrow court for their mad sport of running the bull. They had probably shoved peas in its ears or driven an iron-pointed stick into its body to enrage it. Now the goliath ran straight toward the rabble gathered at Donovan's door.

Screaming, people rushed in all directions, but their efforts to disperse only confused the bull. It found itself in an enclosed space with no apparent way out, the storm only inflaming it further. Shaking its head to clear the rain, the bull shifted first in one direction, then another, and pawed the ground. Finally, it turned toward Strickland and Donovan, still pinned to the side of the building.

Strickland tried to raise his tipstaff, but the crush of bodies bore him inexorably back. Seeing his opportunity, Donovan wrenched out of the officer's grasp and began to inch away. Chase watched him go. There was nothing he could do. He crushed his own panic, letting the wave of fleeing people wash by. Farley and the rest of Strickland's band were swept away. The bull, alone now in the center of the court, lowered its head and made as if to plunge after the scattering crowd.

Chase reluctantly drew one of his pistols and approached the beast. Raising the pistol, he clicked the cock with his thumb. He sighted the massive head, made sure of his opening, and slowly squeezed the trigger. The hammer fell. Flint struck against the steel frizzen, sending a shower of sparks into the pan. And Chase held his breath for the eternal moment between the flash of priming powder and the roar of the main charge.

The bull fell to its knees, face buried in thick mud. Blood oozed from its wound and mingled with the rain and filth to form a dark puddle on the cobbles. The mob had dispersed into alleys and shop doors, leaving only the officers, a few unconscious bodies, and the costermonger still scrabbling in the muck.

Strickland was cursing again and clutching at an injured wrist. Of Donovan there was no sign. Chase put away his pistol and sighed heavily.

❧ ☙

At dusk in Temple Gardens the barrier between past and present turned fluid and ghosts walked. Here and there if Buckler looked closely he caught a glimpse of knights filing toward the ancient round Church, heads bowed in penitence. He might see a lawyer, aged and crow-like, bending toward the peacock courtier at his side or a group of clattering students on their way to a revel in the Hall.

Buckler didn't mind the spirits. In fact, he preferred their company to that of the general run of human. For the ghosts reminded him that man's petty cares, so all consuming in life, would one day become nothing more than fit matter for an amusing story.

Failing lasting glory, the best one could hope for in death was anonymity. To be remembered as a villain was not a fate that appealed to Buckler. Even less would he like to be the butt of some jest for centuries. And in the Inner and Middle Temple, memories were long, men of law having a tendency to speak of long ago events as though they had happened yesterday.

They still talked of the day in 1669 when the Lord Mayor, summoned to the Reader's Feast, dared to enter the Temple bearing the City Sword aloft, blatant provocation since neither learned society acknowledged itself as part of the City's jurisdiction. Determined to humble him for his temerity, a group of irate students struck down the sword and chased the Lord Mayor into ignominious retreat. Buckler thought of this fellow anytime he felt inclined to self-importance—which wasn't often these days.

Most evenings he took a solitary walk about the grounds, dressed in a voluminous coat and wide-brim hat. After long days spent huddled over his desk, he needed the air to reinvigorate a dulled brain. Usually, he had to force himself to leave his fireside, and some days he just couldn't manage; the lethargy was too strong.

Now he paced slowly through the rain-freshened gardens and the various courts and small streets, utterly familiar and prosaic territory that regained its mystery with night's advent. He was thinking of the Constance Tyrone affair, his clerk, Bob, having just told him of Bow Street's ill-fated foray into Bethnal Green. The evening papers had vaunted the news in a mixture of gleeful satire and outrage, making much of the bovine "accomplice" that had allowed the Irishman to escape. The outcome, however, was no laughing matter: there was still a killer on the loose, whether or not the authorities had seized upon the right man in Kevin Donovan.

Buckler was curious too about the fate of Penelope Wolfe, though he knew himself to be well out of that muddle. Learning of her husband's disappearance, he had wondered what she would do. Possibly, the absence of a feckless husband might not make that much difference. Buckler had asked Thorogood what on earth had driven her to marry Wolfe in the first place; he couldn't imagine a more ill-suited pair. In typical fashion, Thorogood had shrugged and delivered himself of a bit of wisdom courtesy of the ancients: something about overmastering passion conquering all reason, as Buckler recalled.

Entering Fountain Court, Buckler came suddenly upon one of his colleagues, Mr. Leonard Crouch, rising young luminary of the Bar in spite of, or perhaps because of, his unremittingly obnoxious efforts to bring himself into view. Buckler wished he could retreat, but Crouch had seen him.

"Ah, Buckler." At the sound of his voice any lingering ghosts fled in dismay. "I've just been round to the Grecian to see Thompson. Wanted to tell him my news, a good bit of luck. Seems I'm to be briefed in the Ship's Bank matter."

"Well done," said Buckler.

"Not that Fortune is entirely responsible. All it takes is a word, my friend, a word in the right ear, and the thing is accomplished."

Carrying a wine glass in his hand, Crouch still wore a long, black gown and white neck bands, but had removed his wig. He always took pains to appear older, for he worried that prospective clients would not entrust their delicate affairs to so young a man. Accordingly, he had modified his stride to a dignified walk and styled his hair in a fashion more suited to a man of fifty than to one barely in his thirties.

They strolled together toward the fountain, passing Middle Temple Hall, an Elizabethan structure with its oak double hammerbeam roof. Smoke from the Hall's central open fireplace was pouring out of the roof's decorative cupola.

"As for you, Buckler, 'tis well and good to make a name for yourself, but I wouldn't defend any more corpses were I you. One such case has a sort of piquancy. Any more, however, and you stand in danger of making yourself ridiculous. Not a very lucrative field either, as I rather think you won't find a steady supply of dead men in need of your services. Unless you decide to represent the victims of grave robbers." He gave a bark of laughter. "I tell you this as one devoted to your interests, of course."

Buckler tried to look suitably somber. "Of course. But who was to know? Perhaps other grieving relatives will be emboldened to seek redress for their wrongs. It is indecent to imprison a dead man for debt, not allowing him a Christian burial. Justice was served."

"Justice? It's not about justice. A pretty word, but we do a job, my friend, defending or prosecuting as the case may be. We owe it to ourselves to get ahead in this business. Which means working toward one day taking silk and finally making something of our lives. It's a contest, Buckler, as much a sport as a bout in the ring or a run on the turf, but with even more at stake. Only a few win."

Buckler nodded and leaned against the fence. If he had to listen to Crouch, he might as well be comfortable. But perhaps his companion would take himself off, for the evening grew markedly chill, and Crouch, creature of cramped chambers, convivial pubs, and stuffy law courts, was hardly the type to appreciate fresh air. He loitered, however, raising a finger to Buckler's face.

"Never give quarter to the enemy. That is why the Corsican Rogue has been so successful. I tell you, if you spot weakness, you must pounce on it, throwing all at a breach in the lines. That is the course we must follow to win this accursed War. And that is how I intend to prevail in my personal affairs."

"Brilliant, my boy." Ezekiel Thorogood popped up from behind the fountain and stood applauding gently. "Perhaps you should advise Wellington. Though I hear a waiting game is more to his taste."

Silhouetted against the shooting water, Thorogood took a handkerchief from his pocket and removed his spectacles to wipe the spots. Then he dabbed his brow and pronounced, "*Non nobis, Domine, non nobis, sed Tuo Nomini da gloriam.* Not to us, O Lord, not to us, but to Thy Name give the glory."

It was the old battle cry of the Knights Templar, intended to rouse the monks' blood as they charged into the fray against all infidels. Crouch, taken aback, gaped at Thorogood, but true to his calling made a rapid recovery.

"Behold. The perfect illustration of my lesson: knight errant and respectable attorney." He bowed to Thorogood. "Or should I say knight error and rapscallions' attorney."

He smiled at his own wit, adding, "Consort with his like, Buckler, and when I am K.C. you will still be here whiling away bootless hours in these gardens."

"He shall indeed be in a garden by the time you are a King's Counsel," replied Thorogood. "Resting comfortably beneath a fine headstone. Be off, Crouch. I need a word with Buckler."

Without another word, Crouch turned on his heel and hurried back toward the coffee house, completely forgetting to moderate his stride.

"Well," huffed Thorogood, "you can thank me for ridding you of that priggish boor. But why the deuce can't you be in your chambers when a man has need of you? I am far too old for pursuit."

"Oh, did we have an engagement? Remiss of me."

He chuckled. "None of your cheek now. I thought we might have a little chat is all."

Buckler looked at him in patent disbelief. "A social call? I knew there must be a reason why any respectable barrister would as soon sit down to dinner with a housebreaker as consort with you attorneys. What is it, Thorogood? Not another affair that no sooner sends me into the hell pit of Newgate than it evaporates?"

"Strange circumstance that, though the object was achieved. An innocent man was set free, and justice was served, however circuitously."

"Justice? It's not about justice; it's... Now you've got me quoting that ass Crouch."

"Do be careful, Buckler. I should hate to have to drop your acquaintance. I'm far too old to make new friends." He paused. "Would you be interested to know the status of the Tyrone matter, especially in regard to young Mrs. Wolfe?"

"Has the husband returned then? I hope they shall live happily ever after."

Thorogood's shrewd glance raked his face. "By Jupiter, I didn't realize she had struck you so. A distinguished looking woman, I agree, but irrevocably leg-shackled. Too much spirit for you anyway."

Buckler knew better than to deny it. "I find many women striking, but married ladies strike me with fear rather than admiration."

Thorogood laughed again and gripped his shoulder briefly with a large hand. "No, Jeremy Wolfe is still missing and likely to remain so if you ask me. I fear my friend Mrs. Wolfe and her daughter must contrive on their own. Which is not entirely a bad thing, one reflects, as Wolfe could make matters most unpleasant for her should he choose to exert his prerogatives. Appropriate her funds or even take the child."

"How does she manage anyway? An independent income?"

"Her father makes her a small allowance, and she writes the odd piece for publication, yet I believe she has ambitions in quite another direction."

"Indeed?"

"She wants to write biography, something like Boswell did with Samuel Johnson, I suppose. Take a renowned subject and record the particulars of his life in order to offer up a living portrait."

Buckler didn't comment, focusing his gaze on the sky. It was that indescribable color that one only saw just when darkness gained the ascendancy while the last of the light lingered. Thorogood's next words snapped his attention back.

"Actually, I came to tell you of an intriguing visit I received today from Mr. Jedidiah Merkle. To speak of another beetle-headed man of law. Worse than Crouch, I vow."

"What did he want?"

"Difficult to fathom, friend, but clearly there was some thought possessing that little mind. He spoke in riddles. From what I could gather, he desired to inform me that should Mr. Jeremy Wolfe's wife find herself in any need, his 'esteemed client' is willing to come to her aid. Merkle didn't explain why this unnamed client is prepared to assist a woman who is presumably a perfect stranger."

"Did he say where Wolfe is?"

"No, but I have the greatest faith we shall find out in due course. Come, I've a fancy for a short stroll, then possibly some refreshment at a local establishment. What do you say?"

Thorogood led the way toward the river at a brisk pace. "The days grow short and all the shorter for me, I fear. I'm not getting any younger, my dear Buckler." He coughed.

"I waste no pity on you, old man. Fit as a stoat and married to a handsome widow much your junior." Buckler looked at him in sudden suspicion. "Whenever you start to play on my sympathies, it's usually to induce me to take on some dubious scheme for which I might receive the grand remuneration of several chickens or a cask of ale. If I'm lucky."

Thorogood kept going, his reply floating back. "May I remind you that our last adventure was reported by all the major papers, and you came out something of a hero. Moreover, those chickens made quite a sumptuous feast. *Pecunia non olet*."

Buckler halted. "Quite right: money does not smell, but the chickens certainly did. By the by, where are we going? I've already had my walk. I'm more than ready for that refreshment you mentioned. Besides it's cold and will be even colder by the river if that is your destination."

"Just a trifle farther." Thorogood's portly figure hurried toward the Temple stairs, starting down. He didn't look back.

"Watch it," Buckler called, exasperated. "It gets slippery just there. I don't fancy explaining a broken limb to your wife." Hurrying to catch up, he followed the lawyer down the stone steps.

Thorogood turned to address him, all trace of his habitual good humor banished from his countenance. "You were right, Buckler. I do have a matter for your consideration. You see, I've been approached by a man with wife and child. He has been wrongly accused of a heinous crime. He is poor and of an unpopular faith."

Buckler sighed. "Another one, Thorogood? But couldn't we discuss the matter in more comfortable surroundings?" He shivered in the sharp wind blowing off the Thames and pulled his hat lower on his head. Below them the black river tumbled by.

"He is being made a scapegoat. The authorities need an arrest to save face, and the government wants a hanging to placate the mob."

"Wait. I begin to understand. Is this innocent man Irish by any chance? By the name of Donovan?"

Thorogood remained silent.

"God save us if it isn't the Tyrone business again. The man is as good as gallows meat according to the news sheets. I thought he was on the run. Here is my best legal advice: tell him to leave the city—escape to Ireland or make his way to America."

Thorogood took his arm. "You know as well as I he has not the funds. He has a family. They will be hounded night and day. He wants to submit to the authorities, yet rightly fears for his chances of obtaining a fair trial. He has a story to tell, but he needs help."

"Why do they always seek you out? Surely, you did not become successful by helping the likes of Kevin Donovan?"

"In my younger days I was quite ambitious in some ways not unlike your friend Crouch, I'm ashamed to say. But my Hope has shown me the way of truth. Embracing her faith, I must needs embrace a new mode of life." He held Buckler's eyes. "Besides, I'm far too old to cope with such matters on my own. I've need of you, friend. At least listen to Donovan's story before you judge."

"You humbug! I suppose if I'm to meet this fellow we shall have to descend into some rookery?"

"Actually, we need only wait here. For I believe that is he in yonder boat." He pointed.

In the twilight, Buckler could just distinguish the silhouette of a waterman making landfall. A second indistinct figure slouched at the rear of the craft.

Thorogood stepped forward. "Come. This won't take but a few minutes of our time, and we shall soon reward ourselves with a steaming bowl of punch."

Chapter Twelve

Ezekiel Thorogood, his wife, Hope, and their brood of children lived in a comfortably respectable neighborhood surrounded by country lanes and extensive fields in Camden Town. In fact, everything about the Thorogoods was comfortable: their rambling house, their large garden with fruit trees, and most of all their offspring: a boisterous, uninhibited bunch left to grow in a tumbling sort of way.

Hope Thorogood had herself brought three children to the marriage, and added to her husband's five theirs was a fine family indeed. She was a handsome woman in her forties, wide shouldered and somewhat thickset with rich corn colored hair, piercingly intelligent eyes, and a round, pretty face. Hope, whose name had been inspired by her birth on Christmas Day, was always busy with some charitable project or other. She had a talent for making the most of people that the ablest general might have envied.

Hope also had enormous courage. Born and bred a Quaker, she had defied family and community to marry her second husband. While nominally she had become Anglican, her essential outlook was unchanged, though she had learned to take pleasure in dancing, music, and the theatre, all of which had been forbidden in her previous life. Watching her and Thorogood together, Penelope could easily understand why she had risked so much to marry him. They had that rare sort of perfect accord—not that they didn't argue, for Hope was a spirited woman. Yet watching the genial Thorogood preside proudly at the dinner table opposite Hope, herself wreathed in smiles, Penelope thought there could be no greater felicity known to humankind.

Penelope had met Ezekiel Thorogood half a year ago at a meeting of a literary society of which they were both briefly members. Sitting next to her one evening, Thorogood had kept her entertained through several hours of dull poetry. Every time the speaker's flights of fancy flew too far for good sense, Thorogood would give a gentle cough as if to nudge him discreetly back. During the interval Penelope and Thorogood struck up a conversation and had been firm friends ever since.

She and Sarah dined frequently with the Thorogoods, and Penelope was happy to give her child a taste of real family life. Here Sarah unbent far more than usual and could be seen to romp with the other children. Here Penelope could relax, knowing she too could laugh and talk freely.

But tonight it was different, for there was another guest, Mr. Edward Buckler. Absurdly, Penelope felt resentful of Mr. Buckler's presence, as if somehow he were snatching a treat meant for her lips. Thus, she maintained a dignified, stilted demeanor quite unlike her usual frank enjoyment. And she knew that Hope, perfectly aware of her feelings, was sympathetic but amused.

With the children upstairs at supper, the adults were enjoying a quiet moment in the drawing room before their departure for an evening at the Philosophical Society. The Thorogoods' drawing room was a cozy, informal apartment with its writing tables scattered about, chairs drawn near the hearth, and pianoforte in the corner. A huge fire burned in the grate, and Thorogood had deposited his bulk in the wing chair close by. His wife, poking absently at her tambour frame, sat next to Penelope on the sofa. Edward Buckler sat across from them. He looked as uncomfortable as Penelope felt.

Remembering his disheveled appearance at their first meeting, Penelope was surprised to find he was an attractive man. He'd had his thick auburn hair cut shorter in a style that favored his long, narrow nose, lean cheeks, and pale blue eyes. Buckler was a trifle less than average height, but carried himself well, at least when he wasn't crawling about on his knees in his dressing gown. She had shared this joke with Hope, so tonight when the barrister came in, Penelope had caught her eye and had to repress a smile. But now Penelope found herself unaccountably tongue-tied and awkward while Hope, placid as always, pretended not to notice the stiff wariness of her guests.

Hope leaned forward to thrust her bag of threads into her husband's hand. "Here, my dear. Will you separate these for me?"

Obligingly, Thorogood took the bag and dumped it out on the Pembroke table at his side. "Why ever do you let them get in such a state?" he asked mildly. He looked up. "Buckler, take note. Ladies are eminently practical about most things, but every so often there's an inexplicable lapse. Were this my embroidery bag, I'd find a different way to store the materials so as not to be forever left untangling them."

Hope smiled. "The children like to play with them. Besides, the performance of such tasks keeps you quiet. My goodness, but you have been restless today, sir. You don't have to tell me there's business afoot."

Thorogood turned a limpid gaze upon her. "I'm sure I don't know what you mean, madam." Penelope noticed that he carefully avoided looking at Buckler, applying himself once more to the tangled threads.

Hope said to Penelope, "You see, my dear, what happens when the poor creatures try to keep a secret? It makes them horribly nervous, I'm afraid. And guilty, as is only right if they don't intend to honor us with their confidence."

"What makes you think I am keeping something from you?" said Thorogood.

"Oh, I can always tell. You've been like a bear in a cage all day. And I saw you whisper to Mr. Buckler when he arrived." She gave her tambour a strong jab. "I tell you, sir. Whatever scheme you have hatching, do me the kindness to remember that winter is coming on. You must not be getting chilled or over…over enthusiastic."

Buckler's lips twitched. "Listen to her, Thorogood."

The two men's eyes met.

Curious now, Penelope said, "Indeed. You must be watchful of your health."

Thorogood had recently recovered from a severe cold that had lingered for more than a month, seeming likely to descend to his lungs. Hope's careful nursing had avoided this calamity, yet she was still uneasy on his account. Thorogood, however, hated to be reminded.

"Nonsense, I am quite recovered. Mrs. Wolfe, I understand from my wife you've been engaged in a new pursuit. I had hoped to hear more of it."

"You mean my work for the St. Catherine Society? Yes, I have been supervising the women so that the directress, Miss Minton, may attend to her other affairs."

"That's kind in you," said Hope. "But does Miss Minton know…" Too late, she understood that her remark might cause embarrassment.

"She knows I am Jeremy's wife, but she really does require assistance. Apparently, the Society has been deserted by its usual patronesses."

Thorogood exchanged another look with his friend. "No doubt they fear the taint of scandal. Not admirable, but then it takes a courageous sort of person to ignore the world's whispers."

Buckler said, "Or a fool." He added, "You've heard nothing from your husband, Mrs. Wolfe? Do you suppose he doesn't realize that Bennington's alibi cleared him completely? There's no need for him to remain in hiding."

"It isn't Bennington's alibi that proves his innocence," said Penelope without thinking, then paused, dismayed. She would not betray Daniel Partridge.

Thorogood sat up straighter. "If you know something more of this matter, ma'am, we'd be most interested to share in your knowledge." He raked a hand through his hair, making one graying strand stick up.

Familiar with the expression on his face, Penelope knew she was in trouble. "It's only that I have encountered the Runner investigating the matter, and I suppose we've come up with a few pieces of the puzzle. But I'm not at liberty to divulge all at this point."

Thorogood was opening his mouth to protest when Hope interceded. "You will not bully her, sir. I'm sure I don't know why she should tell her secrets when 'tis obvious the two of you harbor one of your own."

Buckler looked abashed, but Thorogood just opened his eyes wide and addressed his wife: "I certainly acknowledge the sacred nature of information imparted *sub rosa*, yet it must be advantageous to ally our forces."

"Should Mrs. Wolfe choose to do so," said Hope. "And one wonders if you mean to reciprocate. Anything else would be less than fair play."

"I always play fair, madam." He bowed to both women from his seat.

Buckler gave a choking sound, but subsided under his friend's glare.

Thorogood said, "I was curious merely. Surprisingly, in all my years in the profession, I've yet to have conversation with a Bow Street Runner. What sort of man is he, Mrs. Wolfe?"

Whenever anyone asked her a direct question, she was apt to blurt the truth before she thought how it might sound. "Keen witted and, I dare say, honorable, but he's arrogant at times, too quick to see the bad in people without acknowledging the good. I rather think his work has made him cynical. Yet he doesn't lack for humor."

She was aware of how personal her description sounded, as if she knew Mr. Chase far better than she really did. Feeling warmth creep up her face, she stared down at her lap, then looked up to encounter Buckler's suddenly serious eyes.

Hope opened her mouth to step into the breach, but Penelope forestalled her, hurrying on. "I met Mr. Chase in the church after Constance Tyrone's funeral. He is determined to discover her murderer, and I…I want to help. It isn't only about finding the truth for Jeremy's sake anymore."

"You mustn't put yourself in jeopardy, ma'am," said Buckler.

"Indeed, Penelope, be careful. Perhaps I should accompany you when you visit this place."

Penelope smiled at Hope. "You have more than enough to keep you well occupied." She turned to Buckler. "No doubt that man Donovan will be apprehended soon, sir. Do you believe he is the one?"

"I rather think not," he responded carefully.

Thorogood said, "Just what have you and this Chase fellow discovered, my dear? Surely you can tell us. It could be important."

Omitting all mention of Partridge and his pamphlet, Penelope told them of her encounter with the Tyrones and her experiences at the Society, ending with the discovery of Constance's boots. Absorbed in her tale, they listened without moving.

"But you see," Penelope finished, "it seems so strange for her to have substituted the slippers for the boots and departed again. Mr. Chase believes a carriage may have collected her, for she certainly couldn't walk in the street like that."

Thorogood slapped his hand on the table. "By Jove, that's it! This is just the confirmation we need, Buckler."

Hope said, "I trust you will explain that remark, Mr. Thorogood, though I've a notion what you will say, and I cannot like it!"

"Now, my love…by Jove, look at the time. If we don't take care, we shall be late to Mr. Coleridge's lecture."

Ignoring this gambit, she looked accusingly at Buckler, but he held up his hands. "I tried, ma'am, truly I did. One may as well shout into the wind."

Penelope said to Thorogood, "You are acquainted with the Irishman, sir?"

"Yes, my dear. Donovan approached me for legal advice, and I took him to see Buckler. At present he is in hiding, but I have hopes of convincing him to surrender." He glanced at Hope, who was starting to sputter. "No, no, madam. What would you have me do—turn away an innocent man whom the authorities would as soon hang as look at?"

"How are you so certain of his innocence, sir?"

"Why, because Donovan's never so much as set eyes on Miss Tyrone, my love." His flashing gaze swept around. "Her slipper, however, is another matter. That he found in the Society's garden."

"If she were attacked in the garden, why deposit her in the middle of the road?" asked Hope.

"Perhaps the villain wanted her to be run down so as to obscure the facts yet further," ventured Penelope.

Thorogood shook his head. "It's difficult to obscure hand bruises about the neck. No, I rather think the hackney was mere coincidence. What say you, Buckler?"

"I say someone should be asking who had access to the church grounds and also had a motive for killing Miss Tyrone."

"Let us take a ride to St. Catherine's tomorrow," said Thorogood. "To see the layout of the place for ourselves. Maybe do a little digging in the garden, eh?"

"Leave the dirty work to Mr. Chase," said Hope.

❦

"Yes, sir," said the proprietor of the Bull's Head, "the lady what you describe has been here. And with the gentleman." He managed to look sly while still maintaining an air of respectful attention.

Chase stood in the taproom, nearly deserted this early in the day. Only a few old men gossiping over their beer and one or two incorrigible drunks sat at the plank tables. The landlord, one Evan Royster, had a wet cloth slung across his arm. He was a substantial man, not fat but bulky, with nondescript features and dirty brown hair the color of the water in his bucket.

"About how many times?" asked Chase.

Royster made a big show of stopping to consider. "I'd say near a dozen. They started coming in the spring. I recall clear as anything on account of the lady bringing my wife a hot-cross bun for Good Friday. She was real kind, no height in her manner at all. Her friend always bespoke our private parlor and the finest grub. My wife used to plan bits as she thought might tempt the lady. Plump her up like, not that she needed a blessed thing more than what God already gave her." He permitted himself a brief chuckle.

Chase looked at him. "She's dead. I am a Bow Street officer investigating her murder."

Royster's face fell ludicrously, and he took a step back. "Well, I'm that sorry for the lady, but if what you say is true, it's nothing to do with this house. Why, I don't even know her name, nor that of the gentleman."

"They came here a dozen times but never made themselves known by name?"

"I didn't inquire. 'Tisn't polite when someone's trying to meet on the quiet like. I had most of my dealings with the gentleman anyway, and we understood one another. He wanted to woo his lady love with none the wiser and was prepared to pay well for the privilege." Royster shot him a hopeful glance. "Only right, isn't it, to compensate a man?"

Reaching into his pocket, Chase ostentatiously jingled a few coins. He would have to cross this man's greasy palm with silver, but he wanted to make sure to get his money's worth.

"So you'd describe their behavior as lover like?" he said, watching Royster's face carefully.

"I can't say as I ever saw nothing untoward, but why would a fine looking man like that bring a lady to a tavern, respectable establishment or no? No ring on her finger."

Chase didn't comment.

The landlord gave him a knowing, conspiratorial glance. "We understand these things, isn't that so, sir? My wife would have it the gentleman was telling the truth that he and the lady had business to discuss. But I know the look a man gets when he's hot on a woman's scent, and he had it." He laughed again, comfortably, and moved away to refill a patron's mug.

Royster had not asked Constance Tyrone's name, nor inquired about how she died. Clearly he didn't want to know. For the moment Chase preferred to leave him in ignorance to avoid any premature gossip.

The landlord returned. "I can't think what else I can tell you, sir, and I do have my chores to attend to." He waited.

"When was the last time you saw them?"

Royster frowned, trying to remember. "Oh, end of October or thereabouts. Don't recall the exact day."

So far everything he had said confirmed Partridge's story. Chase handed him a coin and let himself out into the narrow passage.

Picking his way toward the door, he nearly fell over a woman crouched on all fours scrubbing the stone floor. Middle-aged and tired, her face bore the remains of prettiness. Her hair, tied back in a careless knot, was still a vibrant gold. She had been so intent on her work that she didn't notice him until he loomed above her.

"Beg pardon, sir," she cried, jumping to her feet. "Do have a care you don't slip." She gave him an anxious look, whisked her pail away, and flattened her body against the wall.

Chase smiled at her. "Are you Mrs. Royster? I was just speaking to your husband in the taproom."

She gave a bob and smiled back uncertainly. "You've refreshed yourself? I hope you tried our dark brewed. The patrons seem to like it most."

"I shall have to give myself the pleasure another time, Mrs. Royster. Today I've come to inquire about a lady and a gentleman who had been frequenting your establishment. I'm a Bow Street officer, John Chase by name." He bowed politely.

Her eyes grew round. "Pleased to make your acquaintance, sir."

When Chase told Mrs. Royster of Constance's death, she said, "Oh that poor dear. She was a true lady. What happened to her?"

"We don't know everything yet, ma'am. But whatever you can add will be of help." He made a guess. "Were you perhaps the one to serve when they visited?"

"Yes, sir. They always took our private parlor, and I'd bring their tea. Miss Constance liked to pour out for her friend, so I'd just leave it."

"She told you her name?"

Mrs. Royster looked surprised. "Why yes, sir. Once her gentleman friend was behind time, and we had ourselves a bit of a chat." Her face softened. "She was worried that I looked done for, after me to rest." Briefly, her hand drifted over her stomach, and Chase saw that she was pregnant. With her slight frame and voluminous apron, her condition hadn't been readily apparent.

Her eyes glistening with tears, she continued, "She was the one what worked hard, always bent over those papers fit to make your head ache. Planning a school for poor children and their mams, she was. Ah, a saint, that one, and I won't hear nothing said against her."

"Your husband received quite a different impression of the lady's presence here."

She dashed tears away with her sleeve. "What do you expect? To him, there's only one reason to put a man and woman alone together. Besides, you can ask my friend Polly Welles over at the York. She'll tell you same as me."

A sense of anticipation stealing over him, Chase leaned closer. "What would she know of this?"

"I didn't tell Evan because he'd just claim the York be stealing our custom, but Miss Constance and her friend used to meet there from time to time. Not so often as here, of course."

Now that is something Daniel Partridge forgot to mention, thought Chase. Curious, that. Chase would call upon Polly. Thanking Mrs. Royster, he took himself off.

Ten minutes later he stood in the taproom at the York, requesting to speak to Mrs. Welles. The rather stern-faced man behind the counter, presumably her husband, gave him a clouded look, but obliged by calling his wife in a voice that practically vibrated the rafters. The woman who presented herself a moment later presented a strong contrast to her friend Mrs. Royster. Strolling casually toward them, Polly Welles emanated confidence. She too had left her youth behind, but life seemed to have been kinder to her. Her cheeks were unlined, her eyes still bright.

"What are you shouting for?" she demanded of the man behind the counter. "I'm up to my elbows in pickles this morning." True enough, a strong, sharp odor had wafted into the room with her.

The man jerked his head at Chase. "This gentleman is asking for you. What's your business with my wife, sir?"

Chase nodded pleasantly. "John Chase, Bow Street. I'll take just a few minutes of her time, if you please, and she can tell you all about it later. It's nothing that reflects poorly upon Mrs. Welles or this establishment."

Polly's husband thrust out his jaw, seeming inclined to argue. She said, "Oh, give over, do, love. You'd think he had something improper in mind. We'll have our little talk over there where you can keep your eye on us."

She pointed to a corner table. Turning to Chase, she gave him a grin and a broad wink. "Not such a bad thing to have a jealous husband after all these years. He looks fierce, but he's a gentle sort unless someone trifles with me."

"One can hardly blame him for being careful, Mrs. Welles," Chase replied gallantly, earning him a delighted laugh from the woman and another glare from the husband.

Declining her offer of refreshment, he followed her toward the table and sat across from her. She regarded him with friendly interest.

"I've just been speaking to Mrs. Royster at the Bull's Head," Chase began. "She told me of a conversation the two of you had about a certain lady and gentleman frequenting both your establishments."

She knew immediately whom he meant. "Yes, sir. They's unusual, you see. We don't often get folk of that stamp. Literary sorts, yes, as well as artists, players and such. But no gentlemen quite so genteel, and definitely no ladies."

"Mrs. Welles, you must have heard of the woman who was strangled and trampled in the street near here?"

Smile fading, she nodded.

"She was the same woman who had been coming here and to the Bull's Head with her friend."

The color blanched from Polly Welles' face. "Was it him? Did he harm her?"

"I don't know yet, but I can promise you I intend to find out. Will you help me by answering a few questions?"

"Of course, I will." Her brows snapped together. "Ask me. Though I don't know anything to the purpose."

Her story was much the same as Mrs. Royster's. Constance Tyrone and Daniel Partridge had taken luncheon at the York some four or five times. Again, they bespoke a private parlor and seemed to be hard at work. When Polly had entered the room to serve, they were always engaged in earnest discussion.

"I never saw him so much as touch her hand. Still, when he looked at her, he had such a light in his eyes. I would have thought they were brother and sister but for that."

"What of the lady?"

She considered. "I don't know. Oh, she liked him, sir, but she wasn't the type to go for a little pleasure on the sly."

"You've been enormously helpful, Mrs. Welles." Chase smiled at her. "One more question: when was the last time you saw them? Try to remember the exact date if you can, please ma'am."

"Let's see." She stared fixedly at the wall behind him. "It wasn't too long since. In fact, must've been about a fortnight ago."

Chase's heart began to pound. Partridge had said he had last seen Constance Tyrone back in October.

"Are you sure, Mrs. Welles? Can you pinpoint the day?"

"Yes, I can," she cried, jumping to her feet. "I keep a record of our best paying regulars, so when next they stop with us I always know what we served. That way I can tempt 'em with a new dish or two."

She walked quickly across the room and went behind the counter. Her husband, watching her curiously, started to ask a question, but she shook her head at him. Returning to Chase with a logbook, she flipped to the appropriate page.

"Here it is, sir. The lady and gentleman were here the afternoon of Monday, 11 November. Tea that day with fritters and plum cake." She looked at him. "When did you say she passed on, poor soul?"

Chase didn't answer, instead pulling the book closer and reading the entry for himself. And there it was: Monday, 11 November. Daniel Partridge had tea with the victim on the last day of her life.

Watching him curiously, Polly Welles said, "Nothing out of ordinary happened. Just talk as usual."

"How long were they here?"

"Oh, a couple of hours, say from a trifle past two to about four."

Chase stood, holding out his hand and smiling down at her. "I am grateful for your assistance, Mrs. Welles."

Once outside, Chase wended his way through the traffic, a cold drizzle slapping at his face. He would seek out the curate Thaddeus Wood at St. Catherine's to find out if he had remembered anything more. Maggie saw the victim leave the Society about two o'clock that Monday afternoon, but no one so far had admitted to seeing her return, even though the boots proved she must have. And Partridge had lied. He was, in fact, the last known person to see Constance Tyrone alive. What else might he have neglected to reveal?

Entering the churchyard, he caught a movement out of the corner of his eye. A figure in a dark coat lay prone under the rosebushes that lined the wall.

The man was scratching among the leaves while grumbling, "Bloody thorns, blast the mud..."

Chase approached with a cautious step till he came up behind. "Are you in need of assistance, sir?"

Chapter Thirteen

Buckler had encountered no trouble following Donovan's directions through the churchyard to the garden. He had stopped by the reception area of the St. Catherine Society to call on Penelope Wolfe, but was informed by a suspicious old woman that Mrs. Wolfe had "gone off." Thus dismissed, he turned to his true purpose.

The grounds were all but deserted in this inclement weather and for good reason. With everything so tangled and muddy it was difficult to move about. Moreover, since the Irishman could not remember exactly where he'd found the slipper, several clumps of shrubs all needed to be searched. At least that was what Thorogood had decreed, and it was left to Buckler to worry about the practicalities. He had already worked his way along the ivy-covered wall toward a shed obscured in the overgrown foliage, but for all his effort, had discovered precisely nothing. He did not even know what he hoped to find, anything out of the ordinary he supposed.

Well, there was nothing here but very ordinary mud, rotting leaves, and insects. He had turned over enough rocks now to be unmoved at the crawly things that skittered away at his inspection. Lying on his stomach on the damp ground with his head sticking under a bush, he was about to admit defeat.

But when the figure materialized above him, shadowing what faint light filtered through the storm clouds, he too felt like skittering into some kind of shelter.

"Are you in need of assistance, sir?" the man inquired.

Water spilled from Buckler's hat brim into his eyes as he rolled over to confront a harsh-featured, implacable face. "Just... having a look around."

"I'll help you up, shall I?"

A hand extended to haul Buckler to his feet. Buckler brushed himself off, grimaced at the mud stains on his coat, and used his handkerchief to mop his face, thus gaining a few moments to salvage his composure. When he felt slightly more presentable, he looked at the man and wondered what explanation to offer.

"I came to call upon a friend at the St. Catherine Society, but found her out."

"You've taken her absence rather to heart," the man replied, gaze flicking toward the muddied knees of Buckler's trousers. "Or did you expect to find her under that bush?"

Buckler forced a smile. "You are mistaken, sir. My motive for being in so...uh...singular a position is professional. I am Edward Buckler. A barrister."

"I own I had a rather different impression of our eminent gentlemen of the Bar. I am relieved to discover, after all, that you barristers do occasionally venture into the real world and can only hope your client prizes such strenuous effort on his behalf. You do have a client, sir?"

The certainty flashed into Buckler's mind that this was the Bow Street Runner whom Penelope had described last night. He said, "John Chase, is it not? You are the officer looking into the Tyrone matter?"

"If I am?"

"Why, then I am pleased to make your acquaintance." He held out his hand.

Chase took it. "Why are you here, Mr. Buckler?"

The rain had begun to fall more thickly, and Buckler was forced to ignore the rivulets running down the back of his neck. "You are aware, Mr. Chase, that my original connection to the matter arose from Mrs. Wolfe's consultation on behalf of her husband?"

He nodded warily. "I have long wished conversation with Mr. Jeremy Wolfe. Dare I suppose you are privy to his whereabouts?"

"I know nothing of him. Rather, I have been brought into the matter again, purely coincidentally."

"I don't much believe in coincidence, sir. You had best explain yourself."

Buckler hesitated. He did not feel entire confidence in the Runner's integrity, despite Penelope's belief. However, he thought that John Chase's expertise would prove more efficacious than his own unskilled attempts at investigation.

Chase said, "Must I remind you, sir, that this is a murder inquiry?" He pulled out his watch, frowning at the raindrops splattering on its crystal. "Blast it, man, if you've got something, let us have it. I've work today."

"What would you say, Mr. Chase, to the missing slipper having been found somewhere in this area on the morning Constance Tyrone's body was discovered?"

"First, I should express myself curious as to the source of your intelligence." Chase stepped closer.

"I imagine you are well able to turn your curiosity in the proper direction."

A spark ignited in the officer's eyes. "Ah, so the Irishman surfaces. Assuming I am willing to credit what you say, Mr. Buckler, what precisely do you seek?"

"Have you considered the implications, sir?"

"They fairly jump out at one. If Constance Tyrone were attacked in the garden that night, the culprit must have had access to these premises after dark. Ergo, another visit to the curate is in order—for starters."

"Exactly. Shall we finish here first?" Deliberately, Buckler resumed his task.

But as he lifted yet another thorny branch, Chase addressed him casually, as though resuming an earlier conversation. "If you barristers strayed from your sacred precincts more often, you might learn something more of the world's ways. Perhaps then your colleagues would not be so quick to influence credulous juries to evade the law. Silks, fine cambric wipes, Nottingham lace, any item of luxury—all plummet in value just so jurors may avoid a capital conviction."

Buckler strove for patience. "Do you truly expect them to send a poor man to the gallows for stealing a bit of cloth?"

"Why, Mr. Buckler, is not the majesty of the law at risk if mere men are allowed to trifle with it? I should think the law ought to be changed if it be wrong." With hair plastered to his head, the officer's beak nose was more prominent than ever. Fat raindrops struck it and rolled down to drip off its end.

"This is an absurd conversation," Buckler said tightly. "And why do I seem to be the only one looking for clues in the mud whilst you remain on the path?"

"Miss Tyrone's other slipper was not dirty. If she walked through these grounds, she assuredly kept to the path. Ho, this is interesting. I've never remarked this shed amid all the shrubbery."

Chase pushed open the rickety door and stepped inside, his feet crunching over leaves. Entering behind him, Buckler took a moment to adjust both eyes and nose to the interior. All seemed long abandoned. Several up-ended pots had spilled their contents of withered cuttings. Spades, pruning tools, and bags of transplanting soil were scattered about.

The officer seemed particularly interested in a pile of old sacks in one corner. He bent to retrieve one that nearly disintegrated in his grip, leaving a handful of fibers.

"You've found something?" asked Buckler.

"I discovered similar threads on Miss Tyrone's clothing along with some leaves. I suppose that might suggest she was here. Not that this means your client may wriggle free."

"Why should he lead me to a murder scene? No sense in that, sir."

Chase looked up, irritated. "What makes you believe the word of a man who would say anything to save his skin? And this may not be where Miss Tyrone was killed."

"She had no key to the gate in her possession, I understand, and thus could not have entered the premises after the curate locked up. She must have returned from her errand in the afternoon and never left unless she was in the habit of walking around London with only one shoe."

"Anyone could have tossed the slipper in the churchyard before I ever examined the body. We have only Donovan's word for where he found it anyway."

Buckler let out his breath in a frustrated sigh. "Still, it seems likely she was killed right here on the grounds and her body transported to the street to make her death appear a random assault. Surely you've noticed that Donovan is hardly of a size or strength to move her or to have throttled her so viciously in the first place. You should be seeking elsewhere."

"Pull in your horns, sir," Chase advised with maddening calm. "I do have someone else in mind, not that it's any of your affair." He moved away to examine the door, pulling it shut. It stayed closed, but barely.

"What is it?" asked Buckler.

"This shed is hardly secure. I cannot see how Miss Tyrone could have been held prisoner here, so where was she between say four o'clock and her death sometime after midnight?"

Buckler looked blank.

Chase's gaze was still on the door. "But if we were wrong in the time of death… If she died earlier, say before dark, when anyone had access to the grounds, she might have been hidden."

Buckler interrupted. "Then how was the body transferred to the street late that night? The person who moved her would still require entry to the churchyard."

They looked at one another. "You are correct," said Chase.

After another quick glance around, he stepped out and set a brisk pace toward the church, his boots sloshing through the puddles on the path.

Buckler followed. "Wait," he called. "I shall accompany you."

❧ ❦

Chase and Buckler entered St. Catherine's. The day's chill had permeated the walls, and Chase could hear the thin whistle of wind from without and the sound of rain striking the roof. They walked into the nave, their footsteps echoing. Chase suppressed a twinge as the damp seemed to sink into his aching knee.

A voice came out of the emptiness. "May I be of service?"

Thaddeus Wood wore a black cassock, slightly wrinkled and dusty, which hung on his thin limbs, scarecrow-like. He had apparently been cleaning the tall mahogany pulpit, for he held a rag in one hand and polish in the other.

Wood came forward. "What brings you to God's house, Mr. Chase? Mind your step, gentlemen. The roof is leaking. I've set out pots to catch the water."

The warning came just in time for Buckler, who slid and nearly tripped over one of the pans in his path. He recovered, shooting Chase an uncertain look.

After making the introductions, Chase said, "I'd like to go over your memories of the final day of Miss Tyrone's life, sir. Something may have occurred to you that will prove useful."

"I fear I cannot tell you anything more than I already have. May I ask if your investigation has borne fruit?"

"We are beginning to achieve results."

"Good news indeed. Yet I am not truly surprised, for God rewards any sustained effort." He regarded Chase with his clear-eyed gaze. "You are a man who understands that simple truth, I believe."

Not one for religion as a general rule, Chase was always a little leery of those who invoked the Lord in all too human situations. Too often he had known men to use God as a cloak for hypocrisy or an excuse for failure.

He said abruptly, "We need to know of anyone you recall seeing on the church grounds the afternoon and evening of the murder. Anyone at all, sir."

"Just those I have already mentioned. I am afraid the details are indistinct since that day was much like any other. Miss Tyrone's death has been a terrible blow. I fear many of my flock will suffer at the loss of one who fought so tirelessly for the poor."

"Your own duties must keep you much occupied in the parish, sir." Chase was well aware that most curates were paid only a pittance for their labors while their superiors garnered the real profits of the living.

"Yes, the rector has entrusted much of the daily business to my hands. You see, Mr. Stonegrate is also in possession of the livings for several other parishes."

Buckler spoke for the first time. "Your flock is happily blessed in so devoted a shepherd."

"The Church is my life. Though the labor is hard, the rewards are great." His smile lit up the dimness.

What rewards? Chilblains? Thrice darned socks? Try as he might, Chase did not understand men like Thaddeus Wood, just as he had never understood his own father. Watching Wood pick up one of the pots and pour some of the excess water into another vessel, he observed, "No doubt the Reverend Mr. Stonegrate looks to his own reward?"

Wood looked stricken. He kept his eyes on his pans as if fascinated suddenly by the plink of the drops striking the metal. Buckler cast a frowning glance at Chase and asked quickly, "I take it the rector is not much concerned with the St. Catherine Society?"

"Miss Tyrone was essentially autonomous in her activities. The work she did was important and she herself an exemplary Christian."

"I won't argue with you there, sir," said Chase, "but I should like to inquire if you ever saw Miss Tyrone accompanied by a gentleman friend? Dark, handsome fellow?"

Buckler raised his brows. Chase ignored him.

Wood said fiercely, "She had no gentleman friend, sir. Miss Tyrone was a virtuous woman devoted to her calling in life. I will not for a moment countenance the wagging of foolish tongues. Spiteful people who never once in their lives possessed a spark of imagination to pity the suffering of others, or lifted a finger to aid the unfortunate."

The curate's growing passion had smoothed his speech and burnished his cheeks with color. For the first time Chase could understand how this rather meek man might command the respect of a parish. "Friendship comes in many forms," he reminded Wood. "I did not mean to suggest anything dishonorable."

The curate nodded, self-consciousness returning.

Buckler asked, "Whom do you recall seeing that last day?"

"I encountered Mr. Bertram Tyrone in the churchyard about half past three. He had been round to the Society and found his sister gone out. We exchanged a few words before he went on his way."

"You actually observed him take his departure?" said Buckler.

"No, for I went back into the church, but he said he'd see her at home later. Why should he linger?"

Chase exchanged a glance with Buckler, then said quietly, "Anyone else, Mr. Wood?"

"Just the Tyrones' coachman and Mr. Strap, the surgeon. I saw them walk down the path together and out the gate about five. The coachman came every day to collect Miss Tyrone. As for Mr. Strap, I believe he had an appointment which, of course, she failed to keep."

"You locked up about half past five, is that right? Was anyone left on the grounds?"

"It's hard to say, Mr. Chase. Miss Minton often departs earlier, at perhaps four, so as to get home before nightfall. The doorkeeper, Winnie, normally locks up the Society buildings and goes out through the Church after a short interval of quiet prayer. But she apparently went home ill that day, so I assume one of the other women closed up."

"Fiona, I think," murmured Chase and was surprised to see Wood give a faint start, his hand clenching on the rail at his side. Suddenly alert, he said, "You know Fiona, do you not?"

"Indeed, sir."

"Did you see her leave?"

There was something more here. The curate had withdrawn again behind a carefully wooden face and was ostentatiously checking his pots for about the fifth time. Buckler, looking rather like a drowned fox with his red hair straggling over his collar, stood regarding him, his expression intent.

"No, I didn't see Fiona leave," Wood admitted at length. "I returned to my own lodgings soon thereafter. She must have slipped out unnoticed."

"There was no one else on the grounds that night so far as you know?"

"Only Mr. Stonegrate. He was in his office working all that evening, Mr. Chase. He fell asleep by the fire. I found him there the next morning after—"

"After you discovered Miss Tyrone's body?" said Buckler.

"Yes," Wood whispered, bowing his head. "I was extremely grateful for his presence, as you can well believe. It was a terrible moment."

"I shall have to speak to the rector, of course," said Chase. "When do you expect him, or perhaps you can provide his direction?"

The curate looked unhappy. "As it happens, sir, he is in his office this afternoon. Shall I see if he is able to receive you?"

"If you think our dirt will not offend him," put in Buckler. "I fear the inclement weather has left its mark." He gave Wood a charming smile.

"No matter, Mr. Buckler. It is only to be expected, after all. If you'll excuse me, gentlemen, I shall inquire."

A moment later Wood was back. He escorted them through the vestry and down a short corridor, where he rapped on a door and stood aside, bidding them good evening.

A blaze of light and warmth greeted them, and for a moment Chase could not see. Slowly he made out a roaring fire and a man sitting at a large desk. Garbed in full wig, frock coat, and breeches, the Reverend Mr. Horace Stonegrate was gray-haired and fleshy, particularly around the jowls. In spite of his surplus flesh, there was not a hint of softness about him.

Though the furnishings were modest enough, the expensive wax candles indicated that the rector was a man who liked his comforts.

"You're from Bow Street?" Stonegrate said. "What may I do for you?" Pointedly, he didn't rise, his expression disapproving as he took in their mud-spattered attire. Magnified by his spectacles, his eyes were hard.

"John Chase, Bow Street, sir." He paused, adding deliberately, "And may I present Mr. Edward Buckler, barrister of the Inner Temple?"

Chase had marked his man well, for Stonegrate's manner underwent an immediate thaw. Rising ponderously to his feet, the clergyman ushered them to two chairs and faced them again across the desk.

"Well, gentlemen, your business must be pressing indeed for you to call on so bleak an afternoon. Not that I mind the diversion, for I've had my nose to the grindstone for some hours. Writing my memoirs, you know. Friends tell me 'twill make as good a read as any novel and imbued with much sounder principles! Mind, I don't intend to publish, at least not in my lifetime. If, after I am gone, the family overrides my wishes and makes the manuscript available, I shan't have a thing to say about it, now will I?"

Having directed this extraordinary speech at Buckler, Stonegrate folded his plump fingers and awaited his reply.

"Indeed, sir. Your family will presumably wish to bequeath your work to posterity," he managed.

Unable to help himself, Chase put in, "So I should burn the thing before you die if you truly disdain exposure to the public gaze."

Buckler gave a little cough into the silence that met this remark, but Stonegrate never blinked. Apparently the rector had selective hearing.

Stonegrate fixed his flat-eyed gaze on Buckler. "Well then. Your time is valuable, sir, and I shall not waste it. My curate tells me you're here about the Tyrone matter. A tragedy. But we must always remember that God's design is inscrutable, yet merciful."

When no one commented, he went on, "Still, fine family, the Tyrones. Not at all the kind of people you'd expect to be touched by something so…unsavory." He shook his head sadly, removing his spectacles to wipe them. Without the distortion of the lenses, his eyes were much smaller and, if possible, even colder.

Sighing, he replaced the spectacles. "In fact, I was acquainted with Miss Tyrone's mother many years ago. She was a handsome creature and her daughter much the same. Miss Tyrone came to me about three years ago with a proposal for the St. Catherine Society, the purpose of which was to help distressed females keep to the path of virtue."

"An enormous undertaking for a young woman," remarked Buckler. "I suppose she had help?"

"Miss Tyrone was associated with many of the most influential ladies of the ton. I thought it a noble endeavor and turned over two buildings on the church property for their use, as a favor really to her father Sir Giles and the other families.

"After a while, however, most lost interest in the project—not Miss Tyrone, I'll say that. Yet I regret that her work became something of an obsession. Instead of being content with rendering what humble assistance was practicable, she began to get more extreme notions."

Chase broke in. "I presume you mean her plans for broadening the education of the women and children in her charge?"

Stonegrate threw him a look of dislike. "Yes, and the less said about that foolish and unchristian scheme the better."

Flicking a piece of mud from his sleeve, Chase drawled, "Just so, sir. Then perhaps we might discuss the evening of the murder. I understand you yourself were…here?"

The rector's jowls quivered with indignation. "I mislike your tone, Mr. Chase. Yes, I chanced to be here working on a sermon and, quite worn out with my efforts, fell asleep on the sofa by the fire. My curate roused me in the morning with the news and what a shocking awakening it was."

"Do you sleep soundly, sir? That sofa looks quite comfortable." Chase rose and strolled across the room as if to inspect it.

"It is," snapped Stonegrate. "A man whose conscience is at ease may rest peacefully most anywhere. If there's nothing further, gentlemen, my work awaits." He got to his feet to begin edging them toward the door. Quelling the amusement that had swept across his face, Buckler stood also.

Chase, who still waited near the sofa, did not budge. "One more matter, sir," he said at his most bland. "Did you happen to notice at what time Fiona departed the Society that evening?"

"Fiona? No notion. You had better ask her if you think it important."

"It likely isn't." Chase joined them at the door. "She's rather a pretty wench, wouldn't you say, sir? But no doubt flighty, always thinking of her suitors." He observed the rector closely, but could discern nothing, not even a flicker. Stonegrate merely seemed impatient for them to be gone.

"Many young women are like that," he agreed.

Buckler said, "But not Constance Tyrone?"

The rector offered a short, braying laugh. "I should think not, sir. I've had reason to reprimand many a poor fallen creature for her carelessness, intemperance, or even lust. Miss Tyrone, however, did not possess those particular faults."

"A paragon, in fact?" said Chase.

"I made no such claim, sir," said Stonegrate somberly. "Her besetting sin was pride, and the ancient wisdom is as true in these modern times as it ever was. Pride goeth before destruction."

Chapter Fourteen

"Mama, mama." As Sarah's plaintive voice cut through her abstraction, Penelope looked up.

"You're not listening to my words, Mama," the child said reproachfully.

"I am sorry, sweet." Penelope stroked the little girl's dark hair back from her brow. "Mama was thinking of her work." Grimacing, she looked down at the page in front of her. Nonetheless, she laid down her pen and pulled Sarah into her lap.

"What did you want to tell me?"

The child thrust her face closer and whispered, "I like the dragon, Mama."

Penelope banished the lurking smile that would surely offend Sarah's dignity. "Oh, I see. He amuses you, is that it?"

She nodded. Jumping down, she picked up a parasol and ran to engage the dragon, otherwise known as her rocking horse. After several wild leaps and a few jabs, she stopped suddenly and looked at her mother. "I shall tame him and ride him to the river, but don't tell anyone 'cause it's a secret."

This time Penelope permitted herself a smile. "I'll not tell a soul, darling, though maybe you'll want to share your game with Frank later."

Ever since Sarah had heard the story of St. George, the dragon had fascinated her; she invariably insisted upon a revised ending in which it wasn't slain. Penelope hadn't the heart to insist it was an evil creature deserving of death, for she supposed that to a child the dragon must seem compellingly exotic, more interesting even than the knight come to kill it.

Sarah did tell Frank about her game when she and Penelope arrived at the Society later that morning. The two children immediately dubbed an old, peeling stool their dragon and retreated under the table ostensibly to plan their next foray.

"Little imps, eh ma'am?" said Maggie with a grin. "I like to see 'em so full o' spirit."

She and Penelope were sitting on a lumpy sofa across the room, Maggie with her baby in her lap. They were alone with the children, for everyone was immersed in the preparations for St. Catherine's Day in two days' time. Since Catherine was the Society's patron saint, the women would attend church together and participate in a procession. In the past the Society had also hosted a small reception for its patronesses, a tradition Constance had initiated to encourage contributions. This year, of course, the event had been canceled, but the women had pleaded to be permitted to bake their "cattern" pies and join the march. Even the children, who found Maggie a more lenient guardian than the regular nursemaid, were enjoying the break in routine.

"I like your son, Maggie," Penelope said impulsively. "You've done a fine job."

Her face reddened with pleasure, the freckles standing out. "Thank you, mum. I'm right proud of him." She bounced the baby on her legs, but her eyes were on the two children now edging toward the "dragon" hand in hand.

"He surely enjoys your little girl, Mrs. Penelope. When I see him playing so carefree, seems there's nothing he won't be able to do."

"He will do you credit one day."

"If I've anything to say to it, he will." She cuddled the infant on her shoulder, rubbing a caressing hand up and down the tiny back. "I'll have no sluggard for a son. Not like his father."

It was the first time Penelope had seen any hint of bitterness in the cheerfully irrepressible Maggie, but it was gone in a flash.

"I'll apprentice him to a prosperous trade. Nothing dirty or dangerous," she continued after a moment. "How to raise the wind for the indentures is what I don't know, but I'll manage somehow."

"I make no doubt you will, Maggie. With forethought a mother may accomplish much for her child."

Maggie shot her a grateful look. "What about Miss Sarah, mum? What do you see in her future?"

"Happiness, I hope, and the wisdom to make sound choices, regardless of what they be."

"Beg pardon, Mrs. Pen. Surely you're anxious for her to marry well and become carriage folk? What could be better for a girl gentle bred?"

Penelope laughed. "Nothing, I suppose."

"Why what else? How's she to be protected? This world's a cruel place for an innocent on her own, and a girl is no match for a honey-tongued rogue." Sighing, she settled the sleeping infant in the rough wooden cradle at her feet.

They lapsed into silence, each busy with her own thoughts. At length Penelope said, "Some women choose never to be married, Maggie, and often for excellent reasons. Miss Constance, for instance."

Maggie looked dubious. "She wasn't like the rest of us."

Smiling in reply, Penelope wished, not for the first time, that she'd known Constance and wondered how the Society would fare without her. Elizabeth Minton possessed great strength of character, but Penelope sensed she lacked Constance's unique quality that had inspired those around her with intense devotion. It was all the more commendable that Constance had maintained such a bruising pace in spite of frail health.

Just then, the door opening, the surgeon Reginald Strap entered. He wore leather gloves and a driving coat. The wind had swept his pale hair from his face so that his sculpted features and prominent forehead seemed etched the more distinctly.

"Your pardon for the intrusion, ladies." He offered an elegant bow. "I wanted to look in on Mrs. Skirl, but she's not at her post."

Maggie stood, bobbing respectfully. "We're in a bit of a pother what with the preparations for St. Catherine's Day. I imagine Winnie's helping to bake pies in the kitchen. Shall I fetch her for you, sir?"

"No need, Maggie, is it? I shall go in search of her myself. How are your fine children? Still robust, I trust?" He stooped over the cradle and patted the baby's downy head.

Beaming, she curtsied again. "All hale, sir, thank the good Lord."

When Mr. Strap looked at Penelope, Maggie hurriedly performed an introduction. "A pleasure, ma'am," he said.

Penelope rose and curtsied. "Good day, Mr. Strap. I am glad you've come to see Winnie, for she looks far from well of late."

"Yes, she ought to keep to her bed, but I'm afraid she cannot manage without the few shillings she earns here."

Maggie said, "Miss Elizabeth makes her go easy."

"A good thing. You are fortunate in so considerate a mistress." He hesitated. "Perhaps if Mrs. Skirl is occupied, you might tell me where I can find Fiona. I should like a word with her as well."

"Is she ill?" asked Penelope with concern.

Strap looked grave. "I must say I do feel some disquiet for Fiona. Nonetheless, a severe depression of spirits can only make matters worse. She must strive to get the better of it and so I shall tell her."

Having edged over to inspect the surgeon, Sarah was now tugging insistently at her mother's dress, so Penelope lost the opportunity to probe further.

"This is my daughter, Sarah," she said. "Make your curtsy, love." But Sarah retreated behind Penelope and stayed there, peeking out flirtatiously and withdrawing again the instant Mr. Strap glanced her way.

"Why, she's charming, ma'am," he exclaimed, reaching down to pinch the little girl's chin. "And probably keeps you most busy."

"She does indeed, sir."

"Well, I must be off if I'm to locate either of my quarries before luncheon." With a courteous nod for Maggie and another bow for Penelope, the surgeon was gone.

"Have to wonder," Maggie mused when the door was shut, "why a pretty gentleman like that hasn't been caught yet." She shook her head in disgust. "All them fine ladies must be blind."

"Perhaps he hasn't discovered the right lady."

"If he were to come round here on Monday, I couldn't answer for his safety what with all the St. Catherine bonnets!" She giggled at Penelope's confusion. "Don't you know, mum? They say that spinsters put their first pin in the bonnet at five-and-twenty, the second at thirty, and the last at five-and-thirty when the bonnet is done. You'll see the bonnets the women made in the procession, though some call it a Frenchified custom and won't stand for it."

She sent Penelope a mischievous glance. "Shall I make you one, mum? If you wear it and fast and pray, perhaps a good husband will come your way."

"I'm afraid I already have a husband," Penelope said, laughing.

"What's that to say to anything? I've one myself, lot of good it does me, but I'll be marching just the same!"

⁂

Later that afternoon when the pies were finished, Penelope joined the others in the sewing room. Leafing through the Bible to find an appropriate passage, she sensed the women's barely repressed excitement, but they had promised Miss Minton that if permitted their festivities, they would work all the harder. Penelope found their obvious anticipation oddly endearing, for she knew well enough that their pleasures were few. Only Fiona did not seem to partake of the general good humor, for she sat a little apart, staring fixedly at the movements of her deft fingers.

"Did Mr. Strap find you earlier?" Penelope asked, wondering what ailed the girl.

"Yes, thank you, mum," Fiona answered in a low voice.

Nora's sharp gaze swung toward the girl. "What did he want then, love?"

"Nothing particular."

Penelope was sorry to have raised the matter when she saw how all eyes in the room had fastened on Fiona. The girl's hands began to tremble, her throat working with unshed tears.

Nora said, "You're pale as milk." When she reached over, Fiona flinched away and gave a little cry, unable to prevent the tears pouring down her cheeks.

"Let us remove for a moment." Penelope helped her to her feet, saying to the others, "Carry on, will you? We'll soon return."

Ignoring the speculation that broke out, she guided the girl into the corridor. As Fiona's sobs intensified, Penelope hugged her, aware of her narrow shoulders and fragile bones, and wondered with horror whether she was getting enough to eat.

After a minute or two, she pressed a handkerchief into the girl's hand. "When you are feeling better, I do hope you'll tell me what's amiss. I should like to help if I can, Fiona."

"What has occurred, Mrs. Wolfe?" It was Elizabeth Minton, who had returned from an errand.

"I cannot tell, ma'am, but Fiona is most distressed. I think I should escort her home."

Coming forward, Miss Minton gripped the girl's hand. "What has destroyed your peace, my dear? You must tell us."

"Please, mum," Fiona stammered, "just let me go home. I promise to do better tomorrow."

When Miss Minton looked as if she would press further, Penelope said, "I do think it best, ma'am. She lives nearby, does she not? I shall accompany her."

A few minutes later, her arm around Fiona's shoulders, Penelope was guiding her down the path toward the gate. The weather had turned chilly, yet it was a bright day, the smoke that usually covered London in a great black pall temporarily dispelled.

Reaching the gate, they had to step aside for a heavyset cleric just entering. His eye falling upon Fiona, he immediately drew back. She had started forward, but after that first involuntary glance, he looked through her as if she weren't there and made as if to walk on. Only then did he notice Penelope.

"Pray pardon us, sir." She tugged at the girl's arm. Seeming to have shrunk even further into herself, Fiona allowed Penelope to lead her into the street.

Curious, she asked, "What is wrong, Fiona?" The girl merely blinked back, a dazed expression in her eyes, and Penelope decided she'd better get her home at once.

Fiona's rooms were above a chandler's shop which also offered "bits and pieces of old cloth, metals, and papers," according to the sign in the window. They walked up three flights of stairs, finally reaching a low-roofed garret room.

It was clean, bare, and bitingly cold, with only a rusted iron bedstead, a small table, a washstand, and one Windsor chair. A shelf on the wall held cutlery, tin cup and plate, and her few articles of clothing. Yet Fiona had obviously made an effort to render her room more pleasant. Several old prints from books were tacked to the wall, and a rather pretty green bowl, presumably for flowers, sat atop the table.

"Step in, mum, and sit down." She pulled the chair to the center of the room. "I beg your pardon. I have nothing to offer you."

"Don't trouble yourself," said Penelope gently. "Shall I go now, Fiona?"

"No, no. Sit, oh please do."

Rather than disquiet her further, Penelope perched on the chair and waited. Fiona had withdrawn again, staring off into space as if she had forgotten Penelope's presence. Then seeming to come to herself, she looked over and tried to smile.

Penelope was utterly bewildered. "Who was that parson by the gate? I couldn't help but notice how he upset you."

Fiona looked at her. "Mr. Stonegrate, the rector. He was good to me once, but no more."

"Good to you?" Penelope echoed, a terrible suspicion taking root.

"Mr. Strap don't believe me neither. He thinks I'm that wicked, and maybe I am if they say. It must be so." She stared down at the floor.

"What nonsense, Fiona, as if you could be." She fumbled for words. "Are you saying that you and Mr. Stonegrate had some sort of…friendship?"

"We did no harm, mum," Fiona cried, shivering violently. "I was proud to be singled out by such a fine gentleman. He said I could be easy, nothing wrong in it if my heart was pure. But now he looks at me like I was poison."

Penelope rose and led her to the bed. Drawing Fiona down, she chafed her hands, trying to warm them, then removed her own gloves and slid them over the girl's fingers.

"No, mum, you'll be chilled," she protested.

"Don't argue. You shall wear them." Next she unwound her scarf and wrapped it about Fiona's shoulders.

Fiona began crying softly. "You're so kind, Mrs. Penelope, and I don't deserve it. Miss Constance was kind too, though she said it was wrong. But he done worse, she said."

"Constance knew?"

"Yes'm. She meant to speak to Mr. Stonegrate, though I begged her not to. Only she died before she could."

Penelope's mind was racing. What if Constance had confronted Stonegrate, threatening to expose his misdeed? It was a terrible sin to take advantage of a girl like Fiona. And he a man of the cloth, a fact which sickened Penelope all the more. Fifty if he's a day, she thought bitterly, and she less than twenty.

She slid an arm around Fiona. "Miss Constance was right. You are not to blame, but he is. Very much so. But why is Mr. Stonegrate offended with you if she never found an opportunity to speak?"

"It's on account of the sickness what he says I got by spreading my favors around. I swear to you I never did. I've not lain with anyone else." She pulled away. "Where I come from we used to celebrate St. Catherine's Day too. All us workhouse girls would walk the streets, singing and chanting for a husband. In fun, you know. And one of us got to be the Queen and march at the head wearing a pretty white dress. It was me one year."

Penelope was bewildered. "Sickness, Fiona? I'm afraid I do not quite understand you."

Fiona raised eyes swimming in tears. "How should a lady like you understand?" she said simply. "It's the French pox, mum, God's punishment for the wicked. I got it, and Mr. Strap says perhaps the rector does, too. Perhaps I'll die of it, though Mr. Strap says he will try to physic me."

"No, Fiona," she whispered. But the girl spoke no more than the truth. Penelope's father had taken the unusual step of warning her about the disease once it had become clear what sort of man she had married. So she knew that there was no cure for syphilis and that people sometimes did die after a long and terrible illness. "Oh, how could this happen?" she cried.

Penelope meant that she didn't understand how or why such tragedies occur, nor why an innocent like Fiona was invariably the victim. But the girl took her literally.

"I just wanted a bit of fun, mum, and he were so different. It was like being in a story for a little while." Fiona's gaze held a desperate appeal.

Surveying her gloved fingers, she added, "And he had such soft hands, Mrs. Penelope. I never before saw the like."

❦

"Though God can do all things, He cannot raise a virgin after she has fallen," said Thaddeus Wood, his voice ringing out. "This we learn from the story of St. Catherine. Lo, that a truly chaste woman need not fear even torture and death."

Above his head blazed an enormous Catherine wheel suspended over smaller, more subdued windows. It seemed to Penelope, sitting in the hard pew, that the vibrantly colored glass provided the only source of light in this gloom. She shifted, trying to find a comfortable position with Sarah sound asleep in her lap, and could not help but to throw surreptitious glances at the other women of the Society, all clustered together in the half-empty church.

Elizabeth Minton was there, remote yet listening intently. Fidgeting and giggling, Dorrie and Nora looked as restless as Penelope felt, but Maggie displayed rapt attention, an uncharacteristically pious expression on her face. Though huddled and shivering, Winnie too kept her watery eyes fixed on the curate's face, ignoring the assorted rustlings coming from the others. And at the rear of their little group sat Fiona, rigid and emotionless. Penelope had tried to catch her eye to give her an encouraging smile, but the girl was again locked within herself.

Other young women dotted the pews, though not many, for the old ways had long fallen into disuse in staunchly Protestant England. Besides, workers were not permitted time off from their labors for celebrations that now seemed merely quaint. A shame, it seemed to Penelope. For centuries St. Catherine's Day had been observed by girls hoping to wed. It was also believed that wives who marked the day with fast and prayer might thereby be happier through their husband's reformation, desertion, or death—in which case the woman would be free to try her chances again. That is if one were so inclined, she thought wryly.

She made an effort to return her attention to the sermon. It wasn't that the curate was a poor speaker, quite the opposite. The change in him had astonished Penelope. Afire with evangelical zeal, he was no longer a halting, awkward young man. When he spoke of St. Catherine's defense of her virginity and her faith, his voice vibrated with a passion that startled even a slumberous old man in a corner pew.

Yet Penelope had noticed that some of the women in attendance seemed to be enacting some rite quite separate from what went on at the altar. Every few minutes a single girl or sometimes two together would leave their seats and make their way to an alcove at the rear of the church. Trying not to crane her neck too obviously, Penelope had seen them file up, stand for a moment facing the wall, and return to their places. Finally, she had to lean over to Maggie and whisper a question.

"You see, mum, there's a statue of St. Catherine back there next to a small niche. The girls, bless 'em, drop pins into the niche for the saint and say a prayer for a husband."

"Does Mr. Wood know?" asked Penelope from behind her gloved hand.

"I dunno, mum. They try to keep it quiet."

"Do you know the prayer, Maggie?"

A fleeting grin crossed her face. "I done it once or twice myself. It goes like this:

> St. Catherine, St. Catherine
> O lend me thine aid,
> And grant that I never may die an old maid.
> A husband, St. Catherine;
> A handsome one, St. Catherine;
> A rich one, St. Catherine;
> A nice one, St. Catherine;
> And soon, St. Catherine."

Penelope smiled, looking at the faces around her: serving maids, apprentices, and daughters of the French Huguenot silk weavers and silversmiths who peopled this district. All filled with hope at the thought of a fine husband and possibly an easing of their burdens. There was Elizabeth, alone in her spinsterhood; Maggie, whose roving husband had left her with two small children; Fiona, ill and abandoned; Winnie, old and careworn. And Penelope herself, perhaps at this moment no better off. With Jeremy gone for who knew how long, she must shift for herself. Still, she had Sarah, a blessing well worth the sacrifice of anyone's precious virginity.

"Our prospects may not be that bright just now, my darling," she murmured, tightening her grip on the child. "But will one day be better, I vow."

Sarah stirred, nestling further into Penelope's shoulder. In the pulpit Wood had reached the climax of his sermon.

"Who can find a virtuous woman?" he thundered, "for her price is far above rubies."

Chapter Fifteen

Walking out into radiant day had done much to lighten Penelope's spirits. Following the service, a group of women proceeded deep into the East End to participate in a traditional procession. They began at St. Katharine Cree in Leadenhall Street and traced their way south to Rosemary Lane or "Rag Fair," a street in a predominantly Irish and Jewish district where they continued their march arm in arm.

It was not an area Penelope would ordinarily have visited, as it bore a reputation for great poverty and crime. While the lane itself was reasonably wide and clean, street-sellers crowded the sides, and uncountable alleys and dark courts branched off between the high-storied shops and lodgings, disappearing into thick shadow beyond.

As the ever-growing throng of merry makers swept down the street, Penelope slackened her pace, relishing the colorful scene. Old clothes and boots and brightly printed cheap muslins were heaped against the buildings. Coats, frocks, and pantaloons swayed gently in the breeze. Merchants joked and wrangled with their customers, who fingered the satin of a waistcoat or the velvet of a jacket wistfully. Women hawked warm elder wine, and boys hoisted heavy trays offering sponge cakes.

They were close enough to the Thames that its cold wind chafed Penelope's cheeks, but carried also the tantalizing aromas of spices and frying fish. The roisterous cries of children rose above the din as they went a-Catherning, begging for apples and beer with their bowls outstretched. Some of the women, dressed in white, had crafted fanciful hats of paper that towered above the crowd like ship's masts.

Penelope wandered dreamily, absorbed in her surroundings. She admired the way these people were able to abandon themselves to uninhibited pleasure, putting aside pressing anxieties. And for once she was able to do the same. But, looking around, she realized suddenly that in pausing to watch a small boy blissfully consume some oysters purchased from a stall, she had been separated from her companions and now found herself swept by the foot traffic to the mouth of an adjacent court. It was a mean, dirty place with rickety houses listing drunkenly. A tavern stood at the far end. From somewhere a dog was barking.

She was about to start back when four men came noisily down the alley behind her. They came to a halt as she faced them, their conversation ceasing. One gave a tentative smile; the others wore shuttered expressions. All seemed unsure. Perhaps they just wanted to pass on their way to the tavern, she thought, and moved aside. But the men stood still, so Penelope backed up one step, then another. She fought the urge to run, keeping her gaze locked on their faces.

One, a burly, red-bearded creature, took several hesitant paces forward, and the others emulated his lead, approaching in silence. Penelope's mouth dried. She clutched at her reticule as if it were some sort of weapon. And just as she was about to attempt a scream she knew would emanate only as a croak, she heard, or imagined, a familiar voice behind her.

Astonished, she spun round, and indeed there was John Chase emerging from the tavern. He was accompanied by a shabby man of diminutive build who wore a battered leather cap.

Mr. Chase seemed equally if not more surprised to see her. Still, he took in the situation immediately and strode forward. His companion followed, hands buried in coat pockets. The four men had stopped their advance and stood sizing up the newcomers.

"Mrs. Wolfe?" Chase said. "It is you. What brings you here? I trust you've no business with these boys?"

"What if we got business with her?" grunted Red-beard. The others moved in behind their leader.

"Then I would say you've led a long and happy life and should be well content to end it."

The men looked confused. Before they could reply, Chase's companion spoke. "It's a hint, boys, and I'd take it right quick, mind you." He scuffed his toe in the mud with an absentminded air.

Red-beard watched the officer a moment; then to Penelope's surprise the four men slunk away, disappearing into the tavern.

"Smarter 'n they looks," commented the little man.

"Stirring up a hornet's nest, eh Mrs. Wolfe?" said Chase. "That could have been trouble."

"You exaggerate, Mr. Chase," she said coolly, though a queer trembling reaction had started in her abdomen. "I'm here for the St. Catherine Day celebrations, though I seem to have inadvertently wandered away from the others."

"Let me escort you." He reached for her arm.

She pulled away, annoyed by his condescension, and gazed pointedly at his companion, who cleared his throat and stared right back.

Chase sighed. "Forgive me. Mrs. Wolfe, may I present Mr. Noah Packet. Mr. Packet, Mrs. Wolfe."

"Pleasure, ma'am."

Before she could respond, Chase interjected, "Mr. Packet was just leaving. I'll see Mrs. Wolfe home."

"By all means, Chase." He sent a courtly bow in Penelope's direction. "You go on now and play the gallant. I'll be off." He tipped his cap and sauntered away.

Chase turned back to Penelope. This time he managed to take her arm and spin her around. "This is no place for you. You are well out of your element here."

Penelope let herself be guided. "I told you. I am here for the procession. Though very likely I was not in any real danger from those men, it seems fate produced you at an opportune moment, sir."

"I do not believe in fate."

"Why not, at least for today? St. Catherine is the patron saint of spinners, and the Fates spin out human destiny."

"Have it as you will."

Back on Rosemary Lane, Penelope looked around for her friends, but the procession was well out of sight by now. Though she had no intention of admitting it, she was glad of Chase's presence. They stopped in front of a clothing stall.

"You've an interesting friend, Mr. Chase," she observed. "Does he live nearby?"

"Packet?" A gleam of humor lit his eyes. "I imagine he has recourse to several domiciles, all of which he strives to keep unknown. He's a prig, you know."

"Prig?"

"A thief, madam. But good company nonetheless."

"You are friends with a thief?"

He grinned. "You see, Mrs. Wolfe, he's useful. Makes it his business to know what's in the wind and profits mightily thereby."

"Oh," said Penelope. "Have you learned something new?"

"Something I've discovered for myself. Daniel Partridge met Constance Tyrone that last afternoon." He waited as if to gauge her reaction.

"Perhaps Mr. Partridge did not dare to tell you. Why don't you ask him?"

"Easier said." He laughed in derision. "The clever fox has surrounded himself with protectors. He's hiding in plain sight. And just today one of the magistrates at Bow Street dropped a word in my ear. I am to let our distinguished lawmaker alone." Again he gave her that assessing look.

"We know that Miss Tyrone returned to the Society that day, sir, and now that Donovan claims he found the slipper in the churchyard... Where did Mr. Partridge go afterwards?"

"To a meeting with supporters. He remained there in full view of at least fifty people until around nine o'clock, after which he reputedly spent a rather pleasant evening with your husband. I am unable to account for their precise movements, however."

"There is another possibility. The rector of St. Catherine's, Horace Stonegrate."

His face froze in surprise.

Voice lowered, she told him Fiona's story, fighting the color that wavered in her cheeks at the mention of such intimate matters. Chase's expression darkened as she spoke of the girl's despair, but he looked skeptical about her claim of prior innocence.

"Bound to say that, isn't she? If Fiona truly has infected the rector with the pox, he might make matters most unpleasant for her, not that that would remedy his little problem."

He laughed, then held up his hands at her glare. "Peace, Mrs. Wolfe. I grant you 'twould be worthwhile to speak to Mr. Stonegrate again, especially as it appears the murderer must be closely connected to the victim. Stonegrate was at St. Catherine's that night. Wood, too, for that matter."

"And Mr. Stonegrate has a possible motive if Miss Tyrone did approach him on Fiona's behalf."

Chase nodded. "I should tell you that Packet has just given me the particulars of another romance gone sour. Bertram Tyrone and his intended have decided they won't suit. Tyrone was in deep to the moneylenders apparently. He had no choice but to go along with the proposed match."

"Indeed?"

"Of course, he has allowed her to do the crying off, but Packet says the truth is Tyrone's the one who wanted out."

"Somehow that fails to surprise me," she replied, thinking of what Ambrose had said of his brother's betrothal.

She was just about to ask if he planned to interview Bertram Tyrone again when Chase exclaimed in surprise, "Perhaps you hit the mark after all, Mrs. Wolfe."

"I beg your pardon?"

He peered across the street. "I meant perhaps you were right about fate, else why should I suddenly encounter Donovan's wife? Over there."

Penelope caught only a glimpse of a shrunken woman in a shapeless gown before Chase was off in pursuit. He had her in moments, drawing her aside. She cowered, raising one supplicating hand, but her other arm kept a firm grip on a steaming cattern pie. Though Penelope couldn't hear their conversation, she read the fear in the woman's face as easily as if it were shouted.

Suddenly Penelope was startled out of this engrossing drama by a quick movement to her right, and she stiffened, apprehensive that the men from the front of the tavern had returned and would find her alone.

It was a man, but not one of whom it was possible to be afraid. Slight and prematurely wizened, he had a thin face and preternaturally bright eyes. He had emerged from the alley at her back to stand stock still not three yards from Chase and the woman. By the stricken expression on his face, she knew instantly this must be Donovan himself.

Without thinking she called out, "Mr. Chase!"

He turned, coming face to face with Donovan; rather than rush him, he said, "Don't run, lad. No more now."

"I ain't hurt nobody. If I go to gaol, who'll look after her?" Donovan gestured to his wife.

"You must worry about yourself now. The next one who catches up with you might not be so considerate." Chase took a step closer.

A few people had stopped to watch, but he waved them away, keeping his attention focused on the Irishman. And when Donovan didn't move, Chase put a hand on his shoulder and ushered him toward a waiting hackney coach. The Irishman went without protest, not looking again at his wife.

"Come, Mrs. Wolfe," said Chase as he gave his prisoner an arm up. "I'll see you home after a brief stop at Bow Street."

Penelope barely heard him, for she was watching Donovan's wife. Left alone in the street, the woman had already begun to shuffle away, her pie still clutched in one hand.

❧ ❧

"Lie to your wife. Lie to your priest. But lie to your lawyer, and you'll hang," hissed Ezekiel Thorogood. He kept his voice low, for there were sharp ears everywhere at Bow Street.

Buckler had watched his friend's exasperation mount as Kevin Donovan first wept, stuttering incoherently, then lapsed into stubborn silence. Donovan claimed he was home with his wife and child on the night in question, miles from St. Catherine's. He said he didn't find the slipper in the churchyard until fully the next morning, later pawning it. And that was all he would say. Now they had only a few minutes before the prison van would arrive to transport him to Newgate.

It hadn't taken all that long for the magistrates to commit the Irishman for trial at the Old Bailey. And if the attitude of this court were anything to go by, the outcome of the trial could not be in much doubt. Sighing, Buckler stared up at the grime-blackened ceiling and thought longingly of his own cozy chambers. He was doing no good here.

There were familiar faces sprinkled throughout the court. Penelope Wolfe sat with Thaddeus Wood and Elizabeth Minton, who had both testified. Donovan's wife, Annie, lurked at the back as if ready to flee should the law decide to collar her as well. John Chase lounged in a chair nearby. The magistrates, officious and grim, still sat at the table behind the bar, frowning over from time to time. Ignoring them, Thorogood persisted with his questioning.

"Why didn't you tell us your wife was once a member of the St. Catherine Society? You lied about never having met Constance Tyrone."

"I didn't think 'twas any matter," quavered Donovan.

Thorogood rolled his eyes at Buckler. "Acquaintance with a murder victim must be said to matter, my dear fellow. Establishes a connection, you know. And with the testimony of Miss Minton…"

Silence. Then, "She was against Annie from the start."

"Why on earth should she be?" Thorogood gripped the man's arm. "You must do better than that. At least a dozen people saw you in that thieves' ken close to St. Catherine's on the night of the murder. Moreover, what of the scratches on your face?"

"I didn't think all those people would remember me." He turned away sullenly.

"My boy," said Thorogood. "Witnesses are wont to appear from thin air when there's a chance to look important and share in a reward. I can only think that is Joan Snowden's motive, unless you lie to us there as well. Why should she identify you as the man bending over the body in the street? Now give over."

The tears welled again. "What if the truth gets me hung all the same?"

"Then you are no worse off," put in Buckler. "Now tell us, were you at the tavern that night?"

"If I was, it wasn't to hurt anyone."

"Why then?" said Thorogood.

"For work. A fellow had need of a few men to help fetch some goods. I swear it had naught to do with Miss Constance."

"Go on," urged Buckler.

"We went out of town a ways. We did the job, and the man give us our money."

"How did you receive the scratches?" asked Thorogood.

"The boxes were hidden in the bushes. I fell once, and the brambles marked me."

"I don't suppose your friends would verify your story," said Buckler.

Donovan stared at his feet. "Who knows what was in them boxes? Nobody'd take a chance speaking up just to save my neck, now would they? Anyway, afterwards we hied ourselves back to the tavern for a few more drinks. I went home in the morning."

"But first you decided to walk through St. Catherine's church-yard," Buckler reminded him. "And discovered—"

"The slipper," whispered Donovan.

"You hadn't heard of Miss Tyrone's death?" said Thoro-good. "Why did you go there?"

Donovan merely looked at him with eyes stupid with misery. Thorogood was just drawing himself up for another attempt when John Chase came up. "Time to go, Donovan."

Nodding, the Irishman stepped toward the officer with an oddly trusting air.

"We've not completed our business," Thorogood said.

Chase smiled. "Magistrate's orders." He addressed Buckler. "I trust your valued exertions may not prove so much wasted effort, sir. Mr. Donovan's position is unenviable."

"That's as may be," snapped Thorogood. "Though how we are to prepare a defense if continually interrupted, I'm sure I do not know. You people have put the saddle on the wrong horse, sir, in spite of what has been heard today."

"That remains to be seen. Good day, gentlemen."

He led Donovan away. A sly-faced little man, one of the reporters who had descended upon the inquest, followed them out, engaging the Runner in conversation.

Thorogood gave an indignant huff. "I'll warrant the Irishman's innocence expresses itself even to that coxcomb, yet God forbid any such notion should be admitted. Where's Mrs. Wolfe?" he added, glancing around. "I should like a word with her."

"I caught sight of her and the curate escorting Miss Minton from the room a few minutes ago. Miss Minton seemed distressed, though she hid it well in the box. Of course, she was more than credible."

Thorogood glared. "Obviously, Buckler. But that doesn't mean Donovan murdered Constance Tyrone."

"Pax, Thorogood. I know that. Now let's be off before the magistrates have us evicted. I feel myself fortunate those basilisk stares have not frozen me to the spot."

Thorogood turned to the bench and bowed, and the two men flowed out with the crowd into the chill air.

"We must think this out," Thorogood said as they paused outside. "Walk with me, Buckler."

"I don't know how you come by this fondness for foot travel." But he tightened his scarf and accompanied his friend down the street.

They worked their way toward the Thames, walking in silence for a while, Buckler sniffling and Thorogood marching on seemingly unaffected. Emerging from Catherine Street into the Strand, they passed the enormous façade of Somerset House and approached St. Mary's Le Strand. The street teemed with carriages driven very fast; on the walkways pedestrians also moved so quickly it was obvious no one could spare the time to linger in spite of the enticements offered by stationers, drapers, and booksellers.

As they walked, Thorogood mused. "Near as I can determine several main points tell against us, the least of which is Donovan's possession of the slipper. I think we can cast doubt that he took it off the body. Thank goodness Constance Tyrone's gold cross didn't turn up with the slipper in that pawn shop."

Buckler was busy with his own speculations. Donovan had not been straight with them from the first, so why believe his latest story? The scrapes on his face looked particularly suspicious in light of the attack on Constance Tyrone only a few streets away. And Elizabeth Minton had revealed a possible motive for murder. Not only had Donovan known the victim, but he had reason to bear her a grudge. Even without Joan Snowden's testimony, damning enough, the case against the Irishman was gathering momentum.

As these thoughts trooped through his mind, Buckler's unease grew. And gradually he became aware that something else was making him uncomfortable. It was like trying to recall an elusive memory hovering just out of reach.

"You will have to shake Miss Snowden," Thorogood went on. "Were I the prosecutor, I should think twice about putting that one in the box. Did you mark how hesitant she was when that old bagwig bullied her into identifying Donovan?" He looked over. "By Jupiter, Buckler, you aren't attending to a word I say."

Buckler had stopped in front of a confectioner's bow window as if to admire the pastries piled in sumptuous splendor. Casually, he turned. A few yards away a young woman in a vulgar parrot green dress had also halted, but looked away when she caught his eye.

"Thorogood, do you see that woman there? She was at Bow Street."

"What nonsense are you talking now, Buckler? Who?"

"Shhh. That one there by the bookseller. Let's see if she follows."

Shaking his head, Thorogood murmured *sotto voce*, "This may be a main thoroughfare traversed by thousands of people, but far be it from me to discourage your fancies, friend. Lead on."

They passed St. Clement Danes and neared Temple Bar with the woman still a few paces behind. In spite of Thorogood's professed skepticism, Buckler had to reprimand the older man several times for peeking back too often.

"You're right, Buckler," he whispered, "and should she follow us into the Temple, we shall know of a certain. Then we may ask her what the devil she means by it." His eyes gleamed.

"I suppose she might work there. A laundress perhaps."

"Have you ever seen a laundress dressed in such fashion? For heaven's sake, now that I believe you, stop trying to convince me otherwise."

Buckler chuckled in reply. Passing under an old half-timbered structure, they turned into Inner Temple Lane and paused. The noise from Fleet Street faded.

After a moment they heard the woman's footsteps. As she rounded the corner and saw them there, she froze, looking just like one of the figures in Mrs. Salmon's waxworks a few steps away.

"Have you business with us, madam?" said Thorogood. "If so, cease your skulking and approach us direct."

Anger flashed in her face, but she smiled slowly. "If I've something to say, are you willing to listen?"

A wind had whipped up so that even in this sheltered area, the cold was fierce. Buckler said, "If you've something to say, my good woman, please do so at once. The day grows less and less salubrious."

"Not unless we first come to terms. I tell you, sir, you'd best be more polite if you want to learn what's only to your advantage."

Thorogood gave Buckler a warning glance. "Why, yes ma'am. You were present in Bow Street court today, were you not?"

She nodded. "You're the lawyers for the Irishman. If any man seems fixed to become gallows meat, it's him. Only I might be able to help if I've a mind."

"For a price, I take it?" Thorogood asked.

She tossed her head, sending her earrings dancing. "What did you think? Ain't worth nothing without you pay for it."

"I must say your logic escapes me," said Buckler. "What say you, Thorogood? Shall we walk on?"

"Perhaps we might give the lady a few minutes, my friend. Do be more conciliating."

"You're one to talk of conciliation," he muttered. "You who practically devoured Donovan today."

The woman watched this interchange warily, shivering in her thin dress and pelisse.

Buckler was shivering himself. "We had better take this conversation indoors then. Will that suit, madam?" He gave a slight bow.

"Yes indeed, you'll be much more comfortable there," added Thorogood in a hearty tone.

She smiled, a dagger smile it seemed to Buckler, and gave a nod of gracious acquiescence. "Suits me, sirs, so long as you act respectful."

Since Buckler's clerk, Bob, had laid a substantial fire before he left, the chambers were inviting. Even so the woman chose to retain her pelisse, though not averse to perching on the armchair closest to the warmth.

She turned to Thorogood, intercepting his longing glance in the direction of the pipe he had left on Buckler's mantel. "Cozy place, you got, sir. If I were you, I don't suppose I should ever stir from my fireside." Her gaze took in the silver tea service, the rows of leatherbound books, and the faded but expensive Turkey carpet.

"My friend Mr. Edward Buckler, barrister of the Inner Temple, is resident here, ma'am. I am Ezekiel Thorogood. Will you be so good as to tell us your name?"

"It's Deborah Blister, sir. Happy to make your acquaintance." She nodded at Buckler.

"You mentioned you had some intelligence for us," he prompted, leaning forward.

"First, won't you remove your wrap?" said Thorogood. "Perhaps a cup of tea?"

She hunched her shoulders and folded her arms tightly across her bosom. "Nothing, thank you, sir. I got something as might be of interest to you. I need to know what you'll give me for it."

"That must depend on what it is," said Buckler.

"Well, I won't tell you till we come to terms. Who's to say you'd play me square, gentlemen or no. Fact is, that's all the more reason to be leery."

"You expect us to haggle over something unseen?"

"You must view the matter from her perspective, Buckler. We could easily appropriate her possession and refuse to pay her. What recourse would she have? You are quite right to be cautious, ma'am."

Now she looked at Thorogood as if he were either a Bedlamite or some devious Machiavelli. Yet there was something so disarming in the old lawyer's good-humored face that even Deborah Blister was not immune to its appeal.

"I'm glad you take my point, sir," she said grudgingly.

"Certainly I do," was the reply. "Shall we agree upon ten shillings as earnest of our good faith? Once we have heard your story, we may negotiate further if so desired by both parties."

Buckler choked. "Ten shillings before we have knowledge of what she sells? I must say, you drive a hard bargain, Thorogood."

He lifted his brows. "'Tis only fair. Does that satisfy you, Miss Blister?"

In spite of herself, the woman offered a fleeting smile in return, this time quite genuine, and Buckler caught a glimpse of a different person entirely. But then she held out a rather grubby hand. "I'll see your silver."

Thorogood placed the coins in Deborah Blister's palm and sat back. Avoiding his gaze, she slipped the money into her reticule. And when she removed her hand again, she held something that glittered in the firelight—a delicate cross of filigree work dangling on a gold chain. She passed it to Thorogood.

"It'll cost you more to keep it," she said anxiously.

Thorogood didn't answer her. He had turned the cross over to examine the back. "Can't quite make out the inscription, Buckler."

Buckler took it. "C.T. 1809. Constance Tyrone. The clasp is broken."

"You must tell us how you obtained this, Miss Blister," said Thorogood, his voice gentle. "I think you know this cross belonged to a young woman who was murdered."

She gave a little shudder. "I got nothing to do with that, nor my friend neither. You're welcome to the thing before it brings me bad fortune."

"How much do you want?" asked Buckler.

Avarice kindled in her eyes. "I might've pawned it, you know. I warrant it's worth…two pound."

When Thorogood nodded, she released her breath and relaxed in her chair.

"Gad, Thorogood, she'd only get a fraction of that from the Jews." Buckler sighed. "Let us hear your story, Miss Blister."

Now that she had prevailed, she seemed deflated, more vulnerable somehow. "A friend gave it me and told me to keep it dark."

Buckler asked, "When was this exactly?"

"About a fortnight ago. He said it belonged to a dead lady, and I was to hide it till it weren't so warm."

"Until the hue and cry died down," Thorogood said.

She looked at him. "That's right. Only I saw this." She pulled out a crumpled piece of paper. It was the handbill offering a reward for information about Constance Tyrone's death.

"And you thought you'd get a piece? Why haven't you gone to the authorities?"

Though Buckler had spoken dispassionately, Deborah Blister had heard the underlying contempt. "I didn't want no truck with them!" she cried, throwing him a look of utter disdain. "As if they'd believe me anyway. Like as not, they'd accuse me of putting the lady to bed with a shovel, or they'd think it were my George what done it."

"George, I take it, is your friend," said Thorogood. "Will you tell us about him?"

But she had jumped to her feet, sweeping the muddied hem of her gown dangerously close to the fire. "Friend?" she spat and pivoted so suddenly she almost fell over a low stool. "That low, dirty bastard is no friend of mine!"

Buckler righted the stool. "You and er…George had a falling out?"

Her fury died, leaving her eyes sad. "I caught him doing the mattress jig with another woman, so we parted company. And good riddance."

"Where did George get the cross, Miss Blister?" Thorogood said quietly.

For a long moment Deborah Blister stared into the fire, as if troubling memories were uppermost in her mind; then she turned back, grinning with a chameleon-like shift of mood.

"You might say he come by it in the way o' business," she said.

Chapter Sixteen

Buckler sipped a tankard of ale and studied his surroundings. The Old Cider Cellars tavern preserved its dubious reputation, though it wasn't as bad as he had expected. The entrance on Maiden Lane was a dimly lit façade flanked by a pair of pillars. Two doors opened onto a cramped staircase that led down to the low-ceilinged chamber where he waited.

At one end of the room was a platform that dated from the days when the place was a kind of concert hall where performers led the audience in bawdy songs while guzzling cider instead of ale or liquor. Today, while the "harmonic meetings" continued, the primary entertainment offered was the means to drink oneself into a stupor. Even at this late hour the rows of tables in the long, narrow room were clogged with patrons: a few St. James's bucks, medical students, farmers on a visit to the Metropolis, any number of criminal types, and whores on their last patrol of the night. Apparently John Chase had taken his instructions to heart, for Buckler caught only occasional glimpses of him mingling with the mob and looking for all the world as comfortably disreputable as the rest.

Deborah Blister, who found occasional work as a barmaid here, swung by every so often to check on Buckler, otherwise engaged in repelling the advances of numerous prostitutes. He had been sitting so long that the dense smell of smoke and stale beer had permeated his clothes and hair. He would no doubt stink abominably at Donovan's Old Bailey trial tomorrow.

"Have another?" Deborah set down her heavy tray. She looked tired. Escaping from its pins, her hair hung limply about her face, and sweat stained her dress in dark patches.

"Not yet. I would like to be able to converse should your friend ever show up. Another drink just might make my tongue too thick."

She laughed. "Have it your way, sir, but I thought you gentlemen was bred to hold your liquor."

"No man holds it very long." He threw a significant glance at the exit to the privy as several patrons stumbled out, one dragging his lady friend. Buckler was reminded suddenly of the Porter in *Macbeth* who claimed that drink induced urine, a red nose, sleep, and lust but unfortunately unprovoked the ability to perform.

Apparently, something of the same thought had occurred to Deborah, for she said, pursing her lips, "Fools. Ale ain't all they can't hold."

Tray on her shoulder, she swept away to an adjoining table where she raised her voice in shrill flirtation as she plied a group of students with foaming tankards. When a student reached over and rubbed her behind, she gave her sharp smile and pressed closer to the caress. The man pawed her again and handed her a coin.

Buckler turned back to his own drink, thinking it was time to give up and seek his bed. But then he looked up to catch Deborah's eye. Though she still stood in the circle of the young man's arm, there was a sudden intensity in her gaze. She gave a slow nod toward the door and sidled over to Buckler.

"There he be," she hissed under pretense of picking up the mug. "The one with the doxy on his arm."

Her fingers came down on Buckler's arm, squeezing it against the rough planking of the table. Taken aback, Buckler pulled away and assessed the man she'd indicated. George Kite was tall and well formed with a blunt-featured, high-colored face. He wore a fur-trimmed cloak and heavy boots. This was clearly not his first stop of the night, for he swayed where he stood. And he did indeed have an obvious harlot in tow.

"What do you mean to do?" said Deborah. "He can be mortal nasty, specially if he's drunk which I can tell you he is."

Buckler smiled at her. "I shall merely make some attempt at conversation. Do not fear I shall mention your name."

A quick scan of the room revealed that John Chase was nowhere in view. Buckler considered whether he ought to wait for the officer, but decided he couldn't risk it. Kite didn't look to be settling in for a long stay. In fact, the woman on his arm seemed to be tugging him back toward the door. Quickly, Buckler got to his feet and picked up his coat; before he could change his mind, he made his way to where the man stood arguing with his companion.

"A word with you."

Kite looked down. "Whatsis? Who's the little worm?"

"I need to speak to you," Buckler continued doggedly. "In private."

"Listen to 'im," he said to the woman at his side. "This little worm here thinks he's got something to say to George Kite."

The woman gave a titter and took a step back. "Let's go, George."

Calmly, Buckler stated, "It's about Constance Tyrone."

Several things happened at once. Kite snarled, and his massive fist sailed toward Buckler's face. Then Chase materialized, running toward them. Scenting more than she had bargained for, Deborah Blister suddenly screamed a warning from across the room: "Run Georgie! It's a bloody trap!"

Kite halted in mid swing and gaped at Deborah, who was pushing her way through the onlookers. He was confused, but after one blank instant he recovered enough to retreat up the stairs. The prostitute was gone just as fast, swallowed up by the crowd. Buckler was left to face Deborah Blister's scathing eyes.

Before he could respond, Chase grabbed his shoulder. "After him," he yelled. He pushed Buckler toward the stairs and dashed up himself, taking several at a time, but favoring one leg.

Emerging onto Maiden Lane, they could see no one, but footsteps echoed in the darkness.

"Over there," said Chase. "Don't let him get away."

He started out at a run. Struggling with his coat, Buckler followed, certain they would soon lose Kite in the maze of streets.

"We shan't nab him," he gasped as he caught up with Chase. "Why the devil did you scare him off like that?"

"Perhaps I should have let him draw your cork."

Buckler slowed and pressed a hand against the stitch in his side. "'Twasn't needful to charge out like the damned cavalry."

Chase, however, seemed barely out of breath when he paused, stooping for a moment to massage his leg. They were at the opening to a small court where a single lamp sputtered. The footfalls ahead had gone silent.

"Which way?" said Buckler eagerly.

Motioning quiet, Chase was advancing into the court when from above came a creak. He pointed a finger. "Up."

"What do you mean?"

"Up," Chase repeated and gestured toward an open door in the building ahead where they could just make out a rotted wooden staircase. "An abandoned lodging house, sir. He's trapped above, so if you would be so kind as to chase him down, I shall collar him at the bottom."

Buckler stared at him in disbelief. "Wait a minute. Why me?"

"I would go myself, but I took a knee wound in the navy and I've just aggravated it, more's the pity. But don't fret yourself. He's running scared." The Runner reached into his greatcoat and thrust a pistol toward Buckler. "Here. Take this."

Buckler shook his head. "I thank you, but no. Some proficiency with a blade I possess. Pistols, however... And I've no desire to shoot the man in any event."

He entered the building and proceeded to the foot of the staircase. Clutching the rickety iron rail, he began to ascend, his only illumination the flickering from the lamp outside. He took one cautious step, then another, finding that he had to slide his feet up one at a time. As the wood groaned, he cursed softly. There was no sound from George Kite.

A moment later Buckler nearly tumbled off the stairway when the banister disappeared, and his hand came down on air. Twisting back, he pressed his body against the wall. It took a great effort of will to continue.

When he reached the landing at the top of the stairs, he halted, peering into the pitch-black of the corridor. But then he heard the roof creak above his head and noticed for the first time that an open window beckoned practically at his elbow. Kite had escaped that way.

Buckler climbed out on the ledge and reached up. Carefully grasping the edge of the roof, he drew himself up into the cold darkness. For an instant he hung over empty space, terror coursing through his body.

Straining, he hauled himself to safety and knelt to get his bearings. The sky was surprisingly clear, glimmering with stars that nonetheless afforded little light on this night of a waning moon. Foolishly, he checked for the Great Comet as if its presence might suggest some sort of omen, favorable or otherwise, but it didn't seem to be visible.

With no idea which way to go and a fear of stepping off into nothing, he waited, groping around with his hands. Thus, he was still bent down when he felt wind rush over his head and looked up to see Kite swinging a length of banister.

He struck again, lower this time. Buckler sprang away, praying he chose the right direction and wouldn't topple off the roof. The heavy shaft slammed into the spot he had just vacated, tearing a hole and sending shards flying.

"Chase, he's not running!" he yelled as he dodged yet another blow.

This time he rolled down the incline and darted behind the crumbling remains of a chimney. His eyes were beginning to adjust. He could make out the bulk that was Kite prowling like some beast as steam clouds of breath billowed from his mouth. It was all Buckler could do to avoid the advance of the bigger man. He could only dodge and retreat, praying for somewhere to hide or some weapon to defend himself and berating himself for the rejection of the Runner's pistol.

Kite came on, grim and determined, wielding the heavy bar back and forth. All Buckler had for a weapon was scattered rubble which he occasionally hurled in his opponent's direction. Then he was out of roof.

Looking back over the brink, Buckler could make out another landing a few yards below. He caught his breath as Kite lurched forward, and there was nothing for it but to jump across the chasm. The adjacent roof rushing up to meet him, he landed with a crash. One leg went through the decayed slates up to his thigh, and he felt pain shoot all the way through his back. With a lunge he tried to free himself, but he was caught as surely as if a trap had been sprung.

Buckler craned his neck to see where Kite must be. And from somewhere overhead, the man roared in triumph and leaped, the folds of his cloak spreading like great reptilian wings.

As Buckler tried to shield himself, Kite struck the weak roof. It collapsed. Buckler's leg came free, but he crashed through to the floor beneath, landing amid a pile of slates and clouds of lung-choking dust. Dazed, he attempted to rise, his head whirling. Kite lay in a moaning, semi-conscious heap beside him.

"Good work," called Chase from below.

❧ ☙

Shimmering in the lamplight, the gold cross drifted gently back and forth. George Kite stared at it, then looked away. "What do you want? You ought to be fetching me to a surgeon." He winced as his fingers probed his injured arm.

Chase had hauled Kite out of the collapsed building and now stood over him as he sagged against the lamppost. "A surgeon shall be obtained for you in due course; then you may enjoy a trip to the watch house and a wait for morning—and the magistrate."

"You got no proof, or we'd be on our way to the stone jug even now." Kite glanced around as if hoping to summon some aid, but the street was deserted.

"This lovely trinket here links you to a dead woman. A murdered woman."

Kite snarled, "This is that bitch Deb's doing. I'll pay her in like coin."

Buckler stepped out of the shadows. "Chase!"

"No, you won't, Kite," said Chase calmly. "Because if anything were to befall Miss Blister, Bow Street would know where to look. Now hear me. Tell us what you know, and maybe we put in a good word for you."

"I ain't the one as put away the Tyrone woman." He coughed up some phlegm and spat on the pavement. "All you got is a slut's word for it I ever saw that bauble before. Who'll mind her?"

"I for one," said Buckler. "Nor do I intend to keep the intelligence to myself."

Chase smiled, holding up the cross. "You may not wish to exhaust my friend's patience—or mine."

As his eyes lingered on it, Kite shifted uneasily, his pallor obvious even in the faint light. "I'll speak if that will get me shut of you. It was Crow."

"Who's Crow?" asked Chase, his tone casual.

"An acquaintance. They call him the Crow on account of his hand having only three fingers and looking like a bird claw."

"This Crow murdered Constance Tyrone?" said Buckler.

Kite kept his eyes averted. "'Twas a particular wet night as I remember. Not a good night for digging, but there was to be none of that. He said it wouldn't take more than an hour or two, and we'd share in the profit."

"You needed more than a gold cross to make murder worth your while, eh?" said Chase. "But just who was supplying this money? And why?"

"I told you. We didn't harm her. She was supposed to be dead already. Crow was sent to clean up like."

Meeting Buckler's startled gaze, Chase said softly, "Who sent Crow?"

"A gentleman not best to cross, Crow said."

"A gentleman?"

"That's right." Kite went on, his voice low, almost singsong. "Me and Crow meet up at the Fortune o' War pub in Smithfield. It was raining hard, but we were able to borrow a spring-cart on the way. Crow said the Watch had himself a full bottle of gin and would like as not spend the night in his box."

"Old Tom," muttered Chase.

"So we make for St. Catherine's," said Kite. "We stash the cart, and Crow goes up and opens the gate."

"He have a key?"

"I dunno. I was behind him. Either he had one, or else it wasn't locked. He's a lousy cracksman with his hand and all. Anyway, we go in. It was black as pitch with no moon to speak of, but I could see we were in a garden with some buildings hard by. Crow heads down a path until we get to this little shed. He says, this is what we come for, Georgie, and steps inside. And I follow.

"It was bloody cold in there and dark. Crow pulls out his lantern and I was on him about lighting it, but he says we got to see. Then he points. Here's our meat, Georgie, he says." Drawing his cloak closer, Kite shivered and fell silent. Buckler seemed frozen.

"You found Constance Tyrone," prompted Chase.

He chewed on his lip and avoided the officer's eyes. "One corpse is like another. I start to take off all her traps as always. No sense being transported for prigging a bit of cloth if it's the body itself you're after—no felony in that. But Crow says leave her. He gathers a few sacks to cover her and douses the lantern. I haul her out the door, and we head back to the cart. It wasn't easy going what with them prickly bushes."

"Where were you taking her?" asked Buckler harshly.

"Crow was told it wasn't no matter. Long as no one ever saw her again. Only it went wrong."

"What happened?" said Chase.

"We were in the street heading for the cart when Crow up and runs off."

Both Chase and Buckler leaned forward.

"Maybe he heard that bloody carriage coming. The coach come down on top of me, and it was all I could do to save myself. When I go back for her, she was no pretty sight and me there alone."

"You removed the sacking to make it look an accident and stole her cross," said Buckler.

"It must have come loose when she was hit. I picked it up is all and why not? She didn't need it."

"Stop lying!" Buckler shouted. "The clasp was broken. You yanked it off the body."

He loomed over Kite, but Chase held him back.

Buckler subsided. "What did you mean, Kite, when you said Constance Tyrone was *supposed* to be dead?"

Lifting his sleeve, Kite wiped the sheen of sweat from his brow. "Until the carriage hit her, she was still alive," he said distinctly. "I felt her twitch in my arms. Scared me so bad I dropped her right there in the middle of the street."

❦

The air bore an acrid smell of charred wood, the odor lingering although it had clearly been weeks since fire had destroyed the structure on Church Lane. John Chase and fellow officer Dugger Farley stood silently before the remains, a breeze whipping at their coats. Even at the height of the work day, men and women loitered in front of the lodging houses. A knot of children huddled on the pavement at their games, and a band of roving boys swept by, paying scant heed to the Runners. Not many respectable folk passed through this part of St. Giles north of Broad Street. The rookery was poor and dangerous: the residence of the destitute, the haunt of thieves and coiners. George Kite's friend Crow had lived here.

All that remained of the building was the foundation, the cellar, and an occasional blackened half wall. The rest had tumbled in upon itself to lie in chaotic rubble. Chase ventured into the ruin, wood crackling under his boots as he moved through what were once rooms. He knelt down, and his fingers sifted through some ashes. Nothing was recognizable; any artifact or usable piece of furniture had long since been looted.

"It seems your bird has flown," said Farley.

Dusting off his hand, Chase turned back to him. "Flown or roasted, I wonder. Let's go inquire of the local tavern keeper."

"Maybe have a drink," added Farley hopefully.

They chose a direction at random and walked slowly down the street. In this area there was sure to be a public house every block or so. Someone should know something.

"You mean to tell me what's afoot?" asked Farley.

"You didn't ask before."

"Got something to do with that cove Kite what you brought in last night, don't it? The one that ain't recalling his own name this morning. What about this Crow?"

"I had hoped he might shed some light on the Tyrone murder."

"Tyrone? We got the man as done it. Remember? You were the one what snabbled him. It's old business."

"I am not so sure we did get the right man, Farley."

"It's flying in the face of Providence to look elsewhere once the solution's been offered so neat. You never learn, Chase."

He only nodded in return, thinking of Buckler, who battled today for Donovan's life at the Old Bailey. God knew it didn't take long to condemn a man to the scaffold. Chase hoped to find some answers before it was too late.

Tugging Farley's arm, he indicated a small gin shop. The façade was so drab they had almost passed the place before realizing what it was. But the stink of stale spirits hovered about the doorway despite the wind. Near the entry an obviously intoxicated man was urinating in a puddle.

The two Runners pushed inside. The room was small, dark, and crowded. With only three tables and a few chairs, most of the customers stood jammed together, engaged in serious drink and little talk. They stared at the intruders with unabashed hostility.

From behind a low counter a withered figure, who might well have been man or woman, watched as Chase approached.

"How about that drink, Farley?"

He shook his head.

"I need some information about the fire in Church Lane," said Chase to the crone.

The tavern keeper turned away with a snort. Lips tightening with annoyance, Farley was about to press the inquiry, when a patron at one of the tables motioned for Chase to join him. About fifty years old, this man had dark eyes in a long, pale face. Gray hair, neatly combed, curled against his collar, and thick sidewhiskers nestled against gaunt, pitted cheeks.

Chase stepped over a prone figure and sat as he was bid. Farley remained at the counter, surveying the room, his blunderbuss displayed conspicuously.

"If you need to know something, you come to me," said the man. "William Knot by name. This is my place. What do you want?"

"Good day, Mr. Knot. John Chase, Bow Street. I've no quarrel with you or yours except that I need to know about the fire."

"Well said, Mr. Chase, but we'd best be quick. Folks round here tend to cut up rough with strangers." It was said without any threat.

Chase kept his gaze steady. There would be no trouble here without this man's leave. "How long ago did the fire occur, Mr. Knot?"

"Let me see. Today be the sixth. Less than a full moon back." He thought a moment. "The twelfth day of November to be exact, a Tuesday morning early. I was roused from my bed as were we all." He gestured at the room, and several men nodded.

Chase did not let the revelation show in his face, nor look to see if the date had registered with Farley. It was the very morning Constance Tyrone had been found dead.

"The place was done for by the time anybody got there," Knot continued. "Toby Stubbs was yelling in the street, and one of his lady tenants was escaping buck naked from the window."

Chase heard a few muffled chuckles.

"Quite a sight it was. The fire patrol was called, but Toby didn't have no insurance."

"Did the rain put out the fire?"

"Naw, storm was over by then. Fire just burned 'self out, but not before three people found out firsthand what hell be like. What a stink of flesh."

"A man named Crow lived there," said Chase, observing him closely.

"Aye, the cripple. He was burned worse of all. I heard tell he'd likely been soaked in oil."

"Arson then—and murder."

"Yes sir," he replied cheerfully. "Ain't no doubt whatever 'bout that."

"Who would have reason to want Crow dead?"

He gave Chase a shrewd look. "Perhaps you'd know better than us. Like I said, he were burned beyond knowing. Maybe 'tweren't Crow, after all."

"Surely you could tell by his deformed hand."

"That's the strange thing," whispered Knot, drawing closer. "This corpse didn't have no hand. Burnt clean off. The Coroner called it suspicious circumstances, but nobody ever come to ask till now." He gave a raspy snort and grinned at Chase as if he'd just made a fine joke.

"Did no one observe anything unusual that night?"

"Them as was asked said no." He looked away in pointed dismissal.

Chase laid a coin on the table. "Much obliged, Mr. Knot."

"What do you make of it?" said Farley as they emerged.

"I would say someone wanted Crow out of the way." Almost to himself he added, "And without George Kite's cooperation, it seems my friend Buckler and his client will be on their own."

Ignoring Farley's look of puzzlement, Chase strode down the street, wind whistling in his ears.

Chapter Seventeen

Buckler gradually became aware of the sounds around him. Thorogood's stertorous breathing and impatient movements. Coughs, sneezes, and murmurs from the gallery. The whisper of silk as a lady shifted in her seat. The tapping of the warder's shoes as he escorted a prisoner from the dock. The polished tones of an advocate, rising and falling in counterpoint to the judges' interpolations.

His eyes focused, and he glanced around the Old Bailey to find that the current proceeding was lumbering to a close. The court always made Buckler think of a great mouth wherein was performed the Law's deliberate mastication of its victims, chewed well and digested in a seemly manner. It had eaten well this day. Already a half dozen cases had been decided and all in victory for the Crown. Now it would be Donovan's turn, and Buckler could only hope the law had had its fill.

The cluster of journalists stirred and sat forward. Perched in their midst was Fred Gander, whom Buckler had encountered at Newgate while visiting his client. Pertinacious even for his profession, Gander had been hounding Donovan trying to get exclusive rights to his life story—and presumably to his gallows confession.

Scanning the crowd again, Buckler glimpsed Annie Donovan near the rear; she clutched a pale-faced, unnaturally still child who could not have been more than two. The woman herself looked dazed. He also noticed for the first time that Penelope was present in the gallery among several other women. She smiled at him, but he thought she looked worried. He wished suddenly that he could talk to her and tell her of his strange encounter with George Kite. It would have to wait.

"Buckler," said Thorogood. "It's time."

Well aware of his friend's abstraction on trial days, the old lawyer took Buckler's arm and steered him through the court. Nearing the seats set aside for counsel, they almost collided with the prosecutor and his junior who had just finished speaking with the Tyrone family.

Mr. Latham Quiller, serjeant-at-law, was a narrow, clever man who well knew his own worth. Men of his stamp seemed always to find success at the Bar, and Mr. Quiller was no exception. But his real talent lay in convincing everyone, justices included, that his was the voice of reason upholding the majesty of the law while his opponent was all too apt to indulge in inappropriate histrionics. No one ever seemed to realize that Quiller himself was the master of those despised machinations but accomplished them under the guise of logic. Neat trick that and well worth the large fees he commanded.

"Good day, Buckler," he said, smiling benignly. "This shouldn't take long, what? I've another trial coming on and needs must manage this one expeditiously."

"Only so long as necessary, sir." Then he caught sight of the man at Quiller's side. "If you've other obligations, you can always have Crouch here stand in your shoes."

Buckler hadn't known Leonard Crouch would be junior counsel. No doubt he was thrilled to work with the well-known man in the hope that some of the luster of the coif, the cap worn to distinguish serjeants, would rub off. Unlike his companion, Crouch looked a trifle nervous, and his palm was damp when he shook hands. "Well met, Buckler. I believe this is the first time we've faced one another."

After a few more courtesies, they retired to their respective places, and Buckler was able to return to his thoughts. Instead of reviewing strategy as he'd intended, he found himself wondering why he never felt fully at ease in his work. It wasn't nerves anymore, though he still got the flutters before every trial. No, the problem was that he never felt entirely a part of this world.

Thorogood had once said that Buckler possessed the gift of advocacy, but of a different sort. Men like Quiller, or even Crouch, knew the rules and enjoyed playing the game with great forensic skill, yet they approached it with an assured impassivity which Buckler lacked. He supposed that was what Thorogood had meant when he said juries sensed a thinner skin in Buckler and either hoped to see the opposing counsel draw blood or conversely threw all their empathy on his side. Buckler only hoped today would bring the latter. He reached up a hand to straighten his horse hair wig and stood to face the bench where sat the judges and other officials, including the Lord Mayor and his aldermen.

Frowning, Mr. Justice Worthing glanced down at the papers in front of him and ordered the prisoner to be placed in the dock and the indictment read. Buckler's heart sank, for he knew what that look meant. The judges had any number of cases pending during this session and, like Quiller, would seek ways to avoid prolonging this one. This was hardly beneficial to Buckler, whose best hope lay in time to create doubt in jurors' minds.

Arm gripped by the gaoler, Donovan shuffled in, defeated already. He didn't look at anyone with the exception of one anguished appeal in Buckler's direction. When the people in the galleries caught sight of his pitiful figure, hisses of disappointment and contempt broke out.

Rising to open for the Crown, Quiller bowed first to the Bench, then the jury. Buckler could see the interest spark on the jurors' faces as they took in his lean, elegant frame and powerful voice. As he detailed the evidence against Donovan, rustles erupted anew, and Buckler felt the full force of the crowd's condemnation. Donovan felt it too, for he released his grip on one of the iron spikes that fronted the dock and shrank back.

Quiller called his first witness, Elizabeth Minton, who came forward with great dignity.

"Will you explain to the court, madam, when and how it was that the accused's wife joined the St. Catherine Society?" the prosecutor began.

"It was February last. Annie had left Mr. Donovan. She was a silk weaver in Spitalfields, but couldn't get work; her husband also lacked employment. She came to beg of assistance."

"Were financial difficulties the only reason for the separation?"

"No. Annie told us her husband was over fond of spirits and gambling and on occasion struck her."

"Struck her? In justifiable chastisement perhaps, Miss Minton?"

Her eyes narrowed. "I would not say so, sir. My impression was that Mr. Donovan would get drunk and lose his temper. She said she feared for her child's safety."

Quiller let that sink in, then continued. "How long was Mrs. Donovan employed by the Society?"

"About three months, until she decided to return to her husband—against our advice."

This time Quiller asked the next question quickly before the jury could react to the idea of women advising another woman to remain estranged from her lawful husband. "When did you and Miss Tyrone first meet the accused?"

"In early May, when he came to collect Annie and to ask Miss Tyrone for a loan to enable the family to begin anew. She gave him a few pounds, primarily for the sake of the child."

"Will you tell the court what happened that day?"

"Yes. We were helping Annie get the baby's things together when I noticed Mr. Donovan had Constance's reticule in his hand. I asked him what he was doing."

"Was anything missing?"

"No."

"How did Mr. Donovan respond?"

"He became enraged. He swore at us and said we were trying to turn his wife against him. He also said he would get his own back sometime. Then they departed."

"He said he would 'get his own back sometime'? Those were his words, ma'am?"

"Yes."

Well satisfied, Quiller returned to his seat, and the jury watched Buckler expectantly to see what he would do. The reaction to Elizabeth Minton had been so favorable that he dared not do much.

Buckler walked forward. "May I offer my condolences for the loss of your friend? I have heard that Miss Tyrone was a woman of vision profoundly committed to the service of others."

Surprised, she looked into his eyes, giving a slight smile. "You describe her well."

Smiling back, Buckler said respectfully, "Miss Minton, you've told us that nothing went missing from your friend's reticule. Can you say for certain that Mr. Donovan intended to steal?"

"No."

"Is it possible he merely picked it up, thinking it belonged to his wife? You were, after all, engaged in gathering Annie Donovan's belongings."

She looked doubtful. "Yes, I suppose it is."

"Is it also possible that Mr. Donovan's anger stemmed from the sting of an unjust accusation?"

Miss Minton's gaze flew involuntarily to the accused. "Yes." Buckler had judged the witness well, for her innate honesty forbade she answer any other way, though she clearly believed otherwise.

The second witness was Thaddeus Wood, who testified to finding the body and, at Quiller's prompting, speculated that Constance Tyrone must have been engaged in a charitable errand the night she was killed. After Quiller had finished, Buckler approached.

"Was Miss Tyrone often abroad in the parish late at night?"

A look of confusion crossed the curate's face. "No, she generally went home with her family's coachman at dusk."

"Indeed, he came to collect her that day, but she wasn't there?"

One of the judges broke in. "Of course, she wasn't there, Mr. Buckler, or she'd have made it safely home. Make your point, please."

"My lord," Buckler said earnestly, "the coachman's presence indicates that Miss Tyrone had not informed him of an alteration in her routine. Since her family expected her home, a charitable errand such as my learned friend Mr. Quiller has suggested would have been most unusual." He turned back to Wood. "Is that not so, sir?"

The curate looked unhappy, but had to agree.

Buckler bowed. "No further questions."

Returning to his seat, Buckler deflected a knowing glance from Quiller. It said his opponent knew what he was up to and dared him to try. Only Quiller was wrong. Buckler did not intend to suggest Constance Tyrone had been in the street after dark for some disreputable reason. No, he had other ends in view.

The victim's brother Bertram Tyrone took his turn next. Pale and ill at ease, he made a poor witness in spite of Quiller's efforts to soothe him. As he fumbled through his story, the jury watched sympathetically. He reported stopping by the Society that afternoon only to find his sister out, then returning home late that night to discover his sister still absent, her bed untouched. He had awakened his father.

"We decided to wait until morning before summoning the authorities in the hope of her return."

A ripple of surprise swept the court. One would expect the Tyrones to have reported the disappearance immediately, and if it was fear of scandal that had prevented them, it didn't look well.

"No one noted her absence at an earlier hour?" prompted Quiller.

Bertram's voice shook. "My father was at his club, and the servants thought…they thought she was sitting with a sick friend."

"Ah. She had plans to do so? Perhaps this friend resides near St. Catherine's church?"

"I don't know…it was a misunderstanding. My brother Ambrose thought Constance had said as much, but the visit must have been proposed for another evening."

Meeting Thorogood's raised brows with a slight shrug, Buckler toyed with the idea of probing further. But it would be a blind shot, for he had no idea what troubled Bertram Tyrone; it might only be the man's very obvious grief that agitated him so. On the whole Buckler decided he had little to gain and much to lose if he antagonized the jury by pursuing him.

The watchman, Tom Vim, testified, after whom came Constable Samuel Button. "Right," said Button as he dug for his occurrence book. Awkward, sweaty fingers thumbed the pages. "Your pardon, milords. I have it all writ down, just as it happened."

"Commendable," said Quiller.

"Yes, sir, here it is. I was called to the body at approximately half past six in the morning on Tuesday, 12 November."

"You identified her?"

"The curate did that. And I immediately sent round to Bow Street." Looking relieved, Button closed the little book and returned it to his pocket.

Quiller moved closer. "What of your investigation, sir?"

"Well, sir. I reckon Mr. Chase of Bow Street could give a better account. I'm just the parish constable and—"

"The court has need of your observations, Mr. Button," interrupted Quiller, turning toward the jury. "After all, you were the first to reach the scene."

"Well, sir, truth be known, my notes are kind of jumbled." Button retrieved his book and began speaking rapidly. "I first thought she'd been run over by a coach until I saw the marks on her neck."

"What kind of marks?"

"Why, she'd been throttled."

Buckler listened as Quiller strove to bring out the most gruesome details, all the while subtly maneuvering himself about the courtroom to direct the jury's glance in the direction of the Tyrone family: a stiff Sir Giles, a hot-eyed and miserable Bertram Tyrone, and the younger boy, Ambrose, languid and detached.

With the examination-in-chief concluded, Buckler faced the constable. "You have told us that you and Mr. Chase were able, rather cleverly I should say, to approximate the time of death?"

"'Twas really Mr. Chase," said the constable, looking pleased. "You see, he noticed her clothing wasn't so wet as you'd expect given the rain. Which told us she'd likely been attacked after the storm had passed."

"Or at least," amended Buckler, "the dry clothing indicates that the victim did not lay exposed during the rain. She might have lain elsewhere, I suppose?"

Worthing barked, "What is your meaning, Mr. Buckler?"

He bowed, saying apologetically, "I shall take another tack, my lord." He went on after a moment. "Did you not remark, Mr. Button, upon Miss Tyrone's inappropriate footwear and lack of a hat?"

Button nodded sagely. "Indeed I did, sir. I recall speaking of those matters to Mr. Chase. She had no key either."

"Yes, I understand her keys were later found inside the Society's rooms. Is it not possible then that she did not plan an excursion but was called out, or perhaps brought out, unexpectedly?"

Quiller rose with a fluid motion. "This is pure speculation and leading the witness besides. We do not know why the victim was dressed as she was. Further, I submit that counsel's words 'brought out' lack clarity."

"I beg your indulgence, my lord," said Buckler. "If you will allow me to rephrase?"

Worthing nodded curtly.

"What did the victim's mode of dress suggest to you, Mr. Button?"

"Why, sir, we didn't know what to make of it. Especially when Mr. Chase saw her shoe—the one that wasn't lost, I mean."

Buckler heaved a silent sigh of relief. "What of her shoe?"

"No mud, sir. How'd she walk in the street without dirtying her shoe?"

"How indeed," he murmured.

For the first time Buckler caught a fleeting expression of uncertainty in Quiller's eyes, and Crouch, who had not yet learned to hide his emotions as well, looked incredulous. John Chase had testified about the shoe's lack of mud at the Coroner's inquest, but no one had apparently made much of this particular since. If Buckler could get the jurors to question the prosecution's version of a street attack on Constance Tyrone, they might at least be induced to question the other "facts" relating to the case.

But Buckler needed John Chase on the witness stand. For instance, Chase could tell the jury about the sacking in the garden shed and the corresponding threads found on Miss Tyrone's person. Better yet, with the testimony of George Kite or his friend Crow, Buckler might suggest that she was attacked on the church grounds and left for dead, hours before Joan Snowden had supposedly seen Donovan bending over the body.

Worthing's sarcastic voice interrupted his thoughts. "Are you quite finished, Mr. Buckler? The court awaits your pleasure."

"Yes, my lord." Buckler thanked Constable Button and returned to his seat to await the next witness, the proprietor of the tavern where Donovan was seen on the night of the murder. With an avuncular smile, Quiller waved his junior onto the floor, thus demonstrating to all and sundry that his case was proceeding so well he could afford the possibility of error. Giving Buckler a pitying look, Crouch stepped forward smartly, his black robe billowing at the ankles. As he led the witness through the questions in ponderous detail, Buckler found his attention wandering to where Penelope sat with Elizabeth Minton at her side. Both women listened intently, occasionally exchanging glances when Crouch said something pompous.

The tavern keeper offered nothing beyond what Buckler expected. Donovan had arrived at the tavern around nine o'clock, joining three other ruffians for numerous rounds of drinks. They had suddenly departed en masse about half past eleven only to return about two. All the men were drunk and belligerent, yet "in high fettle" about something. At that time, the tavern keeper had noticed the scratches on Donovan's face.

When Crouch finished, Buckler said, "Can you tell the difference, sir, between scratches made by fingers and those made by say—bushes?"

"No," the man was obliged to admit. Buckler thanked him.

After the tavern keeper came Joan Snowden, the prostitute. Buckler settled back to watch Quiller adroitly sidestep such awkward points as to what Snowden had been doing alone in the street at that hour and why she had not gone to investigate what the hackney had struck, nor summoned any help. It was well done, Buckler thought. Also, someone had clearly coached Snowden, for, attired in a respectable gray stuff gown, she kept her eyes turned down modestly.

True to form, Quiller kept his questioning short. "So, after the hackney struck Miss Tyrone, you saw a man looming over her. Have you identified him, Miss Snowden?"

Her voice shook a little. "Yes sir, I have. Him." She pointed at Donovan, and a volley of excited chatter broke out.

The pointing finger seemed to remind everyone of the insignificant man in the dock. It had been easy to forget about Donovan, but now all eyes turned in his direction.

"It's a lie," he quavered, looking in mute appeal at Buckler as if wondering why he didn't do something.

"Have you something to say, Mr. Donovan?" said Worthing. Receiving a barely discernible shake of the head, he glared upward. "Those in the gallery will be silent if they don't wish to be ejected immediately. Now we must inquire if there are further questions from my brother Mr. Quiller?"

"No, my lord." Quiller bowed.

Buckler stood. "Miss Snowden, although the rain had stopped, the night was foggy and the lamps afforded little illumination. Is that not so?"

"Yes…that is no, sir. I could see just fine."

"I am glad to hear it," he answered, regarding her gravely. "You see, in this case a man's life depends upon your ability to see well and to relate what you saw with accuracy." Moving away from her, he turned a little toward the jury.

"The tavern keeper has told us that Mr. Donovan left his establishment in the company of three other men. But you saw only one man leaning over the victim's body?"

"Yes."

"Miss Snowden, you testified at the Coroner's inquest that the man you saw stooping over the victim's body looked 'uncommon big.'" Buckler motioned at Donovan. "Please take another look at the accused. Would you describe him so?"

Her eyes remained on Buckler's. "It's the same man."

"Can you describe for us where precisely you were when you saw the hackney approach? How far away? Ten yards? Twenty?"

"Dunno exactly. Perhaps ten."

Buckler waited a moment, then said, "According to the watchman, Mr. Vim, the weather was too inclement for him to see a body lying in the middle of his route. Yet you identify Mr. Donovan and even oblige us with particulars of his appearance." He looked toward the dock. "Thank you, Miss Snowden. In other circumstances I am sure my client would be flattered."

A general laughter erupted, and hope flickered over Donovan's face for the first time. It was likely the one time in his life when he was glad to be such an unprepossessing specimen of a man. Glancing at the jurors' faces as he sat down, Buckler could see they had taken his point. Thorogood nodded approvingly and folded his hands over his belly.

The surgeon Reginald Strap repeated the medical evidence presented at the Coroner's inquest. Crouch questioned him briefly, merely establishing Strap's work with the Society and questioning him about Constance Tyrone's injuries.

When Crouch was finished, Buckler addressed the surgeon. "You had an appointment with Miss Tyrone on the afternoon of Monday, 11 November?"

"Yes, but she wasn't there, unfortunately. The Tyrones' coachman awaited her also, and we sought her out together."

"Where did you search? Might she have been somewhere on the grounds?"

"We checked her office and had a quick look in the garden. Also, the coachman asked the other women if anyone had seen Miss Tyrone." Meeting his gaze, Strap added gently, "We had no reason to believe she would hide, you know."

Buckler let that pass. "Was this a routine appointment, or was Miss Tyrone ill?"

"Routine—although it is true her health had deteriorated over the last few months; her friends and family all wished to persuade her to reduce her activities."

Buckler nodded. "Mr. Strap, you've told us that the precise cause of death is difficult to gauge. The victim may have died of asphyxiation due to the attacker's throttling, or the fatal blow might have been delivered by the carriage fracturing her spinal column?"

"That is so."

"Alternately, the victim's neck might have been broken by the attacker, not the carriage?"

"Yes."

"Did you note anything to indicate the relative timing of these injuries, viz the bruises left by the strangling and the broken neck?"

The surgeon's gaze sharpened. "I am not certain I follow you, sir."

"Allow me to restate the question." Buckler pitched his voice a trifle higher. "When you examined the body, could you ascertain how far apart the two injuries occurred, if we assume for the moment they were not simultaneous?"

Now Strap looked puzzled. "No, I could not."

"In your opinion, is it possible that Miss Tyrone could have survived a throttling to lie gravely injured for some hours? And then was killed when the carriage struck her?"

"Highly unlikely."

"Why, may I ask?" Buckler quelled the shaking in the pit of his stomach and forced himself to speak confidently.

"She was strangled, man. Her windpipe was almost crushed. Besides, think of the weather. She would have died of exposure."

"But if she were sheltered somewhere, all but dead but not quite, and later moved to the street?"

"Unlikely," he said again.

Buckler pressed on before Quiller could object. "Yet we hear of condemned criminals pronounced dead on the gallows only to revive."

"I suppose that occurs rarely, or at least might have done before the invention of the drop scaffold. And such 'resurrections' appeal greatly to the popular imagination, I don't doubt."

"Still, based on the medical evidence as you observed it, might Miss Tyrone have lain injured but alive for a time before the carriage struck?"

"Yes."

He was opening his mouth to continue when a vociferous "Ahem!" burst from Thorogood. As Buckler glanced his way, the old lawyer gave an almost imperceptible shake of the head and took out a handkerchief to pat his weathered cheeks.

Buckler turned back to Strap and thanked him for his time, grateful he had avoided the pitfall that besets even the ablest of counsel, the one question too many that risks an answer that might destroy all the good one has just accomplished.

Mr. Justice Worthing looked keenly at Buckler. "The court will presume you have some purpose in these questions that will be revealed at the proper time."

"I do indeed, my lord." Buckler resumed his seat. Ostentatiously engaged in blowing his nose, Thorogood did not look up.

The pawnbroker to whom Donovan had sold the slipper ornament testified, and again Quiller allowed Crouch to do the questioning, which was soon accomplished.

Buckler stood to address the witness. "Is Mr. Donovan a regular client of yours?"

The pawnbroker agreed.

"What sorts of goods does he bring to you?"

"Just about anything. Old clothes, bits of cloth, iron, occasionally a broken ticker."

"Nothing of value generally?"

"No, sir."

"So you must have found it rather curious when the accused brought you an obviously expensive piece of trimming."

"I did, sir."

"But he brought nothing else? Not the victim's matching slipper rosette for instance? Nor her filigree gold cross?"

"No."

Buckler looked at the Bench. "Nothing further, my lords."

Friday was waning into late afternoon. Finally, Quiller questioned his last witness, the Bow Street officer Strickland, who related the story of the arrest attempt and the subsequent riot in Bethnal Green. Buckler disliked the Runner, a truculent, beefy type, on sight yet could tell the man's blustering appealed to the jury. As Strickland would have it, Donovan had done no less than willfully touch off a destructive rampage that was only put down by the officer's heroic intervention.

Even Quiller seemed annoyed after a while, for the witness insisted upon saying more than was required. Then it was Buckler's turn.

"When you arrived to arrest the defendant, was he not inside his house?"

"Yes, but—"

"Answer the questions as they are put to you, sir," snapped Worthing.

Ignoring Strickland's glare, Buckler continued. "Did the accused address the crowd in any way. Exhort it to anger or violence?"

"No, but it was his fault. If he hadn't—"

"Did you search the lodgings of the accused after he made his escape? What did you find?"

"Nothing," muttered Strickland.

When Strickland stepped down, it was time for Buckler to present the defense. Since he was not permitted to address the jury on Donovan's behalf, Buckler had a prepared statement to be read into evidence. Also, several witnesses to character were at hand, and two women from the Society, Maggie and Fiona, were prepared to testify about Constance Tyrone's boots to show that the victim had returned to her office in the afternoon.

But it seemed he was to have an opportunity to collect his thoughts, for the jury, pleading fatigue, issued a request for an adjournment which, in an unusual move, Mr. Justice Worthing granted. The judge instructed the bailiffs to take charge of the panel and to ensure that no juror speak to anyone on the matter at issue.

A clamor broke out as the chattering and laughing observers got to their feet and surged toward the exit. A group of richly dressed ladies and gentlemen strolled by the dock to get a closer look at Donovan, who was absently fingering some herbs strewn on the ledge. Since a heavy band of hair had fallen across his face, Buckler could not tell if he was despairing, impatient, or merely exhausted by the rigors of this long day. Buckler himself could suddenly feel every one of the bruises he'd earned last night in capturing George Kite.

Resolving to go and speak to the Irishman momentarily, Buckler said to Thorogood, "What do you think?"

He flexed his shoulders. "You have contrived well so far, I'd say. Made them sit up a bit, given Quiller pause. But I cannot see what good will result without you offer the jury some bread with the jam."

"I know." Buckler stared down at his hands.

Thorogood smiled. "There's time yet, Buckler. If you can get Kite or his friend in the witness box, Donovan may skip out of here a free man. Perhaps Mr. Chase has discovered new intelligence."

"If not, what then? You apprehend as well as I that things can easily turn sour. We may have raised some questions, but even such doubts may not prevent a guilty verdict, especially when the victim was young, beautiful, and virtuous."

"Wait and see, Buckler, wait and see." He glanced at the dock. "*Vincit qui patitur*. He prevails who is patient. If you're lucky, that is."

"Oh, I am patient enough, but luck may be another matter." He looked up. "Or maybe I'm wrong. Here is Chase now."

Pushing his way through the crowd, John Chase had caught sight of them. If all has gone well, his timing couldn't be better, Buckler thought.

Chase approached, stepping around a cluster of people. He looked tired, and there was a large, black smudge across the front of his trousers.

"I bring bad news, Buckler," he stated flatly.

Chapter Eighteen

Penelope came out of the Old Bailey and stood on the curb to look about for a hackney. The exodus from the court had been accomplished quickly, no one wanting to linger in the dark December evening. Streaming into the street and calling to acquaintances, people generally conducted themselves with the cheerful good humor of children let out of school.

By Monday it would all be over. Mr. Buckler had scored several hits today, but Penelope knew he needed to give the jury something more substantial than speculation about the timing of the crime. He needed to suggest why someone else might have killed Constance Tyrone. If not Donovan, who? Without another explanation upon which to seize, the jurors would surely condemn the Irishman. She had seen it in their faces.

As a man shoved by to grab a hack that had stopped a few feet away, Penelope swore inwardly and shook out her shoe, which had landed in a puddle of some indeterminate substance. Thinking perhaps she might have better luck farther down, she was turning away when a familiar voice hailed her.

"Mrs. Wolfe. Might I be of assistance?"

It was the surgeon Reginald Strap. Drawing up his gig, he gazed down at her, his handsome face a little stern, as if he disapproved of her standing alone in the street.

"I was just looking for a hack, Mr. Strap. No doubt one will soon present itself."

He reached out a hand. "Allow me to offer you a lift, ma'am, for it is far too cold for you to stand here."

Penelope said doubtfully, "I should not dream of troubling you, sir."

"No trouble, I assure you. I shall be glad of the company. This has been a rather wearing day."

She took the outstretched hand. It was hardly the time of year for an open carriage, but when Strap tucked the thick rug about her she began to feel warmer.

"How obliging you are." She gave him her direction. "I am anxious to return home to my daughter. I do not think Sarah finds our landlady a congenial companion."

He laughed, looking far more approachable. "Your daughter strikes me as someone rather exacting in her likes and dislikes."

"An understatement, sir. She has definite ideas on most subjects."

Strap tooled the gig around a dray that was blocking the way. "And not too shy to express them, I warrant." He stole a glance at her. "Has she, I wonder, inherited this trait from her mother?"

Why, he's flirting with me, Penelope thought. The sensation was rather pleasant, though she couldn't think how to answer him.

Crowded with Strap on the narrow seat, she could feel her companion's body heat. Her shivers subsided, and she began to enjoy herself. Slowly, they moved away from the congestion around the Sessions House to turn down Ludgate Hill. Fleshy clouds teemed above their heads, the sky hanging low.

After a moment Strap observed, "Donovan's counsel seems to be holding his own rather well. I must say I thought the matter would be wrapped up more swiftly. The evidence against the Irishman is compelling, do you not agree, Mrs. Wolfe?"

"I do not believe Donovan to be the culprit."

"May I ask why?" he asked, surprised.

"It seemed to me Mr. Buckler was able to suggest otherwise, sir."

"Oh, you mean the notion Miss Tyrone may have been attacked earlier than supposed? I see the barrister's intent, I think. Presumably Donovan has got a firm alibi for earlier in the day."

"Your own evidence did not refute such a possibility, Mr. Strap."

"No, but my perspective is based solely on the medical evidence as I observed it. Unfortunately, that evidence is liable to misinterpretation, just as the human mind is ever prey to suggestibility. The jurors seemed to be swayed by Mr. Buckler's tactics, and I fear that's all they were, the feints of a clever lawyer trying against all hope to save his client from the gallows." He broke off, his hands tightening on the reins as he edged into the flow of traffic.

She said, "Your feelings do you credit, sir. In spite of your admirable composure on the stand, I am sure you do not forget that Miss Tyrone was a close friend of many years. You must be anxious to see her murderer brought to justice."

"I am indeed," he replied gravely. "But not so eager that I should be prepared to see an innocent man hang."

Penelope nodded. "Will you tell me something?"

"Of course, ma'am," he said, his expression lightening. Again she had the sense he found her attractive and wanted her to know it.

"One of the young women at the Society recently spoke to me of an…illness she's contracted. She says you have examined her, sir, and I thought you could tell me what she might expect in future."

"You refer to Fiona. I am glad she has confided in someone. She is in great need of our care at present. The disease is in the early stages, and the effects vary widely with the individual. 'Tis too soon to tell how the poison will affect her."

"Poison?"

"Forgive me, Mrs. Wolfe. Such matters are hardly fitting for a lady's ears. But like a serpent's venom the venereal 'virus', as it is often called, contaminates the entire system. Fiona's illness began with a chancre, uncomfortable perhaps but not serious.

Now I believe she has progressed to constitutional symptoms: headache, fatigue, and skin eruptions."

"What happens next?"

He smiled at her. "We treat her. We have had good results with calomel. Her situation is by no means desperate."

"Will she be able to marry and have children?"

"Perhaps. Though there is a risk of infection for the foetus, of course." He laid his hand over hers for a moment. "Why do not you come and see the venereal ward at the hospital where I am employed? We enjoy occasional visits from ladies engaged in charitable endeavors, you know. And you might thus be able to reassure Fiona, help her realize there is hope for a favorable outcome."

"You are very good, sir."

"That's settled then." He turned onto St. Martin's Lane and guided the gig toward her doorstep. Aware time was short, Penelope decided to ask the question that had been troubling her. "Mr. Strap, I've wondered. I had heard that a person with this disease sometimes becomes unbalanced. Might this person become a danger to himself—or others?"

He looked at her curiously, then enlightenment dawned. "Fiona? No. That's not what you mean, is it? You are thinking of her lover. Ah, but you see, ma'am, syphilitic madness only occurs after a person has been infected for some time. If the man of whom you are thinking has committed an irrational act, it wasn't because of this disease."

He had no time for more as, suddenly, he was pulling up short. Reaching out one arm, he steadied her as her body was thrown forward.

"What is it?" she asked.

His gaze swept the gutter. "I beg your pardon, Mrs. Wolfe. Just a mongrel cur I did not wish to hit."

And there cowering in front of the wheels was the sorriest specimen Penelope had ever seen, a filthy, terrified dog seemingly enthralled by the fate that had almost overtaken it.

"Oh, well done, sir," she cried, clambering down from the carriage. "You have sharp eyes, indeed."

"Mind what you're doing, ma'am. You'll muddy your skirts."

But Penelope had bent to examine the dog more closely. Utterly quiescent, it looked back with no gleam of hope in its eyes.

❧

The mongrel pup settled into the basket Penelope found for it and didn't move. Afraid it might die, she worried about what to tell Sarah, who had developed an instantaneous and passionate attachment to the creature. Sometimes its watery, nearly blind gaze seemed to follow the little girl as she bustled about her "chores," occasionally stopping to pat it. Mostly it just lay there, unable to take more than a few feeble licks of the beef tea they offered.

Penelope didn't need the added aggravation the dog brought, particularly today. This was Monday, the day Donovan's trial was to have concluded. Only no trial could ever be necessary now as, to her consternation, she had discovered when perusing the morning newspaper.

Her attention had first been caught by a story about slayings on the Ratcliffe Highway in Wapping. A linen draper, his wife, their infant son, and the shopboy had been found brutally slaughtered, a bloody carpenter's maul the ostensible murder weapon. That such horrors existed in the world gave Penelope an indescribable feeling, as if she had lost all connection and could no longer understand herself or anyone. This feeling terrified her almost as much as the thought of that murderous hand hovering over the infant's cradle.

Her unease persisted through the morning as she toiled at her little romance, such trivial work it seemed. Now she had an errand to perform, though she hardly felt like venturing out alone. Sarah would have to spend the day in Mrs. Fitzhugh's parlor, and Penelope could only hope the child would remember to be discreet about the dog.

Several hours later Penelope stood in a dusty hallway, waiting for a response to her knock. Just as she was about to give up, the door opened to reveal Edward Buckler's clerk.

"Yes?" His tone was polite, but somewhat uncompromising. He kept the door open only a crack so that his face was framed in the aperture.

"I'd like to see Mr. Buckler, if you please," said Penelope.

"He's not here at present, madam. Shall I give him a message?"

She felt a keen disappointment. "No, I thank you. I need to speak with him in person. Do you expect his return soon?"

"Couldn't say, ma'am," the clerk said stiffly. Taking a step back, he prepared to shut the door.

"Wait. Have you any idea of his destination, sir? My business is urgent."

"I couldn't say," he repeated, then met her gaze, looking a trifle sheepish. "He's taking the air, miss. Might be anywhere in the gardens or walking the streets. He didn't say when he'd be back."

Thanking him, she turned away, feeling dejected and more than a little cross. But as she started down the stairs, the clerk edged the door wider. "You might try the bridge, Blackfriars that is. Mr. Edward has a fondness for that particular spot."

Flashing him a grateful smile, Penelope went out into the afternoon.

❧ ❧

She found Buckler leaning against the parapet. He was motionless, staring down into the water. The footways were crowded with pedestrians, and a line of carriages rattled over the bridge. As she approached, Penelope felt the first splatters of rain and glanced up to see the sun struggling through sullen clouds. It would only be a matter of time before any brightness was gone.

She didn't call out, not wishing to startle him, but instead touched his shoulder. "Mr. Buckler."

He looked at her without surprise. "Hello, Mrs. Wolfe."

Suddenly, she felt uncomfortable. "I wanted to speak to you about Kevin Donovan. What are you doing here?"

"Admiring the view. Have you ever noticed how the river looks just as rain is coming on? Gray with shadows chopping the surface. I imagine the River Styx would appear much the same."

She joined him at the parapet to gaze down at the wherries, skiffs, and barges transporting people and goods over the great waterway. "Less crowded perhaps."

"Perhaps. But could the Underworld be much different?"

He gestured to the smoke curling above the city's rooftops, a black, man-generated haze that mingled with the growing storm. Occasionally, a spire or chimney would appear, only to be engulfed again as the fog shifted.

"Consider what goes on below that curtain," Buckler observed in the same apathetic tone. "The dreariness, the squalor, the torment. It's madness, presided over by a king who is himself certifiably mad and whose son, our Regent, turns traitor to his political friends, then makes merry, indulging his own private brand of insanity. You are raising a child here, Mrs. Wolfe. Surely you've at least thought of this."

She understood all too well, but said, defiantly cheerful, "I think you over indulge fancy to serve a metaphor. After all, those boats down there hold flesh and blood men all going about their business, some happily. They are not Charon bearing souls to the land of the dead."

He smiled. "You will soon be wet through if you stay here."

"So will you, and the prospect doesn't seem to disturb you unduly. Besides, I told you. I wish to talk to you of Donovan."

Turning away, Buckler said quietly, "Read the papers, did you? Well, I saw for myself at Newgate. At least they had cut him down by the time I arrived."

A little shocked, Penelope realized what was wrong with Buckler: he didn't care for Donovan; she rather thought he didn't care for anything. "What will you do?" she asked.

"Do? What is there to do, Mrs. Wolfe? I once defended a man whose corpse had been imprisoned for debt, but in general a lawyer's responsibilities cease with his client's life. The only issue remaining is whether Donovan's body will be given to the surgeons for dissection or buried at a crossroads with a stake through his heart."

"I cannot agree. There's Annie Donovan, who is very much alive and must live with the shame of her husband being branded a murderer. Not to mention the fact that if Donovan didn't kill Constance Tyrone, whoever did is still a free man."

His eyes met hers, then slid aside. "Donovan is dead. I do not know why when he had at least a chance at an acquittal. But apparently he didn't think so, or he was guilty after all and committed self-murder out of remorse. That's what the papers claim, is it not?"

"Yes," she said, angry at him.

"What matter in the end? The man was likely guilty of any number of hanging offenses. As to whether or not Constance Tyrone's killer remains free, that too is food for conjecture. He might well have died in a fire the very night of the murder." Buckler related George Kite's story and the subsequent investigation of the mysterious accomplice Crow.

After taking several furious steps away from the balustrade, Penelope swung back. "My goodness, that is one way to dispose of a body, especially one that shows inconvenient signs of life. Simply toss it under an oncoming carriage."

"Kite is certainly villainous enough."

"How it hurts to think of her suffering," she said bitterly. She stared into the river for a moment. "I don't know, Mr. Buckler. If Kite is to be believed, the real villain is someone else—the man who killed Crow and started the fire to cover his deed."

He looked away again. "You may discuss the matter with Mr. Chase."

"Does it not pique your curiosity in the slightest?" she asked, unable to mask her growing irritation. "Especially now with Donovan so fortuitous a scapegoat. How do you suppose he managed to get a rope into the ward? One assumes someone would have seen him and informed the authorities."

"A journalist called Fred Gander paid for a separate confinement. And Donovan didn't use a rope. He fastened his own neckerchief to the rail used for hanging up bedding, this in spite of his leg irons. The authorities care only that he has cheated the gallows and robbed them of their spectacle."

"The newspapers reported that this journalist was one of the last people to speak with him. Gander claims he solicited an interview which the paper intends to publish in installments. You ought to see him, sir."

Buckler shrugged. "He won't tell me anything he can reserve for a hungry public. You know, last confessions of a murderer sort of stuff."

In spite of his air of studied indifference, Penelope had noticed his sudden tension. "You fear that Donovan did confess to Gander and you will look a fool, isn't that so, Mr. Buckler? You thought you might have swayed the jury."

He didn't answer.

"Let me tell you something else, Mr. Buckler. Even if Donovan did admit to killing Constance Tyrone, he might have acted under coercion, or else that newspaper offered him money. He—"

"Of what avail is money to a dead man?"

Tears pricked Penelope's eyes. Why should she mind about any of this anyway? She would do better to go home and attend to her own business. "Perhaps it wasn't for him but rather for his family."

"Did he strike you as that altruistic? I must say he did not me."

"This might have been the one time in his life when he could do something," she cried. "Maybe he wanted to make amends, though it's clear it matters not one whit to you." She pulled her pelisse around her. "I cannot believe that Mr. Thorogood will feel as you do. I shall speak to him, and perhaps also to the newspaper man."

"Can't you leave it alone, Mrs. Wolfe?" he said dully.

The rain began to fall faster now. A sudden gust of wind blew a scrap of paper into the air. Buckler watched it spiral slowly down, then picked up a pebble lying at his fingertips and sent it after.

"I'm going now, Mr. Buckler. You had best get out of the storm yourself." Over her shoulder, she added, "If Gander means to publish a farrago of lies just to sell papers, somebody ought to care."

Left alone, he stared again into the rushing river. Penelope took it all too personally. She didn't understand the constant flow of misery that passed his way like so much filthy water under this bridge. But he knew he had to ready himself for whatever brief next required his skills. John Chase, a professional, would also proceed to his next inquiry.

The sun stole out of the mist to sparkle briefly on the river. And yet, as he watched, the darkness was rolling in, a heavy mass of cloud that rumbled on the horizon.

Chapter Nineteen

Amelia Fitzhugh stood at the door, her lined, sour face even more sour than usual. "I trust I've made myself clear, Mrs. Wolfe. No animals are permitted in this house. Certainly not a disgusting, sickly cur like that."

She pointed at the little stray dog that didn't seem to realize its fate teetered on the brink—or maybe just could not bestir itself until calamity actually struck. In any event the dog had done little but lie in its basket over the past fortnight.

Sarah tugged at her mother's dress and whispered, "Tell her, Mama."

Giving the child's shoulder a reassuring squeeze, Penelope smiled determinedly at Mrs. Fitzhugh. "Perfectly clear, ma'am. As soon as we can find the pup a home, it will be gone." She met the other woman's gaze. "You wouldn't have me put it in the street?"

Mrs. Fitzhugh glanced again toward the animal and pursed her lips in distaste. "As long as we understand each other, Mrs. Wolfe. It looks half dead anyway."

As Sarah's eyes flew anxiously to her face, Penelope replied, "Nothing good food and rest cannot fix, and truly the dog does no harm, ma'am."

"I'll watch him careful for you, Mrs. Fitz," said Sarah. "He won't chew the carpets."

The landlady permitted herself a small rusty smile. "You do that, Miss Sarah." She addressed Penelope. "A few days, Mrs. Wolfe. I shall give you until after Christmas at any rate."

After the door closed behind the woman, Penelope said, "Remember, Sarah. Ruff may not long remain with us." Nor would Penelope be surprised if she and Sarah were ejected along with poor Ruff, for this contretemps over the dog could easily serve as a perfect opportunity for Mrs. Fitzhugh to rid herself of a female lodger possessed of a small child but no husband to lend her countenance. Penelope doubted that the landlady fully believed her stories about a Mr. Jeremy Wolfe and his pressing engagement out of town.

She turned back to her work, struggling to regain her concentration. It was hard to fathom that Mrs. Fitzhugh could feel such concern about one mite of a dog who wasn't causing anyone any trouble.

Today Penelope had heard a report far more worthy of disquiet: a second round of unthinkably vicious slayings in New Gravel Lane near the Ratcliffe Highway, presumably perpetrated by the same villains. This time the victims were the proprietor of a public house, his wife, and a serving woman, all with heads bludgeoned and throats cut. A particularly gruesome detail was the publican's partially severed thumb, which hung from his mangled hand as if he had grabbed at the attacker's knife in self-defense.

What the motive could be no one knew, but as the news spread all of London gave way to panic. It was said that many citizens had armed themselves with blunderbusses and watchman's rattles as people sought a means to protect themselves. The days were short at this time of year, darkness coming so early and so totally, that those who could stay locked indoors did, some even keeping a weapon at the ready.

It seemed to Penelope the authorities floundered in their attempt to make sense of the killings. Unsurprisingly, she hadn't seen John Chase since Donovan's trial and presumed him immersed in the investigation of the Ratcliffe matter. Nor had she heard from Edward Buckler since the day on Blackfriars Bridge, though she had finally received word from her father. *My dear daughter*, he had written. *I pray this finds you and the child in health, and I think often of the time when events may prove so fortunate as to see you both with me...* Jeremy, of course, was not mentioned; still, this letter had more in it of warmth than she had expected. That night she had lain awake for hours.

And yet, in spite of ample time for reflection, Penelope had come no closer to determining who might have murdered Constance Tyrone. No one else seemed to care any longer; in fact, of Fred Gander's proposed series of articles about Donovan, only the first two had appeared. The public had lost interest in the wake of newer, more sensational crimes. But Penelope finally had an avenue of her own to explore, for she had heard from Elizabeth Minton that Mr. Stonegrate was back at St. Catherine's.

It occurred to her that visiting a man she half suspected of murder was hardly a sensible course of action, though truly it could not seem real that anyone would be capable of such an act. She pictured Stonegrate's wide, fleshy features. Could a man kill, then stand to deliver a sermon before a large congregation? Would not his act be reflected in his face, God striking him down for his blasphemy?

She looked over at Sarah, who knelt at the dog's side, patiently feeding it scraps from their luncheon. Her expression was so pure, intent with every fiber on her purpose, that Penelope wanted to freeze the moment, keep her safe always. She did not want Sarah to have to look into people's faces and wonder what lay beneath.

And Penelope thought of the person—or persons?—who had committed the murders on the Ratcliffe Highway. How must his face appear as he walked about the city going about his affairs? One might dismiss the usual goblins that inhabited childish nightmares. They seemed quite benign in comparison to a human creature who could murder so savagely. Did it make him happy to realize he had terrified an entire city? Penelope doubted any ghoul had ever accomplished so much.

☙❧

Slumped against the seat of the hackney, John Chase put a hand to his unshaven chin and rubbed. Since the beginning of the

Ratcliffe affair, he had been on day and night duty, tracking down rumors until he was so exhausted he could no longer discern a tale from truth.

He had just come from an emergency meeting of the Shadwell and Whitechapel magistrates called by Harriott of the Thames police office. The panicked and bloodthirsty mob assembled outside had made it impossible to keep heads cool and deliberate; no coherent course of action had been proposed. Now Chase was on his way to his lodgings for some rest.

As the coach neared the Covent Garden area, the Friday traffic thickened. Knowing it might take another twenty minutes to go the short distance that remained, Chase decided to walk. He banged on the roof and jumped down into the street when the driver halted. After paying the man, he strode away, his hat pulled low for protection against the drizzle.

He was traversing the piazza when his attention was drawn to a large assembly in front of the portico of St. Paul's. There were working men, aproned shopkeepers, merchants clad in their sober coats, and others of more dubious appearance. Some sort of political gathering, Chase judged, possibly one of the recent meetings in support of liberty of the press.

Moving through the throng, he glanced up idly to descry Daniel Partridge—tailcoat, top hat, shiny boots and all. Voice pitched to carry, he was giving a speech, and judging by the reactions of the wildly cheering spectators, he made a good job of it. His remarks complete, Partridge acknowledged the applause with a smile and wave of his hand, then retreated through the crowd which parted willingly, hands extending for him to shake as he passed.

Chase caught up with him. "Mr. Partridge."

He turned, his public smile fading. "Chase. Did you wish to speak to me?"

"I should be honored." Chase bowed.

Partridge's lips tightened, but he said, "Come. My carriage is close by. We may converse there."

They didn't speak again until seated in the M.P.'s gleaming town carriage. Mindful of the coachman on the box, Partridge kept his voice low. "Well?"

Sitting opposite, Chase leaned back and stretched his legs, his eyes sharp on the other man's face. "For someone who prides himself on being a man of the people, you are deuced inaccessible, sir. I tried to see you several times until the magistrate warned me, gently, that I mustn't badger the Great Man."

"You gave up rather easily. I must say I didn't expect that."

Chase suppressed a pang of guilt, for he had been forced to abandon the Tyrone matter. "I never give up. I merely defer. In case you hadn't heard, we have been occupied."

"Ah, the Ratcliffe murders," Partridge replied, his expression changing. "A truly terrible business. Any progress?"

"Not much," Chase admitted. "Mr. Partridge, I want to know why you lied about seeing Constance Tyrone on the day she died."

The M.P. closed his eyes briefly. "I was afraid you would suspect me, but yes, I was with her. After our meeting I drove off, left her standing outside the York."

"Chivalrous of you."

"She didn't want a lift, damn you. 'Twasn't far to walk. In any event, she was not…slain…until later that night. I cannot know what she did after we parted, nor why she was out in the street so late. I only wish I did."

Chase looked at him. "What would you say to your lady friend not having suffered the attack after midnight as originally thought? It seems the time was much earlier. Shall we suppose soon after you were with her, between four and six that afternoon? You were, in fact, the last known person to see Miss Tyrone alive, excepting the murderer of course."

Partridge lost so much color that the faint grooves on his cheeks stood out starkly. "What can it matter now? You caught the man who killed her. I heard he was to be condemned, only he cheated the gallows." He stared blindly out the window. "He ought to have suffered more, much more."

"Yes, had he really murdered Miss Tyrone, but I don't think he did."

"You do not believe I was the one?" He put one shaking hand to his immaculate cravat and tugged. "I loved her. I could never have harmed her."

"I have yet to learn that loving someone will prevent an eruption of violence," answered Chase, smiling grimly. "Quite the reverse, in fact."

"This makes no sense. *The Source* has been running a series to relate the Irishman Donovan's final interview and full confession. Are you telling me it's all a hum?"

"I think Donovan probably tied it on good to get money for his family, yes."

Partridge put his head in his hands, then raised blazing eyes. "If you are right, I'd damned well like to know what you mean to do about it. I want her murderer caught and punished."

Chase laughed. "You have a strange way of showing your desire to cooperate, sir. But you can start now by telling me exactly what took place between you and Miss Tyrone that final day."

Slowly the fire died out of Partridge's face, and he took out his pocket watch as if recalled to the time passing. The last rays of sunlight illuminated the rich color of the squabs behind him.

He spoke, voice weary. "Constance was distressed by some news I brought her. It was a matter of some delicacy, Chase. I judged it unrelated to her death so decided not to inform the authorities at least until I saw what you were able to turn up. When the Irishman was arrested, there seemed no point—"

"No point in revealing intelligence that may shed light on a murder, one you claim you are eager to see solved?"

"I'm telling you now so have done, man. My time is short." He closed the watch and leaned forward. "There was a young woman called Ursula who had been employed by the Society. She fell ill and went to Greenwich to seek treatment from her brother, an apothecary, but was never heard from more. I put some inquiries in train for Miss Tyrone and discovered word of the girl."

"And?"

"She had returned home, unfortunately to become the center of local tattle. The sort of talk that could have been ruinous to the Society's reputation had it come to anyone's ears here in London. I'm sure that's why Constance was so disquieted, setting aside, of course, her concern for her friend."

"Gossip of what nature?"

"That is another reason I chose not to tell you, in the event that report lied."

Chase understood: a gentleman did not tarnish a lady's reputation even if he knew ill of her. Except in this case the woman was not a lady, and men like Partridge were not often so protective of those not of their own class.

The M.P. hesitated a further moment, looking a trifle embarrassed. Finally, he said, "Her brother put it about that she suffered an attack of influenza and died. Perhaps the influenza did kill her were her constitution already weakened, but rumor held that she had contracted the French disease."

"She died, eh?" murmured Chase. He remembered Penelope telling him of Fiona having syphilis. Now another female, too?

"Miss Tyrone insisted that Ursula was a rather special *protégée*, a true sister, cut of like cloth. In any event Constance outright refused to countenance the tale. And that's not all. I hated to be the bearer of this part of the story. Very... distressing, though the Lord knows such iniquity is common enough these days."

A chill brushed across Chase's skin. "What do you mean, sir?"

"Why just this, Mr. Chase: the resurrection men got the girl. The body was dug up and extracted two days after it was buried."

❧ ❧

The Reverend Mr. Stonegrate was not pleased to see her. As Wood ushered Penelope to a chair, the rector turned from the bookcase where he had been selecting a volume and gave her a long, level look. She felt her color fluctuate, but stiffened and met his eyes boldly.

After the curate bowed himself out, she spoke. "Good day, Mr. Stonegrate. I thank you for giving me a few minutes of your time."

He inclined his head. "Wood tells me you are connected with the St. Catherine Society, madam. How may I be of assistance?"

"I should like to speak to you of Fiona, sir." Penelope sat very still, awaiting his response.

Outside wind whistled through the trees, sweeping onward to rattle the windowpanes. Stout walls repelled the drafts, however, and a large fire warmed the room. Stonegrate strolled to the hearth.

"Fiona?" He lifted the poker to spread the coals more evenly. "Ah, yes. I'm at a loss to know what you would say of her." Dusting off his hands, he faced her.

Now it was Penelope's turn to regard him steadily. "I think you do know, sir."

Stonegrate flinched back, a mixture of fury and shame evident in his expression, but then he was coming forward to loom over her. Penelope looked up, appalled to see the glisten of tears behind his spectacles.

When he was sure she had noticed, Stonegrate shifted his gaze to somewhere over her head. "I have failed," he uttered. "You see I do not pretend to misunderstand you, Mrs. Wolfe."

Overcome by the heavy, sweet aroma of his perfume, Penelope wished he would move away. She had to lean back in her chair to see his entire face, and from this angle his nose jutted in a hard mountain of flesh.

"You admit your wrongdoing?"

He lowered his bulk in a nearby armchair. "If I have allowed myself to be lured into an indiscretion, I can honestly say my intentions were laudable."

Penelope's brows rose. "Laudable? I fail to understand you, sir."

Stonegrate stared down at the carpet. "I only wanted to offer the young woman some fatherly guidance. I never meant for anything of a nearer nature to develop.

"I have prayed and prayed, ma'am, and the answer has presented itself. I should never have permitted the Society to operate here, sanctioned by the Church. A group tainted with radicalism, even a hint of popery. Women who lack the guidance of husbands and fathers can only get into dangerous mischief. I see it now."

"You cannot be serious, sir," Penelope said when she could command her voice. "How utterly despicable—and you refuse to spare poor Fiona so much as one kind word." She sat up straighter and clasped her hands so tightly the knuckles whitened. "You forget that acting against the Society could bring undesirable consequences if what you have done to Fiona were to become common knowledge. I assure you most people would place the blame squarely where it belongs."

"Do you threaten me, Mrs. Wolfe?"

Penelope felt a tiny *frisson* of fear. There was something so implacable in this man's expression that suddenly it did not seem so unlikely he might be capable of violence.

For a long moment there was silence; then the bells rang out heralding the hour. When all was quiet, Stonegrate added more mildly, "Surely it is I who may claim to be the injured party. I do not know what lies the girl may have told you, but there is nothing between us, nothing. 'Tis only that I felt something of pity for her. It can hardly be placed at my door if she sought to take advantage of my kindness. What would you have of me?"

"The truth, sir. You have made Fiona most desperately unhappy and ill. Would to God that if you must break her heart, you might at least have abandoned her before the contagion had a chance to take hold."

He drew himself up. "Contagion? I went to see that surgeon fellow myself after the girl dared face me with her shocking untruths. Not that there was ever the slightest cause for apprehension, but I thought it best in order to silence any slander. Of course, the surgeon has given me a clean bill of health, as they say in the nautical trade."

Penelope stared at him, her thoughts whirling. Something was awry here. Had Fiona lied after all? Determinedly, she went on, "I must tell you, sir, that Miss Tyrone had learned of this matter and intended to tax you with it."

"Oh?" He sounded genuinely surprised. "I came upon her in the churchyard a day or two before her death, and she did mention something about calling, but I am afraid my time was otherwise accounted for. Church business."

"You weren't here at all the day Constance Tyrone died?"

"Yes, yes, I was. I returned in the late afternoon."

She felt a burst of excitement. So he had been here at the relevant time. "Perhaps you might describe your movements that afternoon and evening, Mr. Stonegrate?"

His heavy hands clenched. "By what right do you interrogate me, Mrs. Wolfe? My activities are none of your concern. I have already made the appropriate statements to Bow Street."

"To Mr. John Chase?" she asked innocently.

Starting, he glared at her. "I have told Mr. Chase that I spent the evening here working and afterwards fell asleep. Not, I repeat, that it's any of your affair."

"You were alone?"

Expecting at the least an angry response, she was taken aback when his fleshy lips twisted in amusement. "Why you should imagine I had any reason to wish Miss Tyrone ill I cannot fathom. But yes, Mrs. Wolfe, I was alone until morning when my curate roused me with the news."

"So there is no one to vouch for you?"

Again that sly little smile flickered. "Strangely enough there is. Miss Fiona stopped by in search of forgiveness. She was just outside praying in the church for some hours. You may ask her."

"You made Fiona get on her knees to you?" Penelope gave a short, bitter laugh. "You astound me, sir!" She rose, shaking out her gown. "I shall assuredly speak with her."

Stonegrate regarded her over his spectacles. "You insist upon misunderstanding me, madam. Fiona had no need to beg my forgiveness, for I had given it freely. It is the Lord with whom she must make her peace."

Chapter Twenty

"Fiona is not here, Mrs. Penelope. She's not been well."

Maggie was the only one left at the Society. Clad in a voluminous apron with bulging pockets, she was busy tidying and locking up.

"I'm that glad to see you, mum." She pulled Penelope inside and pushed her into a chair in Constance's office. "You've not been with us much of late."

Nodding guiltily, she answered, "I've been working, and Sarah had a bit of a head cold, I'm afraid. I thought it best to keep her close. Where are Frank and the baby?"

"Lil took them home for me. Frank will be sorry he missed you and Fiona too." Maggie paused. "We've been that worried for her, mum. She's got awful pustules on her limbs and a putrid sore throat. Not eating enough to keep a bird alive either."

"She needs treatment, Maggie. You must convince her."

"We've been trying. Miss Elizabeth thought she'd brought her around, but after Fiona spoke to the rector again and he wouldn't so much as look at her, she changed her mind."

"You know about Mr. Stonegrate?"

"We all of us do now, and Miss Elizabeth is so fired up she talks of seeking rooms elsewhere."

"'Twould serve him right to lose the rents, though he'd like nothing more than to be rid of the lot of us. Miss Minton must not give him the satisfaction."

"Yes, mum." She gave a few half-hearted swipes with her broom and stopped to watch Penelope don her gloves and button her pelisse. "Mrs. Pen? Miss Elizabeth says you don't think the Irish was the one what killed poor Miss Constance. But if not him, who? Do you aim to find out?" Maggie's blue eyes were worried.

"If I can. I wondered about the rector, but it appears he may have something of an alibi."

"The rector?" Maggie gasped. "Eh, but that's hard to credit."

"Is it?" said Penelope, smiling a little. "Yet one can easily fancy him talking someone to death."

Maggie sent a glance around the room to check its neatness. Apparently satisfied, she retrieved her own wrap. "If you'll wait, mum, I'll walk out with you."

She went to the French window to test the lock and peered through the glass. "Dark already and cold too, I warrant." She turned back. "Mrs. Pen, what if it was Mr. Bertram Tyrone? He's a rich man now with Miss Constance's money."

Penelope frowned. "He seems to have loved his sister."

Maggie added eagerly, "Or Mr. Strap? Miss Constance once told Miss Elizabeth how grateful she was to him for his help physicking the women in spite of past awkwardness between 'em."

"What awkwardness, Maggie?"

"Well, that's just what Miss Elizabeth asked her, and she said why that silliness about us making a match. So I reckon he once paid his addresses to Miss Constance and she would have none of it."

"Odd, one doesn't sense that sort of emotion when he speaks of her, but perhaps 'twas long ago. I believe they have been friends for a number of years."

Their eyes met. Penelope said, "Shall I bring Sarah to stay with the other children so that I may pay a visit to Mr. Strap tomorrow? I should like to look over his wards and learn what I can of available treatments for Fiona's sake."

"You best be careful."

"Nothing's going to happen to me in a busy hospital with scores of people on hand. Don't let your imagination get the better of you, Maggie!"

"A woman on her own is easy pickings, mum, no matter how safe you think you are. Do you know what today is, Mrs. Pen?"

"Friday, the 20th of December. Why?" said Penelope, puzzled by the sudden change of subject.

"It's St. Thomas's Eve." She came closer, one hand held over her bulging apron pocket. "Ghosts may walk abroad between now and Christmas Eve, and dreams are mortal powerful. That's another reason for you to be careful."

"Oh, Maggie."

"You may laugh, mum," she said darkly, "but that don't make it not so." She brushed a lock of hair out of her face and marched toward the door.

Penelope followed her out of the office into the anteroom beyond. After another quick scrutiny Maggie was ready to depart. Holding open the front door, she waited, ostentatiously silent.

"Doubting Thomas?" Penelope asked. "Why is he associated with ghosts?"

She broke into an impish grin. "Queers me. I recall my mam telling me so. Maybe it's because St. Thomas refused to believe the Lord could return from the dead, so now all the other spirits got to show they can rise up too. But it makes no odds how it all begun. I got something to give you, if you'll take it."

Reaching into her pocket, she pulled forth a round object which she thrust into Penelope's hand; then she turned to secure the door. The light was so dim that Penelope couldn't actually see the object, but she caught a whiff of its unmistakable odor. Round and hard, it was peeling slightly from being jostled in Maggie's pocket.

"An onion?"

"Yes'm. Keep it safe till you get home and tonight after Miss Sarah's asleep—" Maggie shivered in the piercing wind which struck them full force. "Curate will be locking up shortly. We should hurry."

When they stood in the shelter of the gate, Penelope said, "What am I to do with the onion?"

Maggie eyed her from under the heavy scarf she had wound about her face and neck. "Stick a pin in the middle, Mrs. Pen, eight more in a neat circle around it. After that say what I tell you. Put the onion under your pillow, and you'll dream of him."

"Him?"

"Your husband, of course. True one, that is." Her rhyme recited, she hurried down the street without a backward glance, stepping around puddles and horse droppings.

Left clutching her onion, Penelope watched her a moment, then took herself in the direction of home. When Maggie's gift wouldn't fit in her reticule, she considered tossing it in the gutter, but instead tucked it into her muff. If nothing else, she could use it to fend off an attacker.

Sarah pounced on the onion when Penelope got home, rolling it back and forth across the floor for the amusement of Ruff. Removing her wrap, Penelope turned to her writing table to discover that someone had left her another gift: a cylindrical shape wrapped in oil cloth.

"What's that, Sarah?"

Sarah looked up. "Mrs. Fitz said someone brought it for you. She told me not to touch it and I didn't."

"Good girl," said Penelope absently.

"Open it. I want to see!" Sarah abandoned the onion to jump up and down at her mother's feet.

After Penelope read the note that accompanied the package, she removed the wrapping. Since her desk was not large enough, she spread the portrait on the floor, using two paperweights and some books to hold down the corners. It was excellent work, perhaps the best Jeremy had ever done.

"Who is the lady?"

"Someone you don't know, love," Penelope murmured.

Surprisingly, this seemed to satisfy the child, for she bounced away again to play with the dog, and Penelope was able to concentrate. She sat motionless for some minutes.

He had rendered Constance Tyrone with a sensitivity that stunned.

In the background against a stark sky, an ivy-covered stone wall ascended to a high bell tower. In the foreground stood Constance, clad in a simple, high-waisted gown and pointed shoes. She was vibrantly erect, head thrown a trifle back. Framed by profuse red roses that seemed to bleed from the greenery at her back, from the surrounding stone and sky, she was also serene, yet not ethereal, a woman very much of this world. One could almost see the breath beating at her throat. She possessed strength, both of body and soul, yet Jeremy had also captured a vulnerability in the lips, a wistfulness in the eyes.

Penelope thought first that this was a genuine woman of God, but also someone unafraid of practical action, who would scorn to use her spirituality as a retreat from the world. And in spite of the passion evident in every line of the slim figure, there was no prurience in the artist's depiction.

It amazed Penelope that Jeremy had seen all this—Jeremy, who saw so little. Suddenly angry, she rolled up the portrait and bestowed it safely. She would do as requested and forward it to Sir Giles Tyrone.

Later, when Sarah was finally settled and the dog asleep in its basket, Penelope poured herself a glass of sherry and sank into the faded easy chair by the hearth. As they couldn't afford to warm their tiny sitting room at night, Penelope usually spent her evenings in the bedchamber. For a while she read, but found that the words sat heavily on the page; she was simply too tired.

Finally, she got up, thinking she might as well go to bed early. On the way, however, she stopped to retrieve the onion and carried it to the bureau to rummage for some pins. Feeling decidedly foolish, she was glad no one was there to see her arranging them in the required circle. At least, she thought wryly, she would be able to tell Maggie she had followed her instructions to the letter.

When the pins were in place, Penelope went to the fire and sat down again in the chair. The room was quiet except for the chink of coal in the grate and the occasional creaks of the tenant upstairs walking across the floor. Whispering so as not to wake the sleeping child, she repeated Maggie's rhyme:

> Good St. Thomas, do me right
> And let my true love come tonight
> That I may see him in the face
> And in my arms may him embrace.

Afterwards she placed the onion on the bureau next to Constance Tyrone's portrait and went to sleep with Sarah.

❦

Penelope stood on Blackfriars Bridge, some distance away from Edward Buckler. He appeared exactly as she'd seen him before, alone and ineffably weary. She knew she could not touch him or talk to him, that he would not hear her if she tried.

It was dark and growing darker. With horror she watched the night slip over his unmoving form. She looked away, her gaze pulled to the rushing water below, and experienced a sudden nightmarish conviction that the bridge itself would crumble, dashing her into that frigid tumult.

Suddenly she was standing at the head of a narrow, dimly lit corridor, surrounded only by silence. A row of doors, all closed, stretched out before her, yet she paid them no mind as she moved swiftly toward her goal. She knew the room she sought was at the end of the passage and knew also that it would be dangerous to enter. But she was drawn forward.

It was a plain door, nothing marking its difference from the others. And on the threshold sat the little stray dog Penelope had found in the street. It gazed up at her mournfully, not in warning it seemed, but with its habitually resigned expression.

Before she could change her mind, she opened the door and stepped over the dog into the room. At first she could not see, for the curtains at the window were closed. However, as her eyes adjusted she became aware of clots of blood pooled at her feet, and looking up, she saw the corpses of several women hanging along the wall. Their throats had all been cut, widely, from ear to ear.

A peculiar snorting, snuffling noise broke the quiet. Turning away from the corpses, she peered into a corner and caught the unmistakable gleam of gold and jewels, an enormous glittering hoard. Atop this mound sat a goliath, a winged, reptilian creature covered in thick scales. A dragon. Penelope crept a little closer, but poised ready to flee should the creature move. She noticed that its eyes were old and dulled, its scales peeling to reveal raw, bleeding skin beneath. The sound she had heard was the air rasping in its chest as it struggled for breath.

She backed away and found herself, in the inexplicable manner of dreams, standing at a crossroads on a winter day, one of a crowd who watched a tableau unfold. The sun burned brightly, but the wind gusted, and the skeleton of an oak tree loomed above.

The people were gripped by a feverish gaiety, and looking into their faces frightened her more than anything she had yet seen. She tore her gaze away and focused instead on what was happening, wanting to understand it.

They all watched an aged woman dressed in a shabby black servant's gown who faced them from atop an overturned crate. Her shrunken face alight with joy, she bent to retrieve something at her feet and held it aloft for all to see. It was the little dog, trembling, terrified, in her grasp. As the people murmured restlessly, the old woman took a knife from her apron pocket, slit the dog's throat, and tossed the animal into the dust of the road, blood spilling over the shoes of those at the front. A low groan of satisfaction was wrung from the crowd.

When Penelope began to cry, the crone pushed through the onlookers and came to her. Gripped in her arms, Penelope stared, fascinated, into the woman's eyes. The old woman crooned, rocking her, and smoothed her cheeks with one gnarled hand. Penelope relaxed, drifting almost into slumber.

But the dream shifted, and Penelope was a spectator again. Perched on her crate, the old woman grinned and flapped her arms once, crow-like. Responding with shouts of encouragement and the rumblings of an indistinct low chant, the people jostled closer. Penelope could smell their excitement, but she herself felt oddly removed.

Then she discovered what they were waiting to see, for the old woman swooped down as she had before to take up something at her feet, her face wearing that same look of fierce rapture. It was a small child, who looked fearlessly into the crone's face and smiled. The woman smiled back and nestled the child against her shoulder with one arm while the other groped for the knife in her pocket...

※ ⁂

The arms were around Penelope now, close and comforting. "Hush now, my love. 'Twas only a bad dream," said Jeremy.

Still enmeshed in the nightmare, she twisted convulsively in a futile attempt to escape the encircling grip and find Sarah. But then, in a thrill of awareness that brought her fully awake, she realized she had not imagined the voice.

"Jeremy?" She tried to sit up.

He loosened his hold. "Yes, love. I'm here. You were dreaming."

"My God." She gripped his shoulders and gazed up into the familiar features that became more distinct as her eyes adjusted. "It is you. Where did you come from? Damn you, you climbed through the window again."

He bent closer to whisper in her ear. "All of London is battened down defending itself against monsters on the loose, and you neglect to lock up. That's like you. How I have missed you, Penelope."

The kiss, long, deep, and satisfying, left her trembling. "Let me up," she said after a moment, disconcerted to hear how shaken she sounded. "You'll wake Sarah."

Obediently, he followed her into the sitting room. Getting the lamp lit and finding a shawl to stave off the cold gave Penelope a much-needed interval to accustom herself to his presence. As her bewilderment faded, she found herself wondering what had happened to the anger that usually sustained her when it came to Jeremy's nonsense. She had not had reason to believe him in danger any longer—and every reason to think he would return when it suited him. As indeed he had. Why then this treacherous gladness, this insuperable relief?

Facing him, she clasped her arms under the shawl. "Where have you been this time, Jeremy? I suppose it's too much to expect you to inform me of your whereabouts, or even to send word of your intent to return to us."

"Were you worried, love? But you received my note and the painting?"

"Yes, this afternoon."

"What did you think of it, the portrait I mean?" he asked eagerly.

"'Tis your best work yet, as I make no doubt you are well aware. How could you? How could you so forget your honor as to threaten Constance Tyrone? And those dreadful sketches that have quite blackened her reputation. She didn't deserve such treatment, Jeremy."

He reached under the shawl for her hand. "I assure you I shall undertake to express, and to feel, all the regret you would have of me. But you know I never meant for those drawings to be exposed to the public gaze, albeit only fools would find aught objectionable in them. As for threats, I meant nothing of the kind. I merely sought to pursue an advantageous connection."

"You deny that Mr. Partridge paid for your silence?"

"I deny it utterly," he answered, squeezing her fingers. "Oh, he advanced me some funds to see me through a few weeks. 'Twas only fair since he had desired me to lie low until the furor should abate. I was doing him a favor really, for I might have cleared myself simply by telling the truth about him and Miss Tyrone."

Penelope desperately wanted to believe him, and perhaps he was, in some sense, telling her truth. "I suppose you've heard the Irishman Kevin Donovan has committed suicide to avoid the gallows. But he wasn't the one, Jeremy, I am nearly certain of it. Now with this horrible Ratcliffe affair, no one cares for Donovan anymore, nor for his wife and child left to face the world alone."

His eyes were tender. "Like someone else with whom we are well acquainted, eh? My poor Penelope. You've had a rough time of it, but that is all at an end now."

"Well, it isn't over. I have been thinking of writing a piece about the life of Miss Tyrone. She…she haunts me, Jeremy. You know how I've always wanted to attempt something in that line."

He had already turned away to lead her to the settee. "Perhaps you will then, one day. In the meantime let us talk of our own affairs. I have much to say to you. You cannot but own that I have treated you with all forbearance, but even now I'll not compel you, love—though you are my wife."

"What do you want?" she said warily as she seated herself at his side.

"We cannot go on thus. Now that I am to receive payment for the portrait, I shall be somewhat beforehand with the world. I have come for you and Sarah, Penelope. What say you we go to Dublin? I've an acquaintance there who has promised to put me in the way of some commissions."

Penelope stared at him. "You cannot be serious."

He grinned. "Why not? As I said, I've missed you and my lovely Sarah too. A man and his family belong together, Penelope. You need me, and the Lord knows I have need of you. Besides, I've no doubt we can contrive to keep ourselves tolerably well amused."

The bitterness welled up. "Yes, until something, or someone, more to your taste comes along. I tell you fairly, Jeremy—" She broke off in consternation as a tiny, nightgown-clad figure appeared in the doorway.

"Mama?"

"Sarah!" Jeremy was on his feet in an instant, sweeping his daughter high in his arms. "Hello, my love," he said, his face close to hers.

"I've been waiting for you, Papa," she said clearly, the reproach strong in her tone. "You've been ever so long. You won't go away again, will you?"

"You had best ask your mother that question," he replied, holding Penelope's gaze. For a long moment she hesitated as fear, guilt, and sorrow warred with some other emotion she would not define.

"Oh, Sarah," she said finally, "I am so sorry, my darling."

Chase was trudging up the stairs, his hand resting heavily on the banister, when the landlady, Mrs. Beeks, called from below.

"I'm glad you're home, sir. These days a body sleeps easier with a man in the house. Will you take a bite of supper?"

He turned back. "Just bread and cheese in my room tonight, Mrs. Beeks."

"As you will, sir." Nonetheless, she went on, anxiety clear in her tone, "If I might speak to you about Leo, I should be most grateful. The boy insists he wants to go to sea, Mr. Chase, and how to put a spoke in his wheel is what I don't know—"

But he had already moved into his room, and her only answer was a firm click. Mrs. Beeks stood for a moment looking up at the closed door.

In his chamber Chase removed his greatcoat and collapsed on the bed. For a while he lay listening to the flutter of a light rain against the window. At last he lifted himself up and walked slowly to the dresser to retrieve Abigail's miniature. With no other motive than loneliness, he carried it to his sitting room. Pouring himself a snifter of brandy, he folded his body into an armchair, too exhausted to bother lighting a fire. He was content to remain in the cold and dark, sipping the fiery liquid and clutching the picture. He didn't need to look at it. He knew every detail. Tracing a finger idly around the frame, he drifted…

Chase had no idea how much time had passed when the ghost woke him with a feather touch on the shoulder.

"Do not forget," said Constance Tyrone.

In his state of dream-like acquiescence, he felt no surprise or alarm except that her voice sounded different than he would have thought. Not like Abby's, richly warm, yet strong and decisive. Instead, shockingly, it was Penelope's voice, pitched higher and softer. Chase peered into the dimness, trying to see her more clearly. But her head was bent, black hair falling across her cheek and neck.

"I'm supposed to be done with you," he told her. "More gruesome murders, other fish to fry. The public has a short memory for victims. Murderers, however, become legend."

Without answering, she disappeared, and Chase slipped away again...

The next awakening jarred him cruelly. He gave an enormous start, his entire body stiffening, heart thumping painfully. He thought, please God, don't let it touch me.

Beside his chair stood a faceless shape dressed in charred rags and reeking of decay—George Kite's friend Crow.

One of Crow's arms ended in a blood-red stump. His remaining hand grasped a clod of damp earth which he crumbled in his fingers and sprinkled on the carpet. He tossed his head restlessly back and forth, his flashing eyes alive with rage and betrayal.

"What do you want?" Chase forced each word through a tight throat.

Crow was silent.

Watching the trickling dirt, Chase said, "You told Kite there wouldn't be any digging on the night you were hired to move Constance Tyrone's body. What sort of digging did you mean, Crow?"

"You know."

"You and Kite are resurrection men, aren't you? Grave robbers? That's why the job was perfect for you. Only this time the corpse didn't need to be unearthed." Chase stared up into the shrouded countenance.

"And Ursula. You had something to do with that, didn't you? You and Kite were the ones who stole her body. Where did you take her?"

"You know the answer, mate." Crow laughed, a terrifying sound.

Chase struggled to keep his mind clear. "I do know, must have known without realizing, but I'm too tired. You were killed for your pains, weren't you, Crow? Someone did not want you around to tell the tale."

Crow disintegrated.

Then someone spoke from behind in smooth, cultured tones that he recognized, yet couldn't place. "You are out of time, Mr. Chase, and your suspicions will avail you nothing."

Chase's muscles would not obey him as he tried to turn his head, and he felt himself drifting again, this time into a slumber so deep it was like death. But just before unconsciousness came up to embrace him, he was able to identify the voice.

Chapter Twenty-one

"Ring the bell to summon the handlers," said Reginald Strap. "And have the patient brought in."

As an assistant scurried out, Strap waited, quite at ease, regarding the faces that stared down from the tiers of standings. Packed with surgeons' dressers and pupils, the standings curled in a semicircle around three sides of the room. In the arena at the bottom stood the surgeon, illuminated by the sun pouring through the skylight.

Penelope was aware of the precise moment when he noticed her, squeezed in on the top row, for he looked, then looked again and inclined his head with a slight, ironic smile. Penelope nodded back, trying to ignore the sidelong frowns cast in her direction. As far as she could see, she was the only woman present in the operating theatre at St. Thomas's hospital. It was not a circumstance in which to take comfort.

The crowd hummed with excitement as Strap ushered several important-looking guests to their seats in front. Next, he stripped off his coat and hung it on a row of pegs. After rolling up his shirtsleeves, he donned an old purple frock coat, turned up the collar to cover his linen, and tied on a wide, bloodstained apron.

"Today I shall operate to bypass an aneurysm of the popliteal artery which, as you know, runs behind the knee. We place the ligature in the thigh, tying off the diseased artery and thereby forcing the collateral vessels to take up an increased blood flow. For this purpose, I will use the site in the thigh known as Hunter's Canal, so named, of course, after John Hunter, the first to perform this surgery in 1785…"

As he was speaking, a door at his back opened, and two thickset men entered, supporting a drooping, blindfolded figure between them. It was a woman, drunk or merely stupefied with fear. Wearing a shapeless gown of some coarse stuff, she had a strapping frame and lank brown hair bound at the neck. Her cheeks and arms were mottled with large copper colored blotches. The men lifted her onto a plain deal table swathed in an oil cloth. One of the handlers held her fast at the wrist and shoulder.

Strap approached. "Do you agree?" he demanded.

At the woman's mute nod, he motioned to the handler who assisted her to lie back. Without vision, sounds must be magnified, thought Penelope. The woman could hear the cacophony of voices, the hurried footsteps, the clatter as a dresser dropped one of the surgeon's instruments on the small side table—and her flesh would be shrinking as she waited for the knife to descend.

Strap moved away, and the hospital chaplain stepped nearer to address the patient in a voice designed to carry. "Sickness is a forerunner of death. Are you prepared?"

Giving a feeble shake of her head, the woman seemed to be struggling to sit up. She said something Penelope couldn't hear. The handlers pushed her down.

The surgeon turned to his work, but before he could begin, a pupil called, "Mr. Strap, a question if you please."

Strap was not encouraging. "Yes?"

"Can you tell us the reason for this woman's affliction? Has she been injured?"

The surgeon's eyes flickered over the patient indifferently. "I believe the cause to be untreated syphilitic infection."

Daringly, the questioner called out a second time: "Is it true that the great Hunter, pioneer of the technique you apply today, actually inoculated himself with venereal effluent in order to study syphilis and gonorrhea?" Strap held up his hands for silence. The light seemed to magnify them, and Penelope suddenly realized the strength his forearms must possess. "So it has been said," he replied. "But how foolish a risk for a trained professional. Much better to conduct one's inquiries as Mr. Jenner did, for instance, when he tested his inoculum for the smallpox on a young boy. We all know the happy results of that experiment."

Murmurs of agreement and a few "hear, hears" greeted Strap's statement; the admiration he inspired was palpable. And yet his words echoed hollowly in Penelope's head as she rubbed a hand across her clammy brow. Last night after she had finally managed to tear Sarah from Jeremy, Penelope had tumbled back into bed, only to find troubling dreams that had taken their toll. Now the malaise she had felt all day intensified.

Strap joined the surgeons and other observers clustering around the table. "Enough preliminaries, eh? Let's get on with it." His expression was rueful, as if in apology for allowing any delay. Carefully, he lifted the woman's gown to her hips.

Seeming to forget their intention to give her a wide berth, the men around Penelope pressed in closer. She began to feel stifled, her discomfort made worse by the thought of the woman's coming agony.

Expectation grew heavy as Strap took up his knife and glanced up, saying, "Time me, gentlemen." Several eager spectators hurried to comply, producing pocket watches and holding them aloft. The handlers' grip on the patient tightened.

To Penelope, it seemed as though the light had leached from the rest of the room to isolate the surgeon and the woman in a bright bubble so that the other figures on the crowded floor were somehow dark, indistinct. She heard a hiss of indrawn breath as the pupils leaned eagerly over the railings. "Heads, heads," those in the back cried, pushing at each other to gain a better view.

Then Strap's arm plunged so fast that Penelope caught only the gleam of the knife. The woman screamed, and bright blood spilled over the oilcloth to run in rivulets off the table. Wood scraped against wood as Strap kicked a sawdust-filled box across the floorboards to catch the fluid. He repeated, "Time, gentlemen."

A chorus of voices answered him. As cheers erupted, Penelope found her gaze riveted upon the exuberant, glistening countenances of the men who waved their pocket watches. She felt the crush of bodies sway toward her again, and her vision blurred.

Spinning around, she pushed her way to the staircase at the top of the standings. Head bent and elbows clasped against her body, she clattered down the steps and through the passageway, bursting out into the theatre's small lobby, where she nearly collided with an old woman swathed in a voluminous apron.

"What were you doing in there? Ain't fitting for the likes of you." The woman grinned, displaying teeth reduced to black stumps.

Penelope tried to hide her dismay by speaking briskly. "I've come to see Mr. Strap, but I see he is occupied at present. Is there somewhere I may wait?"

The woman gave her a knowing look. "Why yes, miss, if you'll come with me."

She set off at a clip, leaving Penelope little choice but to follow. They descended to a colonnade that wrapped around the wards. The woman continued, her ragged skirts dragging in the dust.

Penelope's nausea faded, and she began to look about with interest. According to the porter who had conducted her to the theatre, St. Thomas's had been part of a medieval priory destroyed in the early 1200s by fire and rebuilt on its current site on the east side of Borough High Street, Southwark. Named originally in honor of St. Thomas à Becket, the hospital had been closed during the Dissolution of the Monasteries, reopening later under the new name of St. Thomas the Apostle. Early in the last century the crumbling structure had been replaced by three enormous red brick quadrangles.

They had passed into the men's block, her companion, presumably a nurse, informed her. Penelope glimpsed the rows of wooden bedsteads and was astonished by the clamor arising from the patients.

Slackening her pace, the woman threw back a smile. "You get used to it, miss. Lying abed for so long makes some a bit peevish, you might say."

When Penelope caught up, the nurse went on, saying seriously, "But this here's a godly place. Why, we have a rule that all our people go to chapel to give thanks for their deliverance before we send them home."

"Yes, indeed." But Penelope wondered how many patients were actually discharged cured. Seeing this place, she could more easily understand Fiona's reluctance to seek treatment.

They continued to a small side court where the nurse halted. "Here's where the foul wards is for them as got the French disease. Men over there, women just beyond. Around and below us is the warm and cold baths, brewhouse, bakehouse, and the morgue."

"Are the surgeons able to effect many cures for the pox?"

She shrugged. "I seen some as make out. They say your Mr. Strap be the best man for that."

Opening a door, she ushered Penelope forward. "Here we are then, miss. You sit right here, and Mr. Strap'll be along."

Penelope found a windowless room which someone had taken pains to render more elegant. Reposing in one corner was a brass-inlay desk, covered by neat stacks of papers, a lamp, and a walnut standish. Faded but of obvious quality, the crimson and gold Oriental carpet held a dragon motif. Framed testimonials and a painting or two adorned the walls. To her right was a connecting door.

One of the certificates caught her eye, so she stood to examine it more closely. The handsomely framed parchment commemorated Reginald Strap's work for the East London Vaccination Institute for the Eradication of the Smallpox. It was a glowing testimonial to "herculean efforts on behalf of the poor" and "battles waged against ignorance and superstition."

Penelope read it over several times, trying to pinpoint the curious feeling that she was missing something. She had experienced the same momentary disorientation in the operating theatre when Strap had spoken of Mr. Jenner's vaccination experiments.

Turning away, she perused the titles on Strap's bookshelves. Works of science and medicine dominated, particularly treatises on venereal illnesses, although he was also interested in history and philosophy. Not surprising, she thought, for he seemed a man of refinement. In truth, Penelope had been surprised by the roughness of many of the pupils and surgeons in the operating theatre.

But Mr. Strap was almost a gentleman, and she remembered that he had once sought Constance Tyrone's hand. It was a shame he had not approved of Constance's vocation, believing it too much for her frail health. Had he fully supported her endeavors, they might have made a happy, productive marriage and given valuable service to the needy.

Yet, she mused, the "needy" didn't always appreciate such efforts, since uneducated people were often wary of innovation. How had Strap persuaded someone like Winnie to undergo his vaccination? What was it she had said?

"I ain't been right since that doctor dosed me... The Lord never intended such mucking about with a body's innards."

And Fiona had replied, *"Oh, she's talking about the vaccination for the smallpox what Mr. Strap give us. Hush, you silly old thing..."*

Penelope froze, staring at the testimonial until the letters jumped before her eyes. Then she looked down, her gaze focusing on the dragon at her feet. She was standing on the frayed remains of its curled crimson tail. Terror flooded her body.

Hurrying across the room, she picked up her reticule and pelisse from the chair. She could be gone before he returned. Opening the door, she stepped into the deserted corridor, but hesitated. It might be some time before Strap finished in the operating theatre. Even though the cutting was, by necessity, soon over, surely he would need to remain at the patient's side to stitch her up and supervise the dresser. Besides, the surgeon had no reason to fear her.

She would take a quick look around, she decided. With a glance in either direction, she retreated into the office and shut the door. Quelling her nerves sternly, she approached the desk. This time she began riffling through the contents of a drawer. It contained nothing but patient histories and pieces of the surgeon's vast correspondence with medical men all over the world. Try as she might, she could see nothing out of the way.

Aware time was running out, she hesitated in front of the connecting door. What could she say if he caught her in there? Perhaps, if she carried off the situation with aplomb, he would merely think her an inquisitive female.

She turned the knob and went in. Against the rectangular room's long wall she saw the outline of a large window, covered by thick drapes. Along the far wall were shelves which contained rows of glass jars. Several human skeletons posed next to various animal specimens, including a stuffed tiger's head and what looked like some sort of exotic bird. Running along the center of the room was a wooden platform, next to which was a stand for surgical instruments. Strap's laboratory.

Penelope picked her way across the room to stand in front of the shelves. A strong chemical odor assailed her nostrils, making her sneeze. When her eyes stopped watering, she moved along the line of jars, eyeing their contents with fascinated revulsion. Labeled meticulously, the jars housed any number of repellent objects, many preserved in clear fluid. She saw muskrat hearts, the hind leg of a rabbit, frogs' brains, a finch's wing, and various organs of monkeys, bats, eels, porpoises, hedgehogs, and deer.

At the end of the row came the human specimens: an amputated foot, a femur bone with gunshot damage, an ear, and several skulls pitted with "syphilitic caries." Worst of all was the cluster of jars holding foetuses at various stages of development. Penelope clutched at her stomach and gagged.

When she had herself under control, she looked into the last jar. Sitting a trifle forward on the shelf, it bore a label that looked newer than the others. Inside was a hand, obviously a man's, for she could see thick, black hairs waving gently in the liquid. While the thumb appeared normal, there were only two other fingers. They were contorted in the semblance of a claw.

A claw. Buckler had told her George Kite's friend Crow had a deformed hand.

Penelope did not know there was someone in the room with her until Reginald Strap's voice said, "I see you are admiring my collection, Mrs. Wolfe."

❦

Buckler lay motionless in a darkened room and stared at the ceiling. He felt only a bone-deep languor, as if a great thirst were finally slaked and he was to be left alone for the present. This time the depression of spirits had raged for days. There had even been a few terrifying moments when he had considered Donovan's remedy to a cruel impasse, but mostly he had sat back and let the mood pass over him like a tempest. Eventually, he knew he would emerge, blinking furiously, trying to accustom himself again to the light.

The last time he had roused from a bout like this, Penelope Wolfe had caught him in his dressing gown and embroiled him in the Tyrone affair. For a few weeks the sense of having a task to accomplish had brought him out of himself, and he was easier. But he didn't like to recall the way Penelope had looked at him the day it ended on Blackfriars Bridge. She possessed great strength of mind tempered with an appealingly responsive softness. She would not condemn another for his weakness, yet Buckler doubted she could really understand it.

What did it matter anyway, he told himself, for likely he would not see Mrs. Wolfe unless Thorogood chanced to invite them both to dine. Buckler turned on his side to rest his cheek against the pillow. Perhaps tomorrow he would dine at a local chophouse on a good beefsteak and his favorite ale, afterward resuming his evening walk. But not today.

Suddenly, he heard the door from the hallway slam. Now muffled voices broke out, getting louder. One was Bob's; the other, unmistakably, belonged to a woman. A series of thumps ensued followed by staccato footsteps. The door to Buckler's chambers was flung open, and someone marched up to his bed.

"Mr. Buckler, sir. I'm sorry to disturb you, but you got to wake up. Mrs. Wolfe is in horrible trouble. It's taken me so long to find you that I think it might be too late and the poor thing may already be murdered."

"Begone, woman!" yelled Bob, gamely following her. He plucked at the woman's arm. "I shall summon the Watch."

She turned on him fiercely. "Let go of me, or so help me I'll box your ears." She bent over Buckler. "Oh please do get up, sir."

Bemused, he gazed up at her, thinking she looked familiar but unable to place her. In the dim light, he saw a youngish, red-haired woman dressed in a plain gray gown, her chin set at a militant angle. She held an infant in her arms, and a little boy and girl clung to either side of her skirt. As if matters were not chaotic enough, the baby chose that instant to let out a piercing wail.

Buckler sat bolt upright. "What in God's name is going on here?"

"I tried to stop her, Mr. Buckler, but she shoved right by me. She—"

"I recognize you," Buckler interrupted his clerk, looking more closely at the woman. "You are from the St. Catherine Society. Mrs. Foss, isn't it? Leave off, Bob."

Buckler's eyes turned to the little girl. It was Sarah, hair disheveled and face coated with something sticky. She was regarding him with huge, terrified eyes that wrung his heart. He held out his hand and was surprised when the child approached tentatively.

"Where's my Mama?"

"I do not know, but shall we find out?"

Sarah nodded vigorously, and Maggie broke in, fear making her voice shrill, "I told you, sir. Mrs. Penelope has gone to the hospital, and you have to hurry."

"Hospital? Has she been hurt?"

"Oh no, sir. Least not yet, I hope." Tears began to spill down Maggie's cheeks. "And I need m...money for the jarvey. He's waiting at your door, threatening to haul me up before a m… magistrate."

"We mustn't alarm the children, Maggie." Buckler fixed his clerk with a stern look. "Bob, take our guests into the office whilst I dress. Go and give the hackney driver his money and bid him wait outside as he may have another fare soon. Oh, and find something for the children to eat if you can muster it."

He dressed rapidly, glad to note he was steady on his feet, although he could not recall when he'd last eaten. A hasty glance in the looking glass over his washbasin revealed gaunt, stubble-covered cheeks and hollow eyes. His hair looked as if a barber hadn't been near it in years. Sighing, he ripped a comb through it and splashed the stale water from the basin on his face.

As soon as he entered the next room, Maggie came forward to take his arm. "We got to hurry, sir. Mrs. Penelope is with him and—"

"Where's my Mama?" Sarah planted herself in front of Buckler. "I want my Mama!" She crushed the piece of dry bread Bob had given her in her fist and dropped it to the carpet. Fastening her eyes hopefully on his face, she repeated herself. Many times. The boy watched her, open-mouthed, and the baby started to whimper from its place on the settle.

"Stow it, everyone, so I can get to the bottom of this," commanded Buckler, certain he would soon be ripe for Bedlam. Then as the little girl's face crumpled, he said, "Sarah, I didn't mean to shout. Don't cry." He looked helplessly at Maggie, who lifted the child into her arms for comfort. Sarah buried her face and subsided.

When all was quiet and the baby had dropped off again, Buckler addressed her. "Now Mrs. Foss. Tell your story if you please, slowly and softly."

"'Tis all my fault, sir, for going to sweep the terrace and not seeing Mrs. Penelope arrive. I'd no notion she'd already been and gone till I found the child in the nursery with Bet. But 'twas too late. I didn't give her Mr. Chase's message."

Buckler forced himself to concentrate. "What was the message?"

"Why, I was to tell her not to go near St. Thomas's Hospital but to stay safe with us at the Society till Mr. Chase could square up to that villain and get him locked up."

"Villain?"

She looked at him as if he were little better than an imbecile. "That's what I've been trying to tell you, sir. Mr. Chase settled it that the surgeon Mr. Strap was the one as did It. You know. I told Mrs. Pen just yesterday to be careful since the Lord knew it could've been anyone."

Shifting Sarah's weight so the child could nestle more comfortably, she added, "I had to do something, sir. I took the children and headed to Bow Street, but Mr. Chase hadn't been there. They sent me off. Then I remembered you, sir. When I saw you at the trial, Mrs. Penelope told me as you lived at the Temple. I asked about a bit, and someone told me where to go, thank God."

"One moment. Let me think." Glancing over at his notoriously unreliable clock, Buckler saw that it reported the hour as a few minutes lacking three o'clock. He tried to approximate the true time. "What's the hour, Bob?"

Bob had retreated to his writing table, ostensibly to continue his work, but Buckler wasn't fooled. Pulling his own watch out of his pocket, the clerk replied, "Nigh on four, sir. By the time you arrive, the hospital gates may well be shut for the night, but no doubt you can find your way in."

"I had better go straight to Bow Street. Surely Chase will have returned, and I believe I may make the authorities sit up and listen in any case."

"No! We'll all go together. I got a plan."

"We cannot go anywhere with three children in tow, Mrs. Foss. Besides, 'twouldn't be safe."

Her voice rose again. "There's no time to go to Bow Street, sir. Mrs. Penelope told Bet she had some other errands, so I don't know what time she arrived at the hospital. She might've been there for hours."

"I shall go straight there to fetch her then. You remain here with Bob." Buckler got to his feet and looked around for his overcoat. The room didn't look any tidier than usual, even though the clerk had had plenty of time on his hands. The stack of old briefs on Bob's desk was just the same, and some of Buckler's clothing was still strewn across the furniture. He spotted his coat and went toward it.

"Begging your pardon, sir," said Maggie. "You best consider. That Strap's a slick devil. He'll think up a lie sure as sure, and there'd be nothing you could do. Better to go in quiet like and spy out the ground. That's why you need me and the children."

Buckler stopped buttoning his coat and stared at her, nonplused. "A man, a woman, and three children are hardly inconspicuous."

"That's just it, sir." She knelt down and began throwing outdoor clothing on Sarah and the boy. "It's St. Thomas's Day. We'll make out we're a poor family Thomassing for Christmas goodenings."

"That might answer," said Bob. "The hospital, being named for the saint and all, would hardly like to turn away hungry folk."

Maggie smiled briefly. "I mean no discourtesy, sir, when I say no one would question *you*."

Buckler rubbed at his unshaven face, conceding she had a point. After all, he could not go charging into a well-gated enclosure as would Bow Street. He would use her idea to gain access, then find a safe spot to leave Maggie and the children. He hadn't time to devise a better alternative.

"Very well. Bob, I want you to locate Mr. Thorogood. If anyone may goad Bow Street into action, he will."

Buckler strode toward his bedchamber. "I shall get my purse, Mrs. Foss, and we'll be off. No doubt your jarvey will require payment in advance."

Chapter Twenty-two

Chase fixed his eyes on the ormolu and bronze clock ticking industriously on the mantel. Squirming in his uncomfortable low-backed chair, he drummed his fingers on a side table in conscious opposition to the clock's rhythm. On the way in he had stopped to speak to a few of the servants, including the Tyrone family coachman, and now was ready for the older son of the house. More than ready.

No fire burned in the small sitting room, but it would have felt cold anyway with its austere, yet somehow ostentatious furnishings in the Egyptian mode, augmented with a selection of French accessories. The war ground on, but the latest in fashion could always be had. The rich did not suffer. It made him uncomfortable.

He shifted his gaze to the window through which he glimpsed the garden, barren and shadowed in the ebbing light. He had hoped to get to Bow Street by now, and glancing at the clock again, he felt the pull of urgency. Damn his late start. He'd spent all night in his chair by the fire, drastically oversleeping in his exhaustion.

Chase was not sure what to make of last night's ghostly visitations. He'd been half asleep, dazed with brandy. Still, he could not recall ever before having such vivid, disturbing dreams. While with one part of his mind he was ready to dismiss his "revelation," another part knew he had found Constance Tyrone's killer. Besides, he had reviewed every aspect of the crime in the light of his new understanding, a process that only strengthened his conviction of having discovered the truth.

He had hurried to St. Catherine's to speak with Elizabeth Minton and the other women, relieved to leave a warning with Maggie when informed of Penelope Wolfe's plan to visit St. Thomas's hospital. Penelope was entirely too easy to read. If Strap suspected her of edging too close to his secret, God only knew what he might do to protect himself. Then Chase had spent several frustrating hours seeking George Kite, managing at last to obtain tacit confirmation of Strap's employment of the resurrection men in the Greenwich theft of Ursula's body.

However, Chase could not disregard his other responsibilities for long; today, in fact, he was supposed to have attended the Coroner's inquest for the latest Ratcliffe victims. Instead he was here to discover whether Bertram Tyrone had been more than just Strap's dupe.

His thoughts were interrupted by the appearance of Bertram Tyrone himself, who strolled in looking annoyingly confident and well rested. Chase rose to greet him.

"I wasn't sure what to make of your message, Mr. Chase," Bertram said. "Nor of this. Where did you get it?" He dangled Constance's gold cross by its chain.

"I regret not having returned it sooner, sir."

Some indecipherable emotion flickered in Tyrone's eyes; then he smiled, an empty twist of the lips. "We are grateful to have my sister's property restored. Was it found among the Irishman's effects?"

"No, sir." Chase watched him closely. "A woman gave it to Kevin Donovan's lawyers."

Brushing past, Bertram went to an ebony table embellished with winged sphinxes whereon he let the necklace drop. He picked up a decanter of burgundy, splashed some wine in a glass, and immediately quaffed it.

"Where did this woman obtain the necklace?" The glass trembled slightly in his hands. "Was the creature in league with Donovan?"

"No, Mr. Tyrone. She has never met the man."

"Look, it was my understanding that the inquiry had been closed after the Irishman's suicide. My family has suffered enough, Mr. Chase. We certainly do not need Bow Street stirring up a hornet's nest to no purpose. If you have learned something further, let's have it."

"Donovan did not murder your sister, sir."

Tyrone refilled his glass, swirling the wine for a moment. "What possible grounds do you have for that belief?"

"If you would be seated, sir, I will, of course, inform you. You might thereby take your refreshment in more comfort."

Chase gave a bland smile as a flush tinged Bertram's cheeks. The younger man tossed some wine in a goblet and handed it over. Perching on the sofa, he waved Chase to a seat opposite.

Chase took a grateful sip. "By the by, sir, I quite envy you. The bachelor life of a man of substance must be so delightfully unencumbered. You and your crony Mr. Strap contrive, no doubt, to pass the time with pleasure and profit."

Bertram stared at him. "How dare you. I demand to know what you mean to imply, sir."

"Strap is a particular friend of yours, is he not? You even had hopes he would become your brother. 'Tis common knowledge among your servants that you'd been trying to persuade your father to countenance the marriage for years."

"Of what account is this now?" Tyrone demanded.

Chase went on inexorably. "A murder is made up of any number of gossamer strands woven together rather like a spider's web. Insignificant though the single threads may seem, they all lead inward to the heart in which all things are revealed—just as the spokes of the wheel point to its hub."

"You speak in riddles."

"One of the threads in this inquiry is your friendship with Reginald Strap, which, I believe, contributed in some part to your sister's death. What I don't know is whether or not you too are a vicious killer."

"Do you accuse me?" Bertram's face contorted in a rage that was more like agony.

"You were at the Society on that last afternoon, sir. If you recall the trial, Donovan's counsel went to great pains to suggest that your sister was accosted rather earlier than thought and hidden on the church grounds. Had Mr. Buckler been able to present his case, a witness would have come forth to testify to that effect."

"You cannot think that I...I did stop to see Constance that day, but she wasn't there, I swear it." His gaze didn't waver. "And Strap could not be so vile. It is true, we spoke of an... arrangement, but he cared for Constance. My God, he wanted to marry her."

"What arrangement, Tyrone?"

A choked sob burst from the other man and, for a minute or two, he couldn't respond. Chase opened his mouth to push further, but shut it again when Bertram jerked to his feet and stumbled to the decanter. After pouring the wine, he remained by the table.

"Constance had grown ever more unpredictable, almost zealous about her charitable work," Bertram said. "I had come to believe that marriage would be the best solution for her, and Strap, well, he was still interested. Oh, I wasn't blind to the advantages on his side: looking high indeed for a mere surgeon. Yet had they wed, I might have counted on him to safeguard her interests."

Chase eyed him shrewdly. "And to keep Miss Tyrone in line. So what did you do, apply the screws to your sister?"

"Nothing like that. I merely told Strap I should speak to my father, and were the outcome favorable, I might attempt to persuade Constance. They shared an interest in philanthropy, you know. I am certain he meant to afford her reasonable latitude, but he would not have allowed her to exhaust herself."

"So your concern was for your sister's welfare, sir? Though I don't doubt that once Strap had control of her fortune, he'd have made it worth your while, perhaps by guaranteeing you a generous allowance to remove your gambling debts and free you of an unwanted betrothal?"

"Strap could not be so vile," he repeated in a broken voice. "How attack Constance in broad daylight? What possible motive could he have?"

Chase suppressed an unwelcome twinge of pity. "The motive is linked to at least two suspicious cases of the pox among the St. Catherine women. In both instances there is some question as to how the contagion was effected. I can only assume these women were the victims of some sort of medical wrongdoing.

"As for how the murder was accomplished: there were no witnesses. The doorkeeper, Winnie, was ill that day, and all the other women were at work in the adjacent house. After your sister returned from her errand, she repaired to her study, where Strap must have surprised her before she had even removed her cloak, though she did change her muddy footwear.

"She may have fled outside, but not far because her slippers weren't soiled. She very likely just reached the terrace. In any event, he throttled her and left her for dead in the garden shed.

"Then his luck ran out, for, as I've just learned this day, your coachman observed him near where Miss Tyrone was secreted. Were she discovered there, Strap would have been under immediate suspicion. Still, he thought of a clever dodge: the employment of two resurrection men who were to dispose of the body late that night. These men, however, were frightened off when the 'corpse' suddenly twitched." Chase nodded as Tyrone sat forward, his eyes stark pools of horror.

"Yes, you might well be shocked, sir. Your sister was alive. She had been gravely injured in the original attack, but for all that she might have survived had those ruffians not dropped her in the street to be smashed by a passing carriage."

"Chase, I swear I had no hand in her death. You must believe me. You can prove this business about Strap?"

"To my satisfaction but not, I fear, to anyone else's."

"The grave robbers?"

"I believe the surgeon sent one to his eternal reward, seeking to wrap up the matter cleanly. The other claims ignorance of the man who employed them."

"Strap has influential friends, Mr. Chase. He is well respected and clever. You won't catch him out." Tyrone got to his feet.

Chase stood too. "If you believe me, sir, perhaps together we may hit upon a way to bring guilt home to the villain."

"Villain?" said a soft voice. Chase glanced up in surprise to see a slight figure garbed in a dressing gown standing in the open doorway. Receiving no answer to his question, Ambrose Tyrone drifted across the room to join them.

"Good day, sir," said Chase, wondering what the devil more he ought to say. Surely the boy's older brother was the proper person to enlighten him. It seemed to Chase that the truth was the lightest of the debts that must be paid were justice ever to be done to Constance Tyrone and all who mourned her truly. And, if he could help it, such payment would be forthcoming.

Bertram Tyrone stared at his feet as Ambrose reached out to take up the gold cross that lay on the table.

The boy turned to Chase, a pathetic eagerness in his tone. "You bring us news, I think."

"Mr. Tyrone?" said Chase.

At this, Bertram looked up. Even without candles in the lengthening shadows, his despair and self-contempt were plain to see.

※ ⅌

The coach tossed to one side, pitched drunkenly, then righted itself. Hunched against the cold, the jarvey flicked his whip and urged the horses on. He ignored Buckler's muttered curse. Praying they would not be overturned, Buckler cast a glance at the man's profile. Only one glittering eye and a heavy, lowered brow were visible above the scarf wound about his ears. One end of the scarf undulated in the wind.

Buckler clutched at the seat and pondered his situation. Choosing to ride on the box in order to clear his head, he had bundled Maggie and the children into the relative warmth of the interior and paid well above the usual fare in advance. But they raced headlong into darkness, armed only with a half-formed and outlandish scheme. While he knew he had to do something if Penelope were truly in danger, the conventional barrister in him warned that he was not a man of action. It would have been more prudent to approach the authorities.

Wheels rumbled on stone as the coach swept onto Blackfriars Bridge and slowed to merge with the early evening traffic. Buckler had instructed the jarvey to take this route rather than London Bridge, believing they could make faster time even though the other bridge terminated right by the hospital.

As they picked up speed again, Buckler thought of the Thames, an unseen blackness below, and felt his anxiety grow. He could hear Penelope's voice saying, "*After all, those boats down there hold flesh and blood men all going about their business, some happily. They are not Charon bearing souls to the land of the dead.*" And he found himself wondering if she really understood the wickedness of which flesh and blood men were capable. A ride with Charon might indeed be preferable.

He shook off reflection and concentrated instead on keeping his seat as furious gusts buffeted him and withdrew to gather strength for the next onslaught. Trying to judge if rain were imminent, he glanced at the sky, but the mist that had hovered on the horizon all afternoon now nestled lower to land. The lamps on either side of the bridge were a line of frail beacons staving off this night of December 21, the longest of the year. They would be of little use soon, he judged.

Crossing into Southwark, they wended their way to Borough High Street. No sooner had the hackney set them down near St. Thomas's than the driver took up his reins and disappeared into the fog. Buckler and his companions moved ghostlike down the desolate street, the children strangely quiet. Then as the hospital loomed, he raised his eyes to the tall iron gates. The carriage entrances were closed.

When Buckler pulled the bell rope at one of the pedestrian doors, the resultant chime sounded distant, yet it produced an old porter who hobbled up and pressed his face to the bars. He lifted his lantern to throw light on their faces.

"What do you want?"

Maggie stepped forward. "That's no way to treat honest poor out Thomassing on a bitter night."

"It's late. Honest people is gone. We're closed but for the accident gate round the side."

"Well, the hour don't make us any less poor," retorted Maggie. "Nor honest neither if that's what you're saying. My husband and children are tired and hungry."

Seemingly on cue, the baby began to cry, with Sarah and the little boy joining in.

The porter backed off a step. "Quiet them pups down, or you'll have the whole place in an uproar. Right, then. I'll take you through to the kitchen." He turned a lock, and the gate swung back. "Now stay with me and don't let those children wander off, or you'll be the worse for it."

They walked in, the gate clanging shut behind them. Buckler, Maggie, and the children followed the porter's bobbing lantern through an arcade with benches at intervals. They moved toward the cross building where a frontispiece was set over a wide opening. At the top under the pediment was mounted a clock, its face lost in shadows. In the niches below stood the dim figure of Edward VI overlooking other statues of afflicted patients.

As they swept by several wards, Buckler noticed that every other window was bricked in. Penelope could be anywhere, and how was he to find her? He would have to inquire for Strap without making the porter suspicious.

Casually, he said, "A friend of mine was once saved from a gangrene by one of your surgeons here. A Mr. Reginald Strap. Do you know him?"

"'Course I do," growled the porter without turning around. "He's the stiff-rumped one as physics the foul wards. Likes to fancy he's a cut above the rest."

"Oh? I imagine he has a consulting room? In this yard?"

"Naw. The foul wards is beyond the third court. Who'd want 'em near decent folk?"

Buckler exchanged a look with Maggie. "I must get away," he whispered as they approached the kitchen, which was off the passageway stretching under the frontispiece.

"Yes, sir." Forthwith, she doubled over and grasped at her stomach. "Oh my, oh my."

The porter spun around. "I told you to be quiet. What is it?"

"It's my belly," wailed Maggie. "I'm with child, sir, and I fear there be something wrong."

"Mama, mama," cried the little boy, and Sarah resumed her heartrending sobs.

"Help her," said Buckler. He gave Maggie an admiring look.

"What'll I do?" said the porter nervously.

"This is a hospital, man. Fetch a doctor!"

As the porter ran off in confusion, Buckler mouthed a thank you, patted Sarah on the head, and slipped down the steps into the next court.

Buckler wished he knew more about the hospital's layout. That it was built around a series of courtyards reminded him of the Temple, so the place felt eerily familiar. By the light of lamps in sconces, he could see figures milling about. The tower of St. Thomas's church rose to his right, and beside it he could make out a gate, probably the accident entrance which the porter had mentioned. He strode down the colonnade.

No one challenged him as he made his way to an irregularly shaped yard off the third quadrangle. Overpowering odors of must, dirt, and sickness buffeted him. The pox sufferers would be housed nearby.

Removing his overcoat, he folded it under his arm, for if he encountered someone, he hoped to appear at least somewhat respectable. He walked on, but the chill was deadening.

When a ward opened up in front of him, Buckler stepped over the threshold. Obtaining information here might prove to be less risky than confronting hospital workers, he decided.

Perhaps one of the patients had seen Penelope or would know where to find Reginald Strap. He looked around.

Lining the walls were wooden trough-shaped bedsteads, occupied by forms covered in sacking. A single lamp on a bare wooden trestle table provided the only light, a meager fire at one side of the room the only heat.

He looked up at the large plaque affixed to the wall in front of him. It read:

THE INTEREST OF THE POOR AND THEIR DUTY
ARE THE SAME
FOR
CLEANLINESS GIVES COMFORT;
SOBRIETY BRINGS HEALTH;
INDUSTRY YIELDS PLENTY;
HONESTY MAKES FRIENDS:
RELIGION PROCURES PEACE OF MIND,
CONSOLATION UNDER AFFLICTION,
THE PROSPECT OF GOD'S BLESSING, THROUGH CHRIST,
IN THIS LIFE, AND THE ASSURANCE OF
ENDLESS HAPPINESS AND GLORY
IN THE LIFE TO COME.

Suddenly, he heard a faint mewling like the sound a kitten makes when hungry, and he turned to see one of the patients motioning at him. Buckler drew near, leaning over the bench at the end of the bed.

Though the man's chin and sunken cheeks looked human enough, his nose was eaten away to a gaping cavity, his swollen lips contorted in a toothless grimace. The flesh of his face and arms was pitted with deep scars. My God, thought Buckler, recoiling instinctively.

The creature had noted the involuntary movement. "I know you," he croaked. Something like a chuckle escaped his throat.

Wanting to flee, Buckler nonetheless advanced another step. He heard rustles from the other patients as they shifted in their straw, but no one appeared to be paying any attention.

"You're the one as brought me the sweets and the pint of ale that time. I never forgot."

"You've mistaken me for someone else, I fear."

The sick man struggled to one elbow, and Buckler saw that he was young, no more than thirty-five. Sweat-streaked, filthy hair tumbled across his unlined brow. "He looked like you," he said. "You got anything for me? A bit of tobacco?"

"No, I am sorry."

The black eyes darted to Buckler's. "I used to walk the earth like a real man, you know. Ethan Ash's my name."

"I seek Mr. Strap, the surgeon. It is most urgent I locate him."

"Mr. Strap has a consulting room down the corridor. I was there once myself. Or he'd be in the operating theatre. But not now. Come back tomorrow." He enunciated carefully, turning each word over in his mouth.

"If Strap were working late, where would he be?" Holding Ash's gaze, Buckler struggled to prevent his horror from showing.

"Perhaps in the dead-house, carving up some poor cull like them surgeons always do. Only by the time it's my turn, there won't be much left." The mewling noise sounded again, and Buckler realized it was the man's breath whistling through his cavernous nostrils.

"I appreciate your help, sir," Buckler told him, his tone respectful. He began to back away.

Ash did not reply, so Buckler thanked him again and left. With relief, he re-entered the courtyard and stood for a moment to reorient himself. Ash had said that Strap's consulting room was close by. But before Buckler could move, a swarm of porters all carrying lanterns hurried by.

Buckler stopped a man as he passed. "What's all the excitement?" he asked officiously.

"A crazy woman is loose, sir. She's run to ground in the operating theatre."

Chapter Twenty-three

Mr. Strap gave a charming smile. "I am sorry I was delayed, ma'am, but I see you've been entertaining yourself."

"Yes, I have. Your specimens are…fascinating. I hope you don't mind my having a look around whilst I waited." Penelope turned away from the shelves and took a few steps toward the door. Her imagination might be playing tricks, but if the misshapen hand had once belonged to George Kite's accomplice Crow, she did not want the surgeon to notice her interest.

Strap, however, mistook her intention and offered his arm, his lips lifting in another chillingly intimate smile. "Not at all, Mrs. Wolfe. Your interest is gratifying. May I point out a few items of note?"

She took his arm, feeling its solid warmth beneath the elegant jacket. He had removed his blood-spattered frock coat and scrubbed his hands clean. They were well-molded hands, strong with shapely fingers and close-clipped nails. Penelope shivered.

"You see, ma'am," he said as he guided her down the room, "these specimens are essential, the life's blood of a surgeon's inquiries." He pointed at a hyena's head, carefully labeled and preserved in its jar. "Studies in comparative anatomy may reveal great truths of human physiology. And, of course, the unusual or the deformed must always tempt us, though it is, in actuality, the study of the whole and healthy that lays bare the workings of disease."

He allowed a glimmer of humor to surface. "A fact which doesn't stop us surgeons from competing over unique specimens, paying dearly for the privilege of owning them. You know, John Hunter once gave five hundred pounds for the corpse of an eight-foot Irish giant and boiled away the flesh in order to extract the skeleton."

Penelope lowered her eyes. Were she fortunate, he would attribute any show of nerves on her part to feminine sensibility. He mustn't discover what she suspected, even though it was difficult to see how she could be endangered in so public a place as a hospital.

"Our endeavors are often not understood by the public, I'm afraid," he continued after a moment. "At times we face quite hostile resistance. Yet if medical science is ever to relieve the varied ills that beset mankind, such inquiries are vital."

"I make no doubt you and your colleagues render assistance to a multitude of unfortunates, sir." She slowed, trying unobtrusively to retract her arm. Strap allowed her grip to fall, but took a step closer.

"That is my fondest wish," he murmured, his gaze skimming over her face.

She wrenched her arm away under pretense of examining the timepiece pinned to her dress. "The hour advances, and I must think of returning home. It has been a most stimulating afternoon." To her own ears her voice sounded strange, high-pitched and artificial.

Strap's gaze assessed her. "But you have yet to achieve your purpose in coming here, ma'am. Would you not care to discuss Fiona's treatment and view the wards? I think a course of Van Swieten's liquor would do her the most good. Perhaps combined with a regimen of baths and enemas to help purge the system of impurities."

Without waiting for a response, he strolled toward the connecting door, and Penelope relaxed a little. If she could get him out into the wards, all would be well. She even thought she could keep up her pretense of ignorance with other people around. It was only that the flirtatious glint in his eyes unnerved her so much she was sure her dread would seep out and spread over her body like a rash. In that moment, she devoutly wished she had agreed to Jeremy's proposition. Very likely she never would have come here today at all. There wouldn't have been time what with all the necessary arrangements…

His voice intruded. "Why Mrs. Wolfe, viewing my collection must have distressed you. Come sit down in my office, and I shall bring you a glass of cordial."

"No, I had much better go now, sir. Thank you again for a most informative experience."

He frowned. "I cannot deem that wise, ma'am. What if you were to swoon in the street? You ought to rest for a few minutes."

After leading her to a small sofa, he picked up a bottle of cordial sitting on a side table and poured a generous splash. Sipping the drink he brought her, Penelope took a determined grip on herself. At least holding the glass gave her something to do, and the brandy helped. She glanced up, daring one look into Strap's eyes to see if he suspected her, but saw only solicitous concern.

"Thank you, sir. I do believe the suffering of that poor creature in the operating theatre discomposed me more than I had any notion."

Unfortunately, this momentary rally of her courage ceased abruptly when he sat down next to her and removed the glass from her hold. Taking her hands, he smoothed his palms over her gloveless skin and lifted her fingers to plant a gentle kiss on the inside of one wrist. "Ah, Mrs. Wolfe. I do hope you are feeling more the thing."

Penelope pulled away. "I am fine, sir, though some air would be welcome."

"No hurry, ma'am. It is natural that the coarse reality of surgery should disturb you. And I compound the offense with a demonstration of all my beauties. You must forgive me."

"You misunderstand, sir. I found your specimens most intriguing. As for the operating theatre, I admit I did not relish the blood. Yet, truthfully, it was more the spectacle that was so repugnant. It did not seem as if that unfortunate woman was deemed worthy of anyone's compassion."

His expression darkened. "I show my compassion for a patient by operating with all the skill and dispatch of which I am capable. What would you have, Mrs. Wolfe? Crying over her would hardly help and might possibly kill her were I to make an error."

Penelope watched him. She'd retrench in a hurry if she had any sense and get out of this room somehow. But if she didn't catch a glimpse of what lay behind his façade, she might never have another opportunity. After a moment, she spoke. "I cannot imagine you capable of error, Mr. Strap, for I am certain your methods are quite...deliberate."

The telltale tightening at his jaw was so faint she almost missed it. As it was, that and an instinct screaming too loudly to be ignored were enough to tell her her surmise had been correct: she faced Constance Tyrone's murderer. She must leave this place and get to Bow Street.

"I am hardly perfect, ma'am," he said into the silence. "What human being is? I make mistakes and live to regret them. But I can honestly say that to master the challenges of my profession is everything to me. I promise you young Fiona will receive the highest standard of care, that is if she can be persuaded to put herself in my hands."

The rage slicing through Penelope took her by surprise, and she glanced away quickly, afraid it would show. Picking up the cordial, she took one last sip and set the glass down with a snap. "I am quite restored now," she said, rising, "and must return home immediately. Perhaps you may show me the wards another day."

Strap got to his feet. "I confess I do not know what to make of you, Mrs. Wolfe. Did your experience in the operating theatre today give you such a disgust of surgeons that you are inclined to doubt our good faith? Or is it something else?"

Their gazes fused, and for a long moment Penelope was helpless to break away, aware that her fear and her knowledge were plainly revealed. Then her eyes flitted toward the door just beyond Strap's solid figure as she calculated whether she might step around him and how many paces might bring her to freedom.

He studied her, unmoving. "You appear agitated. I must insist you sit down and finish your refreshment. It will do you good."

He took a step closer, and Penelope picked up the glass as if to comply. But she found herself doing something she could never afterward understand. It would have made perfect sense to toss the cordial in his eyes and run.

Instead, she raised the glass and threw it across the room. Spraying its sticky contents all over the desk, it crashed against the wall and fell in fragments to the dragon carpet. With Strap's attention diverted, Penelope darted around him, fumbled at the door, and was out before he could react. She fled down the corridor, retracing her earlier steps. Surely there would be people about in one of the main quadrangles.

Behind her, Strap's footsteps pounded in pursuit, and she had to force herself not to look around. All she need do was find someone, anyone, nurse, patient, or visitor, and she would be safe.

Turning into the large quadrangle, Penelope paused for an instant to get her bearings. She must proceed back through this and the middle yard before reaching the court by which she'd entered. But then she recalled the porter's warning that the front gates would be locked by four o'clock.

The surgeon was almost upon her. With no time to do anything else, she crouched down by a white stone pilaster, praying the gloom would hide her.

To her profound relief, a nurse came out of one of the wards and moved toward the statue in the center of the court. She carried a large basin in her brawny arms; a bunch of keys clanked at her waist.

Penelope was about to emerge from her hiding place when Strap hailed the nurse. "Hi, you there, a pox-ridden lunatic has escaped the foul ward. Inform the porters, and make sure the accident gate is secured. That should be her only means of egress. I believe I can restrain her myself, but assistance may be required."

"Yes, sir." The nurse hurried off to do his bidding.

As Strap's keen eyes began to sweep the shadows, Penelope sucked in air and slouched over. She was so frightened that her brain repeated the same thoughts over and over in an endless circle of panic. She lifted her head, daring a peek. It was a mistake. It seemed Strap looked right at her, his cold stare unerringly seeking out her shrinking figure. Penelope froze, but released her breath when he moved away.

Then she was on her feet, poised to run. Thankfully, her mind had cleared, terror subsiding to a hard lump in her gut. She recalled passing St. Thomas's church as well as the chapel in the adjoining court. Perhaps the pastor or hospital chaplain would help her.

"Come out, Mrs. Wolfe," came Strap's amused voice. "I thought I glimpsed you a moment ago, and I see I was right. Do be reasonable."

Penelope ran pell-mell across the paving stones, bruising her feet in her thin-soled boots. She dashed through the colonnaded passageway and gazed about wildly. To her left was the church, the accident gate at its side, to her right, the chapel. But there were men clustered about the gate, blocking her access, and others approached from the direction of the chapel. No one had noticed her yet.

Moving forward more slowly, she tried not to attract attention. She made it across the courtyard before the shouts erupted.

"Mr. Strap, Mr. Strap. She's there," someone said.

"Yes, I see." Strap's voice sounded quite close, but Penelope did not wait to find out, slipping ghostlike toward the portico between the cross buildings.

But suddenly she knew she wouldn't make it that far, for the surgeon was nearly at her shoulder, his arm reaching out to seize her. She could hear his labored breathing. Just ahead beckoned a stairwell: her only choice. She ducked inside.

With Strap at her heels, she flung herself up the stairs. Gaining the landing at the top, she remembered she had come this way earlier. Surgery was just through the door, with the herb garret beyond. And the church was below. Perhaps she might hide in the operating theatre, then find her way out through the church once the hue and cry died down.

Slipping through the door, she confronted a wall of blackness, stumbled forward, and tripped over a low table. Several objects clattered down with her. Penelope groped with her fingers until they closed around sharp steel. A surgeon's knife. Pain lanced through her hand. With a muffled exclamation, she retracted her fingers only to reach out again more cautiously. This time she grasped the handle.

At her back Strap said, "She's gone in the theatre. Not to worry. Two of you may ascertain that the ward entrance is locked. The rest remain here. Give me that flambeau, will you? I shall go in alone and speak to her. Facing you chaps might scare her out of the few wits she still possesses."

She heard laughter. Another voice broke in. "Watch yourself, Mr. Strap. She may be vicious."

Fleeing through the entrance to the standings, Penelope clambered to the top, then crouched down. Strap entered and shut the door, his long shadow shooting across the wall. Face encircled by torchlight, he went to the lamp on a table and lit it. "You are utterly contained here, Mrs. Wolfe. I've seen to it we shall not be disturbed."

Penelope squeezed her body against the wooden planking and clenched her jaw to prevent her teeth from chattering. The chill air was foul with the unwholesome odor of sawdust and the sweeter scent of old blood.

He continued methodically to another lamp which sat by the wash basin and ewer. Soon he would be bound to catch sight of her, but he paused in the middle of the floor, seeming in no haste to begin his search in earnest. Instead he began to speak in ringing tones.

"Syphilis withers many a life, ma'am. Think of the youth whose one blithe foray into dissipation saddles him with a potentially incurable illness. One that may prevent his seeking an honorable marriage lest he infect his wife and unborn children. A disease that may seem to be vanquished only to break out anew with even more devastating effects.

"You did not accept my offer of a tour, Mrs. Wolfe. If you had, you would have seen what ruin *morbus gallicus* makes of a sound body: ulcers, rotting bones, even at times a decay of the brain leading in the end to madness."

Strap came closer to peer upward. "And what may we offer these sufferers other than the hazardous and worthless 'cures' of innumerable charlatans and the pious moralizing of priests? Of what use is it to condemn a man for his debauchery, telling him his disease is sent as a curse from God? For if he be healed, he will only seek out the means to his destruction yet again."

He reached over and extinguished his flambeau, laying it aside. Speaking more quietly, he said, "Constance assigned far too much importance to the puny claims of the individual. Actually, science requires a breadth of vision that recognizes that humanity's good lies in the pursuit of knowledge. Antiquated notions of morality only obscure our clearer reason—they are a luxury we can ill afford. A pity she could not understand."

Altering his position, he looked directly at her. "But perhaps, after all, this particular weakness is inborn in the female of the species."

As though released from a trance, Penelope scrambled to her feet and backed along the standings, the knife thrust out challengingly.

"I am glad you've come into the light," he called, "for indeed there is nowhere left to hide."

"For either of us. Bow Street is at your gate prepared to charge you with the murder of Constance Tyrone."

"You are overly generous in your estimations, Mrs. Wolfe. The authorities are bound by convention, and who among them has the imagination, the daring, to conceive of my purpose? What evidence could they possess?"

"That evidence exists, sir. You admitted you are human, and humans make errors. Perhaps you have not taken that fact sufficiently into account."

"Stop brandishing the knife so absurdly and come down, Mrs. Wolfe." As Strap leaned his elbows on the railing at the front of the standings, the light burnished his fair hair. "'Twould be child's play to take it from you, but you might prefer the dignity of your own descent."

"John Chase of Bow Street has learned of the grave robber called Crow you employed to dispose of Constance Tyrone's body. It would also be profitable for Mr. Chase to discover more of that loathsome hand I observed in your laboratory. This hand, I make no doubt, you cleaved from Crow's corpse after you had destroyed him."

Strap laughed softly. "What next will your fancy suggest, ma'am? I suppose I couldn't resist the…er, appeal of this specimen? Any murderer worth his salt finds it necessary to come away with a trophy? Nonsense, my dear. Will you step down now, or shall I call for assistance? You will never hold off three men rushing you."

"If I do, what then?"

His eyes gleamed. "Ah, the nub of the matter. As much as I enjoy your company, Mrs. Wolfe, I cannot allow you to spout this sort of nonsense. My professional reputation is at stake, you see. Yet if you are willing to see reason, I believe we can resolve matters to our mutual satisfaction."

"I suspect your 'resolution' involves either imminent harm to my person, possibly with this very knife, or restraint in the foul ward under the guise that I am deranged. I heard you say as much to your minions."

"I am hardly a butcher, madam. I have no need of methods so crude. Why should we not talk further? Perhaps you may understand me better. Come down." He held out his hand and smiled, a wry, winning smile that softened the austere cut of his nose and brow.

She stayed where she was, saying firmly, "If you wish to converse, you may begin by explaining what medical advantage you sought from the barbarous betrayal of those who trusted you."

Surprise flared in his eyes. "I suppose there can be no objection to your knowing the whole, clever girl. And you must tell me more of this John Chase." He indicated the trickle of blood dripping from her hand. "But first you must allow me to bind your finger for you."

When Penelope did not respond, Strap climbed up to the second row. Strangely unconcerned, he adopted the pedantic tone he had used earlier. "Have you been vaccinated against the smallpox, Mrs. Wolfe? I assure you the time is not far off when every person on these islands will be, this in spite of certain foolish and shortsighted attempts to discredit the practice. And the ultimate victory over this blight will be due to one man who dared attempt something new.

"Mr. Jenner has proved that a related, less virulent form of disease may offer protection against the more dangerous one, and he was fortunate to have the illustration ready to hand. I speak of cowpox, which Jenner had observed in the milkmaids, and, of course, it turns out he was correct: those inoculated with the cowpox do not contract smallpox.

"My own theory is similar. In the case of syphilis, I thought first of gonorrhea. But gonorrhea provides no demonstrable immunity to the pox. I tend to concur with recent speculation amongst some of my Edinburgh colleagues that the two may be quite distinct conditions."

He stole a glance at her as if to make sure she followed him. Then his measured voice continued. "So you see my difficulty, Mrs. Wolfe. How was I to find a less virulent form of syphilis that would serve as an inoculant? I decided to create one by introducing the disease to an animal, thereby changing the poison's character. Thus, by passing the effluent through many generations of rabbits, I eventually produced what I believed was weakened venereal matter.

"The next step was to test its efficacy by first inoculating a subject with my modified virus, later following up with an inoculation of live syphilitic matter to see if protection had been achieved. I needed an arena for these experiments, and you must see the aptness of the St. Catherine Society? First and foremost, the women are supposed to be chaste, though in the case of Fiona I clearly misjudged."

Indignation was too weak a word for the emotion welling up in Penelope's throat until the desire to scream at Strap nearly overmastered her. For an instant, she experienced the terrifyingly real sensation of slashing her knife across that smooth, handsome face.

Feeling sick, she said, "'Tis clear your little experiment failed miserably, for Fiona is very ill indeed thanks to you." Then as another thought occurred to her, she gasped, "My God, how many of the women did you deceive? You did vaccinate the rest for smallpox?"

"Oh yes, all but three. Fiona, you know of. Also a female called Ursula who left London unfortunately and later died of influenza. And old Winnie. I thought it might be instructive to observe the progress of the disease in a person of advanced years even if my trial failed."

He added earnestly, "I had every intention of treating all three once my work was complete. Consider, Mrs. Wolfe. Can you maintain I was not justified? Think what it would mean, the suffering which could be alleviated."

"You murdered Constance to protect your secret. She discovered your infamy and threatened to expose you. Oh, how she must have reproached herself, for she it was who had persuaded the women to submit to your care."

His mouth hardened in distaste. "I easily refuted her protests. She became irrational, maddened almost."

"I believe it was she who confounded your infamous reasoning. You were maddened, Mr. Strap, for only a madman attacks a woman in daylight when anyone might have seen. Stay back, or I swear I shall use this knife."

Instead Strap took a careful step up, pausing to get his balance. "Perhaps you will, Mrs. Wolfe, perhaps not. I shall have to take my chances as we are running out of time."

"Stay back," she cried, gathering up her dress. She clasped the knife hilt in front of her heart. A swift sidelong glance told her that a panicked jump over the railing might result in a broken leg, putting her entirely at Strap's mercy. She braced herself.

For an instant as neither moved, there was time for a prayer to form in Penelope's mind. Had Constance too cried out in her extremity? *St. Catherine, I have need of you.*

From the lobby came the sound of a scuffle, a chorus of shouts. She tried to keep her gaze fixed on the surgeon, but when the doors burst open, she couldn't stop herself. Her eyes shifted. She caught a blur of motion as Strap sprang.

Chapter Twenty-four

Chase pushed his way through the ever-present crowd at Bow Street police office. Even at the dinner hour, the proceedings had drawn an audience as clamorous as that of Covent Garden theatre only steps away. In a way, what happened here was as scripted as any drama. Malefactors secured and brought before the weighty force of justice, every detail of their misdeeds exhibited before eager spectators.

It would be hours, Chase thought, before he could get a word with the weary magistrate, now questioning a gentleman and his wife whose carriage had been robbed. Though white and shaken, the pair confronted the bench accusingly, as if the safety of His Majesty's highways was Bow Street's sole responsibility. An officer of the Horse Patrol stood by attempting to tell his version of events.

Watching this scene unfold, Chase felt a weariness that had little to do with his gnawing hunger or the frenetic pace he'd set all day. The sparring match with Bertram Tyrone had been invigorating, yet had provided no lasting triumph. Despite Tyrone's obvious anguish, he could resume his easy pleasures—even without Reginald Strap—and no doubt a sizable inheritance would serve as a powerful palliative for remorse. Now Chase must somehow convince the magistrate to release him from the Ratcliffe murders, which had all London in an uproar, and reassign him to a "solved" crime everyone wanted to forget.

Just then unmistakable bass tones thundered over the din. "Heed my warning, sir! Else you will answer for the well being of my friends."

Peering into a far corner of the court, Chase spotted Ezekiel Thorogood, who loomed over the magistrate's clerk like a wrathful deity about to loose his ball of fire. The clerk, his eyes glazed over, stared stolidly ahead, all but frozen in the stance common to beleaguered public servants.

"What the devil," muttered Chase, moving quickly toward them.

Heads swiveled as Thorogood boomed again, "I tell you, there is no time to lose. Cease your foolish prattle and do something before I inform your superiors precisely what I think of your so-called procedures. Blasted arrogance!"

The clerk, whose name was James Winkle, spun in relief as Chase approached. "What do you know of this?"

Thorogood said, "Chase, thank God. Penelope went to call upon Reginald Strap at St. Thomas's hospital today. She has not returned."

A foreboding seized Chase. He cursed fluently. "I left word that she was not to leave the Society."

"The message was never given. Maggie Foss failed to locate you, so she took little Sarah and her own children off to the Temple seeking Buckler's help." Thorogood nodded at a slight, ordinary-looking man at his side. "This is Mr. Buckler's clerk, Bob Arney."

"They meant to pose as poor folk out Thomassing," Arney said.

"I'm afraid Buckler has acted impetuously," added Thorogood. "They've all gone after Mrs. Wolfe."

"The fool!" Chase snapped. "Of all the…to endanger a woman and children. What did he hope to accomplish?"

"What's this about?" demanded Winkle again.

Thorogood put out a hand. "Mr. Chase, we must hurry."

Chase looked from one to the other. He would have to go in search of Penelope Wolfe, of course. With a burst of excitement, he realized he was glad of an excuse to challenge Strap.

"Listen to their story and believe it," he said to Winkle. "Send for Farley and whoever else to follow me."

Not waiting for a response, he strode to the door. As he passed the bench, the magistrate gave him a squinty-eyed stare but didn't try to stop him. Chase emerged onto Bow Street, where the theatre crowd thronged the pavement and carriages clogged the street in both directions. He looked about for a hackney.

The journalist Fred Gander suddenly materialized at his elbow. "I was beginning to think you were on permanent loan to Shadwell, Chase. Anything new on the Ratcliffe murders? The city's in a frenzy, you know."

"I can't talk to you now, Gander." Chase's glance flew up and down the street, his eyes coming to a rest upon the patrol officer's horse tethered nearby. Coming to a decision, he untied the reins and leaped into the saddle. "Tell Thickery I had need of his horse."

Chase kept a tight curb on the animal as he guided it through the press of people. It was maddeningly slow going, and several times he was forced to ride up on the walkways to avoid traffic. One street seller swore at his back, pelting him with a piece of fruit. A cart with a broken wheel halted his progress for several agonizing minutes until a group of men shifted it out of the way. At last Chase made his way out of the press and headed toward London Bridge.

Increasing his speed, Chase tried to marshal his thoughts. This was not the time to wonder how Penelope might react if Strap frightened her. She was a brave person, apt to speak her mind, as he himself had discovered on more than one occasion. She was also incurably earnest, a trait that was as irritating as it was admirable. At times there was something almost cloying about her professed regard for other people and their feelings. Chase had a hard time accepting it as genuine, for she often struck him as little-girl spoiled, selfish in her own way—not subtle or sophisticated as a woman should be. Still the idea of something happening to her or, worse, to little Sarah...

Chase's mount tossed its head and pranced, sensing his mounting anxiety. Grasping the reins tighter, he headed over the bridge, forced to slacken his pace. When he reached the other side, he galloped up Borough High Street and around the corner to the hospital's side gate, where torches blazed, illuminating a swarm of shadowy figures. Chase was met with shouts.

"Who goes there?" a voice challenged.

"John Chase, Bow Street," he answered, sharp with urgency.

"Bow Street?" said a man, emerging into the light.

He was of stocky build, or appeared so in his ill-fitting gray coat and wide-brimmed hat. "Unlooked for help is the best kind, I'm thinking. I am Henry Badcock, Borough watchman. Right happy to see you, sir."

Chase dismounted. Handing the reins to a hovering boy, he addressed the man. "What has transpired here, Mr. Badcock?"

"Well, sir. I was making my rounds when I heard all the rumpus. I thought it might be accident victims as happens now and again. But I find the porters turning out a woman and she shrieking fit to curdle milk. Then I'm not here but two minutes when they say they got another female up to tricks, a lunatic what escaped the foul ward."

A woman yelled from the darkness. "You keep your hands off my children!"

"That be the woman they was turning out," said Badcock, shaking his head in disapproval. "I was just about to interrogate her when you rode up. Seems her husband is yet somewhere inside."

Chase sprinted toward Maggie, who sat on the ground by the gate, her arms embracing the baby, Sarah and a little boy huddling beside her. An old man hunched menacingly over them. She tried to rise, but another porter jostled her back. Chase shoved him aside, exhaling a deep breath of gratitude that the children appeared unharmed.

Maggie looked up, close to tears. "Mr. Chase, I didn't give Mrs. Penelope your message. Mr. Buckler is looking for her—"

Before Chase could answer, they were interrupted by the arrival of a young man, probably some sort of apprentice. The porters gathered round as he panted, "The madwoman is trapped in the operating theatre, and Mr. Strap has gone in to subdue her. He's not to be disturbed, mind." The youth started back.

"Better Strap than me," said Badcock to Chase.

Chase didn't answer. Going after the apprentice, he caught him by the shoulder and whirled him around. "Where's this theatre? Take me. Now!"

"What is it, Mr. Chase?" asked Badcock nervously.

"Now!" Chase gave the young man a little push. As they ran, he called back to the Watch. "Keep the woman and children here till I return."

From behind he heard Badcock spring his rattle, but it was too late to wait for help. Accompanied by the apprentice, Chase raced down an arcade into the next court, up some stairs, and through a set of doors.

The young man pointed. "That's the operating theatre!" he gasped, eyeing Chase fearfully. He stumbled off.

The group about the door looked up as Chase approached. He saw immediately that Edward Buckler was there, struggling in the grasp of two surgeon's assistants.

"Let me go, you devils," Buckler shouted.

One of them laughed. For men used to restraining patients, the physically ineffectual Buckler posed no threat. They had him bent to his knees with his arms twisted back.

"Let him go." Chase drew his pistol.

They swung astonished faces to him.

"John Chase, Bow Street. Step aside."

"She's in there, Chase. We must gain access." Buckler yanked his arms away and stepped to the door, but the larger of the men blocked his way.

"I've orders from the surgeon to let no one enter. That includes Bow Street." He folded his arms belligerently.

"I said step aside," bit out Chase. "There's no time to argue."

He smirked. "You won't shoot me for following orders."

"Orders be damned." Buckler lunged forward, catching the man's jaw with a crack that sent both reeling to the floor. Only the barrister rose, flexing his hand. The other fellow looked at him and backed away.

Chase gave Buckler a nod of surprised respect. "We shall have to kick open the door. Stand back."

When it burst ajar, they were met by a blaze of light. The surgeon stood in the observation standings, gazing up at Penelope, braced above, a knife clutched in her hand. As her startled, terrified eyes flew to the door, Strap launched himself. And before Chase could bring the pistol into play, the surgeon was upon her, wrenching the knife from her grip. She cried out.

Strap backed along the riser with the blade at Penelope's throat. "What is the meaning of this? You've no business here, gentlemen."

"Release Mrs. Wolfe, Strap." Chase took a step forward.

"Do you think to arrest me, sir?" Strap kept tight hold of Penelope. "You had better have sufficient grounds. Perhaps I should enlist Mr. Buckler in my defense?"

Buckler remained silent, fists clenched. As Chase advanced into the room, the surgeon began to descend from the standings, dragging Penelope. She went limp, but he seemed not to feel her weight.

"Put the weapon down if you value Mrs. Wolfe's life," said Strap. He skirted the room's perimeter, passed an overturned table, and edged toward the door.

Chase could see the shimmer of the knife as the surgeon moved in and out of lamp glow. He knew he must not allow them to leave. "Try it, and I shall take off your head."

For an instant Strap's face burned with pure, immutable resolution, then the shutters came down. "You cannot desire that Mrs. Wolfe should be hurt," he said.

Cutting left to ward him off, Chase scanned the surgeon's now impassive features, praying for a revealing flicker. What would Strap do were his exit blocked? He needed Penelope as hostage; it made no sense to harm her. But suddenly Chase remembered the livid finger bruises on Constance Tyrone's neck. Those were not the marks of cool, deliberate murder, but rather of ungovernable impulse.

Strap took one step and another, still with Penelope thrust in front of him. Always the cool steel embraced her throat. Chase avoided her eyes, afraid of the distraction, but he was acutely aware of her terror.

"Be reasonable, gentlemen," said Buckler, his voice cracking with strain. "We are all civilized men. Mr. Strap, release Mrs. Wolfe."

"No use, Buckler. I shall kill her if you try to stop me—and I assure you I am quick with a knife."

As Strap retreated another pace, his back to the open door, Buckler stood in danger of coming between Chase and his quarry.

"Buckler," Chase said warningly.

The barrister began to edge away, but then a cluster of onlookers appeared at the theatre's entrance.

"Here now, what's all this?" barked the watchman, Badcock.

"Get away from the door," said Strap calmly, not looking around.

"Mr. Strap," someone called.

Feeling himself go very cold, Chase cocked the pistol. No one had grasped the situation. Strap did not mean to escape at all. In another moment Penelope would be dead.

"Please withdraw, all of you," pleaded Buckler and waved an arm to stave them off.

Chase shut everything out, his vision narrowed, consumed utterly with Strap. His mind became still.

Glancing over his shoulder, the surgeon inadvertently loosened his grip. Penelope wrenched herself free. Buckler pushed her to one side, then lost his own balance and tumbled over her crouching figure to land on the floor. As Strap swung in their direction, the barrister managed to thrust Penelope behind him.

Chase saw his opening and squeezed the trigger.

He awoke to bells, clear and jubilant, ringing out their summons to Christmas services. Chase had slept deeply through the night. Morning brought the promise of pleasure to come and the sense that today at least one might lay aside all ugliness and darkness.

Chase dressed in his best suit and spent some time in front of the looking glass arranging his neckcloth. After shaving in icy water that stung his skin, he took himself downstairs to the kitchen.

"Mr. Chase!"

Leo and William jumped up from their chairs to cluster around him in the doorway, where he hesitated with his small stack of gifts. He didn't usually enter the kitchen, and never this early. He wondered if he intruded.

Mrs. Beeks was at the dry sink rolling crust for a pie. Raising her flustered gaze, she said, "Oh, Mr. Chase. I do beg your pardon. You find us at sixes and sevens this morning what with so many guests coming to dinner."

Chase smiled at her. "A happy Christmas to you, Mrs. Beeks. Please don't stop your work on my account."

"I wish you were to dine with us today, sir," said William. "Are you certain you won't?"

His mother fixed the boy with a steely look. "Mr. Chase has a prior engagement, William. You know that." She turned to Chase. "I'll see to your breakfast immediately, sir."

"Not to worry. I intend to share Leo and William's bread and milk this morning, if they will offer me table room."

The two boys nodded enthusiastically, Leo pulling Chase by the arm to the table and William fetching another bowl and spoon.

Mrs. Beeks smiled, yet her tone retained a bit of sharpness when she addressed her younger son. "William, fetch Mr. Chase a pot of fresh tea."

Chase sat, pushing one gift across the table to Leo and laying William's next to his place; then he set aside the small embroidered pillow stuffed with fragrant lavender he had purchased for Mrs. Beeks.

Wiping her hands, she came to lean over her son's shoulder. "Presents, Mr. Chase? You shouldn't have, but it's kind in you."

"And it's not even my birthday. This is capital, sir." Leo lifted up his tiny wooden model of a schooner, complete with two masts and sails, ratlines, and a bowsprit.

Over the boy's head, Chase met Mrs. Beeks' eyes and nodded reassuringly. Her smile had faded, but she laid her hand upon Leo's arm. "Very fine."

She went to take the teapot from William. "Go and examine your gift now, dear."

Needing no further encouragement, William opened the book on antiquities and was promptly lost to all of them.

"What about yours, Mama?" said Leo through a mouthful of bread and milk. He had set his schooner in front of his bowl after indignantly pushing aside his brother's propped book.

"Later, love, when I have a moment to myself. Now I want to give Mr. Chase a trifle I worked for him. I had meant to have it finished some time past." She crossed the room to retrieve a pile of wool which she presented to him a little shyly.

Touched and a little uncomfortable, Chase set down his tea cup to unfold a handsome woolen green scarf. "I shall have no trouble keeping warm with this."

She grinned, looking years younger. "Well, someone needed to do something about that disgraceful moth-eaten bit of nothing you wear. A man can't be doing his job when his neck is prey to every draft."

"I am grateful, Mrs. Beeks." Chase stood and bussed her cheek, bringing an even brighter glow to her skin.

Leo took the scarf and stretched it between his arms. "It's awfully long. I expect you can use it to truss a thief if you need to, sir. Or do you bear some sort of rope for that purpose?"

"Leo Beeks," warned his mother, "you'll spoil my scarf." She took it from him and folded it. "And don't be bothering Mr. Chase with questions at the breakfast table."

Sitting back down, Leo muttered, "How's a fellow to know what profession to take up if he ain't allowed to ask any questions?" He looked at Chase hopefully. "I've been thinking perhaps I'd rather be a thief-taker than a sailor. What is your opinion, sir?"

Chase put down his cup and bent his head to his bowl before Mrs. Beeks could catch his eye again.

At midday Chase presented himself for dinner at the Thorogoods'. Following a fresh-faced, beaming maidservant to the drawing room, he was struck immediately by the house's air of cheerful comfort. The carpeting on the stairway was shiny with age; the pictures on the landing all sat slightly awry. Fingerprints smudged the walls as if small hands habitually reached out to steady fast-moving feet. From below, aromas of roasting meat spiced with sage and onions mingled with a hint of stewed cinnamon apples to drift up in Chase's wake.

As the maid threw open the door, a babble of voices greeted them. In order to be heard above the din, she sang out loudly, "Mr. John Chase, sir!"

Her voice was so penetrating that Chase started and shrank back, but Thorogood was already coming forward to draw him in. The first thing Chase noticed was the roaring fire on the hearth, for the flames shot so high and crackled so loudly that anyone standing too close would surely be scorched. Second, he took in the fact that the room was crammed with bodies, including eight or ten children in all different attitudes: some lolling on the rug next to an old dog, others rolling and tumbling, still others contentedly perching on various laps.

Chase's gaze continued to sweep the room until it alighted on Penelope Wolfe, sitting next to Buckler on a small sofa against the far wall. Engrossed in conversation, they apparently had not observed his entrance.

Pulling him toward the circle of faces, Thorogood boomed: "Another birthday gift for you, ma'am. A genuine Bow Street

Runner, and a fine gentleman to boot, here to dine at your board on Christmas Day!"

Hope Thorogood looked up from refilling a guest's cup with steaming punch and gave Chase a luminous smile. He drew in his breath, arrested by something in her expression that spoke of truth and a frank joy.

"Welcome to our home, Mr. Chase." She put down the cup and approached. "We are indeed glad to see you today of all days."

Chase bowed over her hand. "This is your birthday? May I offer you my felicitations?" He glanced down at the packet of chestnuts he carried. "I wish I had known, ma'am."

"Nonsense." She took the bundle from him. "Look. See what Mr. Chase has brought."

A laughing group of children darted forth to relieve her of the chestnuts, bearing them off to be roasted.

"Mind your fingers," Mrs. Thorogood called after them. She thrust a glass of punch in Chase's hand and embarked upon a bewildering round of introductions, presenting in turn several of Thorogood's grown children, some cousins, and an elderly uncle, all of whose names he promptly forgot.

Then she peered over her shoulder. "Mr. Buckler, Penelope. Do come and greet Mr. Chase. I believe he might stand in need of a familiar face."

They rose from the sofa. "I am pleased to see you, Mr. Chase," said Penelope, holding out a bandaged hand. Chase had gone to her lodgings to see how she did on the day after the dramatic events at St. Thomas's hospital. She looked much better today.

"A happy Christmas, Chase." Buckler was grinning broadly despite the bruise on his cheek earned in the struggle with Strap.

Chase fumbled at his pocket. "Where's Miss Sarah? I have a trifle for her somewhere. Oh well, I suppose I shall bestow it upon someone else if she's not here."

Shrieking, the child danced up and held out her palm. "It's for me; it's for me," she chanted, carrying off her treat. She ran over to join the children who played with the dog, or rather played next to it, as the creature merely sat there, giving an occasional twitch of its tail.

Watching Sarah stroke the animal, Chase commented, "A bit under the weather, is it? I've never seen a less prepossessing dog." He looked at Ezekiel Thorogood. "No offense intended, sir. I am sure it is quite amiable."

Thorogood's rich chuckle sounded. "You ought to address your apology to Buckler, sir, for it is his dog."

Buckler groaned. "You see, it happens already. And I am hardly able to withstand so severe a blow to my consequence. Can you imagine what my colleagues will make of the creature?"

"They will deem you the soul of charity," put in Mrs. Thorogood, twinkling at his look of utter chagrin.

Penelope explained. "You see, Mr. Chase, I found Ruff abandoned in the street when Strap escorted me home from the Old Bailey. Actually, it was due to his sharp eyesight that the dog was not trampled. A small mercy we must be thankful for."

A shadow darkened her expression, but she went on brightly, "Unfortunately, my landlady is not disposed to be hospitable and outright refuses to house the poor thing. So Mr. Buckler has agreed to adopt Ruff, and no doubt he will find the pup very good company. 'Tis the least we may offer as repayment for his efforts in the Donovan matter." She shot Buckler a mischievous glance from under her lashes.

He grinned back. "Yes, I see now I have been fortunate. I take away from this experience a near dead mongrel and an already dead goose, albeit a plump one."

"I for one am grateful for the goose," put in Thorogood, "as it will provide a fine dinner for us all in about an hour's time."

Buckler responded to Chase's questioning look. "Donovan's wife sent the bird. It seems the money Fred Gander paid for her husband's 'confession' has enabled her and the child to begin a better life."

"I am glad of it," said Penelope. "Only, what a tragedy that she must lose her husband to gain this chance. Strap had a good deal to answer for, that's certain, for Donovan was as much a victim as Miss Tyrone and the others."

Thorogood commented, "Yet if the surgeon's experiment had succeeded, he would have been hailed as a savior. The irony must strike one forcibly."

Mrs. Thorogood addressed Chase. "What is to be the fate of the women of the St. Catherine Society?"

"Fiona and Winnie are under the care of a reputable surgeon, ma'am. And according to Miss Minton, Bertram Tyrone has called to express his support of the Society's endeavors. We shall see." He sipped his punch.

"Will you receive a reward for ridding the world of that scoundrel Mr. Strap, sir? I hope the authorities have the sense to see how you deserve it."

He smiled at her. "Recompense is only offered upon a perpetrator's conviction, Mrs. Thorogood. At first the magistrates were even inclined to doubt that so respected a man could be guilty of such infamy. Now I think everyone should like to forget it. The papers have made surprisingly little of the circumstances."

"In truth, they are too full of the Ratcliffe affair," said Buckler soberly. "It looks like a breakthrough has occurred at last. Did you see the account in today's *Morning Post* of the seaman John Williams' examination at Shadwell? The maul used to strike down the victims was found to have originated from the public house where Williams lived. I must say it looks bad for him, though it does not do to judge too hastily. God willing, the nightmare is over."

Strolling away, Buckler went to speak to one of the cousins. And with Thorogood and his wife circulating to ensure their guests' comfort, Chase was left alone with Penelope, who launched into speech.

"I am grateful to have this opportunity for a word with you, Mr. Chase, as I didn't like to speak in front of Sarah when you were kind enough to pay a call the other day. I wanted to tell you that I have seen my husband in but a brief visit. I...I just thought you should know I have his solemn pledge he never meant any harm to Constance Tyrone."

Chase kept his expression impassive. "At any rate," he told her, "I am relieved for your sake that all is well with him." He wanted to say more, to ask her, for instance, if she thought she and Wolfe would make another go of their marriage—but it wasn't his place. His eyes sought out Sarah.

"She will sorely miss her father, I fear," Penelope said, following his gaze. "Jeremy has gone to Ireland. Something about a commission in Dublin." Before he could reply, she went on quickly, "Have you family, Mr. Chase?"

He studied her face. Thick brows over large mahogany eyes and a complexion of a warmer tone than was common in an Englishwoman. The looser hairstyle she wore today suited her admirably. But he must answer her. "Yes, a father and several brothers and sisters. I haven't seen them in years. My mother passed on a few years ago."

"You have never married, I suppose?" She reddened a little, and her eyes grew anxious.

"No."

Glancing at the punch bowl on the table, she made as if to step back. She would give an excuse to move away, Chase thought.

"I have a son in America," he found himself saying. "I should like to have him here with me, but he's only twelve and doing well with his mother and grandfather. Perhaps one day…"

Observing the pity that flared in her eyes, he felt the old crushing sense of defeat flicker, then subside. Deliberately, he smiled. "He's a fine lad."

There was no time for more, for Buckler and Thorogood had rejoined them. "You know," Buckler remarked to Chase. "There's one thing that still bothers me about the Strap business. Who was driving the carriage that struck Miss Tyrone? Was it after all a jarvey too scared to come forward and confess what he had done?"

"Hackneys are often used to transport stolen goods. It's possible the driver was engaged on some nefarious scheme of his own. We shall never know."

Thorogood said thoughtfully, "Buckler, I recall your mentioning the other day that you could almost fancy Death himself drove your hack on the way to St. Thomas's to rescue Mrs. Wolfe."

"Quite a ride, eh?" Chase said, amused.

"Indeed it was. And one must profoundly pity Miss Tyrone lying in the street with such force bearing down upon her."

At this, Hope Thorogood looked up from her ministrations to the elderly uncle. "I prefer not to think of her death in that way."

"Why what can you mean, my love," erupted Thorogood. "As Tibullus says, '*Imminet et tacito clam venit ille pede*': It—that is death—is always close enough; it sneaks up on silent feet. No, no, I see the quotation is not wholly apt, but were we to substitute thundering hooves…"

"Yes, Mr. Thorogood," said Hope, "but do not let us acknowledge it today. Besides, while I am quite unable to cap your Latin, I can think of a much more uplifting sentiment for the occasion."

And with a swift glance all around, Hope quoted softly, "Be thou faithful unto death, and I will give thee a crown of life."

Afterword

Writing historical fiction requires a sort of teetering between the pure, elusive ideal of accuracy and the messier demands of a particular story. Accordingly, while taking this opportunity to tie up some loose bits, I would also like to "fess up" to several instances of poetic license. No doubt you have found more I should have mentioned.

Of St. Catherine:

Although there were several churches dedicated to St. Catherine in Regency London, Curate Wood's church, located in Soho roughly on the site of old St. Anne's, is completely fictional.

I found few specific references to St. Catherine's Day celebrations during this era. However, up until the introduction of the new poor law in 1834, workhouse girls at Peterborough and lace makers in other parts of Northamptonshire and Bedfordshire reputedly observed the holiday.

Because angels bore the saint's corpse to Mount Sinai (where would be established a famous monastery in her honor), Catherine is often associated with hills; tiny, hilltop chapels dedicated to her exist all over England. Actually, the bit of lore about dropping pins in a niche and reciting a prayer for a husband comes from a tale of the St. Catherine chapel high on a hill in Abbotsbury on the Dorset coast. In spite of no path and lots of sheep, I managed to clamber up to this fifteenth-century chapel above the swannery.

The Catholic church removed Catherine of Alexandria from the calendar of saints in 1969.

Of Coffee Houses, Taverns, and Public Houses:

I invented many of the pubs and coffee houses with the notable exceptions of the Grecian, today called the Devereux; the Russian Coffee House or Brown Bear in Bow Street; and the Cider Cellars tavern.

Of St. Thomas's Hospital:

The female operating theatre in the garret of St. Thomas's church did not open until 1821. At the time of this novel in 1811, women underwent surgery in the adjacent Dorcas ward, a practice which must have been disturbing for the other patients. I found it more effective to locate Penelope's confrontation with the villain in the garret theatre, especially since I was able to see it firsthand. Marvelously restored, the theatre is now a museum.

Of the Great Comet:

The Great Comet of 1811 was a prominent feature of the night sky. Napoleon reputedly took its appearance as a heavenly sign in favor of his Russian campaign (wrong move). The giant "fireball" was also thought to contribute to prevailing maladies referred to as Comet Fevers and was credited with producing an unusually fine vintage of port wine.

Of Syphilis (and AIDS) Vaccines:

Oddly enough, just as this piece was completed in the spring of 1997, news reports about the search for an AIDS vaccine began to appear. Since the use of harmless viral proteins had proven disappointing, the focus was turning to more controversial trials that would employ a weakened yet still hazardous live virus.

Reginald Strap takes a somewhat similar approach in seeking an inoculant for the syphilitic "virus" (by which he means poison, as he is unaware, of course, that syphilis is a bacterial infection). Ironically, Strap is ahead of his time, for his notion of weakening the organism by passing it through an animal is well established in vaccine development. And after Jenner's success with smallpox, it seemed reasonable that a Regency era physician might be tempted to seek a preventative for syphilis, still a scourge then, though no longer the dire pestilence it once had been. I thank Stephen Greenburg of the National Library of Medicine, History of Medicine Division, for providing valuable insight into Reginald Strap's experiments.

The quest continues for a syphilis vaccine.

Of British Criminal Law:

It was not until 1836 that a person accused of felony was allowed to make his full defense by counsel. Nonetheless, prior to that date a practice had developed whereby a barrister could cross-examine witnesses and argue points of law, yet could not address the jury. It seems this privilege was granted—or refused—somewhat capriciously. In one 1760 trial, for instance, the prisoner was forced to question the witnesses called to prove his own defense of insanity!

Of the Ratcliffe Highway Murders:

In several key ways, the fate of the Irishman Donovan parallels that of the young man called John Williams, chief suspect in the Ratcliffe murders. Both men commit suicide in prison, thereby "cheating the gallows" before the Law can exact its penalty (Williams never even goes to trial). Moreover, in both cases the evidence against the accused is circumstantial, and the rush to judgment seems appallingly unjust.

Still, Donovan escaped the final indignity visited upon Williams, for on New Year's Eve day, 1811, London was treated to a gruesome procession that wound its way through the streets of Wapping, pausing in turn at the homes of the Ratcliffe victims and at the lodging house where Williams had lived. The focal point of this procession was a cart in which was displayed Williams' corpse, clothed in trousers and frilled shirt. Also featured were the bloody maul and other weapons used in the crimes. The cavalcade ended at a crossroads where Williams was thrust into a cramped, unblessed grave.

Thousands of people watched the interment in eerie silence until the moment when an attendant picked up the maul to pound a stake through Williams' heart and the crowd exploded with curses and howls.

It is easy to imagine John Chase of Bow Street mingling with the throng, keeping a vigilant eye out for pickpockets and other malefactors eager to take advantage of this cathartic moment in the life of a city. It is less easy to envision the presence of Edward Buckler, who probably would have chosen to remain sequestered in the Temple with more congenial ghosts.

As for Penelope Wolfe, even an unconventional gentlewoman of her mettle would hardly dare to brave so public and unsavory a spectacle, though no doubt her curiosity must have presented a severe temptation. This instance is one in which following the rules might be said to redound to her benefit.

To receive a free catalog of Poisoned Pen Press titles, please contact us in one of the following ways:

Phone: 1-800-421-3976
Facsimile: 1-480-949-1707
Email: info@poisonedpenpress.com
Website: www.poisonedpenpress.com

Poisoned Pen Press
6962 E. First Ave. Ste 103
Scottsdale, AZ 85251